RIVERSIOUX

RIVERSIOUX

The Peccary

iUniverse, Inc.
New York Lincoln Shanghai

RIVERSIOUX

iUniverse books may be ordered through booksellers or by contacting:

iUniverse
2021 Pine Lake Road, Suite 100
Lincoln, NE 68512
www.iuniverse.com
1-800-Authors (1-800-288-4677)

ISBN-13: 978-0-595-36885-3 (pbk)
ISBN-13: 978-0-595-81298-1 (ebk)
ISBN-10: 0-595-36885-9 (pbk)
ISBN-10: 0-595-81298-8 (ebk)

Printed in the United States of America

PROLOGUE

Sometime ago a friend mentioned writing his final thesis for Bible College His topic was "living in abject poverty". Seemingly he spent considerable time in the mid-70's living with and observing the lifestyle of the "downtrodden" in Mexico City. Being intrigued I asked him to send me a copy. Recently, when visiting in our home, I asked if he had ever sent the thesis since I hadn't received it. He apologized saying he couldn't find it (common trait amongst my peers and me). I asked if he could orally summarize his findings. The answer so obvious becomes elusive in life's every day travails. Jerry's answer "all persons (poor and wealthy) have the same wants; food, shelter and sex, the order of importance changing with age".

INTRODUCTION

There are many reasons to write a novel; vanity, boredom, wealth, a quest for immortality, and many others. Common sense lays to rest the issue of money, boredom and vanity will come and go, but immortality has always been the human quest. Theology is a byproduct of mans quest for this illusive goal and best left to persons of less geometric mind. However the idea of history being adjusted to my view of reality, although hardly original, attracts fingers to the key board with gusto.

Laziness decrees choosing a subject one has some knowledge of. A subject with the ability to retain enough flexibility to be molded into whomever the story dictates as the fixed mind is overwhelmed by the fluidity of story. For this fledgling author the answer is easy. One must travel far enough back in time that no living soul can dispute with honest vigor the veracity of the tale while being recent enough that a broad but vague recollection does still exist. If successful, my Great grandfather Alanson Baker (wife Mary to a lesser degree) will emerge from this exercise as a living breathing individual with the human fragilities and greatness endowed upon all mankind. Although a work of fiction this tale is to a great extent historically correct. In places the calendar is circumvented to enhance the convergence of historical characters and to protect the identities of 'certain' individuals. Grandfather Alanson in most instances merely provides a vehicle in which to travel through these most historic of times.

Footnote: Grandmother Mary is deserving of her own "tale"!

Eye Of The Needle

At 8:00 AM Alanson awoke startled by the blast of the sandpit work whistle; eighty-five years had taken its toll. Always, it seemed, there had been tasks and events so pressing that sleeping past dawn simply wasn't plausible.

Last night after having struggled to get home, he'd retired early, aching and running a fever. Mary fussed over him as usual. For 40 some years Alanson had been her champion and life's passion. She never forgot! If only he could have returned in kind. He loved her and he showed it in the few ways his soul allowed. Events of childhood had imprisoned his heart. Try as he may the key to unlock this vault remained unattainable. Though obviously present, affection and passion surfaced only after filtering through scar tissue. Still the years had been kind.

"Mary, what time is it dear"? Strange his voice seemed to echo as if through a metal tube. He was here in the present but his voice came from a distance.

Mary leaning over wiped his brow with a damp towel and whispered "it is 2:00 in the afternoon Alanson".

It didn't seem possible. He must have been dreaming about the Riversioux again. Many times, years after watching her steam away without him, her whistle still harkened the new day. The past few days the Riversioux had been playing tricks on his mind. After a half century the paddle wheeler and her "crew" still remained embodied and alive within his soul.

Why was the family here? Alanson strained to remain cognizant. He was sweat soaked and tired, so tired. Voices, children's voices, he was sure he heard children.

"Grandpa, grandpa" a small hand tugged at his pajama sleeve.

"Ora my little cricket is that you"?

"Momma and I have been walking the lane(back and forth—back and forth) all morning". Ora struggled not to cry.

Ora was his favorite grandchild. Always in trouble this one, not because she was naughty but rather because of energy in need of outlet. She must be five years old, he couldn't force reason from his brain. It seemed everything within his skull was afloat!

There it was that tugging little hand again, he was trying but his will no longer overcame the gentle breeze whisking him from shore, the shore that harbored the fading voices.

Mary called her children, Sara, Alanson Jr. and Avis into the parlor as the grandchildren were sent for yet another walk up the quarter mile lane.

She loved this man more then life itself and now he was dying. What could she say; she who had run the family business with shrewdness that had amassed a small fortune. Alanson had always been "there" with his wisdom and vision of the future. He alone had put the ship to sail, together their calculated determination had kept the ship on course and their love had calmed the stormiest seas. If only she could make him see that she understood the pain he endured. He loved her completely, she knew it! She had shared Alanson's love with only one other woman, they had both loved Jane. Still he suffered believing he was less than she deserved. Alanson, the embodiment of human strengths, more then once wept upon her shoulder for his inability to be immersed in spontaneous affection nevertheless Mary understood that like a fairytale princes she had been blessed with true love.

Mary, with a matronly calmness obtained from a lifetime not wasted, sat in the family 'special' chair. Properly erect with hands loosely clasped upon her lap. She addressed her children now gathered in a semicircle on the floor, much like when she read to them as toddlers. Incapacitating grief spasms of the soul momentarily surrendered as Mary verbalized her love for their dying father.

"Explorer we did it" rattled from Alanson's bedroom! Alanson stroked his big horse's neck in affectionate circles.

"Pleases give me a few minutes alone with your father" Mary pleaded more than demanded as she rose to attend to her husband.

She stood in the doorway watching as Alanson caressed his pillow. Love radiated from the old man.

Mary had forgotten. Alanson had three loves in his life. Of the three only Explorer received love unrestrained! Mary still harbored ill feeling towards Alanson's parents and THAT preacher (even though Alanson seemed to have forgiven him) who had rendered forever unattainable certain precious intimacies. She would give anything if just once Alanson would have been able to break loose from the bonds that imprisoned his affection. Yes she was jealous. Though her love for Alanson would never be diminished, her most intimate female desires begged for caresses with the same affection the pillow now received.

Mary didn't realize she was verbalizing her thoughts as she tried to comfort Alanson's sweating form with a cool cloth.

"You are" Alanson attempted to speak but his words trailed off.

Rocking, Mary held his limp but living form tightly to her bosom as he slipped into coma.

He had comprehended her words as he gently slipped into the world between, the world where dream and reality are meshed as one. Never had Alanson completely relinquished to the dream world, this time he wasn't consulted! Why had he fought what he hadn't understood?

The light grew brighter as he lay levitating above his form. Then instantaneously he was whisked away to a point of observation. The light which had been yellowish was now bluish white and blinding; he now was a part of all. Senses were rendered merit-less, he simply was.

A long road stretched out before him, a road which begins with birth and ends in ecstasy. He was nearing the end and it felt indescribably wonderful. Just a little farther and he would be there but below him sat his beloved bereft in tears. "Don't cry Mary, everything is okay".

Why couldn't she hear him?

Freedom lay just ahead yet Mary's crying tugged him back.

He wanted both!

He didn't move but the road forked in front of him anyway. One path led to the beginning and birth. The other led to what he had thought was the end and death but in reality was unrestrained freedom.

"Alanson make a right and enter paradise or make a left to view life one more time and spend another moment with your Mary."

This no doubt was God speaking but nearly everyone had it wrong! The voice came from within. He, Alanson sat before no judge. There was no right or wrong. In fact there was nothing…of human want! Death he now understood was undeniable refuge and its gates were opened in welcome but he found he could not enter. Mary was suffering.

Desperately he wanted to take the road toward death and pass through these gates of peace. In time no-doubt he would but he still had will and his will drew him towards Mary.

Alanson turned left.

Mary felt Alanson's muscles momentarily bulge with youthful vitality and then once more relax as Alanson dreamed on.

CHAPTER 1

▼

The Big Sioux Valley in mid July can be an oven. The humid air is permeated with a sweet decaying aroma distinct to primate prairie wetland. Man can be swallowed up in a land such as this and will be if ones senses are not restrained. Alanson, a dreamer by nature, harbored no inclination toward restraint. On the paddlewheel riverboat, whose chugging cadence still echoed through his soul, he had heard tales of a fertile land with grass so tall it obscured the vision of men on horseback.

Now mid July, the pollen laden grass nodules reached skyward searching for an ejaculating summer breeze, in one desperate effort to brand the next generation of wetland prairie with its own genetic imprint. Alanson reached for his flask of water which he'd filled earlier in the day from one of the numerous wetland springs permeating the valley floor. While indulging in deep quenching swallows he wiped his forehead with his other hand. The flask, a semi-water proof leather container, kept the water cooler than its surroundings as its seeping content slowly evaporated.

Although the Big Sioux River was never far away the suffocating clouds of wetland pollen demanded frequent sips of water to stave off natural restricting of the throat. Earlier in the morning it had been clouds of gnats intermingled with equally large hoards of female mosquitoes experiencing their first Anglo-Saxon hemoglobin that had pestered this wanderer. Now astride his horse (Explorer) he dreamed of home and fortune as the two slowly made their way northward in the sweltering humidity native to river bottom grasslands.

Alanson, short even by mid eighteen-hundred standards, was a stocky well muscled young man endowed with strikingly good looks. With blue black hair, clear dark intelligent eyes and a swagger that manifested determination, one easily recognized Alanson as a man to be reckoned with. Now nearly thirty years of age he was leaving behind his life as engineer\clerk on a riverboat which hauled supplies to trappers and miners in the Dakota and Montana territories. Impelled by dream and desire he had managed to save most of his considerable earnings.

This was America in its teenage years where muscle, courage and planning; laced with a multitude of good luck could pay extravagant dividends. Alanson like America possessed inherent capabilities and a belief in destiny that would remain with him throughout much of his life, both as comfort and tormenter.

He had learned through conversations with prospective eastern investors that a rail line had been plotted and would be built northward up the Big Sioux Valley as soon as a few more federal concessions were granted. The frontier port city of Sioux City held immense promise for Alanson and any other young man of vision but Alanson had endured the restraints of social order long enough. For fifteen years he had studied and sharpened his frontier wit on river steamers, ever increasing his purse while "waiting" for fate to beckon.

Now after twenty-five miles and two days of meandering up the valley, travel fatigue was replaced with a feeling new and exuberating. Standing tall in the saddle a clear stream splitting the never ending ocean of grass could be seen in the distance. A spring fed creek wound it way westward through the gentle hills of western Iowa only to juncture with the Big Sioux as a first concurrence on a journey destined to end in saltwater. The beauty and promise of this juncture brought an involuntary prayer of thanksgiving from his pollen caked lips.

The railroad, although not yet under construction, was already staked out. In front of him, to the north, was the creek; to his right were stakes where the proposed rail line would one day run and to the west was the Big Sioux River. Earlier in the day, about four miles south, he'd come upon the staked plot of a small railroad town.

The day had been grueling and the sun was setting but for Alanson sleep would not come easy this night. When exhausted the mind becomes an extraordinary devise. Exhaustion mixed with excitement tends to release thoughts long dormant in the recesses of ones consciousness. These unorganized thoughts bubbled forth with no rational. Not one to enjoy thoughts that seemed to ordain their own origin and termination Alanson refreshed himself in the stimulating cool waters of the stream. After much scrubbing layers of pollen, sweat and numerous seeds left a soapy scum upon an otherwise pristine stream.

Refreshed, Alanson punched holes through the lid of a tin of beans which he then heated over a small flame. Using Explorer's saddle for a back rest Alanson slowly devoured the beans as the sun slipped behind the Dakota hills less than a mile west of the river. Meanwhile, Explorer was rolling and splashing in the shallow waters of the stream emulating Alanson.

Explorer, exhausted from the day's journey, was left untethered as Alanson attended to business. As loners are apt to do, Alanson began giving himself verbal instructions. "First I'll pace off the distance between the river and the railroad." Already in his mind a plan was forming, "I'll purchase a quarter section encompassing the property adjacent to the creek bordered on the east by the railroad and the west by the river. Then if things are as they appear I'll purchase the adjoining property." He was communing with the creator of this immense land as he paced off the land between the railroad and the river. The evening darkness was settling in as Alanson reached the river. Becoming tired and feeling pleased with his day's toil Alanson started retracing his steps; searching for a patch of willows on a sandy mound he had spotted earlier on his westward trek.

Apparently years before the river had made a bend at this juncture depositing sand and silt in a mound which now was surrounded by a thick stand of willows. Its middle was covered with a soft mound of river grasses. The river was now a hundred yards to the west, still cutting the Dakota river bank on its haphazard search for the course of least resistance. Upon closer scrutiny Alanson became even more impressed with features of the mound. The rise of the landscape would offer drainage during rains and in time of high water offer respite. As he prepared night's camp he declared, as was declared three millenniums before in a valley now housing Rome, "here is where I'll build."

It was time to locate Explorer as the night fog was beginning to rise above the cooling prairie; as if the fog wasn't spectacle enough the lightning bugs were in the process of illuminating the foggy landscape in a way unimaginable to one unfamiliar with wetland prairies. To Alanson this was a welcoming sign from a higher power, however Explorer was not impressed in like manner. He whinnied for attention as Alanson yelled "over here big guy". Sooner then usual he was at Alanson's side gently nuzzling his partner. Both dreamed the night through, one dreamed of warm stables and fresh hay while the other of long anticipated actions of fulfillment.

There are many reasons for one to rise early; Alanson could not imagine anything more pressing than destiny. Ever brightening slivers of yellow and red sunlight peeked around the Iowa Sioux River Breaks chasing the disappearing darkness westward into the Dakotas, the home of the Sioux.

Alanson's' eyes were following the illuminating light rays westward when an involuntarily shiver brought goose bumps to his skin; he rubbed his arms in an attempt to alleviate the discomfort.

Straining his eyes he stared into the foggy terrain where he saw or imagined he saw men on horse back. They seemed to be staring back at him from the Dakota side of the river. He was thankful recent spring rains had swollen the Sioux to near bank levels. From past experiences aboard the riverboat he knew the Sioux was a warrior not to be taken lightly. For the first time of 'many' Alanson was influenced by the river as he gently kneed Explorer, encouraging him to pick up the pace in an easterly direction away from the river.

CHAPTER 2

▼

The territorial boundaries of the Sioux Nation were from the present Chippewa County in Minnesota, west to the Apple River just below Bismarck North Dakota, south to the Niobrara River in Knox County Nebraska, east to the Big Sioux River, north along the Big Sioux River and finally east\northeast through Pipestone Minnesota back to Chippewa County.

The Sioux nation is composed of numerous subdivisions, with the Dakota being the largest distinct division of the group encompassing the Wahpekutes. (Example: Sioux\nation, Dakota\state, Santee\county, Wahpekute\township, band\village) The Wahpekutes were one of several subdivisions of the Santee Tribe.

The Yancton Sioux now occupied the lands west of and adjacent to the Big Sioux. The Yanctons had for sometime been looked upon as friendly toward whites. Under the council of Chief Ioway the Yanctons had sold their holdings below the Big Sioux to the U.S. Government for payments to be made in yearly installments. Although ignorant of letters and figures Ioway knew the value of merchandise and made sure no shortages occurred in the transaction. The band had turned most of the governing over to the military establishment and the Yanctons were now dependant upon government payments. Ioway (named because as a child he had been kidnapped and raised by the Iowas) had recently died and the Yancton were no longer under his 'wise' council.

Inkpaduta was of the Wahpekutes band of Santee Sioux. This band under Wamdisapa (Black Eagle) left the tribal homeland of southwestern Minnesota for less contested hunting grounds along the Missouri in eastern South Dakota in the vicinity of the Vermillion River. This was the tribal homeland of the Yancton, known for congenial relations with all their neighbors, red or white.

The Wahpekutes had lost many warriors in a long running battle with the ever encroaching white hoard. Black Eagle assumed the Yancton, who lived in peace with the whites, would offer little resistance to sharing common ground with their cousins.

Black Eagle hated the whites for taking his homeland but even more for the way the conquered lands were abused. He and his ancestors had lost battles before to superior forces; which never was palatable but it was the way life was intended. He could not understand this conquers attempt to circumvent nature. His beliefs didn't allow for such events, his contempt for the white devil was insatiable.

Strangely he held no such contempt for his Yancton cousins whose short sightedness and capitulation to the whites was obvious. Early on "he" also had been awed by the immunity of the white heathen, it seemed every natural law was being infringed upon yet the whites continued to multiply and conquer. Maybe he was the one who had been misled by the shaman, possibly the whites knew a better way. Time and life had proven his initial instincts to be correct.

Black Eagle instructed the young Wahpetkutes in righteous hate. Inca had learned well and hate for the white-eyes became imprinted within his genes.

As was the custom at the age of twelve Inka went in search of his life's purpose. With a flask of water he headed for the spirit mounds, which lay a ways west of the Sioux River and slightly north of the Missouri, to seek guidance. He understood, from listening to the elders, much suffering must occur before the spirits would deem him a soul of serious intention…Inka was prepared for whatever must be endured.

That he would be plague to the whites-eyes was predetermined, Inka was in quest of divine blessing. He paid proper homage before scrambling up the highest mound where spraddled he laid continuously staring into the sun. All morning and all afternoon he lay with his water flask alongside. Though his body craved liquid his soul craved fulfillment.

Through the night he watched the summer moon rise and then set. Then once again the blazing summer sun appeared and as the day progressed the plains sweltered. Around mid afternoon Inka lost consciousness and drifted off into dreams of peaceful water falls and gentile winter snows. Involuntarily he shivered and crossed his arms over his bosom searching for warmth. His body was void of moisture and sweat no longer flowed from his young frame.

With his arms wrapped tightly around a now shivering and dehydrated frame the vision appeared. Brother badger gently picked him up by the nap of his neck (much as a mother cat). Then firmly grasping his passenger he furiously tunneled through time into the future. In blurring sequences days and nights sped by until the tunnel abruptly resurfaced on a hill overlooking the valley of the future.

An exquisite rainbow encompassing the full spectrum of life's basic colors extended from one horizon to the other. Everywhere there were white-eyes, so numerous they lived in nests like wasps. Inka grasped his ears in an attempt to muffle the din. Peoples and lands had been conquered until all earth was now their domain. No forest or grassland remained; all was blackened with greed.

Then seemingly out of nowhere and yet everywhere grandfather spirit appeared, demanding the whole of Inka's vision. With long raven hair and gentle but sad brown eyes he kneeled stroking a dove perched upon his wrist. In front of him sat a vase with a steamy vapor rising through its cover. All was peaceful.

Suddenly in a celestial rage grandfather grabbed the rainbow, knotted it, looped it around the dove's neck and pulled it snug. Grasping the rainbow in one hand with the dove still flopping in jerky but weakening death throes he smashed the steaming "container of pestilence" with his foot, loosing its contents upon the land. Then as he had appeared grandfather disappeared.

In a vision within his vision Inka observed as insects infested the earth, the once sparkling rivers turned to mud and filth until no living thing could exist within their banks. New incurable diseases ran rampart until once again mother earth was free of mortal subservience…

As the ingredients in the container were being spewed upon the earth brother Badger was scurrying back out his tunnel. Hurriedly he spat Inka from his mouth into the bright sunlight and then spinning around tightly wedged his body in the tunnel entrance.

Inka awoke once more racked in sweat. Dehydrated and weakened he felt for his flask, once located he drank slowly but deeply. His eyes were blurred and his lips were cracked but he was alive and life's vocation was manifest. Whether brother badger would succeed in plugging the tunnel was not clear, whether the plague was predestined termination he did not know. He did know grandfather had shown him the beast, with all his cunning he was prepared to oppose the white-eyed anti-spirit.

Inkpaduta or "Inka" was 10 years old when his band moved from Minnesota to the Dakotas but to him home would remain the Iowa\Minnesota lakes area, the resting place of his Wahpekute ancestors.

Black Eagle had installed in the young Wahpekute braves a strong distaste for all things connected to the white man. Inka now fortified with his spiritual revelation expanded the chief's hate into a vendetta never far from eruption.

Annually the tribe made a pilgrimage back to their 'Mecca" of Spirit Lake to commune with and pay homage to Wahpekute ancestral spirits and every year the trip became more hazardous.

Whites now claimed title to these holy grounds because of a piece of paper purchased from persons who had never walked upon the soil! At first Inka couldn't fathom how even a white-eye could justify such nonsense. Later, under the guidance of Black Eagle, he came to understand that the white-eye possesses no conscience and therefore had been deemed unworthy of a soul by the Great Spirit. He also learned to disregard accepted protocol when dealing with whites for they were little more than debris, debris with no spiritual quality. Now nearly 16 years of age Inka was nearing manhood and anxious to prove his worthiness as warrior and as leader.

The Smith brothers, Tom fifteen and Jim seventeen along with their cousins Gaile and Neal Welch fifteen and sixteen respectively were also nearing manhood. Their parents had bought adjacent quarter sections from a land broker in Illinois, who had purchased the property from the railroad, who in turn had received the property from the federal government as an incentive to push rail service farther west into hostile Indian Territory. Hopefully this would enhance civilization of the western grasslands now inhabited by savages. The government had taken the land from Inka's people.

It was mid July and the small grain harvest was nearing completion. The new turned virgin soil had produced prodigiously. Jubilation was the prevailing attitude as the four boys left the grain fields for a mid afternoon dunk in the clear waters of Lake Okoboji.

As they waded through shoulder high prairie grasses they teased one another about the Boyle girls each claiming to have shared numerous intimacies with the neighborhood girls and with each suspecting the others veracity. As with boys from "Genesis" to present the bravado of these boys of the prairie compelled them to impress their peers with imagined sexual exploits. It was in this boisterous atmosphere that Tom heard playful "feminine" sounds apparently originating from near the lake.

The lakes area had more or less been cleared of savages for a decade; still every so often a few would be seen returning on pilgrimage to their old homelands. It was well known these heathen held no love for the proprietors of their old lands. For this reason the cousins never strayed far from home without firepower.

Inka, (Wanahca) Flower his mother, and (Glega Hehaka) Spotted Fawn his older sister along with the rest of the Wahpekute were on their annual pilgrimage to Spirit Lake. Spirit Lake was a holy place; the perennial resting grounds of the Wahpekute deceased. The past night had been spent in misery, fighting mosquitoes and removing ticks on a typical July wetland night. Finally several hours before dawn the tired band of irritable sojourners fell into an exhausted slumber. They had made camp along the aptly named Rock River.

In a land of grass and fertile soils this unique river cuts a path through multicolored rock formations with the rapids and falls typical of such rivers. Scattered clumps of willow trees dot the shores. In a grove large enough to conceal the small band camp was pitched.

The decimated Wahpekute band now consisted of a mere twenty-three lodges. Once a powerful and feared band they had fallen prey to and were nearly obliterated by white man disease, which they had no immunity to. This fierce band of survivors who had traded brutality for brutality with the superior number and firepower of the whites could find no shaman with medicine powerful enough to stymie the ravages of the biological warfare now being waged.

Black Eagle had been skeptical when a currier was sent to his village under a white flag of truce. His band still had a tenuous hold on southwestern Minnesota and the Wahpekutes unlike many tribes remained robust and healthy. They raided homesteaders with regularity replenishing needed supplies before burning their houses and belongings. The Wahpekutes had adapted well to this new way of life.… Still no matter how many they sent fleeing more replaced them.

One bitter winter day a currier carrying a white flag came offering blankets as a gift for his people. A special day the whites called Christmas. The holy man in black explained that on this day of great joy all peoples were brothers. His band necessarily always being on the run rarely had opportunity to prepare properly for the bitter cold of Minnesota wintertime. The old and children suffered greatly.

Black Eagle promised in return to "initiate" no more hostility toward any settler who posted a cross (symbol of love) above their door as he accepted the gift of smallpox infested blankets.

Black Eagle nurtured this band of survivors with a continual diet of contempt for the whites-eyes as the band regained its' strength. Through natural birth and the kidnapping of youngsters from bands friendly to the whites each lodge was filed with youth, mostly males and mostly Yancton. Each garnered a healthy hatred for all things connected to the whites-eyes.

Giggling, Flower and Spotted Fawn could not contain the relief experienced in the clear cool waters of Okoboji. The waters granted temporary relief from the incessant itch of the mosquitoes bite while also cleansing the body of sweated on pollen and seeds.

Flower, 29, was showing the beginnings of midriff fat, exclusively in the abdomen, so prevalent amongst the prairie tribe females. Still her well endowed femininity was breathtaking as she glided through the water with an otter like grace.

Spotted Fawn was proud of her mother's beauty. Most females of her mother's age no longer appealed to the males of the band yet Flower was the object of many suitors, especially Black Eagle, since the death of her father to the Whiteman's curse.

Spotted Fawn also was in full blossom of womanhood and Flower was pleased, sure that soon once again there would be "youngsters" in the teepee. Flower playfully splashed water in Fawns face, then half heartedly attempted to escape retribution as she ran along the sandy Okoboji beach. Mother and daughter playfully wrestled unaware of the probing eyes upon them.

The boys watched the playful exhibition from a squatting position, concealed by the cover of thick marsh grass. Lust is natural to young males and in the right circumstances is overwhelming. When four teenage boys happen upon a pair of skinny dipping 'heathen' beauties wrestling upon the sands of a secluded lake the outcome is predetermined.

Flower was the first to become aware of the soft but rapidly approaching footsteps as the boys dashed across the waves of sand separating the seclusion of the marsh grass from the water. With a look of terror Flower shoved Spotted Fawn aside as she faced her adversaries. "Run and don't stop" she yelled.

Spotted Fawn needing no encouragement already was distancing herself from the lake with the Welch boys in determined pursuit.

Flower realized this was probably the final chapter in her book of life, a book already filled with too much grief at the hands of white men. Crouched she glared at her attackers as they circled ever closer.

Jim and Tom were now consumed with primeval desire. "Grab her by the hair while I pin her arms" Jim commanded as he ripped off his trousers exposing his aroused genitals.

Tom every bit as excited as Jim knew he'd have to wait his turn but soon they'd "know" he wasn't a virgin. "I get a turn too" Tom gasped trembling with anticipation, barely able to speak. Then astounded they both stared in disbelief as the heathen slut lay down upon the beach spreading her legs in seductive invitation.

Flower knowing no English understood the intent of the two boys. She stretched out on the sand beach writhing in exotic temptation, riveting the boy's attention. Meanwhile her hand searched in the sand for the buffalo rib bone that had pierced her foot while she and Fawn had frolicked just moments earlier.

The boys remained hypnotized by the welcomed but unexpected lust of this primitive harlot.

Always one to boast Jim (grabbing his manhood) announced "once the squaw saw a man's wedge she couldn't wait to be split; now little brother watch me tame this wild Injun."

Intoxicated with lust Jim fell awkwardly upon Flower, in wild thrust he attempted to release the ache of pent up emotion that now boiled within. As he floundered Flower gently reached for his genitals, with knowing hands she brought him to position and thrust her hips upward, engulfing Jim within. Jim was nearly unconscious as Flower folded her body into his. Wrapping her legs around him she ran her hand through his hair while at the same time pulling his mouth to hers. She playfully plunged her tongue in and then out of his mouth.

Jim was experiencing new and unintended emotions; he embraced Flower holding her gently as he playfully reciprocated with his own tongue. Like practiced dancers they moved as one, together in a harmony edited by eons of evolution they rushed towards an explosive crescendo.

Meanwhile Tom in the process of removing his overalls, weakened from witnessing events that surpassed even his wildest adolescent fantasies, lost his balance and stumbled sideways with one leg hung in his trousers.

Noticing Tom's predicament and sensing her chance for retribution Flower unleashed a furious attack upon her unsuspecting assailant. Flower clamped her mouth shut upon Jims tongue while maintaining a firm grasp of his hair. With a fury fueled by atrocities past and present she thrust the rib bone into the small of Jims back, over and over. In fierce rapidity she continued the assault.

Jim's heavy breathing became gasps. He no longer was a raging bull being tamed, he was being slaughtered. He struggled in vain to roll free but the heathens legs gripped him ever tighter as the onslaught continued. With each thrust his life was being drained. With life's energy ebbing Jim attempted to scream for help, filling Flowers mouth with blood which caused her to gag and therefore momentarily release her bite. With tongue freed a hideous animal like scream escaped from Jim's larynx.

The scream caused Flower to release Jim but freed her to attack a gawking Tom. She knew she must be swift and finish her tasks before the other white-eyes returned! She raced toward Tom, who stood petrified...momentarily unable to mobilize his legs, intending to thrust the now shattered bone into his abdomen. Fortunately Tom's legs responded to an adrenalin rush.

Tom's only thought was escape as he fled towards the grassy out bank with Flower in determined pursuit. With fear as motivator Tom easily sped away from the determined but over matched Flower. When safely out of site he collapsed in a heap, whimpering he buried himself beneath the swamp grasses.

For a short time Flower searched for the cowering Tom, thwarted in this endeavor and with time at a premium she raced back toward the beach intending to finish what she had left undone.

The Welch brothers were exhausted. All day they had sweated harvesting the grain and now they were trying to catch the fastest female they had ever laid eyes upon. This vixen that was to be theirs was now a mere speck in the prairie horizon. The boys shook their heads in collective dejection.

Slowly they made their way back to their cousins who they knew would razz them unmercifully for their inability to catch one little injun girl. "At least they will have the other one when we get back" Gaile said more or less to himself between angry kicks at the sand while shuffling his way along Okoboji's beach.

Neal perked up at the mention of the other Indian, in the chase he had completely forgotten about Flower. The boys quickly regained their exuberance contemplating what lay in store when they returned to where the chase had originated. Once again they boasted of what they would teach the squaw when "their" turn came.

A terrified hideous scream, resembling the cry of a wounded kitten yet unmistakably human, chilled the blood within their veins. From that instant and for all time the boys wished this event had never transpired.

The Welch boys were not swift of foot, instead stocky and unusually stout for lads of their age, nevertheless the distance back to the Smith brothers was traversed in short time.

Near incapacitating nausea gripped the boys as they came upon Jim's limp form lying in an ever expanding pool of blood. His tongue dangled like a broken chicken wing as blood continued to gurgle from his gasping mouth.

Brandishing the broken rib bone a naked blood splattered Flower stood above the now helpless form preparing to unleash one final assault.

The boys raced to the grass cache where they scooped up their always primed and ready rifles.

Flower understanding and receptive saw a glint of steel in the waning summer sun as she rocked backward into a pool of white-eye blood. Instantly dead from 2 projectiles fired simultaneously Flower lay motionless with an unmistakable look of defiant contentment etched into her death mask.

The boys grasping their guns relentlessly clubbed the lifeless form that had so recently been an object of uncontrollable lust. As tears welled the boys continued to beat this heathen who even in death mocked them, finally under the influence of exhaustion sense slowly retuned to the boys.

In a frightened trance Tom remained hidden in the thick river grass just beyond the beach. He was crying uncontrollably as the Welch boys lay down their blood soaked guns.

Tom's whimpering reminded them of the motionless form lying on the beach The form that apparently hadn't moved since the final thrust of the heathen's primeval weapon.

Miraculously Jim was alive though gravely injured. As they approached he weakly gasped in an attempt to speak but his nearly severed tongue could form no words. Blood still trickled from his mouth.

The Smiths had always been the more boisterous of the cousins, the Welchs more dependable. If this was not to end in even worse tragedy the Welch brothers would have to initiate some immediate and decisive action.

Neal, sensing the imperative need for action yelled "Tom quit your whimpering and get your butt moving, we need help and we need it now."!

Bending over Jim, Neal struggled to regain control of the situation "Gaile go dip your shirt in the lake so we can wash Jim's wounds."

Gaile already was returning from the lake with water dripping from his shirt, wringing it as he ran. Together they cleansed Jim's wounds, neither being able to look at his lacerated tongue.

Neal in a calm reassuring voice was attempting to bring a sense of hope to the scene when Tom asked. "But what happens if there are more Indians"?

Neal glared at Tom: "God dammit Tom you'd better get your ass moving"!

To a casual observer Jim would appear the ringleader and he was the instigator of most happenings but Neal had always quietly been the alpha male. Jim's dominance ended where critical decision began. "Cut some willows for a carrier while I try to fashion a stretcher out of the Indians dress" Neal said.

Jim, who was beginning to gain reassurance through Neal's demure, managed to nod in approval.

Spotted Fawn returned to the Wahpekute camp completely exhausted, barely able to relate the tale of brutality to Chief Black Eagle.

Black Eagle's rage bordered on madness yet he managed to remain stoic as young Fawn wailed for retribution. His entire adult life had been filled with outrages and though this was only one more episode in a life long drama, this act cut to the bone.

The weight of responsibility rested heavy upon the aging leader; he mustn't let emotion replace wisdom. Once more the survival of his people hung in balance. The whites undoubtedly would blame the Wahpekute squaw for any injury inflicted upon her assailants and they would settle for no less than blood retribution.

"Spotted Fawn there will be a time for retaliation. The time is not yet here. Gather what you have, we must leave this instant."

Black Eagle then turned to face the approaching Inka. "Your mother is dead and if not for her swiftness your sister would also be dead. The white-eyes will be here soon to slay those of us who remain. No time for words now, my son, hurry and pack up!"

Inka so wanted to argue but glancing at Black Eagle the thought disappeared. "In this sacred place the blood of my mother will mingle with that of the white-eyes" he silently vowed while gathering the family possessions into a bundle.

Inka had now lost both mother and father to the white-eye and he struggled to understand the wisdom of continued capitulation…Black Eagle had become his protector since his father's death and many hours had been spent grooming him to become an instrument of retribution. Being under the tutelage of Chief Black Eagle was an honor, Inka would continue to listen and learn until the proper time.

The band although exhausted from their trek east never hesitated in their flight west until they reached the Big Sioux River which they then crossed just above the tumbling waters of the Sioux Falls.

A line of debris on the bank indicated the river had recently receded from a summer flood. Black Eagle gave thanks to the Great Spirit for allowing the river to be crossable, saving his band from retribution of the pursuing white devils.

The Big Sioux, though not the Missouri, is a river of magnitude when in flood. Debris and violent currents make crossing the river unimaginable during high waters. Black Eagle knew that once in Dakota Territory they would be safe. A venturesome white may cross the river on a short excursion and survive but anything more was suicide as this was Siouxland!

With this knowledge Black Eagle pushed his band southward along the west bank of the river for two-and-a-half days until once again high water separated the lands.

It takes seven days for unencumbered driftwood floating upon the river's crest to reach Alanson's' creek from the Sioux Falls. From the Dakota shore Black Eagle and his tired band peered through the early morning fog as Alanson mounted his magnificent horse…then spurred him in a direction away from the river.

CHAPTER 3

▼

Alanson was in a hurry! He planned to be one of the first to purchase a stake in what would become Plymouth county Iowa. As of yet no one had turned a furrow in the Sioux valley but land would go fast once the railroad was for real.

This now was and would be the frontier for the foreseeable future, Dakota Territory was Sioux country. He had observed Dakota's heartland from the deck of a riverboat and he supposed it would be some time before the Sioux would be subdued.

"I wish the sun would hurry and subdue these mosquitoes" he said to his horse and companion Explorer who was in the midst of his morning urination. Pressurized spurts of acrid fluid sprayed forth from a long shivering shaft…as if in the throws of ejaculation. As Alanson watched he silently wished gratification was that easily obtained by man. "Quit dreaming of that filly in Sioux City and get me to the assay office" he said. "If you get us there by evening I'll purchase a pair of Belgian fillies with which to work the land by day and keep your stall warm at night".

He was as close to Explorer as any human he'd met since leaving home at fourteen. He would never go back home. He had broken completely and permanently with his parents.

At a young age he had committed the blasphemy of defying the unforgiving God of his parents. It wasn't that God didn't exist in Alanson's world. There were numerous things beyond his understanding that "maybe" God controlled. He, through observation, knew that the non-believer who worked and planned fared at least as well as the believer who prayed and tithed.

By now, they had traveled south to the small staked railroad village he had noticed on the way north. The sun was rising and gaining strength and Explorer needed a breather. "At this rate you'll being drinking from the Missouri River water tonight." Dismounting he continued on foot letting Explorer take the lead, "I'll spend the next several days signing legal papers and procuring supplies while you can become more intimate with those city fillies. Then if things work out maybe I'll cross over to Dakota City and get acquainted with the new missionary." Even though not a conventional Christian, Alanson enjoyed a theological discussion.

It is hard to determine what a horse does and does not understand but when a horse is your only partner it makes little difference. Alone amidst nature at times a man feels compelled to bring human presence into an otherwise logical world.

Alanson, somewhat by choice and somewhat by circumstance, was for the most part a loner, being more intelligent and observant then most, also a philosopher. He seldom felt a need to explain his tight wad approach to life or his pleasure in good natured mental jousting with the few learned preachers he came across. His peers on the fringe of civilization would neither understand nor care.

Sometimes when feeling the need for conversation he would lock horns with a preacher whose education amounted to "the call'. These encounters usually ended with both condemning the other to Hell, one verbally and the other mentally. Still it did serve the purpose of reaffirming his belief that being mostly solitaire wasn't all that bad.

Being alone in the valley's heat and humidity it seemed good to share these thought with Explorer. "PHETTT, PHETT, PSSSSHT" after a space of 15 feet and a horrible breath denying odor Alanson was brought back to the present as Explorer released a large amount of pent up gas.

Enough for walking he remounted and again they traveled on, each in a personal yet interwoven world.

To their east lay the Loess Hills, a one hundred and forty mile long unique river break. Eons ago, when the earth's weather was in upheaval, these hills were formed by blowing dust and sand. Now these super sized sand dunes were canopied with oak, ash, walnut, maple and cottonwood interlaced with plum and numerous other berry trees. With the Loess Hills to the east and the river grasslands to the west this indeed was a magnificent country to behold. Alanson semiconsciously absorbed this awing panorama while subconsciously dreaming of how things would be when his vision came to fruition.

How many head of cows could be pastured on three hundred and twenty acres of Sioux bottom land? Corn would surely produce astounding yields, which could then be fed to hogs. The hogs, once the railroad was complete, could be marketed locally for shipment to the population back east. A community would materialize around the railroad and if events were properly managed prosperity and settlement would arrive simultaneously.

Yes, he would visit the mission in Dakota City whether the vicar was a man of character or perhaps a charlatan. He was content being a loner BUT to see his dreams mature a community was necessary. He would befriend this man of God and in time, through him, secure a spiritual outpost on the Big Sioux. Sure as night follows day once a church was established settlers with families would appear.

This was the dream possessing his consciousness when the stench of Sioux City signaled their arrival in civilization. It sickened Alanson, though he felt no guilt, that the bluffs just west of Sioux City were occupied with the rotting remains of the Sioux.

Small Pox had and still was wiping out entire tribes. For nearly two decades these bluffs had become the final resting place of diseased Indians. The corpses, wrapped in hides at first but now quite often in white man's garment were strapped to a willow bed held above the earth by four tree limbs, were left to rot on the same bluffs where the great chief War Eagle "friend of the white man" was laid to rest some years before. War Eagles (who broke bread with and welcomed Lewis and Clark) remains shared prime real estate with his perishing band of descendants.

When the wind was right the odor of these rotting corpses would be the first indication river men received that Sioux City was close at hand. Alanson had many times in the past experienced this sickening phenomenon as a river hand, now a southerly wind once more alerted his senses. Alanson gagged, spat and headed for the Bruguier Inn and Saloon where a bath and bed could be obtained.

Morning, which was to be spent, resting, was intuited by the familiar blast of a river boat whistle. Each river boat has a unique call easily recognized by its hands, much like a mother goose calling her gaggle.

Alanson recognized Miss Sioux's whistle (home to Alanson for approximately the past decade). Something was surely amiss as the Riversioux should have been well into Dakota Territory by now. It had been ten days since wishing the crew well as he prepared to pursue his own ambitious dream.

It had been wrenching to leave the closest thing to "family" he had ever known. Shared hardship, common goals and forced proximity creates family; in healthy circumstances genetics supplies these ingredients. Since the Molly's demise and reincarnation as the Riversioux the hands of the paddle wheeler had valued his presence and in their own rugged manner loved him. He, if the crew and boat were intact, couldn't deny the unexpected pleasure the whistle offered.

The inviting aroma of steaming coffee pulled him toward the post restaurant where a few tables roughly hewn from local timber served as a dining area. He had bathed the night before in the posts public tub for the price of a nickel, then spent the night in the lean-to stable outback sleeping in a "nest" of fresh hay as all the posts beds had already been spoken for. A shallow well supplied surprisingly cold water lacking the offensive sulfuric odor common in the valley wells. This morning the well had also provided a refreshing face wash.

With the arrival of supplies aboard the "Sioux" less then two weeks ago meals were an exceptionally grand affair. Crisp well salted pork back was accompanied with flapjacks, maple syrup straight from Vermont, fresh churned butter, cave cooled milk from local cows, tasty whole grain toast seared black on the cook stove alongside pots of steaming coffee. This was followed with apple sauce, dried plums or both. When food was plentiful Alanson, well known amongst river men as 'cautious' with his money, didn't consider partaking in abundance a vice.

Usually not one to leave the table without conversation, for this was where news was attained, Alanson excused himself early. This morning he could not focus his mind until the mystery of The "Riversioux" was solved. The answer was soon in coming.

While walking down the dock toward where the "Sioux" was moored he was hailed in a booming voice "Alanson, you're the answer to this captain's prayer." He would have recognized the voice anywhere for it was a clear crisp voice of unpretentious authority. Captain Jonas Maynard was as good a captain as navigated the mighty 'Mo". He also was as well read and as honest a man as he had ever known. Much value was placed on both virtues by Alanson.

"For a man of supposed talents you don't mask troubles well Jonas. Why aren't you miles upstream?" Alanson asked as they earnestly shook hands.

"Remember how thin and pale John, the engineer who was contracted to take your place, appeared when he arrived. He died the day after you left, Typhoid we think". Jonas did not look well himself but Alanson imagined the burden of responsibilities was probably responsible for his graven appearance. The "Sioux" was under a contract deadline to deliver and that deadline was now placed in jeopardy.

Alanson knew Jonas well. He was a proud individual who would ask nothing from one he lacked confidence in and if confidence was not in question it still would be difficult for Jonas to seek favor from someone of less financial means or professional status. With an honesty that surprised himself Alanson asked Jonas to reinstate him as engineer of the "Sioux".

"Since only a couple of bands of Indians occupy the Sioux Valley as of yet and since I already have the wherewithal and knowledge to purchase a prime site in the valley my most pressing need is to replenish my bank account. Of course my value has risen substantially in the past two weeks! If you can afford me I'm your engineer". They again shook hands as the deal was consummated.

While still in the grasp of handshake Alanson nodded his head toward the horse shoe pit behind Bruguier's Inn. For years Bruguiers pit held the reputation as the home of championship horse shoe. The 'Riversioux' crew, with Alanson and Jonas as anchors, were the perennial and present reigning champions.

As a team the two complemented each other well and together they summarily lay to waste the opposing paddlewheel teams. In truth Jonas was simply a class above Alanson in pitching shoes, a fact that escaped Alanson.

Being docked at Bruguiers led to a mandatory match for Horse shoe superiority between the two, with Jonas always prevailing. With the Riversioux crew as an audience once again Alanson's hopes of defeating Jonas were severely and 'ceremoniously' dashed.

"It seems as if skill once again prevails over luck Alanson but in time luck well surly have its day" Jonas undeniably enjoyed victory but even more so when Alanson was his opponent.

With cheeks of crimson Alanson once again, to a by-now incredulous crew, proclaimed his game was slightly off but wait till next time!

The horse shoe game aside reenlisting with the Riversioux had been a hasty but good decision for several reasons. First of all time spent with Jonas was always time well spent, secondly he knew that Jonas would to the best of his ability assure that his financial goals were more then met and last but every bit as important was his belief that good men doing good things received good rewards. Alanson believed this was the nature of things. Some would call this a faith in God and possibly it was. Alanson couldn't delineate the boundaries.

Also submerged in the mix was a man's fractured ego, still smarting from defeat Alanson 'believed' the time was approaching when he would finally enjoy the satisfaction of teaching the skipper a thing or two about the game of horse shoe!

CHAPTER 4

▼

August 26, 1855 the Riversioux left the security of the Port Of Sioux City in route to Ft. Union, Montana. Times were changing on the river. The once 'semi' hospitable plains tribes were becoming irritable and even aggressive.

In the earliest days of Missouri River paddle wheelers the crews cut their own timber for use as fuel. From the Dakotas northward cottonwood was the only tree available that was plentiful and of adequate girth to satisfy the veracious appetite of a paddle wheeler. Below Sioux City hardwoods could be attained with out great effort but as one moved northward they dwindled to a meager few.

The problem with cutting cottonwood for immediate use was that when green it barely burned hot enough to maintain adequate steam pressure. Therefore the earlier boats operated at less then one half power in the northern stretches known as the Dakota Territory, not only did this add days to an already arduous journey but it also added grave danger.

Later as traffic increased upon the river, permanent crews were procured by the freight companies to cut and stash supplies of cottonwood. The locations, although constantly changing as the river cut new channels, were located at appropriate intervals where the paddlewheel could safely dock to take on their supply of "cured" fuel. This worked fairly well until the plains Indians became envious of the operation and demanded ransom. For a while the boat companies resisted but as their crews began to mysteriously disappear the river tribes were grudgingly rewarded with one of their first capitalistic enterprises outside the fur trade.

Now with the new hostilities many tribes refused to let boats near their shores, while others no longer wishing to exist without the comforts accompanying the fuel trade were eager to do business as usual. The territories of the competing bands continually changed and always overlapped. It would be Jonas's decision where to stop for fuel supplies; the safety of his boat and crew depending upon the wisdom of this judgment.

The pilot, also usually the captain, steered the vessel while keeping in constant contact with the engineer through an intricate system of tingling bells. The engineer at the tingling of the appropriate bell would increase or decrease power to the amount requested.

The upper Missouri being a gauntlet of snags, sandbars and whirlpools quickly weeded out all but the most skillful pilots and engineers. Jonas and Alanson had no peers and as a team tested many times by travail were now legend upon the mighty "Mo". With the impending Indian situation this legend would surely be severely tested.

The Molly Joe (renamed Riversioux) built in 1848 was one hundred and thirty feet from stem to stern. She had a width of nineteen feet and weighed seventy five tons loaded. With a paddle wheel on each side and matched twin stacks she was a breath taking lady churning the turbulent waters of the mighty Missouri. Jonas was rightfully proud of his vessel which had cost him four thousand dollars to rebuild and in which he had at least another thousand dollars worth of repair parts stored within the hold. He had spent nearly his entire inheritance plus he had borrowed heavily from friends and still he was compelled to seek additional investors who shared faith in his abilities.

"Miss Sioux" drafted four and a half feet empty and five and a half feet loaded. Since being unloaded and then reloaded in St. Joe her draft was now less than five foot. The cargo had been unloaded and then partially reloaded in two afternoons by the crew who were then given the next twenty four hours off. Jonas, Alanson and "Fletch" (a professional hunter employed to keep the crew supplied with fresh meat) loaded the final cargo late that evening. Evidently some sort of livestock was in the hold as everyday fresh water and food was carried to the hold by one of the three. The crew were given instructions not to enter the hold by the "old man" himself. Jonas tolerated operational questioning only from his officers and then it had better have merit.

A little more than fifteen miles up river from Sioux City, near the bend in the river Lewis and Clark had named Elk Point, Jonas ordered the hold opened. Slowly shading their eyes eight Negroes emerged from the darkness below and faced the crew. Seven strapping young males and one equally healthy female stood staring at the crew who in turn were left gawking back in disbelief...

Fletch stood to the rear of the raised pilot house with his arsenal fully on display. For what seemed an eternity the crew stood dumb struck. As it dawned upon them that they had unwittingly become engaged in slave running they seethed in a not unanticipated synchronized rage.

While the crew was occupied with thoughts of mutiny the Riversioux was been securely anchored. The retort of a fifty caliber Sharps refocused their attention on the pilot house where Jonas, flanked by Alanson on one side and Fletch on the other, prepared to address the crew.

"Gentlemen you behold three serious men, one professional hunter and two determined river men with everything they posses on the line. I apologize for the trickery involved but for your safety and the safety of the fugitives it was necessary. Listen closely for your options, number (1): you can file past Alanson who will pay you well as you immediately depart by foot, or number (2): you can be part of a just though extremely dangerous cause with ample reward when completed. Of course there is number (3): you can take your chances against eleven well armed (the blacks also bore arms) individuals who have already made their choices".

Jonas had picked this crew with his usual care. These were adventurous men looking to better themselves. Yes, they had been tricked and each understood the deadly stakes of this treacherous adventure but added danger is of little significance to people who every day face dangers most men never experience in a lifetime. The only ingredient needed to solidify support was the reward.

Jonas continued "when Ft. Union is reached Fletch and the free Negroes are heading up the Yellowstone well stocked for the trapping season. The numerous Negroes who have already reached the headwaters have saved all their past year's furs to trade with us IF we get our cargo to Ft. Union by October 1. One third of the profit will be evenly split amongst the crew upon our return to St. Louis".

This would amount to several years' income for one trip! Most of the crew were veterans and fully understood the risks they were signing on to but most also could cipher simple math. These were capitalists and this was a chance of a lifetime.

"We're in" shouted the crew chief, who was spokesman for the crew.

On a riverboat the chief gains his authority by actually being the toughest man aboard. Many river boats construct rings where ambitious crewmen through elimination bouts work their way to the championship. Once the champion is determined he remains chief the entire journey. This is all determined before leaving dock. If a hand feels it impossible to accept the eventual winner as chief he is free to leave with no problem but once underway any crewman challenging the chief's authority is either immediately thrown overboard or locked in the hole until the next fuel stop where he is put ashore without pay.

Jonas felt the bouts may be useful as entertainment but not very proficient as an actual way of determining chief. He found it better to keep a professional pugilist on his year-round payroll and see if anyone was foolish enough to challenge him. Since he attempted to hire men of some reason a challenge rarely occurred. This gave Jonas complete control over the crew through the muscle of the crew chief and his 'earthy' management ability gained the respect of his officers. With control firmly in Jonas's hands there was less chance of conflicting purpose then in similar boats traversing the Missouri, where even the most capable of craft was continually at risk.

Alanson remembered the tranquility of the Sioux Valley, seemingly so distant though now a short days trek away (maybe ten miles as the crow flies). The Big Sioux and the Missouri river share a common valley for some twenty odd miles north of Sioux City until finally developing independent river breaks approximately twelve miles north east of Elk Point. The terrain between Elk Point and the staked railroad village (future town of Westfield, Iowa) Alanson had stumbled upon only a few days prior is flat and easily traversed.

He'd taken great risk in St. Joe smuggling runaways onto the 'Sioux' and when the Indian uprising became the talk of the river he had pleaded with Jonas to let him continue as engineer for just this one last round. Jonas would not hear of it.

Many nights they had discussed Alanson's plans which in reality were as much Jonas's as his own. Finding the ideal homestead and returning to Sioux City with the Riversioux still in need of him was more than luck…this trip and his involvement were predestined.

When leaving the boat Jonas had paid him well but he would not divulge any details about the remaining trip north. This Alanson had understood since he was no longer involved but now he was involved and answers were due.

Jonas was in the pilot house laboriously refiguring a long list of figures as Alanson knocked on the door. Alanson was responsible for and handled the bookwork of the Riversioux but Jonas owned the Riversioux and he alone was responsible for its crew and content; therefore everything concerning the Riversioux passed through his double scrutiny. This was a standard practice on any boat under Jonas's command and in no-way did it reflect upon the ability of or on his confidence in its officers. Competent men striving towards perfection prefer seeing their work verified as even competent persons may occasionally error.

"Jonas I know you are a decent man, some would say noble, but not a man to jeopardize an entire life's savings without some reward this side of the here after. What really waits us at Ft. Union?"

Jonas continued studying the figures in front of him as Alanson spoke. Then he slid back from his cubicle desk allowing his eyes through contact to confirm his words. "Alanson in the past few years we have become more then simple associates, we have become friends. As a friend I wish you hadn't returned to Sioux City so soon but being captain under these particular circumstances I need your experience and must confess I am more than a little pleased you did. Taking on fuel will be perilous and if we do succeed the fuel most likely won't be cured. For the first time in your career you may be operating a boiler room burning green fuel. You will be learning in the worst circumstances imaginable.

Fletch will have the added duty of securing firewood along with supplying fresh meat. We'll all be occupied trying to elude renegade Indians but if by divine wish we somehow make Ft. Union on schedule and then return to St. Louis intact we will all be well rewarded. All the furs procured over winter by Fletch and his troop of free trappers will be ours in payment for their ride to freedom. Two thirds I'll keep for the boat and the other third you, Fletch and the chief can split. If we do succeed in this endeavor, why next summer you can buy half the Sioux valley and have plenty left over to build an appropriate home for such a spread. As for me I'll pay the Riversioux off and have enough left for a down payment on a couple more boats but the odds are great we won't survive to see the coming frost."

Alanson was satisfied with the answer and Jonas didn't feel a need to disclose anymore at the present time.

CHAPTER 5

─────────────── ▼ ───────────────

Fletch was a man worthy of trust but not affable in character. To all acquaintances, old and new, his past remained a mystery. Apparently bitter remembrances from his youth still lingered destroying his ability to bond in the usual manner.

Badgers and foxes have been observed spending weeks together hunting. This works for their mutual benefit. The fox is swift and has a highly developed ability to locate prey while in comparison the badger is cumbersome. On the other hand few predators or prey can excavate a borrow as rapidly as the badger and as a killer the badger has no peers. Together they both eat well. The badger keeps what he catches and the fox keeps his, they never quarrel. When circumstances dictate the time to part has arrived each follows his instinct, never looking back.

Fletch is a badger with cunning. A cold, calculating, killing machine without the impediments naturally acquired from love. Fletch had been an officer on Jonas's boat for nearly 5 years. The 'Sioux' employed three officers, Fletch, Alanson and Jonas. Being one of three in a crew that now numbered twenty five (counting fugitives) is fertile soil from which a bond can spring. Try as he might to resist Fletch felt a growing responsibility to protect Jonas's interest, though not love this uncomfortably was becoming something beyond mutual benefit.

Sitting with his back against the wall of the pilot house Fletch lazily surveyed the deck and passing river bank. The late summer sun accompanied by prairie breezes which rippled shoulder high grasses in hypnotic waves put his mind to ease, as much as Fletch's mind ever allowed him ease. His duty when not hunting was to observe and be prepared.

It seemed his past life spent in London belonged to an individual remembered but long departed. At the age of nine his father had indentured him to a coal merchant. He felt no ill will toward his parents, he felt nothing. He had never seen either of his parents clean, rested or not hungry. Their time was occupied with survival, another mouth simply added to their burden. He spent his final week before indentureship alone with his mother. His father once again in debtor's prison.

He remembered his mother as an elderly woman although probably she had only been in her early thirties. Their final days together were spent huddled in a corner, sobbing and as usual "hungry". He left her fitfully sleeping in a stinking unventilated upstairs room in a tenement house perched above the reeking waters of the River Thames. At the age of nine, Fletch already understood that most anything would be better than what his parents settled for.

Fletch arrived two days before the agreed date of indentureship at the coal yard. Mr. Phillips, the "boss man" greeted Fletch with a cursing for expecting lodging and food when as of yet he had not labored. Fletch, unlike his parents, was as yet feisty and unbroken.

He immediately got in the face of the rotund boss man "why don't you eat the worms crawling from my ass you." "WHACK" some time later he woke up bruised and beaten—but not broken. For a while he laid observing the boys as they loaded and unloaded an unending row of coal wagons. All were being cursed generously but the younger and smaller boys regularly felt the sting of the boss's whip as they withered under the load. With no apparent alternative Fletch grabbed a shovel and joined the apprentices in their toil. Fletch though only nine was gritty, possessing an unusual ability to work.

'Boss' Phillips immediately noticed the new boy's initiative; most of the boys being recruited anymore were so lacking incentive they required a good beating for motivation. He would keep a watchful eye on this new boy.

Fletch made no attempt to rescind the friendship offered by the many boys who admired his grit. In less then six months he was made "tattle" boy, with the responsibility of reporting when the prescribed jobs were done and by whom. Fletch didn't tattle, instead he found ways of cutting corners and when necessary pitching in. In another six months he was made lead boy. He further refined and polished his management skills. If one of the boys was negligent or "sneaky" Fletch would call him out. They would fight it out then and there. The winner was deemed right and all was settled. Fletch didn't lose, although younger than many of the boys he was a fearless fighter with no compunction about using teeth, fingernails, elbows, knees or simply gouging eyes out of their sockets. He was respected by the boys for his honest approach to personnel management.

The boys continually accomplished more and more with Fletch as their lead boy but most everything has its limits. Production, after a while, leveled while expectations didn't.

'Boss' Phillips received a healthy stipend for his new found genius. The yard owners, based upon Phillips's recommendation, continued to up their projections of delivery while simultaneously cutting the work force. When deliveries began to be tardy, and then unfilled, Phillips attempted to retain the profit margin by cutting rations. With less food the boys output slipped even further. Phillips now under pressure returned to what he knew and the boys were beaten unmercifully.

Faced with the result of his previous management decisions Phillips issued an ultimatum, "get production back inline or else". Fletch tried to compensate for the inadequate work force by laboring late into the evenings but ultimately even his Herculaneum attempt fell short.

Being held accountable for his overly optimistic projections Phillips now became the target of stock holder criticism. Excrement demands release and so in front of the assembled boys Fletch was lashed to a wagon wheel, stripped and whipped by the boss man into unconsciousness. He awoke with a clarity of purpose. He had been beaten, starved, and made to live in filth just like his parents.

Fletch was exactly ten and one half years old. He had been beaten and degraded by a fat maggot living off the fruits of child labor. At the age of ten years, six months and one day a fat maggot boss man sucked his final breath. No human would ever use Fletch again.

For several years Fletch roamed the London streets with a band of hoodlums and in short time he rose to ring leader. As the gang prospered Fletch also prospered but as in any group of thugs there are jealousies and natural betrayals. One dark London night a gang leader was robbed, beaten and left to die by his "friends".

Of course Fletch didn't die, but he did change occupations. In his activities around the docks he had become well known as proficient in his line of business and for some time he had been courted by the teamster bosses to ramrod their most raucous night shift. Now in need of occupation Fletch accepted the offer.

He worked the night shift but spent his days listening to sailors talk about America and its opportunities. Soon America became his overriding dream. It was said that in America one could purchase a gun, a set of traps and earn a good living while never answering to anyone!

With his mind made up the rest was simply a matter of time and opportunity. He put his final weeks pay in his pocket and stowed away on the merchant ship

"London Fog" bound for America. Three days into the crossing he resurfaced and busied himself with task aboard the ship. With his gusto and natural ability he soon became an appreciated deckhand.

Fear had long ago been discarded by Fletch so when in the midst of an unexpected blow he climbed the mast and trimmed the sails, saving the ship from possible disaster; his place in the hearts of the crew was solidified. The first mate on this vessel was none other then Jonas Maynard.

Fletch paid little heed to Jonas other then to notice that he was a respected officer…In fact he didn't make any close friends on the voyage but he did manage to procure enemies.

Cowards live with a double curse. First a coward naturally lives in fear and secondly and even more compelling a coward fears recognition. Most cowards simply live a submissive life meticulously avoiding the possibility of conflict while others become bullies preying on the former in a demoniac demonstration of "manhood".

All living creatures have a pecking order. Humans, presently the apparent top rung in God's evolving creation, are no exception. Although not universally recognized, the female by nature occupies the alpha position in human society. Through civilization the number two position is occupied by the individual who manifests an aura of dominance. Civilization, being the creation of the dominant, perpetuates the status quo. Fletch, not a product of "civilization", offered pretense no latitude.

Bullies and their cousins (the pompous elite) despised Fletch for repudiating the accepted norm. His demise was plotted at first individually but when this failed as a group. With each victory his influence with the crew increased as his quarries influence waned. One morning several weeks into the cruise several bodies were observed floating in the ships wake.

Social order was maintained with cordiality for the remainder of the cruise and when the ship anchored in New York harbor the "civilized" passengers deemed Fletch an alpha citizen and the crew hailed him as their leader.

Even though generally admired and looked up to he still acquired no intimate friends during the crossing. The last day at sea before dropping anchor in New York Harbor Jonas sought Fletch out. "Fletch even though you initiated this cruise as a stowaway the officers and crew voted you full pay as deckhand" Jonas said as he handed him a pay envelope. "I have been instructed and personally I am pleased to offer you any position aboard the London Fog other than officer. I hope you will consider accepting the offer" he continued.

Fletch answered with a simple "no thanks". Fletch's dreams were not of wealth and security but rather of freedom and independence. A life confined to the restraints of a ship was not on his list of desirable occupations. With the unexpected bonus of a deckhand's pay by sundown he intended to own a gun, set of traps and a horse. The American west would be his confines!

Wow, New York was a city of contagious energy encompassing a conglomeration of enterprises, some legal and some otherwise but what caught Fletch's imagination was a game being played by "adults". It seemed every grass lot was home to one of these games. The crowds were rowdy and close plays were vigorously contested. He also noticed money exchanging hands once a winner was determined. Being a product of the "streets" with more than average physical ability Fletch reconsidered his 'immediate' departure for the west.

It was in the early 1840's and baseball was being invented on the streets of New York. Baseball being a game of 'equalization' caught the fancy of immigrants fleeing the 'old' system. Fletch would become a part of this early history although not a part that most sportsman would recall with pleasure.

The first organized ball team took the field in 1842 and was soon joined by a covey of others. The early games were poorly organized with rules being made and changed as the occasion rose. Within a year or two rules began to be formalized and teams with better skilled players could with fair confidence be predicted to win.

The New York Knickerbockers, a team of professionals (brokers, bankers, doctors and such) was soon organized and being 'doers' took it upon themselves to formalize a league. The Knickerbockers usually won their contest while Fletch worked the sidelines betting the opposing team's faithful on the games outcome. This was easy income for a spell but eventually bets were hard to come by. Fletch decided it was time to take a more active roll in the games outcome.

New Jersey also was a hotbed of baseball activity consisting mostly of young hardcore men off the streets with time on their hands. Fletches kind of team! He crossed the Hudson to Elysian Fields and soon was a 'star' player on a team of immigrants barely able to communicate with each other. These players possessed skills and grit but not discipline. Fletch rose from star player to coach and in short time to manager. With the new discipline that Fletch installed the team began to win some games and then they won a lot of games.

Fletch made an astute study of the game, the teams and its players and he bet accordingly, sometimes for his team and when prudent against.

Meanwhile across the Hudson the Knickerbockers were nearly unbeatable. The two teams weren't scheduled to meat on the field until late in the season.

Both teams had a great following and the money being wagered on the upcoming contest was astronomical. Fletch was well known for his uncanny ability to pick winners and now had to give points. In New York Fletches line for game day had New Jersey winning by three or more runs which infuriated the New York faithful while on the Jersey side the home team was given a five run handicap with Fletch taking the Knickerbockers. The New Jersey hardcore simply gambled so the bets poured in.

The week preceding the big game practice was intense on both sides of the river as this was the first 'World Series' of baseball. In later years these 'in city' rivalries would become famously known as the subway series.

The Knickerbockers practiced fundamentals and stressed the importance of team play while across the river in Jersey wagering and point spread was the focus. Fletch taught the first known course in shaving points (missing tags, hitting into double plays and the like). The incentive was established, every player on the team wagered heavily on a 4 run Jersey win!

On a warm and sunny fall afternoon the Knickerbockers and the Jersey 'lot' took the field amidst a well deserved fanfare. Bands played spirited numbers as blankets were spread on the raise surrounding the field. Entire families picnicked in pregame festivities momentarily evicting from their minds the previous week's drudgery of sweathouse labor.

The Knickerbockers held hands and prayed for divine blessing in this contest between gentlemen and the Jersey lot while the Jersey lot stared at Fletches hands feverously studying a detailed set of signals. Fletch, the team's catcher, worked out a set of hand signals to relay to the pitcher the pitch expected, from the sidelines he signaled to his batters when to swing away, bunt, strike out or when to simply blow a play when in the field. With Fletches discipline firmly established and this new unsportsmanlike like system of communication the Jersey club was a sports juggernaut.

The Knickerbockers were undeniably physically a talented team and with intimidation as a tenth player their winning percentage was the best in the city. In New York they were the establishment, a team of winners. In business and the professions these men were the elite, used to preferential treatment and accustomed to winning. Their opponents were employees and customers used to receiving instructions and advice. This relationship was not discarded on the field.

Jersey's ball team adopted its manager's character. When the game started the Knickerbockers expecting servitude received disdain. As the Knickerbockers became flustered the Jerseyites gained confidence. By the fourth inning it seemed as if the New Yorkers would be routed. Not satisfied with simply winning the Jersey boys began heckling the Knickerbockers and then their fans.

The crowd (parroting the athletes) also became unruly, hurling debris towards opposing fans and players. The umpires after a prolonged consultation halted play and threatened to rule the game a draw.

The boys of Jersey walked the sidelines apologizing profusely for their lack of manners, promising to be respectful if allowed to continue. In due time the crowd, wanting a game and the respite it offered, was pacified. With calm finally restored the contest was continued.

The delay affected the Jersey team's continuity and now threatened to derail the well oiled machine from 'cross the river'. Their previous precision play became erratic. Routine ground balls were suddenly being booted and mental errors compounded, throws were errant and the game tightened. The crowd was no longer unruly but instead became engrossed in the contest as the Knickerbockers once more seemed on the brink of victory.

The top of the ninth and the Jersey boys had somehow maintained a four run lead but the game now was in doubt. With the three point spread and the total collapse of Jersey those who had wagered were confident 'sportsmanship' would prevail.

Miraculously the Jersey team at the most opportune time reclaimed its composure and sent the Knickerbockers packing with three surprisingly easy outs!

Nearly three quarters of a century later in Chicago a futile attempt to duplicate Fletch and his New Jersey hooligans nearly destroyed organized ball.

Fletch understood when to stop. He left New York with a gun, a set of traps, a horse, half a suitcase full of cash…and a new found religion.

Every street corner seemed to be occupied by a 'man of God'; new immigrants make willing converts. Fletch like thousands of others immigrants was alone and longed to 'belong'. The hucksters cry "If you are lost be found. Jesus loves even the sinner. Come and be welcomed into the family of God" was irresistible. Fletch discovered the family of God within the confines of a tent pitched upon the banks of the Hudson River.

Companionship along with end time tales that would frighten the meanest lot of London was served once a week. Also to the oft used there was an appealing message of unerring judgment where riches would be bestowed upon the just and horrifying damnation unleashed upon the unjust. The message rousted Fletch and his peers from their seats with shouts of amen brother AMEN! Once a week Fletch paid his pew dues, upon leaving half a suitcase of cash legislated the huckster's tent obsolete.

The chatter of feeding crows ended Fletch's summer daydream. The River-sioux was approaching the juncture of the James and Missouri Rivers. In drifts along the shore lay rows of buffalo carcasses now thoroughly decayed and sun dried, the odor was more of leather than rotting meat. Nevertheless crows were in discord, scrimmaging over tatters of hide they had torn free. Fletch estimated as many as five-hundred buffalo must have perished attempting to cross the iced over Missouri sometime the past winter. Soon the whole crew leaned against the deck rail awed by the carnage of nature.

Even 'Explorer' seemed to grasp some significance of the carnage as he stomped and blew air through his nostrils as horses sometimes do when upset. Explorer was on board as more than an accommodation to Alanson. Jonas had installed a buzz saw on deck to rip limbs into useable chunks for use as fuel. He had asked Alanson to purchase three Belgians (Alanson insisted on mares) before leaving Sioux City to assist Explorer in pulling logs on deck. With the unstable Indian situation buzzing fire wood on shore was no longer feasible.

Fletch didn't philosophize much on the meaning of life nor question its unpredictable and sometimes brutal twists. The street peddlers of religion in New York had painted the picture of a blue eyed blonde haired Christ who bestowed wealth upon his worshipers and plaque upon the unbeliever. Having no reason 'or want' to question this doctrine he accepted it and when asked why he could espouse a somewhat comprehendible basis for his steadfast 'convictions'. In everyday life these thoughts never surfaced nor influenced a conscious decision.

Getting away from the confines of the 'Sioux' astride Alanson's' horse Explorer topped anything he had ever experienced. Although he lacked the fron-tier experience of other game suppliers he was well endowed with human experi-ence. He had been stabbed, shot, beaten and left for dead on numerous occasion and he always managed to return in kind, usually with properly accrued interest.

Fletch had managed to pick up some Dutch in New York and some Spanish in Florida. In Louisiana a smattering of French worked its way into his vocabu-lary. All these nationalities had at one time traded with the inland tribes and in the process had left a trace of their language behind.

He was getting a handle on some basic Lakota and the sign language used by all heartland prairie tribes was a quick study. With this background communica-tion, although at times painfully time consuming, was now possible with most any of the upland prairie tribes.

Contrary to common belief amongst the bar stool philosophers animals are an easy quarry when compared to the most cunning of human kind. Fletch long ago had mastered the streets and wildlife with their habits limited to their brain capacity were a quick study. On the other hand the American Indian possessing an ingrained knowledge of animal instinct combined with human intelligence made a worthy and admiral adversary.

Immediately Fletch felt a kinship with the heathen redskin and this kinship was demonstrated many times as a post businessman attempted to take advantage of the natives assumed ignorance.

Fletch knew he had two faults that might some day be his undoing. He could not watch someone be swindled by another who seemingly felt because of his 'superior' social status no crime was actually committed nor could he forget a kindness from one who expected nothing in return. The first made him a sympathizer to the Indians plight and the second kept him loyal to Jonas. Fletch spent little time contemplating the ethics of these issues; they had boarded the ship with him when he left the old world. The class system had never benefited him.

Explorer left the 'Sioux' just as anxious as Fletch. Being an animal of great physical abilities the confinement of a deck was not to his liking. Alanson was a gentle 'master' and Explorer reciprocated with obedient affection but when Fletch was at the bridle he was in his element. Without fail there would be adventure. His ability to travel great distances in record times and his astounding capacity to carry loads usually saved for pack mules would be valued—and used.

Good horses like good men are proud. Not only was Explorer proud but he also was vain. More then once he had allowed pursuers to close ground only to loose them in a sudden burst of speed knowing full well Alanson would never have condoned such behavior but Fletch encouraged it.

On one occasion while actively searching for mischief they happened upon two Indians attempting to pull a large elk back to camp with two Appaloosas but experiencing little success. Fletch knowing the Indians propensity for gambling bet his Sharps against the finer of the two Appaloosas that Explorer could pull the elk to camp by himself. They left camp with a horse in tow and the Redman's admiration.

There would likely be no such mischief this trip as the tribes had suffered long enough. Smallpox was decimating the nation, wiping out whole tribes. Bear, buffalo and elk were becoming scarce east of the Missouri and now the most eastern of the Sioux tribes were being forced to relinquish all holdings beyond the Big Sioux. For the Sioux capitulation was over!

CHAPTER 6

▼

Many forces shape an individual with righteous hate equal to any. Black Eagle planted the seed of hate, Flower's death nurtured the seed and on his death bed Black Eagle assured its maturation. "Inkpaduta your mother carried my child when she was murdered" were his dying words.

Inkpaduta had studied the ways of the white eyes and learned the ways of his late chief Black Eagle. Now twenty one he was known as the most knowledgeable of the renegades, waging war upon frontiersman in general and riverboats in particular. Under his leadership the splintered bands of Dakota Sioux opposing white domination were becoming cohesive. Inka believed it was imperative to shut down the Missouri to riverboat trade; his weaker brethren were becoming enslaved by the opiate of merchandise.

Not trading (they often boasted but through necessity did) with the whites Inka's band had few modern weapons. Providence now offered an opportunity to procure some white-eye fire power.

Fletch felt the presence of watchful eyes as he threaded his way through the mosquito infested marshes bordering the Missouri. Explorer methodically weaved side to side through the marsh grass temporarily brushing the pesky insects off both himself and Fletch only to have them immediately reattach in a frenzied attack. Every few steps the big horse would kick, attempting to dislodge basket sized clumps of gumbo that seemed to be attracted as if his hooves were magnetized.

Swatting mosquitoes and sweat soaked, Fletch cursed the twist of fate which had drawn him into such an inhospitable vault of torture.

At present stealth was not on the agenda as he carefully maintained (he believed) an escapable distance between himself and the concealment of willow thickets.

To rendezvous you first must make your presence known, he was drawing upon experiences from his past. Many times in the back streets of London he had purposely made his presence known to would be assailants, sometimes merely to reason and other times luring them into a predetermined trap. Never had he courted risk for its excitement as had some of his opium inhaling comrades had, nor did he now.

The muscles in the great horse tensed as they approached a thin line of willows surrounding the marsh grass.

In the west a storm had been brewing since early afternoon. This had been an exceptionally hot and sticky day so Inka kept a wary eye on its development as he and a score of braves paralleled Fletches progress. The time was nearing for yet another encroacher to exchange links in grandfather's revolving chain of life, this time as protein for the opossum, the skunk and the crow. When gorged these scavengers would depart leaving the more environmentally sensitive insects and worms to tidy up the Santee Prairie floor.

Inka sensed this intruder as a worthy opponent and surely strength would be attained as he chewed upon his still beating heart. The intruder's horse was an animal more magnificent then any he had ever seen and surely deserving better then its present circumstances. Today would be a good day were his thoughts as he clucked like a prairie chicken signaling his cohorts into action.

Lightening flashed in unison with a deafening crack of thunder causing the horses to bolt, instantly separating them from their riders. Man made plans were rendered useless as instinct preempted strategy. Momentarily conditions favored Fletch, Explorer excelled during trying circumstances, meanwhile Inka and party were left afoot scrambling to locate and then calm their terrified horses.

Inka, who Fletch recognized as party chief, was the focus of his attention. As Inka pursued his stead Fletch pursued Inka. Immediately the big horse and rider were upon the hapless Inka who luckily saw the butt of Fletch's fifty caliber Hawkins careening towards his head. He partially deflected the blow, saving his life but he nevertheless reeled to the ground unconscious. Hastily Fletch strapped Inka's limp form onto Explorer and the three of them rapidly distanced themselves from the recent field of scrimmage.

CHAPTER 7

▼

Alanson figured and then refigured power equations, over and then over again. Since burning the last of the dried hardwoods, except some which he held back for emergencies, fresh cut cottonwood was now 'the' fuel. Maintaining sufficient pressure to propel and stabilize the vessel as they wound their way through the perilous channel was becoming nearly impossible. The river had become a maze of sandbars, ever-changing channels, and floating logs both visible and submerged.

Alanson pulled the emergency cord signaling eminent danger as once again the boiler wasn't maintaining enough pressure to safely maneuver.

Jonas ordered the anchor lowered in midstream and sent Jeff Davis (Goliath sized fugitive slave) to fetch Alanson and 'Stroker', the boiler man to report to the pilot house once things were normalized.

Davis was a young black man of awesome size with a work chiseled physique. His features were etched with life experiences, which like most people exuded a first impression. Detour was undeniably the visible message. He and Stroker entered the pilot house almost but not quite simultaneously, being large men both twisted and ducked to enter the small cabin doorway Alanson watched in amusement before entering himself.

"Why do we always seem to loose pressure as the day wears on" Jonas asked? Everyone including Jonas already knew the answer.

"It takes a great amount of fuel to maintain adequate pressure. With the heat of the day in addition to the heat of the boiler room no man can keep the boiler adequately stoked with green cottonwood" Alanson answered.

"With cottonwood as fuel we need several boiler men" Stroker added shrugging his shoulders. "If we had time a man could probably be trained, IF we had a man aboard with enough mechanical savvy and enough brute strength to train. Which we don't" Stroker continued.

Alanson watched Davis as Stroker explained the situation. His impression of Davis had initially been of a man driven by hate but on closer scrutiny there seemed to be room for more than hate within the big man's bosom.

Stroker had been, even though the crew chief was unquestionably the most feared, the largest man on board the Riversioux but looking at Jeff anyone could easily see this was no longer the case. For some reason this apparently didn't register with Stroker.

Alanson watched as Davis remained nonchalant, visibly displaying no tangible change of expression.

Jonas raised his hand and spoke quietly "Jeff, obviously being physically capable has volunteered to spell you as boiler operator. It sounds reasonable to me".

Stroker, out of character, interrupted "no pekker-wood nigger shares the boiler with me".

Shaking his head Jonas merely nodded yes.

Alanson noticed the emergence of a wry smile on Davis's face as Stroker went into his tirade. As the three of them descended down the stairway toward the engine room Stroker made no effort to hide his contempt for Jonas's decision while Davis displayed a large subservient toothy grin, similar to a face years later displayed on boxes of rice.

There still being several hours of sunlight and with a deadline (with many dollars in jeopardy) to be met Stroker began immediately tutoring Davis. He was an ignorant nigger and the sooner "the old man" realized it, the better.

Stroker demonstrated how to sort fuel for dryness and for density. He explained the bell system, even though technically that was the engineer's responsibility it expedited the process if the boiler man could decipher the signals, He showed and explained the gauges and their uses, location and usage of various air intakes and outlets that controlled fire intensity and a multitude of danger indicators also the engineer's responsibility but valuable knowledge. He then demonstrated the proper way to stoke and feed the boiler. In the intense heat of the day when fatigued many boiler men became careless and were severely burned as a consequence.

Stroker was a good employee who genuinely strived for perfection. He didn't agree with Jonas on the "nigger" issue but he had taken employment on the 'Sioux' and disregarding an order was not indexed in Stroker's book of ethic.

Dusk was settling in and the long work day was ending. "How long before you think you can handle the job" Stroker sarcastically asked?

"Come daylight I'm ready boss man" Davis answered equaling Stroker's sarcasm.

Now Stroker knew this fugitive cotton picker hadn't begun to understand the intricacies of the boiler room but neither was he about to argue with the thick headed nigger so he simply answered "see you in the morning BOILER MAN" as he hurried up the walkway to report to Jonas.

By the time Stroker reached the pilot house he was fuming. "Jonas that nigger learned the basic operation of the boiler room in one short course" raged Stroker "says tomorrow he is ready to solo. I apprenticed for a whole week before I even considered soloing and this big coon says he's ready! The whole bunch"—

Once again Jonas raised his hand to silence Stroker's torrent of temporary insanity.

"Okay Stroker, do we have all summer to school someone" Jonas asked? "Did he ask any questions that would lead you to believe that he didn't understand the job"?

"The black S.O.B. didn't ask anything. He acted as if he understood"! Stroker was in need of relief. He truly wanted things to work out for Jonas and everyone. Didn't Jonas understand that niggers weren't capable of learning complex mechanical things?

"Go below and get a nights rest" Jonas ordered. "Tomorrow maybe we'll each look at this differently" he was still speaking as Stroker slammed the door behind him.

Jonas had dealt with ignorance all his life; still he was uncomfortable with people drawing conclusions from hearsay. Stroker had determined a man because of coloration wasn't capable of learning "simple" mechanics.

He slumped in his chair, exasperated. What a conundrum, Stroker was a loyal dependable employee who possessed a mind capable of finding answers to complex mechanical problems. If given a part with unusual coloring Stroker would examine the part for defects and if none was apparent he would use the part; given a human being of color and he was summarily discarded as unusable.

Jonas wasn't a philosopher who agonized over reasons but instead possessed a mind that came to conclusions in a predictable mathematical fashion; he simply observed and processed what he saw. This gave him the ability to make decisions quickly, and then sleep well with the decision. Essential traits for honorable men in leadership positions.

CHAPTER 8

▼

Jeff was fourteen years of age when he unwillingly left Africa. His name had been Malaika Akomolafe until he became an 'American'. He remembered his passage well, chained in the puke filled hole of a slaving vessel. Malaika had reason to be consumed with hate and for a time he had been but Malaika no longer existed.

He was born in the Benin region of Nigeria during a time of turmoil. Africa was in the wrenching process of being divided by its conquerors. Old traditions were being challenged and found wanting by modern technology and new religions. Europeans were busy 'modernizing' black Africa. Plantations, gold and silver mines, and agri industry complexes rendered the age old village social system obsolete. African tribal hierarchy was in disarray and becoming impotent.

However there were enclaves where strong leadership delayed this cultural downward spiral and Malaika was born into one of these enclaves. He, the son of the village leader, seemed destined for good things. He was well liked and athletic and already at the age of thirteen he towered over most men, even so Malaika sensed all was not right.

Many of the neighboring inland tribes were abandoning their native beliefs and now proclaimed allegiance to Allah. On the coast, under European influence, Christianity was making inroads. 'As a rule' in the past another's religion was of little importance. Many beliefs had survived side by side for as long as time but there was a dark side to these new beliefs. While the former religions were for the most part tolerant towards other beliefs these new Hebrew based religions exalted a jealous God. More troubling was their exclusiveness, leaving non-believers little more than chattel. Muslims converts were now kidnapping infidels for sale to the

Christian slave traders operating out of the port cities of Accra, Abidjan, and Lagos.

Trust among neighbors was disappearing and of-course Malaika was troubled but he lost little sleep over these things. He had greater things occupying his mind; tomorrow he would be initiated into the 'Swashassa', an elite young men's club and an essential stepping stone towards future tribal leadership.

Malaika slept fitfully and with good cause as he full well understood that initiation could be a brutal test. His courage, stamina, and temperament would all be tested. Not that he worried greatly about his courage or physical stamina but the possibility of being tricked and humiliated by jealous rivals as was often the custom wore on his conscious.

At dawn Ebau and Nosha, co-leaders of Swashassa, rousted a weary Malaika from his bed as the long days events were already commencing. The tribe's social structure, consisting of three rings, was gathered around a large fire. First an interior ring of somber elders and holy men in customary dress, next a colorful ring of honored warriors (displaying traditional weaponry), and finally a festive ring containing the remaining villagers.

The village circle parted as Malaika was escorted to the center by Ebau and Nosha where he was then instructed to kneel in a submissive position. He was then undressed and washed thoroughly by several of the more elderly females in the village. When the task of cleansing was accomplished holy men anointed him with an odorous liquid solution. Once externally purified he was ordered to a sitting position.

Next a young virgin in exquisite costume came dancing forward carrying a large vessel of fermented herbs (crushed\ liquefied and reeking). With both hands gripping the container she pressed the concoction to his lips. Malaika gasped for air as the liquid flowed into his stomach. He dared not swallow. Malaika simply let the liquid flow, knowing that if he swallowed his throat, once closed, would resist reopening. Tears welled from his eyes, he felt as if he was aboard a storm tossed sea vessel. Trying desperately to steady himself he stumbled as he was being coached to his feet by the soft voice of his attending virgin. Numbed and dizzy he heard her suggestively whisper "when you return a man I'll be waiting".

Weak and disoriented he was roughly dragged from the throng of revelers by his mentors (Ebau and Nosha) deep into the forest surrounding the village where he was instructed to kneel and wait. He was told he would be met by four warriors from a neighboring village who would compete with him in a gauntlet of travails prepared by the Swashassa brotherhood.

He thought this unusual as neighboring villages were not customarily included in tribal ritual. Malaika strained to reason but dizziness prohibited it and kneeling did provide the rest his reeling body craved.

Was he dreaming or were there voices behind him! Straining to remain cognizant, the conversation seemed to end with cursing and the exchange of money. Malaika heard footsteps approaching from behind as he was struck.

He awoke bound hand and foot surrounded by strangers. Was this a gag? He struggled to free himself and again was struck but this time the blow was meant to induce pain. He was instructed to get up and walk and once again he struggled to resist and once again he was rendered a painful blow. Confused Malaika stopped resisting and did as he was ordered. Was this an initiation trick? He prayed fervently this was the case.

After a four hour forced march his hopes were instantly and brutally crushed. In a clearing he was prodded into a well guarded holding cage already overflowing with young Africans of various tribes and customs. This was a rendezvous point for Arab businessmen dealing in the slave trade.

Malaika knew that both Ebau and Nosha were jealous of his abilities. They had been vying for pre-eminence in the Swashassa and with his inauguration they both would be eclipsed. He didn't want to believe that members of his own village were capable of such atrocity but as he was shackled and forced aboard a slaving vessel any lingering doubts vanished.

Malaika despised everyone connected to this barbarous trade. He hated the guards who imprisoned him as he waited shipment and he hated the Moslem slave traders who delivered him to the port but nothing equaled his contempt for Ebau and Nosha!

Once aboard ship male and female were confined together in one large room beneath the deck. Each individual was cuffed to a chain that ran the length of the vessel with honey pots placed at each end and one in the middle of the chain. The cuffs were connected to the chain in a manner allowing the prisoners (in unison) to traverse the length of the chain. No toiletries were supplied other than the honey pots which were 'intended' to be emptied three times a day.

Females experienced their monthly menstruation and as the trip progressed and weather deteriorated the port holes were closed, honey pots spilled and passengers vomited. The odor became so overwhelming the crew no longer entered the hole to empty the honey buckets. Food and water was simply handed down several times a day. The cargo died from these conditions at a rate of up to twenty percent. Still the profit margins were good and the trip weeded out all but the fit.

No smiling lady brandishing a torch welcomes these immigrants. Upon arrival they are immediately transferred to an auction vessel which lay anchored just outside the port of New Orleans. The survivors are stripped and herded into a holding room where the filth is hosed off.

When clean they are separated by sex and then professionals in human trade further segregate the slaves into small lots of equal physical abilities.

Malaika received individual attention as he had had remained in remarkable good health. Being physically dominant, in the hole he received first food and drink. Though he hadn't demanded this treatment he nevertheless received it. In every society the strong are served by the weak. Structured societies throughout the ages have indoctrinated their subjects with the notion that any alternative leads to chaos and ends in anarchy. Any theorem continually restated eventually becomes an accepted fact. The hole is itself a structured society.

When Malaika arrived the importation of African Negroes for slavery had been banned for some time in an attempt to appease the growing contingency of northern anti-slavers in congress. How ever the abolitionist were not appeased nor did the importation and auctions of slaves discontinue. The business became quasi-clandestine which rendered the imported Negro ever more valuable and insured the dealer a larger profit. It also added an indispensable middle man.

The auctions now took place aboard a roving auction vessel which met the slaving ships out of port where the transfer of cargo actually took place. The 'auction' vessel was acquitted with a slave cleaning room, a bank, restaurant and bar and an ornate auction arena. Small pleasure boats ferried buyers to the auction and then the Negro and his new master back to shore. For this service the auction vessel received a fixed percentage of sale receipts. The operation in reality was quite transparent but local authorities seemingly were 'misled' by the shrewdness of the operation.

On the auction block Malaika was forced to pose showing off his well muscled frame to an appreciative audience of plantation owners and slave brokers. The bidding was spirited and enduring with the winning bid rendered by a prominent young broker.

Adam Davis was the broker's christened name. He was an aristocrat, one of four sons in a prominent southern family. Adam was well mannered and equally well attired. The product of fine schooling and with an understanding of class and social graces, he had never known want.

No gentleman ever stepped with more pleasure then young Adam as the magnificent Malaika paced behind him in docile servitude. Adam, a broker, lived well dealing in human stock but this large nigger was not for sale instead he would serve as promulgation of 'his' social status. To own a slave of such magnitude with a natural inclination for servitude would guarantee the envy of his gentleman friends.

Malaika had been away from his parents for less then three months. At fourteen he still emotionally was a boy, unfortunately he was a boy encompassed in the physique of a man. Tears no longer formed; but his heart ached to be home. He was broken and without purpose. Malaika was raw material waiting to be molded.

Malaika was taken to the Davis Plantation of Mississippi where he would be trained in the social graces of a personal servant. Possessing good intellect and with a want to belong, Malaika became an outstanding student. He especially excelled in the languages where he mastered the King's English with French soon following.

With young Malaika as personal servant Adam looked forward to social affairs as never before. Malaika bowed, opened doors and never once exuded his manhood, which genuinely pleased his young master.

For nearly two years Malaika existed with apparently no purpose other then to serve.

Malaika's life again was abruptly altered when Adams youngest Brother Jefferson (who had been away to military academy) returned to the plantation. Adam, although aloof, never abused Malaika. In truth more then once he was known to object when his friends made Malaika the butt of their jokes. To Adam Malaika was a good servant and a valued property, undeserving of derogatory statements.

Jeff the youngest of the family and apple of his father's eye thought differently.

One Saturday night a month the young sporting 'gentleman' of the community arranged matches between male slaves. Often the contestants were the most physically fit males of the plantation genuinely wishing to participate; other times their involvement was punishment. After being paraded in front of the spectators wagers were consummated. The 'host' plantation would then serve a gentleman's supper for the guests comprised of meats, greens and deserts, followed with plenty of 'spirits'.

Meanwhile the nigger contestants were shuffled to a sorting pen where customarily a religious service was held. The service generally was performed by one of the local plantation parsons who regularly ministered to the slaves. After services the niggers were herded into a livestock pen surrounded by a tall board fence which served as a temporary fight ring.

The fights lasted until one contestant was unable to respond (often mortally wounded). The winner customarily would receive sexual free reign of the plantation for a specified period, death would be preferable for the conquered. Generally only two 'bucks' fought but on special occasions several plantations were represented. Great amounts of money would be wagered when a free for all was the event. Jeff being a 'sportsman' wagered often and lost regularly. Being on a run of bad luck he once again desperately needed cash. Malaika now sixteen was a physical specimen to behold and Jeff salivated.

Quakers (friends) were present in small numbers throughout the southland. This band of worshipers firmly believes God hates violence and abhorrers slavery. Being more moved by the earthly works of St. James than the abstract philosophy of the Apostle Paul, passive action coupled 'with' heartfelt prayer supplied substance for these believers.

From creations dawning man's blood has continually leaked in fanatical acceptance of the idealist sword, sadly ideas do not take root in blood. A battlefield rarely advances an 'ideal' while on the other hand ideals have survived indefinitely if 'one' individual willingly sacrifices his life at the alter of enlightenment. Courage of conviction is 'unquestionably' demonstrated when violence is opposed in a nonviolent manner. This the Quaker believes and he has internalized the doctrine.

As with all theologies there are a few inherent but necessary variables. In the friends book of practical theology every deception imaginable was employed to remain anonymous. Righteous chicanery abounded!

Jeff, being the youngest brother, begged and pleaded until Adam finally relinquished and loaned his big nigger for "just a couple of weeks".

It was common knowledge among the slaves that when violence was about to be perpetrated upon them the parson was the avenue of last resort. Malaika visited the parson.

Four contestants would be featured at this months sporting event with all except Malaika volunteering for the contest.

Each gladiator had 'personal' meditations with the parson several times leading up to the match where plans were laid and finalized. The railroad was alerted to 'book' passage to St. Joseph Missouri. The captain of a riverboat was in-turn alerted that 'freight' was being procured.

Saturday night as the supper festivities were preceding four 'fugitives' vanished into the Mississippi countryside. After dinner the festive young sportsmen found the parson lying unconscious, bleeding from a wound on the head and with blood still trickling from a swollen grotesque mouth.

Later that steamy southern evening, with bandaged head, a 'friend' painfully lisped a prayer of thanksgiving while trudging home.

Approximately two weeks later after shuttling from station to station (mostly manned by Quakers) the four freedom seekers arrived in St. Joe Missouri. The city of St. Joe was an adamantly divided city with a plurality of its citizens harboring pro-slave sentiments.

On the Kansas side of the river however the antislavery sentiment was in majority. In the midst of these Kansas sympathizers was a safe house operated by the 'railroad'. On a Saturday night, after having rested and being fitted with clean cloths, Malaika and his three companions were escorted to the rendezvous house.

The house, rather its occupants, reminded Malaika of a rendezvous on the shores of another continent in his past life. Africans of many cultures were huddled together excitedly, yet obviously apprehensive, discussing dreams of a future life. Back then they were huddled together with no dreams, sharing fears. This was a new life and a new time.

Just inside the door a white man with a tally book recorded the date and name of each fugitive as he entered. In turn each was asked what his free name was to be, what skills he possessed and what occupation was of interest.

Malaika was the last to enter. When asked his name he answered "Jefferson Davis and I want to be a Sioux Indian".

Malaika, (now Jeff) hadn't given any thought to changing his name. The name Jefferson Davis came from somewhere within. But he did understand. Jefferson Davis, his demure and self righteousness, put flame where a dying ember once simmered. Jeff Davis had fathered this free nigger.

Many fugitive slaves already lived amongst the Sioux. He had even heard that a band of mulatto (Sioux\Africans) had established a territory of their own. Jeff had dreams, if he could join up with either he would and if not he would strike out on his own.

Jeff mingled with the other 'guests' as energy long dormant began to rekindle. Making conversation without fear was not immediately possible. He had left Africa merely a boy and if he had dreamed of a future he couldn't remember.

The dreams of a slave can't be verbalized as ears are everywhere. He had seen fellow slaves beaten for revealing secret dreams for self betterment to their peers. Some trouble causers claimed the master employed Christian preachers to replace the Negro dream of earthly 'materialism' with dreams of an afterlife. In any case while the dreamer was beaten the 'nigger' informer enjoyed privilege.

Since stepping off the boat in New Orleans Jeff had always 'sensed' an invisible spirit listening as he spoke and watching as he moved and the spirit reported directly to Mistah Davis.

Jeff had been schooled well in the English language and his usage was impeccable but he had also learned that proper misuse of the language at the appropriate time endeared him to the master. Now free he no longer felt the need to pretend.

As Jeff worked his way around the room making conversation he was astounded at the sophistication of these fugitive slaves! Amongst the field hands mingled Africans of education. At first he was mystified, then he thought about is own education. They, like he had worked the system. There were teachers, practitioners of medicine, accountants, and professionals of every sort. Just as he, they also had been taught skills to enhance the life style of aristocracy. Though education of slaves was legislated illegal, capitalism deemed it worthwhile. The brightest were educated to fill positions more fitting their abilities. Even in slave societies education reaped reward for all. The plantation benefited from in-house expertise and the slave benefited from elevated dreams. To Jeff it seemed most those dreamers were fellow guests.

Jeff enjoyed conversing with the professionals but while making the rounds he found many who shared his dream. Soon persons with common dreams were clustered in small groups. Jeff was amongst a group of would be frontiersman when they made eye contact.

The few females present in the railroad hotel also sought out groups with similar goals. Jenny's dream encompassed a good Christian man, children, a home and a piece of productive farm land. Jenny was wrapped in animated conversation with a small group of aspiring farmers when their eyes met.

Not a small woman, Jenny was pure Ebony with hard well defined muscles that rippled beneath her black sun darkened skin. An obvious fugitive from the cotton fields, Jenny wore her ruggedness with dignity.

She, unlike most of the guests, hadn't run from the master's whip, or for that matter the long harsh days spent bent over in the delta sun. She found satisfaction in her labor and she found solace in Jesus. If not for the sons (and their teenage friends) of her master the seed of freedom never would have germinated.

Pre-civil war Dixieland, with all its perceived gentility, from Virginia on the east to Texas on the west operated more whore houses per capita than modern day Nevada. The female slave was pawn to the sexual whims of the master, his sons, and their guests. The gentile ladies of southern aristocracy possibly were not aware their husbands and sons were rapist and pimps, seeing and not comprehending are a necessary skill in such societies. That many slave babies had light skins, many with family resemblances to the master seemed to go unnoticed in America's bastion of social graces.

Jenny could not remember not being a Christian. The plantation encouraged black participation in the faith of their master and as with other conquered peoples most complied. Religion helped pacify a population whose numbers nearly equaled their keepers. Every plantation made available and encouraged worship services for the Negro.

The Negro minister became the elite of Negro society; effective ministers gained respect and gratuity from the master. The gospel of acceptance with a promise of a blessed afterlife served the master and sustained the servant.

Jenny was a believer who served and obeyed her master. At times she had questioned her seemingly hopeless circumstances and always the written word quashed the inherent sinful quest for reason. When plying the parson on this issue he would paraphrase the 'holy' book "God has a plan beyond human understanding in which we all play a given role, if one unquestionably as a child accepts Gods will, Heaven is your reward". She had heard this over and often, from her first to her most recent sermon. This reconciled the young slave girl until she blossomed into womanhood. The gospel also proclaims the body is a temple and a spiritual shrine which shall not be defiled. Being unable to justify rape and sodomy under the auspices of 'obeying' your master, Jenny fled.

With the unset of darkness she ran. Jenny, a fifteen year old run-a-way was short on plan but long on faith. While still within the sight of the plantation Jenny knelt in prayer. Faith, though usually misrepresented is a powerful tool. As Jenny raised her bowed head a small campfire was visible through the thickening night fog. Expecting an answer Jenny without hesitation walked uninvited into a group of 'runners'. The fugitives, startled by this unexpected arrival, fled leaving their few belongings behind. Bewildered but firm in faith she ate the prepared but abandoned meal and then crawled under a blanket and laid down to rest.

Shortly after midnight she was awakened by two white men, one badly bruised with a swollen mouth. "Where are the others" they asked?

Jenny was confused but answered as best she could "they ran away". The three stared at each other with a bewildered look.

Finally the fellow named Phillip asked "What are you doing here, we weren't expecting a female".

Jenny now completely confused and with a twinge of fear setting in demanded "WHO ARE YOU"?

Phillip and David also confused were not threatened by her presence as there probably had been a change in their scheduled pickup.

The Underground Railroad had many unscheduled passengers and even more no shows. "What is your ticket destination" Phillip asked while placing a reassuring hand on her shoulder.

Jenny, not understanding but now trusting these obvious vessels of God, simply told her story.

Phillip and David through necessity also operated on faith. Phillip did most the talking as David, though improving daily, lisped his words badly. Phillip explained to Jenny who they were and what they did. Though both men were concerned for their booked passengers safety they also were visibly joyful Jenny had been delivered to their care.

Jenny arrived in St. Joseph one day ahead of Jeff.

Jenny strained to stay focused on conversation but found she continually instead focused on Jeff's where about...He was the most self assured African she had ever seen and he was sooo big. She could overhear some of his conversation and wondered how a fugitive slave could speak with such perfect clarity? While these thoughts entertained Jenny's conscious their eyes met once again.

Neither Jeff nor Jenny said a word as they sat staring at one another. Finally he asked "how long have you been here"?

"Since yesterday, I was a passenger on the railroad" she answered with her dark eyes still focused.

Jenny though outwardly calm internally was in turmoil. Though drawn to this seemingly gentle giant her thoughts involuntarily returned to the plantation and her terrifying experiences with the master's teen-age sons. Just fifteen years of age and without benefit of family, having been purchased and separated from her mother at six or seven years of age, she had no practical knowledge of relationships.

Jeff sensed uneasiness had come over them but why? While trying to think of something to say he noticed a small cross on a simple chain hanging around her neck. His breathing became labored as he reached for the necklace.

Jenny was startled by his actions and jerked away, afraid. The kind man with a swollen mouth had given her the necklace. On its back side was the letter "D". He had explained that if she ever got to Southern Ohio he had family there who would offer her refuge. Go to any of the many 'Friends' meeting houses and show the cross.

She was still grasping the necklace with both her hands as Jeff laid a nearly identical necklace along side with tears streaming down his face.

Jenny released her necklace and placed her hands in his as tears from her dark brown eyes mingled with Jeff's.

For some time neither spoke, "how was reverend David" Jeff finally asked? Jenny who had been chilled with memories of sexual servitude only moments ago was now warmed by memories of kindness.

She related her journey to freedom as Jeff listened in astonishment. He and three other strong men, after two weeks preparation had made the same run and they had nearly met disaster but this 'girl' simply relying only on her faith had left after them and had arrived a day earlier!

"How was reverend David" he asked again more firm then he had intended.

Jenny startled by his demanding tone answered "he was as gentle and as kind as anyone should be" she said pointedly, "even with his bruises and protruding lips".

She could see Jeff was struggling to regain his composure so she once again gently squeezed his mammoth hands, this time to reassure her new friend.

Jeff had confided in no-one since arriving in America but Jenny would have to listen as he prepared to unload a burden he no longer could bear. Looking at her with pleading eyes which now betrayed his youthfulness he started "as a condition for his help the reverend insisted one of us strike him on the head knocking him unconscious. He showed us how and even where to place the blow and then he insisted we practice by hitting a stockyard post with an oak branch. Of course no-one was willing to do it so we drew straws and I lost. He demanded we do it and then to erase any doubt of conspiracy to kick him in the face once he was unconscious. He said it was his calling to man the railroad."

Tears unashamedly fell from both as he continued "I saw blood oozing as his head caved from the blow, and then with my eyes closed I managed a kick. We grabbed our things (the 'friends' gave us each a change of cloths and two dollars) and ran. I was afraid he was...dead"! Jeff could not continue.

In other times under similar circumstances Jeff and Jenny would be preoccupied with problems related to adolescents. Instead issues of life and livelihood preempted the psychology of affluence. Jeff just sixteen and Jenny fifteen, products of similar life experiences now sought dream partners.

Sitting and holding hands they discussed their dreams. Jeff espoused his dream of frontier life while Jenny reiterated her love of the land; circumstance had molded an environment demanding a shared commitment. Being free, being young and being in love when the two were whisked aboard the Riversioux the two diverse dreams had willfully amalgamated into one.

CHAPTER 9

▼

In the cool predawn fog Stroker impatiently sat in the boiler room anticipating the debacle of Jonas's 'nigger' experiment.

The stillness that necessarily accompanies daybreak was interrupted by the approaching cadence of Jeff's long stride. Sipping a cup of steaming coffee Jeff appeared carrying an extra cup "Jenny thought maybe my 'partner' would enjoy a hot cup as we discussed the day's agenda" Jeff said as he casually offered the aromatic brew to Stroker.

Stroker seethed but the coffee was welcomed. "Jesus Christ this uppity nigger strolls in here drinking coffee ready to DISCUSS the day's agenda"! Stroker could barely contain himself but managed to ask with sarcastic politeness "are you ready for work and is there ANYTHING we went over yesterday that you didn't understand"?

"I'm ready boss but possibly things will come up we didn't discuss" Jeff replied with a toothy grin while setting his cup down.

"Okay, boiler man, build up steam" Stroker couldn't wait to hear this smart ass nigger's plea for help. He swallowed a large gulp and then with theatrical contempt threw the remaining coffee overboard.

Jeff built up steam using only the greenest fuel, saving the precious elm, oak and dry cottonwood for the emergencies that he had been told would surely arise later on.

The whistle blew and bells tingled signaling the start of a new day. Alanson also enjoying Jenny's coffee pushed the throttle gently ahead to quarter throttle.

Instinctively Jonas 'felt' for the throat of the river as he uncannily navigated through the treacherous morning fog.

Bells tingled continuously as Jonas and Alanson communicated with Jeff stoking the boiler accordingly.

Stroker became more and more agitated as Jeff calmly responded to each bells demand with a cool confidence. Stroker remembered his own schooling under Oscar the big Swede S.O.B. who castigated his every mistake. The sting of those rebukes still smarted after all these years. Stroker could not understand how this run-away cotton picking S. O. B. could manage the technicality of boiler room procedure but God Damn-it he was!

As the morning fog dissipated bells continually sounded as Jonas demanded more and more throttle. The heat and humidity associated with mid summer river travel encompassed and then possessed the boiler room but still Jeff with massive biceps bulging continued to satisfy the incredible appetite of Miss Sioux's boiler with 'green' fuel.

Stroker was becoming less annoyed and more awed as the day progressed. He was as good a man as any on the river and after years of acclimation he still wore down as the heat of the day extracted its toll. What kind of life could prepare a man for conditions as demanding as these? Damn few men survived in these conditions yet this Nigger-Davis apparently remained unaffected as he continued to feed the furnace.

As the Riversioux continued making steady progress up river Stroker began contemplating on what actually was transpiring. He and the crew had a huge stake in getting to Ft. Union on schedule and with two boiler men their chances of success were naturally enhanced many fold. With an understudy such as Nigger-Davis the chances were multiplied even more.

Stroker leaning through the entry way of the boiler room asked "Davis how about taking a break"?

Jeff smiled casually and shook his head no. He was near collapse from heat exhaustion and his body cried for respite but he wasn't about to give the arrogant piss-ant the satisfaction of that knowledge.

"Go and get yourself a drink and God Dammitt that's an order"! Stroker meant what he said.

Jeff managed a nonchalant stroll towards the mess as Stroker's eyes followed him.

In a short while Jeff returned appearing anxious to man the boiler but to his amazement Stroker greeted him with a quizzical yet friendly grin. "Stand and watch big man, if you have any questions just ask" Jeff sensed his sincerity.

As the bells tingled Stroker began explaining not what they meant but rather what to expect next. The bells he explained were actually Alanson's responsibility but a 'good' boiler man should also understand their meaning, so mistakes aren't made through misinterpretation. He talked and Jeff listened.

Stroker was beginning to see Jeff as a boiler man rather than a 'black' boiler man. Stroker didn't realize this change but Jeff definitely did. This wasn't a new phenomenon to Jeff. How many times had whites seen him only as a nigger until he proved his capabilities, even then some remained slave to their prejudice but in time most men ascertain what they witness.

Jeff could see that Stroker was knowledgeable about his trade and he also seemed to genuinely care about the Sioux and her mission. This was good enough for him, his dreams depended upon this mission and now he also had Jenny to think of. It seemed Stroker's job and his dream at least for awhile would share the same path and he really hadn't boarded the Riversioux to socialize.

On the plantation Jeff had asked questions and eagerly learned with fear as his motivator but now for the first time in memory Jeff asked questions for reasons that probably could be described as selfish—if desire for self betterment is selfish.

Stroker found he now answered with measured care for he was a proud man, if Nigger-Davis was going to learn the boiler trade aboard the Riversioux he damn sure would learn well!

When men through work become peers, former prejudice dissipates like fog under a mid-morning sun...Neither Jeff nor Stroker had 'planned' for it, yet both now reaped its dividends...

CHAPTER 10

▼

Fletch was in possession of a dubious prize and now what to do with it was a puzzle? He personally had no quarrel with the Redman and he had sought no confrontation, the battle was brought to him and he had responded. An aurora of unqualified hate seeped from the heathen as Fletch rechecked the leather cords securing him.

Inka was humiliated being strapped to the horse he had intended for his own and why hadn't the heathen killed him?

Fletch also was pondering the days happenings. He supposed he had no more love for civilization than this Redman. Most tribes had at least a few dilapidated guns but he had noticed this band mostly relied upon the bow and arrow...so Fletch began concocting a plan. First he would have to somehow subjugate and then communicate with his uncooperative captive.

His mind drifted back to times gone by. When lead boy for old man Phillips in the London coal yards he had used diplomacy tailored to the workforce. He took measure of his captive and then nodding his head in approval he pressed Explorer to pick up the pace. He hoped he hadn't misjudged his captive's character.

Fletch was searching for an open meadow with which he was soon rewarded. The sweet aroma of fresh buffalo dung mingling with the acidity of urine drew him to a freshly cropped meadow of blue stem grass.

Dismounting Fletch grabbed Inka by his hair, lifting his head to eye level. In comprehendible Sioux dialect Fletch propositioned his securely bound prisoner. With thumb thrust into his chest he spoke. "They call me (Fletch). I am brave, trustworthy and a better man then you. You who are tied to my horse like a female rabbit, what are you called"?

Inkas instincts reigned in his fury. "Play this right and soon the impudent white-eye would be crow bait". He would play this white-eye's game. "I am Ink-paduta, chief of the Wahpekute and the scourge of all white-eyed heathens. They call me Inka, you F-L-E-T-C-H dog puke".

Fletch flashed a boyish smile as he callously rolled Inka off Explorer.

Inka though hurting also was pleased. Another prick or two at this white-eye's pride and he'd soon be freed with white-eyes begging him to test his masculinity. "F-L-E-T-C-H dog puke is brave when the rabbit is in a cage. A GIRL is brave, trustworthy and better then her enemy when her enemy is bound head and foot. Is dog puke a girl"?

Fletch rolled Inka onto his belly. Then while pretending to hump Inka dog style Fletch added more insult. "How does Mrs. Rabbit enjoy being screwed by a puke dog"?

Inka though contemptuous of this cocky little white-eye piece of dog shit did admire his gritty humor.

He was about to answer when Fletch leaned over and kissed him full upon the lips, then he sweetly whispered in his ear "Listen Miss Inka, chief of the bunny tribe lets play a game with real stakes. I will tie my horse to the far tree with all my weapons. Then I'll release you and if sweet bunny rabbit can muzzle this bad dog so be it BUT if I whip your sorry ass so bad you can fight no more you must agrees to my plan.".

Inwardly Inka thought (I don't bargain with white-eyes, I kill them) but smiled as he nodded in agreement. "Breath deep dog puke for it will have to last for eternity".

Fletch knew this would not be a fair match but what fight is. Most Indians he'd known were good wrestlers, masters with knives and usually athletic but they were not pugilist. For this reason Fletch had egged Inka into fighting in an open meadow. With no sticks or stones as weapons there would be much blood shed, mostly by Inka.

Inka was coiled and prepared to spring as Fletch loosened the final knot. Grandfather had touched the brain of this loco Fletch and soon his horse and GUNS would be his booty. Inka made a dive at Fletch who simply sidestepped while landing a bruising blow to Inkas mouth. Bone and sinew cracked as blood exploded from the impact.

Stunned but still upright Inka again rushed Fletch and again met with the same results. Over and over the scenario was replayed. Inka was game and even learning to block some of Fletches blows but had no idea how to retaliate. Fueled by hate but now breathing heavily on increasingly unsteady legs Inka continued to press the battle. Finally being battered unmercifully he swallowed his pride and resolved to continue the fight white-eye style. With new resolve and with his own fists raised he attacked.

Meanwhile Fletch also was contemplating the situation and decided this had gone far enough. It was hot, his arms ached and his knuckles were beginning to swell from thumping the Indian's hard head but more importantly he was still in hostile territory!

This time Inka was prepared to grab Fletch's arm as 'he' side stepped while unleashing a crashing right hook of his own.

Fletch did not side step but instead walked directly into the charging Inka lifting him skyward with a knee to his groin.

Inka fell limp, nauseated and helpless. Moaning with hands grasped between his legs he was barely cognizant as Fletch firmly grasped his head and spoke directly into his face.

"This was fun sunshine now lets conclude our business" Fletch spoke with authority but seemingly displayed no animosity.

While holding Inkas head erect Fletch carefully articulated the proposal.

Fletch explained the 'Sioux's' dilemma and their need for firewood and safe passage. He explained that onboard the 'Sioux' were great stores of ammunition and guns. He proposed a dozen rifles and a small amount of ammunition for each catch of wood delivered along the route and with safe arrival at Ft. Union the Wahpekutes would be supplied with enough ammunition to mount a major war.

Jonas had given him the authority to use what ever means needed. Now he hoped the 'old man' was serious.

Inka listened in disbelief as this Fletch who could have killed him twice but hadn't now offered him the means to drive him and his kind from the Santee homeland. Most surely grandfather spirit worked in a mysterious manner. Bruised, bloody and nearly beaten to death Inka whispered a prayer of thanks while shaking hands with Fletch consummating the bargain.

They then determined to meet in three days where the Missouri dips southward to juncture with the Niobrara. The 'Sioux' would be anchored on the south side of the river where Fletch with four men would meet Inka on the shore opposite from where they were moored.

They raised their hands in salute as they each returned to their own kind with an unbelievable proposition.

Inka despised this white-eye who had twice nearly killed him but he also grudgingly respected him. He would use him for his purposes and in due time he would be dealt with. In the span of two full moons he might possess what he had thought would have taken years to accumulate. No he didn't trust this 'Fletch' but the reward was so great he must see it through.

Upon returning to the Wahpekute village Inka related how he, even after continually being beaten while secured hand and foot, had managed to escape from the white-eye. Once loose though already severely beaten, he had defeated the white-eye, nearly killing him! Then grandfather spirit grasped his hand as he was about to deliver a death blow. The words uttered from his lips were not his own but the words of eternal grandfather. In return for firearms white-eyes life was to be spared and the boat was be given safe passage to the Yellowstone. Grandfather obviously possessed white-eye's mind as he had agreed.

Once the Wahpekute accomplished grandfather's task, they would destroy the boat and kill all its occupants! They would attain enough weapons and ammunition from the boat storeroom to successfully defend the Dakotas and reclaim the home of their ancestors, Spirit Lake.

Inkpaduta had been hand picked and groomed by the late Chief Black Eagle to be their leader and the Wahpekute eagerly followed.

Meanwhile Fletch was having second thoughts. Not that 'he' didn't think his bargain reasonable but he wasn't sure this is what Jonas had in mind. Jonas being a man of peace would balk at such a proposition. With the Wahpekutes being known as renegades Jonas would not okay supplying them with the means to escalate their uprising. Something a little more palatable would be needed to sell the idea to Jonas.

He would tell Jonas the meeting was in four days. One more rendezvous with the savage Inka would be needed before this deal came to fruition. Hopefully the Indian was enticed enough to show.

CHAPTER 11

▼

Jonas was beginning to be concerned as Fletch had been gone for quite some time. Through the years Jonas had known many capable men who had perished at the hands of the Sioux. Still Fletch WAS different.

He had received a most heartening report on the big run-a-way slave Jeff Davis which is what he had anticipated all along. In choosing his crew, character was as paramount as job ability. Once the port at Sioux City was behind them the Riversioux became a civilization its own.

Alanson was a thoughtful individual who as second in command Jonas felt he was well served. Stroker was big and strong with a work ethic second to none. He was mechanically inclined and willing to learn. Though a social Neanderthal he harbored no meanness within. Yes Stroker also was a good crew member. Big "Rube", his hand picked bouncer\ crew chief was what he appeared, a thug who did what he was paid to do therefore he also was a valuable crew member. Fletch remained the wild card in the deck!

Fletch was a loner with a past that remained elusive. Jonas remembered how he got to America and also how he had demonstrated his worth while in route. Still he preferred to know where and what shaped the character of his nucleus crew. Since Fletch didn't discuss his past Jonas was compelled to accept him on performance. Perform he did! He had never encountered such a hunter or fighter. Physically he was certainly adequate but not overwhelming nevertheless he performed with grit and a coldness that was at times chilling. He killed with no remorse, though he had never been known to provoke a situation. Jonas knew Fletch had a sense of right and wrong, it simply varied from every accepted norm on earth. He was confident Fletch was fond of him and the crew in his own way. That was the catch; Fletch did all things according to his code.

As Jonas was occupied with these thoughts Fletch was sighted approaching the river bank.

For some time Fletch rode parallel to the 'Sioux' looking for a spot where the river made a sharp bend forcing the current shoreward. When the channel made contact with the bank the 'Sioux' moored just long enough for Fletch to lead Explorer up the loading plank.

Though thankful for a temporary haven of rest neither Fletch nor Explorer was anxious for an extended repose.

Alanson shook hands with Fletch while they exchanged reigns of the great horse.

Explorer whinnied as Alanson led him to his stall. Alanson knew that when Explorer was with Fletch he enjoyed a freedom he would never experience with him. He could tell his big horse enjoyed Fletches episodes and this pleased him. He cared deeply for his horse but he was who he was and anyway Explorer was plenty enough horse for the both of them. As Alanson combed the stickers from his hide Explorer reciprocated with a gentle nuzzle.

Fletch explained to Jonas that the Santee Wakpekutes were now under the leadership of Inpaduta as the late trouble causing Chief Black Eagle had passed on. Black Eagle had hated the white man but Fletch assured Jonas that Inka was a man of honor and one who could be negotiated with.

He explained how the two had met while stalking the same herd of deer. Together they had laid in an abundant supply of venison for the Wahpekute band and the 'Sioux'. Later around the friendly confines of a camp fire they had negotiated an agreement for fuel wood and a safe passage to the Yellowstone. The fee hadn't been determined as of yet but in four days they would meet again and finalize the agreement. He, Jonas and three others were to meet Chief Inkpaduta and his band at the Niobrara juncture to finalize the agreement.

To Fletch this wasn't a fabrication or even misstating the truth. Truth was a term people used when common sense wasn't adequate; he simply was doing what was best for the 'Sioux' and her crew. That is what he had signed on to do. Now he had to come up with a way of satisfying the needs of both Jonas and Inka while at the same time shielding both of them from the 'truth'. Satisfying Inka should be rather easy since he only wanted weapons and would have little interest in how they were obtained. Jonas on-the-other-hand could be a problem for as far as Fletch could see he always was concerned with a broad range of circumstances that wasn't warranted. He didn't give a rat's ass if the Wahpekutes had enough guns and ammunition to prolong their inevitable capitulation. In fact he sympathized with their plight even if their present circumstances necessitated them being mortal enemies. Deceit was foremost on his mind as he walked toward the mess hall prepared to enjoy his first real meal in some time.

The James River is a peculiar River in that it meanders more than six hundred miles to negotiate less then a three hundred mile route on a venture that begins east of Mandan North Dakota and ends at its juncture with the Missouri near Yankton South Dakota. The topography of this region offers the river no sense of resistance leaving it free to traverse broad expanses where in fact a shorter route would offer superior drainage. In late summer it is common for the river to become stagnant, relinquishing the decaying fragrance accompanying such happenings.

On-the-other hand the Niobrara is a stream of contrast. It rushes from the Rockies to the Missouri marked with rapids, fueled by torrents of rushing water steadily cascading toward the mighty Missouri River.

The stretch between the mouths of these rivers often becomes treacherous with sandbars appearing and disappearing within hours causing the stretch to be well known as a burial ground for paddleboats. If two paddle wheelers should happen to meet anywhere near this stretch the pilots engage in serious discussion concerning location of sandbars, whirlpools and other conditions of concern.

The St. Joseph on its way down stream was the bearer of bad news. There had been a major rise in the Niobrara due to recent heavy rain storms in the Rocky Mountain foothills causing sand to build up to such an extent the Missouri was now simply oozing through the wide Missouri basin with no apparent channel.

C H A P T E R   12

▼

JONAS

Jonas was the only child of Chauncey and Helen Maynard a respected Quaker family in the Philadelphia vicinity. Chauncey, a second generation master carpenter, practiced his father's trade customizing and fitting timbers in the Delaware River Boat Works. Jonas a third generation apprentice studied under his father, but stories of the sea captured his imagination.

Chauncey, content with life and having no desire to graft Jonas as a mere extension of himself encouraged Jonas to apprentice mornings in the ship yard and school at The Philadelphia Nautical Institution in the afternoons. In the yards he learned the physics of ship building while in the afternoon he studied the science of the sea.

Jonas being a conscientious student earnestly studied and generally retained what was presented. While showing scant interest in experimentation he excelled in deciphering the better of proposed plans. 'He was comfortable with tried and true methodology'.

Joneses ability to recall details pertinent to a particular situation coupled with his unpretentious self assurance were prerequisites for leadership. Rearing, schooling and aptitude rendered Jonas well qualified for leadership responsibilities.

With his parents blessings at the age of twenty one Jonas signed on as a junior officer aboard the frigate 'London Fog'. The freighter maintained scheduled rounds between London and Philadelphia and it was during this period that Jonas became acquainted with Fletch; he filed Fletch in his memory bank.

In the port pubs paddlewheel riverboats were the talk of adventurous young American seaman. Jonas being young and inquisitive was not immune to such gossip.

The Mississippi River was becoming a hub of transportation with the paddlewheel being its modem. River cities were prospering and expanding at phenomenal rates. Rivers provided natural roadways through an otherwise formidable landscape. Qualified pilots were few and the demand was great, river pilots could name their price!

The crème-de-la-crème of pilots navigated the Missouri, where both river and residents remained hostile. The Sioux (with the Notable exception of Chief War Eagle) hadn't been gracious hosts to Lewis and Clark and things definitely hadn't improved.

Below the Port of Sioux City the river is masculine in nature sporting a deep channel that procures a straight determined and completely unimaginative course while from Sioux City northward the Missouri becomes feminine in attitude with a treacherous channel continually shopping for a course, trying every variance, but genetically incapable of decision. Sandbars regularly appear and disappear with no apparent explanation.

Numerous are the pilots navigating north to Sioux City, few are the pilot who traverses beyond but those who do and survive the adventure fall in love with this whimsical lady.

Early in Joneses fifth year at sea he returned to find his father had succumbed to a major Cholera epidemic. Jonas, not willing to leave his mother alone, resigned from the London Fog and seized an opportunity to pilot a riverboat making daily excursions between Philadelphia and Trenton New Jersey.

Six months later his mother also died. It appeared, since she seemed in reasonable health, she simply wasted away wishing to join Chauncey. This probably was the case but Jonas never-the-less harbored guilt, believing he could have placed more value on his mother and less on his occupation. Needing a change in life, Jonas sold the family business and departed for St. Louis.

For the following eighteen months Jonas apprenticed as pilot on various paddle wheelers based in the Port of St. Louis.

In his second year of apprenticeship, while moored at the Port of Sioux City, Jonas was granted the opportunity to apprentice as pilot on a north bound paddlewheel. The upper Missouri stole his heart!

Upon returning to St. Louis he harbored intentions of purchasing his own boat but this was the fall of eighteen forty eight and freight demand was booming. Even with proceeds from the family business he still lacked the funds necessary to purchase a boat since established shipping firms were now actively bidding on riverboats still in production.

With his hopes temporarily thwarted Jonas spent the winter off-season securing loans from business associates and friends. By spring Jonas had secured enough financing to purchase a rebuilt but somewhat dated paddlewheel from an ex-associate at The Delaware River Boat Works.

MARY

Mary George was eight years old when the wagon train formed heading west in search of California gold. The George plantation still retained considerable value and produced abundantly but as the family expanded and the land eroded changes were needed to sustain a life style appropriate for a family of prominence.

The Georges and several other wealthy Virginia plantation owners booked passage on a west bound wagon train in which Mary, her parents and baby sister would accompany to St. Louis. Once in St. Louis the landed entrepreneurs would split off and head for Texas while the plebian forty-niners continued on to California.

Mr. George had in his possession bank notes of substantial value plus a dozen slaves. The ventures goal was to purchase, clear and initiate operations of a branch plantation in East Texas.

Mary remembered farewell kisses and tears as they parted. For most train participants the trip to St. Louis would be arduous but for Mary it held promise of excitement and new adventures.

The George wagons were well provisioned and accompanied by slaves who would perform services not unlike at home. Departure was a carnival of insuppressible excitement for young Mary who proudly sat between her parents who exuded their own unsuppressed glow of optimism but for the slaves there was an aura of sullenness which precedes the heartbreak of fractured families and the prospects of added drudgery.

Character is an illusive thing and its origin even more so. Mary, reciprocate of favored circumstances, at an early age was not comfortable with her inherited nobility. She loved both her parents and her Negro caretakers. While she willingly obeyed her parents and with earnest pleasure studied the social graces necessary for a life of southern aristocracy, she gained her zest for life from black persons in bondage.

In most circumstances sincerity breeds respect but the 'system' prohibited either. Still she was young and youth has a noble dream.

Mary possessed another trait which was sustainable. In figures and the transaction of business she was a prodigy.

Also accompanying the train was a young Christian couple who made regular stoical visits spreading the gospel to each wagon while at the same time soliciting financial support for a proposed mission in The Nebraska Territory. In a short time their spiritual energy was mainly focused on the wealthy and then exclusively.

Mary's parents being the elite of the elite warranted their preferential diligence and they, accustomed to preferential attention, received this attention as matter of fact.

The Georges and the reverend relieved the monotony of wagon train life by discussing the lofty subjects of theology and politics while the reverends wife kept young Mary current in her schooling. This routine continued uninterrupted until the wagon train pitched camp on the banks of the Mississippi River waiting to traverse the mighty aorta of the new world.

After restocking their dwindling supplies the bulk of the train planned to follow the Missouri River west to St. Joseph where an experienced wagon master had been procured to guide the train west through hostile Indain country.

Without warning Cholera struck! Hundreds died with whole families perishing within hours! The City of St. Louis was quarantined. The few supplies made available were left at the outskirts of town where healthy members of the train retrieved them. For Mary anarchy and panic suddenly replaced excitement and adventure.

Mary's family was not spared. Mother, father and baby sister all became ill while Mary unexplainably remained in robust health.

Meanwhile the young missionaries were not negligent during this time of strife. Every possible means of care was employed, but to no avail. With death imminent the young 'mercenaries' (who also remained healthy) became desperate to retrieve some dividend from their investment.

The parson hastily penned a letter to Mary's grandparents detailing their circumstances, leaving out no detail of the effort extended in behalf of the family they had grown to love. Official appearing documents along with the un-cashed bank notes were inserted into a communication requesting Mary become a ward of the young Christian couple. An addendum requested a generous yearly stipend, as the young couple was much more adept in furthering the gospel then their own financial being, was added.

The pastor hurriedly paraphrased the content of the letter to the dieing man, requesting he sign it. In the interest of his sole surviving offspring William George carefully penned his signature to the document, dated August 23, 1849.

Young Mary was now in possession of three wagons containing finery of all sorts; silverware, jewelry, and clothing plus a substantial amount of cash from her fathers' cash box—but the slaves had vanished.

Her new custodians immediately went about pursuing financial arrangements in her behalf. The pastor secured transportation across the river intending to sell Mary's excess possessions but unfortunately because of epidemic fears commerce with 'foreigners' was temporarily banned within the city limits of St. Louis.

The Riversioux was in the process of being loaded for its maiden journey as the chagrined Pastor Cheney returned to the St. Louis docks.

For a substantial figure an agreement was arraigned with the captain guaranteeing transportation for four wagons, livestock and three passengers. Freight of less priority was unloaded and put back into storage. Though the cash outlay was substantial the reward would be even greater.

The Reverend Cheney, now being a man of means, suddenly had acquired a head for business. St. Joseph was the final rendezvous of the 'forty-niners' before entering Indian Territory, a natural sellers market for wagons and livestock.

Another letter was posted to the George family back in Virginia requesting all further correspondence be forwarded to St. Joseph Missouri,

Later in the day the Riversioux docked in East St. Louis to pick up its last minute cargo.

Though unsure of circumstance, Mary (resilient by birth), boarded the paddle wheeler Riversioux with her usual unshackled anticipation.

ALANSON

1849 was a year of infamy in St. Louis. Not only did Cholera strike but four months prior the boiler of a paddlewheel had blown near the St. Louis Levee initiating a fire that leveled fifteen square blocks. All government buildings were destroyed along with many boats in harbor. Numerous other boats were partially damaged.

One's misfortune is another's opportunity and Jonas being skilled in boat rehabilitation was quick to take advantage. The Molly Joe, christened only two months earlier, was one of the boats badly damaged in the disaster.

For a 'song' Jonas purchased the damaged riverboat 'The Molly Joe' which was equipped with the latest in river technology and had been especially designed to traverse the upper Missouri.

Immediately a gang was assembled to refit the lisping paddlewheel. Jonas's intentions were to retain the best of the construction workers as boat crew with Alanson being foremost.

Alanson was born in western Pennsylvania, the son of John and Elizabeth Baker. The Bakers were a hard working Pennsylvania Dutch farm family of modest wealth.

In appearance church was the cornerstone of family life but in practice church was client to appearance. A quite formality was the families prevailing image.

When young Alanson, as boys will do, challenged the family norms with actions 'uncivilized', Elizabeth gently censored 'the young rascal' and continued her façade of gentility. Upon returning home gentility succumbed to rage as Momma embarked on a dialogue of unending 'truisms' concerning tyrants and punishment. Alanson being too young to comprehend the language fully grasped the message.

With appearance being virtuous in the Baker household, cleanliness; manners and ethics publicly blossomed while privately wilting.

To the passer-by Sunday, being the Sabbath was a day of rest and reflection on the Baker farm. If one could pierce the seclusion of the barn John would be seen methodically performing weekly maintenance on farm equipment while Alanson laboriously pitched the week's manure.

In later years Alanson never claimed mistreatment; except for appearance sake he was sure he should not exist. In fact Alanson harbored few memories of his early childhood. His youth which was spent upon a stage of make believe left few highlights.

From puberty on memories abounded! Some were pleasant with the others being learning experiences.

The Shepard of the Baker church flock was approximately forty years of age with a barren wife perhaps fifteen years his junior.

In this church's doctrine children when attaining the age of responsibility (early teens) are enrolled in religious Education. After a year of intense schooling each student goes before the minister who asks pertinent questions concerning virgin births, trinity and so forth. Upon answering the questions correctly, while maintaining a proper attitude of sobriety, the young adults are recommended to the deacons for church membership. A recommended student is not denied membership.

The next procedure is baptism by immersion. Baptism by immersion is a somber ritual (separating literalist from papist) which involves the believer being totally immersed in water and then 'lifted' once again by the attending preacher. Sacred words of ancient origin are solemnly recited over the immersed body.

Upon emerging the believers soul is miraculously and gloriously cleansed of all previous sin; then through atonement 'of the blood' ever lasting life is attainable. In protestant vernacular this process is labeled 'born again'

Being thirteen years of age Alanson was enrolled in religious education…

On Sunday evenings Pasture Satterday conducted the classes while the Wednesday evening classes were conducted by his wife Jane, the pastor being occupied with 'The Weekly Wednesday Evening Prayer Services'.

Never known to smile in casual conversation the Reverend scorched the congregation with righteous rage on Sunday mornings. On-the-other-hand Mrs. Satterday appeared to be joyous by birth but sobered by circumstance, Alanson looked forward to Wednesdays while dreading Sunday.

Preacher Satterday asked Alanson to stay after class the first night of R. E.…and every subsequent class. Alanson, only thirteen, was innocence personified. The Reverends massaging hands were unexpected, uninvited and unwelcome. If only it would have ended there.

Alanson left class physically hurting, confused and harboring misplaced (but very present) feelings of guilt. He walked around the section many times with his mind in disarray before finally returning home. Should he tell someone? In the past his mother usually worried what others would think when confronted with 'his' problems. Maybe this would be different? Then again maybe 'he' had done something the preacher misinterpreted?

When finally reaching home all he did was cry; no he did do one other thing. He kneeled and he prayed as never before! He fervently prayed 'this' would never happen again.

Of-course the next Sunday it did happen again. When asked to stay after class he had anticipated Rev. Satterday wished to apologize and make things right but instead this time he was also threatened.

Arriving home crying he was chastened for disturbing his parents Sunday evening Bible studies. Chastened or not he could not help but cry. Finally being 'greatly' annoyed Elizabeth asked what was the matter with him? Alanson wanted to tell but really didn't know how. Finally amidst a flow of unending tears a partial story emerged.

In horror Elizabeth insisted he never repeat this lie again! What would people think? As usual John sat with his arms folded piously saying nothing.

For the first time in his young life Alanson began to 'think' beyond the perimeters of the parochial ghetto imprisoning his mind.

In time even horror becomes routine. With an escalating 'health sustaining' loathing for the preacher Alanson learned to tolerate Sundays but now Wednesday well THAT was another day!

On a warm July evening the R. E. room appeared in desperate need of cleaning so Mrs. Satterday asked Alanson to stay after and help straighten things up a bit.

Alanson noticed that as the curriculum advanced 'the' Mrs. Satterday's dress and mannerisms were becoming more and more interesting. Standing erect with good posture the absence of undergarments wasn't too conspicuous but when leaning over to pick up 'numerous' dropped objects the absence became inescapable.

This evening teenage boys fantasized as Mrs. Satterday taught the class with an unmistakable throaty lust and lust is very communicable in the teenage years. After class young teenage boys rushed home in search of relief…all except Alanson.

With the reverends damnations bellowing down from above, Alanson and Mrs. Satterday engaged in adulterous behavior upon the cool R. E. floor.

For the next six or seven months every Sunday evening Alanson descended to the furthest depths of Hell, pacified with the knowledge ascension and 'rapture' followed on Wednesday.

He shared neither event with his parents.

After the Christmas Pageant Mrs. Satterday asked Alanson to help put the seasonal decorations back in storage. Happily, with expectations Alanson followed her to the R. E. Room. She was crying as the door closed. "I'm having a baby" were her words.

She explained the pastor hadn't shared beds with her since their wedding night, quickly adding "I have a plan but I am so worried about you"

Alanson had never considered the possibilities of birth or babies but being young the prospects didn't seem that daunting.

"What are your plans" he asked with growing excitement.

Mrs. Satterday explained that ever since discovering her pregnancy she had been borrowing from the church offering plate. It really was quite easy since it was the duty of the pastor's wife to hand the collections over to the church treasurer after having herself counted the receipts.

Her younger brother James hadn't wanted her to marry the Pastor in the first place and he had always wanted to go west. Now financially sound they were leaving for St. Joseph Missouri this Wednesday evening. She would fain sickness in the afternoon and ask one of the mothers to teach R. E. class. She was quite sure the pastor wouldn't miss her till breakfast the next morning.

"I'm going with you" was Alanson's reply.

Jane (Mrs. Satterday) at first tried to dissuade him but after looking at Alanson and considering the special circumstances of his home life finally relented, neither had reason to remain.

Alanson wouldn't be missed until breakfast either for other then at meal times his presence seemed to be an unwanted embarrassment. Since relating the details of his relationship with Rev. Satterday and his parent's reaction he was most comfortable spending his days outside and his nights alone in his room.

Alanson had a few details to tend to before departing:

Thursday morning after becoming completely exasperated at Alanson's late arrival for breakfast Elizabeth Baker entered Alanson's bedroom. Horrified she ran screaming through the house with Alanson's farewell note. "HOPEFULLY YOU WON'T FIND MY RUNNING OFF WITH THE PREACHER'S WIFE TOO EMBARRASING".

Towards the front of the R. E. room stands an easel which holds a large folder containing sheets of writing paper. During class the folder is opened and the instructor meticulously prints Bible verses of special significance on the sheets of paper for students to copy and memorize for their upcoming inquisition.

Sunday evening the bereaved pastor opened the binder prepared to fill the folder with Biblical condemnations of adultery.

In large letters was Alanson's parting epistle:

> With his rod Moses split the sea,
> using his staff to set men free.
> But Satterday's rod split my ass,
> making it painful for shit to pass.

> (read—Leviticus: 20 verse 13)

Years later Alanson considered both messages rather childish; but of-course at the time he was a child.

Jane, her brother James and Alanson shared an apartment upon arriving in St. Joseph. Due to the added stress soon after arriving Jane went into an early labor where she experienced difficulties. Sorrowfully the baby didn't survive. These were difficult times for young Alanson and for his house mates; Alanson being a child himself reacted in a childlike manner and moved to a boarding house.

Alanson, needing to support himself, hired on as a dock worker by day and with Jane's insistence attended classes at night. Mondays and Wednesdays he studied surveying for his own enjoyment and on Tuesdays and Thursdays he studied accounting…In short time he gained a reputation as a responsible clerk as well as dependable deck hand. Soon he began accompanying freight shipments to insure no fraud was perpetrated in route or at destination. This was the frontier.

Meanwhile Jane began receiving courtiers and soon a proposal, which she accepted. Jane's new husband-to-be was a Quaker. After marriage the two moved across the river to Elwood Ks. where a small community of Quakers already resided.

At first Alanson was simply jealous of Jane's new love but as Jane blossomed and her happiness bubbled forth his jealousy faded.

Alanson arrived in St. Louis several days before the great explosion. Having gained a reputation as an honest and bright young clerk the city secured his employment to eliminate fraud and help facilitate the many settlements being negotiated.

It was during these negotiations that Alanson and Jonas first became acquainted.

CHAPTER 13

▼

Having made numerous changes, structural and otherwise, Jonas decided to rename his rebuilt Paddlewheel.

What separates average riverboats and average pilots on the Missouri River is it's juncture with the Big Sioux. Below the Sioux River many pilots and most paddlewheels routinely make rounds while above The Big Sioux only skilled pilots with custom built boats dare venture. Jonas intended to be one of the 'few' so in the summer of 1849 the registry of the "Molly Joe" was changed to the "Riversioux".

The Riversioux was seaworthy and Jonas had a crew. Due to the disaster many tons of freight piled in harbor warehouses and the freighting future appeared bright.

The "friends" were an active group in the St. Louis area, occupying several meeting houses. Jonas when in the St. Louis area attended and contributed, financially and intellectually.

It was at one of these meetings prior to embarking on his first voyage aboard the Riversioux that Jonas became acquainted with The Underground Railroad.

Following fellowship, in a conversation revolving around the ethics of slavery, Jonas espoused a firm stance condemning any and all involvement in human bondage. He was then encouraged to accompany the group to a member's home for further discussions and coffee.

Upon entering his friend's home he was surprised by the bevy of activity and the presence of twelve Negroes. His public stance on suffrage along with a reputation already garnered gained him the confidence of this secretive Christian organization, the St. Louis depot for the Underground Railroad.

Twelve slaves from a west bound wagon train had managed to escape during the chaos of the recent cholera epidemic. Being aware of the Quaker stance on slavery the group sought refuge in the first friends meeting hall they encountered. Now with newly printed papers of freedom they sought transportation north, eight planned to make connections at the Kansas terminal for eastern passage while the remaining four were heading north to become free trappers. That evening Jonas booked his first 'railroad' passengers.

Possessing forged papers with still drying ink the fugitives slipped into the belly of the Riversioux. Extreme precaution was taken to obscure the fugitives from sight as any Negro in transport was by nature suspect.

Alanson as Jonas's new clerk and part time deck hand intended to make a good first impression upon his new employer. His primary responsibility was to ensure all freight was accounted for and properly secured. On his initial inspection upon leaving harbor he immediately became aware that some freight had been shifted into new positions.

Alanson attempted to do another inventory but with the freight being shuffled it was impossible for him to be confident all inventory was accounted for. What would the 'old man' think of a clerk who bungled his the first day out! He fretted over the situation for some time and valiantly tried to come up with a reasonable solution but with no feasible alternative he finally decided to report his findings.

Alanson entered Jonas's cabin with trepidation. "Captain we have to anchor immediately and re-inventory our freight, something is amiss and I think we better determine what that something is before we get any further from port" Alanson spoke apologetically.

"Sit your self down Alanson and have a cup of coffee" Jonas interrupted, "you haven't miscounted. I booked a dozen free Negroes for transport late last night. They take almost no cargo area and it pays very well. If I had waited for the government authorities to do their paper work and check documents we would still be in dry dock this time next week. With my last minute commitment to the pastor I simply couldn't wait. Alanson I am truly sorry you weren't notified and for this I apologize".

Alanson was satisfied with the explanation but he still was not pleased. "Captain if I'm to have responsibility I also must to be aware of ALL transactions, if that isn't possible I'm afraid this job isn't either". He was turning to leave as Jonas's hand rested upon his shoulder.

"Just a minute Alanson, I hired you because of your attention to detail and I am not going to loose you for fulfilling expectations. From now on I assure you all freight procurements will pass through your hands".

Satisfied they shook hand, shared a cup of coffee and with growing excitement discussed the Riversioux's inaugural trip north and of-course through St. Joseph, Missouri.

Alanson left Jonas feeling anxious to visit Jane in St Joseph but right now he was heading into the hole to seek out his 'freight'.

After a prolonged game of hide and seek the fugitives were coerced out of hiding.

The Negroes told of their trip from Virginia and the cholera outbreak, then how on his death bed 'Master George' had signed their papers of freedom. They also mentioned a little orphan girl (Mary), who they swore they hadn't abandoned until she was under the protection of a young missionary couple.

Alanson as of yet didn't really know the 'young missionaries' but his gut feeling was to sympathize for the girl.

Alanson was puzzled. The twelve slaves were below, the missionaries and little girl were above and everybody including the skipper told a different story! He believed the skipper hid the truth (if he knew the truth) for good reason. Meanwhile he would attempt to befriend this little girl named Mary.

Instead Mary 'befriended' Alanson. Alanson happily escorted her everywhere, except the hole, carefully answering her many questions as they went. He gently questioned her but she said nothing derogatory about her custodians. He noticed she gave them no praise either. He did sense apprehension but who wouldn't be apprehensive in her circumstances.

He found he looked forward to their walks. She was the trusting sister he'd never had and with Mary there 'refreshingly' was no pretence. She looked up to and trusted him in a way no-one ever had and it felt good. Still though he continually tried he never could determine her destination, she didn't seem to know and the pastor wasn't certain since he had undertaken his new 'responsibilities'.

On the third day out of port Pastor Chaney approached the now inseparable pair and instructed Mary to run along to Momma Cheney as her school studies had been neglected all to long. "Mary will not be dawdling with the likes of deck hands in the future; the girl needs a stern hand. Am I understood?" Rev. Cheney 'preached' to Alanson.

Alanson's heart sank. He wanted to throw the pious bastard over the railing but what would that accomplish for little Mary?

Though they shared the same small vessel for the entire trip they never again managed to converse in private but he did manage to slip her a note...CONTACT A. BAKER % THE RIVERSIOUX AT ANY PORT ON THE MISSOURI RIVER IF EVER YOU NEED HELP.

The trip up river to St. Joseph is an easy stretch of river to navigate. A relatively straight channel with ample flow isn't a great challenge but is a great training course. Jonas put the Riversioux and her crew through every rigor imaginable. Their combined performance left him pleased and confident.

Meanwhile the fugitive slaves remained secluded with their aloneness broken only by Alanson's occasional visits. He spent hours in conversation with them and the 'skipper' attempting to make heads or tails out of the entwined destinies of the Riversioux's passengers.

When the Riversioux docked in St. Joe Alanson believed he had most of the pieces in place. His quest had been for understanding not confrontation and his new knowledge only added to a growing admiration for his skipper's quite courage.

Alanson determined he for the most part harbored the same desires as Jonas but he pursued another antidote to life's dilemmas and that answer was capital. Capital can be slow to accumulate but he was young and time seemed non-ending. Of-course if that preacher ever harmed little Mary—well there are things which can't wait!

CHAPTER 14

▼

Like tundra warming under the summer sun St. Joseph sprouted with renewed energy. Until a short while ago an ever shrinking frontier trade and a dependable but slowly expanding farm economy afforded a niche for the port cities business establishment. Now wagon trains rolled in to St. Joe, the last chance to replenish supplies before a 1700 mile trek through Indian Territory, in a seemingly never ending stream. Paddle wheelers were moored in dock loading and unloading supplies continually. Business was good and fortunes were being realized.

As the Riversioux was being secured to the dock a ruckus in, then in front of, the "Wharf Pub" caught the attention of her deck hands. A buffalo hunter and an Indian were embroiled in a brawl with the pub patrons. Though greatly outnumbered, the two seemed to have the upper hand until the gathering crowd of spectators sided with the pub's patrons, and then together they assailed the two with renewed ferocity.

After a ferocious battle the Indian was finally subdued and then bound. The Riversioux crew watched as the vanquished Indian was brutally dragged down the dock with a lariat looped around his neck. With the situation finally under control and to their liking things turned festive with the increasingly boisterous crowd yelling in chorus "injun catfish bait—injun catfish bait". In their frenzied jubilation the bleeding frontiersman lying in front of the pub was ignored.

Fletch checked his feet and hands for movement, nodding his head in satisfaction he painfully managed to right himself enough to lean over his saddled horse with a fifty caliber Sharps. Two pistols, an assortment of knives and another rifle protruded from the saddle. With a deafening roar the hand that had formerly grasped the lariat was sent reeling into the river, leaving a murky cloud as it spun downward out of sight. Blood spurted in rhythmic cadence from the recent but now frantic merry-makers severed wrist. "Anyone wishing to continue with this party pick up the lariat, otherwise this party is over" Fletch spoke with calm authority through his busted mouth.

Confused and disoriented the crowd scurried for safe haven. With the refuge of distance they reassembled hastily assessing the new circumstances.

The crew from the Riversioux took this all in not knowing what had precipitated such a happening. Seldom had a docking been so dramatic! Meanwhile the frontiersman brought both his and the Indians horse alongside the "Sioux" where they now conferred before what appeared a final showdown. The crew stared in disbelief as Jonas lowered the ramp and invited the two aboard, horses in tow.

"I still have a job for you if you're looking" Jonas offered in the restrained manner only Jonas Maynard was capable of.

"If this ship is ready to sail, you've hired a sailor. We can hash over any details later" Fletch sported a sheepishly grin through his disfigured and still bleeding mouth.

Jonas ordered the plank raised; with bells tingling the Riversioux generated an ever increasing wake as it made its way towards the Kansas shore.

Alanson and crew were introduced to Fletch as Jonas explained their prior acquaintance.

"What was all that" Jonas asked?

"I and Mr. Red Buffalo" pointing at the Indian "got into town yesterday with a wagon plumb full of Buffalo hides. We sold them this morning after running up a sizable tab at the bar last night. Well Buffalo went over to settle the bill, since he isn't good with words seemingly a misunderstanding occurred. Being an ignorant Indian the bar keep thought he might fleece him. Buffalo is plenty savvy and I guess in retrospect maybe a bit overly cocky anyway when the bar keep grabbed for his pocket book Buffalo grabbed the bar keep by his throat. That's when I arrived.—Well you saw the rest".

Jonas remembering the 'London Fog' shook his head in the affirmative. "You and Buffalo go below and clean up. We'll discuss employment after we reach the Kansas shore".

Jonas had plenty on his hands already as Pastor Chaney and his wife were more then a little upset for not being able to disembark in St. Joe.

Jonas assured and then reassured the Reverend that he and his wagons would be transferred back to St. Joe at no extra cost. Cheney was still assailing Jonas as they touched the Kansas dock. Little Mary stood alongside watching, assessing her future.

Alanson noticed a mature grimace replace a childlike innocence as Mary followed the Cheneys down the loading ramp. As their eyes met Alanson attempted a reassuringly nod. Remembering his own childhood experiences he swore softly to himself "best leave her alone preacher". It was an empty threat, meant to soothe a troubled conscious. He had no idea where they were going.

Alanson harbored his own skewered vision of ethics; his were rigidly focused but somewhat detached from conventional morality. Jonas took great risk transporting fugitive slaves; while Alanson admired his moral courage he at times questioned his wisdom. He and Jonas for the most part shared beliefs but not remedies. He could (with clear conscious) temporarily sacrifice contemporary ethical standards to enhance personal wealth. Wealth was the mechanism that fueled change. One day "he" would have the means to make real difference. Still if he found that little girl was mistreated. Well…some things can't wait!

Alanson was fairly confident he understood Jonas, but seriously doubted Jonas understood him. Meanwhile his knowledge of Joneses involvement in the Underground Railroad would remain his secret.

Jonas was now making arrangements to have the Chaneys ferried back to St. Joe and was still being righteously admonished in the process. Cheney was "horrified" to have shared quarters with such unprincipled desperados.

Jonas held a distinct advantage over most in determining character. He did not waste time weighing or considering motives. Instead he observed the obvious, drawing straight forward conclusions. He had supposed the Cheney's phony 'Christians' upon their first meeting. This caused him little bother for as a Quaker, judging others "moral" worth was left to higher authority.

Meanwhile Fletch and Buffalo were becoming acquainted with the run-away fugitives below. Buffalo by request of the fugitives already had decided to accompany the trappers north. The fugitives were sincerely grateful for the experienced company while Buffalo was simply grasping for continued existence. Nothing was asked nor was any reason offered as to why the Negroes remained secluded. In the present world Fletch, the Indian, and the run-away slaves were all outcasts and details weren't necessary.

While peering out the port-hole one of the fugitives noticed Mary walking down the gangplank with the missionaries. The others were called over to observe as the one pleasant memory of servitude walked down the plank securely in the care of a Christian couple. Prayers of thanks rose from "Sioux's" belly. With their past properly ended, their future needed tending.

Buffalo stayed below getting better acquainted with his new business partners while Fletch went seeking Jonas to discus his employment. Jonas was still engaged tending to the seemingly grievously wronged Chaneys so Fletch approached Alanson who was in the process of disembarking. "Do you want company" Fletch asked?

Alanson really didn't, but answered "sure" anyway. He planned to look up Jane where he'd hoped to work a meal out of his visit; still Fletch was a character he did want to become acquainted with.

"I'm going to visit some old friends I haven't seen for some time, if you are game for such come along" Alanson offered.

Fletch had entertained the notion of booze and a whore house but 'old friends' struck a nostalgic chord. He couldn't say why, discounting Buffalo and Jonas who really weren't old friends, he didn't have a one! "I didn't clean up for nothing, lets go" Fletch said as he fell in along side Alanson.

Samuel and Jane lived a short distance from town. Alanson enjoyed visiting them for several reasons; first Jane would always be special and secondly the small dairy farm they operated 'together' seemed to comfort him. He had always enjoyed the farm back in Pa. if not the home, Sam and Jane had intertwined farm and home in a way that enhanced both.

Alanson gave a short, partially factual, account of his connection to Jane as they walked.

Fletch added nothing to Alanson's knowledge of his past but he did display enthusiasm toward the 'Sioux' and an admiration for her skipper. On the frontier many don't elaborate on their past. Alanson hadn't been exactly honest with his own account.

They were at the door.

A vibrant young lady welcomed them. Alanson was astounded by the changes in Jane. Not only was she the picture of contentment, she also was expecting child and from the looks not too far in the future.

With their past comfortably behind them they now truly were friends. Jane hugged him with genuine affection, then turned to Fletch and hugged him also.

"It is so good to see you. Samuel will be so pleased". Jane was one big gracious smile. "Come in and introduce your friend" she said while holding the door.

Fletch was introduced as an old friend of the skipper and a new hand on the Riversioux where HE now was employed as clerk.

It felt so good to be in the company of this vibrant and lovely lady. Alanson could hardly imagine she had once been 'the' Mrs. Satterday.

Meanwhile Jane was just as impressed with Alanson. The frightened and confused boy now was the clerk on a paddlewheel and he had become a strikingly handsome young man!

Both admired the other while shedding unashamed tears of affection, and then hugged once again, understanding each was indebted to the other for their present circumstances. No words were needed nor spoken as they silently took inventory of each other.

Meanwhile Fletch stood watching the exchange, self consciously shuffling his feet. Alanson had told him she was an old family friend but it appeared there may be a little more to this.

"I am cooling a pie in the window and it is probably ready to be cut" Jane finally added giggling good naturedly at Fletches obvious uneasiness.

"I explained we were old family friends, I suppose families aren't as FRIENDLY where you come from" Alanson added as he winked at Jane.

Fletch really didn't give a rat's ass what was or had been between the two but the pie being cut he did care about. This was Dutch apple pie with a tantalizing sweet cinnamon aroma Fletch hadn't experienced before.

"I've been roaming these Kansas prairies since early spring and haven't tasted sweets in all that time. Never have I smelled anything as grand as that pie and I am about to loose patience with this small talk" Fletch said while feigning savagery. If he didn't have such a shy impish grin his blackened eyes and swollen face might have been more convincing.

Jane intuitively liked Fletch. She couldn't wait for Samuel to meet her guest.

Samuel had always been fond of Alanson, even when he was still a jealous boy. This would be a good day.

Reading her mind "where is Sam" Alanson asked?

"He's doing social work since as of yet we have little money with which to tithe" she answered and then quickly added "nobody can highjack a work tithe"! She and Alanson again laughed; this time until tears streamed down their faces.

"These are strange birds" Fletch thought but he was glad he had come.

After pie and coffee Alanson told Jane about the little girl (Mary) and his fears for her.

Being a victim of somewhat similar circumstances, though she tried to hide it, her concern showed.

"I knew I should have done—something". Seeing Jane's concern the words simply escaped.

It neared 6: 00 pm and Samuel was home.

With loving hugs for his wife and honest handshakes for his guests Fletch and Alanson instantly understood Jane's satisfaction with life. A loving family needs no marquee.

The "family" concept was attempting to enter Alanson's psyche, while Fletch simply remained pleased to be included.

After supper the guys visited while Sam and Jane milked the cows and then they all pitched in to finish the remaining chores. With the work done a general tour was made of the farm with Sam proudly detailing his plans for the future.

Alanson listened while taking mental notes. Sam's notions were solid and workable but noticeably imprisoned by scale. No dream was beyond Alanson's reality!

With a final cup of coffee and heartfelt farewells their evening visit concluded. Alanson headed for the 'Sioux' while Fletch accompanying him still entertained other notions.

Alanson at Fletches request stopped off for a round at the tavern before heading back to the Riversioux. Fletch immediately became a little more rowdy and just plain more assertive then Alanson was comfortable with. He quietly exited at first opportunity.

As Alanson hit Main Street and turned left toward the docks he saw Jonas escorting the eight fugitives planning to go east through the darkening streets. He decided to follow. As he had suspected they tuned into the Quaker Hall and meeting them at the door was none other then Sam.

With his suspicions verified, Alanson returned to the 'Sioux' with a reinvigorated feeling of self-satisfaction.

Later in the evening Jonas returned. Alanson was sitting on the deck smoking, a rare indulgence for Alanson but this had in-deed been a rare and a gentle evening.

"I met one of your friends this evening" Jonas said sitting down along side Alanson.

It was a warm Kansas evening with a variety of frogs croaking their individual songs of romance. A slight breeze cooled by the waters of the Missouri somewhat restrained the mosquito's population. A custom made evening for congenial conversation.

Alanson smiling inwardly asked "and who would that be"?

Earlier in the evening Samuel and Jonas had had their own conversation concerning Alanson. He'd learned much about his new clerks past and nothing he'd learned detracted from an opinion he had already formed. Now was the opportune time to make a new proposal.

"Samuel and Jane attended the friends gathering tonight. I was late as I had to escort the Negroes to the station. By-the-way Jane sent the remaining apple pie along with me. She said you and Fletch already had your share so I suppose it's up to me to finish these last few pieces" Jonas said with a teasing grin.

"Just like you Quakers, always full of public pronunciations on the straight and holy but when sharing Jane's apple pie is the devil's temptation you're revealed as pathetically wanting."

Alanson thumped his pipe on the railing, dropping the remaining tobacco coals into the water below and watched as they floated southward sizzling and crackling in seemingly a determined effort to thwart the inevitable. After sucking a deep breath of warm musky air Alanson slowly exhaled, smiling and waiting for Jonas's response. Meanwhile the final ember exploded in a kamikaze salute while skirting around the cross river ferry which also was snuggled in harbor for the night.

He knew things about Jonas and vice-versa. Probably neither would ever know the extent of the others knowledge which made little difference. Both existed comfortably with the other.

"Jesus said what you do unto the least you have done unto me also. Since you're absolutely the least I've met in some time I guess I'm morally obligated to share" Jonas finally answered while handing Alanson a slice.

They enjoyed each others wit even though there remained a shield around Alanson's inner self. After talking to Jane Jonas had a better grip on what made Alanson the cautious man he was.

"Blackie, our engineer tells me he is retiring upon our return to St. Joseph. He is willing to train his replacement and I would like you to be that man". Jonas paused and continued since no answer was forthcoming. "As you know it is second in command and a considerable raise in salary".

Alanson had no doubts about the offer. Of-course he wanted the job! He knew he was 'destined' for greater things. He also knew he had never taken a job that he hadn't performed beyond the former employee's ability.

"Thanks for your confidence Jonas, I welcome the offer and will endeavor to maintain the Riversioux as the best operated paddlewheel on the Missouri".

Two men with differing dreams shook hands as the contract was sealed. Jonas was a man of easily definable character. Neither morality nor ethic varied with time or circumstance. On-the-other-hand Alanson always searched for underlying reasons and pondered over the far reaching effects of "any" decision. Still in most cases similar conclusions would eventually be reached.

Alanson excused himself with "time to hit the sack" where in actuality a night of sleep prohibiting pondering was at hand.

Jonas continued to relax, enjoying the solitude of the 'Sioux'. With all the responsibility of a fledgling business and pressing 'social' commitments Jonas remained content. When the day was done he usually could look back and be satisfied with the days tally. He was mentally making the tally when Fletch boarded, somewhat tipsy but coherent...

"Sit down Fletch it seems time to discuss your position aboard the 'Sioux'. You don't have to commit to anything. We would have taken most anyone aboard under similar circumstances. ARE you looking for employment"?

"Skipper maybe youse think I don't owes anything but ahh disagree. In any case I'm interested in what you've in mind and yes I am vaailable". Fletch slurred his speech, some-what from an evening of pleasure and some-what from the beating he had absorbed earlier in the day.

"First I insist on no alcohol on board. Your time ashore is yours, on board your time is mine" Jonas placed a hand on Fletch's shoulder while looking him in the eye. "Is that agreeable"?

Fletches eyes never wavered as he answered "sounds fair skipper. So what's we talken bout"?

"I'm looking for someone to negotiate fuel contracts with the various tribes of the upper Missouri and a purveyor of fresh meat, a professional hunter".

"Stop there skipper, if the pay is right I'm your man". The slur had disappeared.

A job as meat supplier in the Dakota Territory was a dream job. Freedom and independence with a regular pay check.

Salary negotiations were completed in short time.

Fletch finding a cot, passed out after devouring the remaining slice of Jane's pie.

With the day completed Jonas leisurely walked back to the captain's quarters feeling pleased. His crew was not only complete but he was confident he had the makings of the best damn crew on the Missouri! Stretching out on the mattress which he had brought with him from his parents home in Philadelphia he almost instantaneously fell into an unencumbered sleep.

The sleep was unencumbered but short lived. Before the first rays of sunlight broke the Missouri skyline Jonas was roused by a frantic James. "Jonas bounty hunters are in St. Joseph and will be at the meeting house by the break of day. Do you have room on the Riversioux for our guests until they leave"?

Jonas still drowsy struggled to answer. "How many souls are we talking about? Stretching and drawing a deep breath he continued "never mind how many, just get them over here"!

"We have eighteen; they are getting their things together as we speak and hopefully they will be here any moment".

As Jonas dressed Jim continued "I'm sorry Jonas but I simply didn't have any other options".

"We all have our responsibilities and we all do the best we can James". Jonas was beginning to get focused as his thoughts now permeated in clusters. "Hurry, bring them and a half dozen saddled horses if you can; meanwhile we'll be working on a solution. Don't worry Jim once you get them onboard no harm will come their way".

Jonas sounded the alarm as James hurried down the gangplank.

When the crew gathered Jonas explained that he had just contracted to provide housing for some black fugitives until they could be transported back to their rightful owners in several days time. Newly apprehended run-a-ways had just been brought in and the local facilities were already filled. They would be disembarking momentarily and all hands should report immediately to their work stations.

Jonas adjourned the crew while asking Fletch and Alanson to stay.

"Fletch can you and Red Buffalo make a hunting excursion into Kansas with the four free blacks for three days? I'm afraid their may be trouble if they remain on board".

"No problem skipper, I'll roust out Buffalo and we're on our way".

"Alanson I would like you to go with the hunters, I would feel much better knowing you are along and we also are flat running out of room"!

"It will be a vacation for me Jonas but are you sure you know what you are getting into"?

Jonas assured Alanson it was simply a last minute opportunity to gain some much needed operating capital.

Alanson thinking about the Underground Railroad and the dangers involved was about to speak when Fletch returned with Buffalo and the fugitives.

He held his thoughts, Jonas was in command and though they were still in the process of really getting acquainted he found he already respected Jonas's judgment.

Fletch and Buffalo gathered supplies for the outing while Jonas and Alanson readied the boat for their guests.

When dawn broke the cross river ferry from St. Joseph was rocked by the wake of a paddlewheel under full throttle south bound.

Buffalo explained he was a Nishnabe'k (the people) Indain, commonly called Pottawatomie by the white man. They had been traveling steadily since departing

Elwood and were now nearing the Delaware River when the aroma of meat roasting upon a campfire drew them to a halt.

Buffalo was aglow, these were his people camped here.

Alanson and Fletch watched silently as Buffalo and the Pottawatomie talked.

Finally Buffalo explained "these are my people who have been starving on the white man's reservation in Osawatomie, they say if they must starve from now on they will starve as free people. They will make their home on this river and run no more, Grandfather spirit has sent a buffalo as an omen of good things to come. Please join us as we partake of what is ours".

For three days Alanson and Fletch stayed as guests in the Pottawatomie encampment. They were told of how the tribe had been forced to walk from their former tribal lands near Twin Lakes Indiana, six hundred and sixty miles, to Osawatomie Kansas.

This was in "38" and remembered by the Pottawatomie as the trail of death (five percent of the tribe died in transit, mostly children).

They had been forest and lakes people and not familiar with the prairie therefore when they finally arrived in Kansas they starved and many more perished while waiting for promised provisions which were never forthcoming.

Red Buffalo had lobbied the elders of the tribe to leave the reservation but they had refused. As they slowly starved while pleading for help he struck out on his own where he met Fletch.

Neither Buffalo nor his black partners (Pottawattamie, as most upland tribes, are a welcoming people) returned to the Riversioux. Buffalo once again was with his people and his people were once again 'Nishnabe'k' THE PEOPLE.

Alanson having swapped stories and shared hospitality for three days with these embattled peoples parted with a new sympathy for and lifelong admiration for the hapless Redman, never suspecting that a century and a half and six generations later in a local Indian hospital a young Pottawattamie maiden would give birth to his granddaughter.

Upon returning to St. Joe Alanson was relieved to see the Riversioux moored at the dock and all was peaceful. Even more satisfying was the calm reliability of the skipper.

When asked what had transpired in the past three days Jonas replied he had been enjoying Jane's home cooked meals for the past day and a half and he now found it quite difficult to leave.

Samantha Lee
6th generation Descendent of Alanson

CHAPTER 15

▼

Jonas called a meeting of the officers and the crew chief to discuss the river situation. He had considered waiting for the river to establish a navigable channel as the crew and boat were his principle responsibly. He had founded his reputation on this premise but with his 'special' cargo and the imposed deadline traditional decisions were superceded. Still without the crew's input, unilateral decision wasn't in Jonas's repertoire.

In the cool of morning the crew's brass gathered inside the 'Sioux' pilot house.

Jonas explained the situation and shared the information garnered from the pilot of the St. Joseph. Seemingly the 'sandbar' ahead was much more then the usual bar which could be traversed in a day or two of strenuous effort.

Jonas being both pilot and owner of the Riversioux enjoyed much more latitude in decision making then most pilots. These were the times that tested the wisdom of such concentrated power.

"My conscience urges me to recommend we tackle the river and continue" Jonas began. "Personally the thought of abandoning these Negroes is unconscionable. We all have a considerable financial investment in the success of this venture but more relevant this is the finest crew on the Missouri. I believe if we wisely and efficiently use our combined talents this river will NOT thwart the Riversioux".

Jonas had considered how best to present the argument for continuing. Pride and competition are the stimulus that throughout history have driven men to victories considered unattainable. He had learned this while attending the Philadelphia Nautical Institute. "Everyman has an obligation to speak his mind, then we'll vote on a course of action" Jonas concluded.

Believing he knew his crew Jonas was fairly confident of the outcome.

Surprisingly Stroker was the first to speak "Last week I'd of said let the niggers fend for themselves and save the crew. We've done as much as anybody would do. We got them the Hell out of Dixie and away from the bounty hunters. TODAY I say "nigger" Jeff is part of the crew and if those other niggers are half what he is we'll whip this measly stream. We're in this thing together and together by-God we'll all get rich. I vote Hell yes"!

Stroker hadn't expressed his feelings about the big man. He was glad Jonas had forced the situation. He was proud to be training the best damn boiler man on the Missouri River.

Fletch had been pondering the bargain he'd proposed to Inka. As of yet he hadn't come up with a palatable way of fulfilling his end of the bargain—until now. Jonas had just thrown a pitch in his wheel house and this old Jersey ball player was ready to take it down town!

"Skipper I'm fairly certain the Santee can be persuaded to help, I suppose I would need to meet with them again to iron out a few details. Seems they are in desperate need of rifles and ammunition for hunting and all. If we could supply them a dozen rifles and a little powder I'm fairly certain they would lend a hand. I vote we finish what we started".

Jonas didn't know much of Fletch's past but he kind of understood his thought process. His gut told him there was more to Fletch's proposal then being articulated. Still his priorities were always tailored toward the welfare of the Riversioux and his judgments, although definitely not mainstream, were usually sound.

Through travail he'd learned that to survive in this business trust was essential. He was surrounded by people who had earned his trust.

Alanson, always fascinated by human reasoning, watched the debate with amazement and a touch of humor. Stroker was praising the same niggers he had yesterday thought useless and now Fletch was indicating he could get the very Indians impeding their mission to expedite it.

He truly sympathized with the plight of the run-a ways slaves, still his conscience could survive with the Negro making his own way under the present circumstances BUT there was no way he was turning back! With all the potential profit to be realized from this enterprise his dreams would be nearing reality. "I vote we continue" Alanson added.

Rube lived up to expectation. "No piss ant river stops this boat. The crew votes we quit farting around and get on to Ft. Union"! Rube rarely missed an opportunity to reiterate his 'manhood'.

In two days the Riversioux was at a stand still. The crew was witness to a phenomenon unique to the Missouri amongst large rivers. As far as the eye could see
the river meandered through the tall wetland grasses. It was awesome, beautiful
and more then a little intimidating.

Jonas felt confidence draining from his crew as they gazed upon the imposing
sight. As chief operating officer it was compelling he dispel the gloom. If fear is
the nemesis of efficient operation, then action is its antidote. When capitulation
is unacceptable attack is the primeval response.

Jonas once again called a meeting of officers. They were instructed to each
pick two crew members, asses the situation and report back with a plan of action
within twenty four hours. When they returned Rube would take the remaining
crew and do like wise. The 'Sioux' was never left unprotected.

Fletch would meet with the Wahpekute Santee chieftain Inkpaduta the following day in an attempt to enlist his help.

Leaving the meeting the crew already was vigorously arguing the merits of
their (yet non-existent) plan amongst themselves. Competition elbowed doom
aside.

Jonas was pleased with the mood swing, but held little faith in any team coming forth with a workable plan. Many schemes would surely emerge and some
when dissected and amalgamated might produce 'a plan'. Morale was his immediate focus.

The Negroes would be given the task of measuring the distance between
where the channel ended and where it once more became navigable.

They were summoned and Jonas explained what he needed. The group
needed no motivation but their dissatisfaction with the process was not subtle.
"Mistah Jonas you spose us negraws are capable of such tasks without a
boss-man"? Jeff was the spokesman. It hadn't been missed that everyone (except
the colored) were being asked for opinions.

"I have no illusions about your ability to reason. What we don't have is time
for social engineering! Your plans will be rejected and your time wasted. Either be
of help or go below".

Jonas didn't enjoy his decision. "Jeff you are the crew leader, report to Alanson
for a cram course in surveying".

"We will do our part Mr. Jonas" Jeff did understand. Though he was in "free"
territory he remained black. Jonas saw things as they were and made decisions
accordingly. He would see to it his crew didn't let the skipper down. "Thanks
skipper, don't worry about this crew".

As the blue eyes of Jonas and the ebony eyes of Jeff met, if there had been doubt it was being erased. With a parting handshake both felt confidence gain momentum.

Jeff thought back to the Quaker who had risked his life for his freedom and even demanded a beating so he could continue to help others. He thought also of the jeopardy Jonas presently placed his beloved "Riversioux" in. He had been wronged by many and helped by a few. It was his choice. He could be one of the many or one of the few. He regretted having been the 'crowd' spokesman. He determined in the future he would use more consideration before drawing a conclusion.

Jonas, whose intentions had been to motivate the crew, had succeeded but now he also found himself motivated.

Jeff searched out Alanson. He reiterated for Alanson his discussion with Jonas and his own ignorance of surveying.

Alanson never traveled without his surveying equipment. Surveying was a hobby with dividends. Many times he had picked up day jobs when the 'Sioux' was in port. "Help me fetch my equipment and we'll go through the basics" Alanson said motioning Jeff toward the storage compartment.

Alanson set up the surveying scope on the bow of the boat while Jeff assembled his crew. Class began. The scope and its various settings were explained. Charts were gone over with Alanson explaining their uses. Then with hand signals markers were placed at intervals along the shore line by Jeff's crew. Calculations were made which determined geographic position and distances. Jeff watched, and then asked Alanson to go through the procedure once more.

Carefully step by step Alanson explained the procedure once more.

"How about I give it a try" Jeff asked?

Stroker had bragged 'excessively' on Jeff's ability to soak up detail. Still this was a little more complex then pitching wood into a furnace. Shrugging his shoulders Alanson moved aside.

Alanson pointed out three trees at various distances, the farthest being some 200 yards distance. "Give me the geographic location of and the distance between each tree, and then the total added distance from the first to the last tree." This was asking a lot but what Jonas asked was considerable more.

Jeff, except for a few calculating errors, was flawless.

Alanson walked Jeff through the calculation process one more time and that was it.

Smiling Alanson handed Jeff the scope. "If you break it you bought it" he added shaking his head in pleased admiration. "That's the basics; class is over unless you have questions".

The new technology intrigued Jeff…"When we get through this river channel situation I would like to learn more if you have time"?

"You and your crew get the channel mapped and it will be a pleasure". Alanson was sincere. He enjoyed surveying. Sharing his interest would be fun, with a quick study like Jeff it was something he looked forward to.

Alanson walked up the catwalk to the pilot house where he could see the skipper sitting alone.

"Come on in". Jonas was sitting with his hands behind head, feet resting on the instrument panel. It continued to amaze Alanson how the skipper could remain relaxed under seemingly any situation.

The only time he was 'really' comfortable with life or its human occupants was when he became so involved that they became temporarily secondary. Someday he hoped to discover the cause for this malady and maybe overcome this troublesome social handicap but right now there were things more pressing upon his mind.

"We have an exceptional talent aboard this vessel that it appears we aren't making full use of" Alanson said while sitting down across from Jonas. "That Jeff is some quick learner and one shouldn't overlook his pure brute strength either. I really think we could better use his talents in alleviating our present predicament"?

"Alanson, when Jeff found you he was just coming from here. He and all the Negroes clearly made the same point as you. Of-course their thoughts are equal to anyone's. Thoughts aren't wrapped in skin coloration"!

Jonas was becoming a little exasperated having to explain his reasoning. He considered Alanson and possibly young Jeff at least his equal if not more intellectual then he.

"When the crew finds out that "niggers" are being consulted, we lose our credibility to command. Have you forgotten Strokers reaction to simply being asked to 'teach' a Negro? Stroker quite likely is above average. Most men never get past the color. That is the way it is, I don't like it but its still fact. If this was a year long cruise maybe—"

Alanson raised his hand to bring Jonas's explanation to an end. Smiling he cut in "alright skipper I get the picture. Still it wouldn't hurt to have him report back after his survey is completed. Surveying gives one another perspective".

"Alanson you're probably right. Have Jeff report to me before he leaves" Jonas always appreciated Alanson's input and that's precisely why he received it.

"Its still early Alanson have you got a moment" Jonas was pouring two cups of coffee.

"Always have time for coffee". Alanson answered reaching for a cup knowing they were about to have one of their 'conversations'.

"I've wanted to get your opinion on this for some time. Our conversation about Jeff leads right into it. I'm afraid war is how this slave issue will be finally settled. One can't help but feel it. Do you see any other solution"?

"I wished I didn't agree but I believe you're right skipper".

We've seen the issues divisiveness right here on the Riversioux's deck! I'm a Quaker. You know we are pacifist. I would do almost anything to end slavery but trading slavery for butchery certainly won't advance mankind".

Alanson interrupted "no reasonable person wants this war but if war is the only debate the southerner understands lets get it on. I admire the courage of you pacifist and four hundred years from now, possibly, they might even listen. You know, I never knew a Negro personally until I was aboard this boat but common sense led me to believe no-one should be bought and sold like a horse!

I believe on this particular issue passivism is the wrong avenue". Alanson sipped his coffee and then continued. "I don't hate the southerner but I do have contempt for the whole slavery concept. From where I stand if a person stands in the way of another's freedom, well I guess that pro-slaver becomes collateral".

Alanson was fairly certain this conversation wasn't over. The two had been together aboard the 'Sioux' for six years now. Sometimes their conversations had been known to continue for weeks; Captain Jonas wouldn't be out of steam just yet.

"Well that all sounds good BUT remember Jesus died for an idea. One life sacrificed for all mankind. There is a difference between dieing for a cause and killing for a cause.

Killing, even the most superficial of men have been known to kill for an idea, on-the-other-hand only the most dedicated of mankind is willing die for an idea. One concept evolves from mans highest nature while the other from his most base".

Alanson shaking his head was silently forming words for his mimicking 'talking hand' "please not another sermon"?

I know you aren't easily persuaded by theology but maybe you CAN do math. One life as compared to hundreds of thousands of lives! That's what this war will come to. Nothing is as brutal as a family feud. When and if, you come back from your honorable war tell me the morality of brother butchering brother. The thing you chest beaters don't understand is the reality of your wishes? Hundreds of thousands dead and wounded verses hundreds of thousands shackled in slavery. Sorry I'll be a pacifist and let you balance the end tally sheet".

"How about a refill you pacifist asshole" Alanson didn't want the 'old man' to blow the rivets in his boiler. He enjoyed an argument but at the same time didn't want passion to be replaced with anger.

"Pour you blood sucking maggot" Jonas smilingly demanded holding up his cup. Jonas looked forward to these discussions. SOMETIMES he set Alanson up. Alanson was always on guard but when drawn properly in, he would forget and reservation was flung away. These were the times that became memories. In general conversations Alanson remained cautious trying not to appear superior; usually he ended up being condescending.

"Have you heard from that sweetheart back in Philadelphia lately?" Alanson changed the subject. "You can't expect her to wait for ever, of-course since she's a Quaker also I suppose sacrifice is in her nature"?

"At least SOMEONE cares about me. I haven't seen females beating a path to your heathen hovel" Jonas retorted.

"Gotta go rub Explorer down, give some more thought to your asinine argument and later on we'll have another go at mankind's social problems right here in Miss Sioux's pilot house" Alanson said rising to leave.

"Do you good to commune with that horse of yours, you both can lick your ass without bending over". Jonas reached for his day book preparing to make the days entries. "Always pleasurable talking with you Alanson" Jonas added with unmistakable sincerity.

Alanson noticed Jeff was leaning against the railing engrossed in the currents as they twisted their way through the debris. "Want to take a little walk in the cool waters with me" Jeff asked as Alanson grabbed the rail along side him.

It was hot and the water looked inviting. "Sure, let me role up my pant legs first" Alanson answered already in the rolling process. He then lowered himself over the railing; momentarily he hung contemplating the distance to the water before dropping. Meanwhile Jeff grabbed the rail with one hand and swung over, dropping gently into the water. Being nearly seven foot tall he still held the railing as his feet were planted in the Missouri River sand.

Jeff had a reason for asking Alanson to accompany him. Fascinated by the ever changing currents he had begun studying the rationale for the changes. The rationale he believed he now understood, how to apply the knowledge he was working on.

"Notice how a small channel is formed toward the lower end of each log that lays perpendicular to flow and then disappears a short distance down stream. What would happen if many logs were laid in sequence, one just behind the other? I wonder if a channel could be produced using the river's own energy? Maybe we could do an experiment with a few logs? With your math skills I'll bet we can predict how much of a project would be involved to manufacture a channel".

Alanson was already processing the idea and liking the results. "Let's get a log and lay it nearly perpendicular but slightly tilting downstream, measure the log, then time how long it takes to produce a channel. Then we will measure the depth and length of the new channel"

Big Jeff had already begun the process of positioning a log. It wasn't a great task moving the log if one used the current as a propellant. Size and weight he found was very useful in controlling its movement.

Jeff simply braced himself as he let the current maneuver the log into place while on the other hand Alanson, equally powerful, found himself under, on top of, and along side the log and still the log managed to procure its own course.

"There's one experiment completed' Jeff laughed. "It is going to take a whole bunch of Alansons to get this job completed".

Alanson immediately turned red with embarrassment. It always annoyed him when determination couldn't overcome physical size. This wasn't the first time this had happened. In the past he had usually found a way to be equally as useful as the bigger guys. This he was determined would be no different.

They spent the next several hours measuring and timing. To their delight the effect on the channel was multiplied with growing dimension as more logs were laid end to end and multiplied once again when a new row was added below the first row. "Okay, we have enough data to make a projection" Alanson said scribbling the last of many figures. "If you have a couple of hours I believe together we can come up with a fairly accurate calculation".

They both were beginning to get excited by the time they boarded the 'Sioux'.

"Jenny was baking up some sweets when I left. How about we go below and grab a snack as we figure" Jeff invited. In their excitement they had not been paying attention to time. The sun was getting low and Jenny already had supper prepared when they arrived.

Lord it smelled sooo good. Alanson would have been disappointed had he not been invited to sit at the table, which of-course he was.

Jenny offered the blessing, giving thanks for freedom, for friends and for Jeff.

Alanson, not an eye closer during prayer, watched his big friend's dark face blush crimson. He once again saw the benefits of 'family'. The concept was beginning to become secured within his consciousness. Jenny like Jane was in full blossom. Love radiated as the two made small talk.

Alanson thought of his parents and how his bitterness was now reduced to sympathy. It must have been obvious he was daydreaming.

"Are you becoming too tired to work on the formula tonight" Jeff inquired?

"Oh, no I was just thinking" he answered. It seemed there was some disappointment with his answer.

Jeff did his best to hasten the calculations but his prior aptness now turned into complete ineptness.

Jeff's mind obviously was elsewhere. Alanson finally becoming exasperated excused himself, taking his figures with him. Tell-tale giggling followed as he departed.

At dawn Alanson excitedly presented Jonas with his calculations. If enough workers were available the task of channel engineering would probably take (depending on Jeff's crews findings) no more then two to three days!

Jonas, visibly relieved, nevertheless instructed Alanson to keep his calculations to himself for the time being.

The three man crews began checking in as Alanson was leaving, ready to 'study the problem' and come up with a working mans 'common sense' solution. Jonas issued a prepared pep talk before sending the men on their way.

Each group was to report their recommendations to Alanson, who would record each group's findings and then present the plans to Jonas. Jonas would study the plans and from them draw a formal blue print of action.

Jonas was confident he had sounded sincere, leaving the impression of great expectations. The crews departed in high spirit.

Jonas pulled Alanson's calculations from his desk drawer to recheck the math. He was nodding his head in approval as Jeff knocked on the door. Laying the papers aside Jeff was motioned in.

"Skipper I apologize again for my immature actions yesterday" he said while noticing the papers on Jonas's desk.

"We all have come to conclusions we later regret, I believe we both can move on" Jonas answered while picking up Alanson's calculations.

"Unless I am completely wrong you and Alanson have 'the' workable plan. Alanson says it was your idea; he simply helped with the math. It would be best if the whole crew was credited with the idea" Jonas continued "Is your crew ready for work"?

"Ready and willing and don't worry about my feelings. Unless (I'm) completely wrong 'we' have no issues" Jeff said while turning to leave.

With a smile Jonas placed a reassuring hand upon Jeff's shoulder while adding "no Jeff we don't have issues and for your peace of mind this skipper after many painful lessons now usually does his worrying 'before' making decisions. It adds pleasure to the evenings".

Fletch was waiting when Inkpaduta and his band approached. Uneasiness momentarily gripped him as he was surrounded by two or maybe even three hundred festive braves. He had no idea how Inka had gathered such a band but since he was still alive they probably at present meant him no harm. He motioned for his recent sparring partner to meet with him 'alone' down near the river bank.

Inka, haughty and ferocious appearing, indicated a large cottonwood tree as the spot for rendezvous.

Inka had spread a story amongst the Sioux of how he had defeated the white-eye. How he cunningly had extracted a deal for guns and powder in exchange for the begging white-eye's life. He boasted of how he in the near future would drive the white-eyes from their lands forever. He soon would acquire great fire power which he would share with any who accompanied him. Inka believed in what he preached. Many disenfranchised Sioux wanted to believe as they made a festive ring around this pitiful white-eye who was hasting his own kind's demise.

Fletch didn't move, he simply sat as Inka motioned him toward the tree. He was getting a 'read' on the situation. Inka, like him, had told some cock and bull story about their 'get together'. His band looked to him as a mighty conqueror. Inka had dug his own hole, now let him dig his way out!

"Shall we discuss bunnies and dogs under a tree or discuss weapons on the river bank my dear friend". Fletch spoke amply loud for all to hear.

Inka's band looked at each other in bewilderment.

Of-course no-one except Inka understood such nonsense. Inka though furious with Fletch's response now had too much at stake not to see this through.

"Dogs and bunnies under a tree, are you loco"? Inka demonstratively threw his hands in the air as he nevertheless nudged his pony toward the river bank.

Greetings fucked rabbit". Fletch was really beginning to dislike this Indian.

"Have your fun puking dog, I (Inka) will honor my word and deliver you and your boat to Ft. Union. Then we will see who laughs but enough small talk. When do we get our guns" Inka demanded.

"Maybe you don't" Fletch had to do this right "there is a problem".

"Are you blind as well as foolish, don't you see all these Indians white-eye" Inka pointed toward his band. "You are loco if you think I came here to play more of your childish games".

"It seems we both have a problem. I will up the reward for you BUT I first need your help". Fletch explained the Riversioux's problem. He also explained that if they didn't get in route soon everything was off and the Riversioux would be returning to Sioux City.

"What do you have to offer" Inka demanded.

Fletch pulled a Colt pistol from his saddle and fired four shots into the water with out stopping to reload.

Jonas had recently purchased several dozen Colts from the now defunct Colt Firearms Company. Samuel Colt had sold the army a thousand revolvers for trial. The Army, living up to its reputation for always being a step behind, believed it to complicated for the regular army and could see no useful combat application for the weapon. No more orders were forthcoming. Colt Industries having invested heavily in anticipated sales to the army in short time became insolvent.

Mr. Colt was presently raising money to reopen the factory, this time with civilian sales its targeted market. Jonas, at Alanson's request, purchased the factories remaining revolvers and ammunition. Fletch had raided the store room!

Neither Inka nor any of his band had ever seen a weapon such as this.

"What do you think bunny boy" Fletch asked reloading the weapon?

"Twelve of those'" pointing at the revolver "plus the twelve rifles and ammunition" Inka answered attempting to mask his excitement.

"Deal" Fletch offered his hand which Inka theatrically declined.

"We'll meet here tomorrow at the same time. Bring two of your band and I'll bring two men from the boat. We'll finalize the agreement". Fletch was obviously enjoying 'telling' Inka.

"If it wasn't for the weapons you would already be fertilizer in some squaws maze patch dog puke but that can wait. Be here!" Inka commanded as he spun his horse to leave.

"If you were only the slightest bit pretty I'd still be humping you bunny boy" Fletch blew a kiss as Inka kicked his horse in the flanks.

Inka was under no illusions. The Riversioux was a virtual fortress; a fortress containing enough weaponry to make the Wahpekute invincible. Patience, Black Hawk had stressed patience and he had listened. The time was nearing and Inka salivated.

The band of warriors fidgeted uncomfortably as Inka explained the 'new deal'.

Labor is not in the Sioux warrior's resume, work is for females and cowards. Still the reward far out weighed the embarrassment. They would show up prepared to do whatever necessary. The band spent the evening celebrating the upcoming annihilation of the heathen white-eyes.

As evening drew its curtain over the Dakota Missouri more then the Wahpekute had dreams.

Alanson envisioned land, capital and status. The day was approaching when the quest for money would become secondary to its proper use. Society was beset with intolerable wrongs. He hoped soon to combat these inequities with the same weaponry that had imposed them.

Fletch lay basking in Inka's humiliation. Once more he had played the cards dealt and come up a winner. He held no animosity for the Redman but this Inka in time would have to be removed. Fletch gently fell to sleep anticipating the occasion.

The fugitives also had a dream. For the first time they would be laboring for their own betterment. The opportunity would not be squandered.

Stroker basked in the blossoming of his protégé, ashamed he'd been so blind but proud he no longer was.

Jonas was staying up late studying the plans that had been submitted. He was impressed. The crew had come up with some ideas of merit. Jeff's plan still 'was' the plan but the crew's ideas when incorporated greatly enhanced the total. Jonas was pleased to finally be doing what he did best. He would spend the night constructing the most feasible plan of action.

A knock on the door awoke Jonas from his solitary activity. He had expected the interruption.

Opening the door Jeff announced "we have the measurements skipper". Jeff though he tried couldn't restrain a satisfied glow of accomplishment.

Looking over the detailed report Jonas was pleased "would you have enough energy remaining to help me finalize the plans for tomorrow"?

Nodding his head in the affirmative Jeff answered" I've been used some rougher in the past".

As Jonas was studying Jeff's measurements he handed Jeff an estimate of the man power and equipment available. According to the survey figures approximately seven eighths of a mile in a total three and a quarter mile distance would need to be channeled.

At 2:00am the two were satisfied with the work agenda. Fletch, Rube and three men of Rube's choosing would stay aboard the Riversioux. Alanson would lead one crew, Jeff would lead the Negro crew and Rube would lead the 3rd crew.

The Indians would be the engine, using their ponies with ropes to pull and float the trees into position.

While the Indians transported the logs the two white crews would be using wedges and bars to loosen logs for transport. Jeff's crew would be kept busy filling gaps under the logs with sand. When not busy they all would be 'digging' river channel.

The 'Sioux' being only partially loaded 'only' needed four and one half foot channel depth to navigate.

Alanson try as he may, couldn't come up with an exact formula. Each addition to log length multiplied the effects of natural channeling plus each additional barrier placed downriver multiplied the effects again. This was log rhythm and he didn't posses the math ability or necessary charts to accurately calculate a time schedule but mathematically this job could complete itself in a short dramatic fashion.

The over riding complication would be in implementation. Jonas would need all his formal personnel schooling plus all his life experiences to prevent chaos. The work detail would be comprised of Negro fugitives striving to obtain freedom, Free Indians desperately clinging to freedom and free white men (many with no empathy for either).

Jeff assured Jonas 'his' crew would not respond to verbal abuse. Physical abuse he would tend to personally. Jeff wearing no shirt on this warm summer evening flexed his massive muscles in a youthful and unmistakable demonstration of intent.

"JESUS CHRIST JEFF" Jonas seldom swore but being a believing pacifist the words flowed involuntarily. On this note they called it a night.

Returning to the Sioux Fletch explained to Jonas the need for a dozen revolvers at their rendezvous with Inkpaduta. Jonas though uncomfortable with the possible ramifications (and wondering how Fletch had obtained the colts) of the impending bargain saw no alternative. They would hand over the twelve pistols but would with-hold the ammunition until the Riversioux was safely above the Niobrara.

Inka and 2 braves were waiting along the river bank when Jonas, Fletch and Rube arrived. Anger seethed from Inka as Fletch "arbitrated" the meeting.

Jonas felt ice sickles forming within as eye contact was established with Inka. They were dealing with a man possessed! He now understood Fetch's insistence that Rube be included in their party.

Inka recalled the teachings of Black Hawk—patience, patience and timing. Now was the time for patients, later there would be a time for retribution. Ink-

paduta, though consumed by hate, suffered with pleasure. The more the humiliation the more pleasurable would be the coming day of reckoning.

The Wahpekutes received the 12 revolvers with one shell in each. The rifles
and ammunition would remain aboard the Riversioux until the job was completed.

With the bargaining completed Inka withdrew to the river woodlands where
his burgeoning party awaited. Twelve shots echoed up the river valley followed by
whoops of excitement. Satisfied with their revolvers the party made their way
toward the 'Sioux'. As of yet the concept of labor had not penetrated the bands
festive mood.

The sight of men straining to free logs while stranding in the shallow waters
immediately sobered the band of warriors. There were three crews toiling at the
task. One crew was comprised of the dark skinned ones and among them was a
man of preposterous size.

The buffalo man was not totally foreign to the Plains Indian. A number of
run-a-way slaves had been joining various bands of Sioux for some time but amal-
gamation had not gone well. Dissatisfied with their status in the tribes the
Negroes now had formed their own band and were presently contesting for hunting grounds with the old established bands. Many young Sioux females accompanied the black man.

Jeff's heart jumped as the Santee braves began to appear along the shore.
These were truly free men. Sitting astride their ponies 'bare back' every visual
effect exclaimed freedom. More and more braves arrived until the river bank was
lined with Indians. Jeff watched as Fletch approached their leader. Even from his
distant vantage point their animosity was apparent. Fletch seemed to be explaining what the Indain role in the process was to be. He then demonstrated their
proposed job by tying his rope around a loosened log and pulling it into a staked
area.

Jeff had not gone to bed after leaving Jonas's office instead he and his and crew
had labored through the early morning hours staking the proposed channel. This
had already put the job ahead of schedule. Stroker had assisted.

Fletch's demonstration was interrupted by several shots from the 'Sioux'. Inka
had sent several dozen of his band to check the status of the 'Sioux' while the
crew labored. Warning shots from her hull satisfied their curiosity.

Fletch was losing patience with Inka but there was a job to be done. Each
glared at the other with an understood promise of a future reckoning.

Work commenced with the Indian doing what was necessary but not one bit
more. The braves refused to dismount, leisurely sitting astride their mounts while

the crews hooked and unhooked the lariats. When the log was ready to be pulled the braves kneed their mounts into action dousing the crews with muddy water. This childish prank never ceased amusing the braves.

More then once the crew needed restraining and reminded what was at stake; on the other hand the job was progressing rapidly with the logs being pulled at great speeds in an attempt to drown the lowly "workers".

The day progressed with the Sioux's crew providing humor for the Indian. The effect of humiliation was offset by the progression of the task. As the logs were lined vertically to the shore, each downstream from the other, a current was developing, continually more prodigious.

By late afternoon both man and beast was exhausted. Jonas could see that sometime tomorrow the Riversioux would be once again upon her way. He called the day of labor to an end as the 'Sioux's' whistle blew.

All day Fletch had been away. Not only did Jonas think it wise to separate Fletch from Inka but he also was planning an evening feast for this diverse crew in an attempt to foster some semblance of solidarity.

Fletch was occupied grilling elk and white tail deer over an open pit along with a plentiful supply of potatoes and corn. These would be accompanied with a side dish of dried apples. By four thirty pm the meal was ready. Fletch motioned for Rube to whistle for the men.

Fletch also, at Alanson's request, set up stakes for horse shoe. After the meal before an audience of more then two hundred puzzled Indians, eight equally puzzled Negroes and of-course a boisterous crew Alanson was again ceremoniously thrashed.

"Maybe next time Alanson" Jonas teased.

"My game is slightly off but NEXT time we'll see who smiles". It seemed like plain 'luck' should cede him a game sometime but it also seemed luck always cozies up to Jonas Maynard! Alanson harbored great respect for the 'old man' but on these occasions it was difficult restraining reactions he'd later regret.

When men work together and then feast together they once more become boys. These men who seemingly could not live in harmony would for a time play together. The Santee braves laughed as they explained how sorry they were the paddlewheel's crew had gotten soaked. They had attempted to restrain their horses but their horse just didn't like white-eyes. Tonight they would have a talk with their horses and tomorrow they would surely be more civilized.

For the moment their divergent goals were forgotten and boys were satisfied being boys. Fletch who hadn't been a part of the work scene didn't understand what the joke was all about.

Inkpaduta had waited for this moment. The Santee had been scripted for this moment. Inka had pastured a spare horse in a clover patch along the river bank since early in the morning. Clover is a legume, legumes are laxative.

Inka was being prodded by the Santee to "demonstrate" for Fletch what the laughter was all about. The crew members 'unwittingly' soon were also demanding a demonstration. Inka, shrugging his shoulders, reluctantly agreed if Fletch was willing.

Fletch did not like the position he was being put in but unable to quell the demands also reluctantly agreed.

The river was lined with spectators as Fletch looped the lariat from Inka's spare horse around the log.

The boat's mirthful crew waited impatiently for Fletch to be soaked as they had been.

Everyone except Inka was astounded when Inka kneed his mount. Fletch immediately was inundated with flying horse shit and left gasping for breath amongst never ending bellows of gas.

The Santee rolled in laughter as they gestured at the hapless Fletch while they playfully held their noses. Fletch washing off horse dung in the river didn't laugh. Jeff whose crew had suffered all day at the hands of the Santee didn't laugh and Jonas didn't laugh.

Fletch smiled directly at Inca in a manner that sent chills through a gathering which until this point had been contending with an uncomfortably hot summer's evening.

Each groups need for the other and Jonas's insistence on non-violence saved the evening from further deterioration. Groups of tired men slowly made their way back to their respective domiciles.

Fletch finally finished cleaning the final layers of dung off was in the process of currying Explorer when he was surprised by a brigade of Negro workers heading back up river.

Jeff couldn't restrain a grin when he saw Fletch still cleaning in the river. The prank did have humor, if not the prankster.

The crew of blacks was carrying wedges, shovels and the like. "You're heading the wrong way" Fletch teased.

"I believe the job sight is this way" Jeff replied pointing up river. "Since it is a cool pleasant evening the men decided to finish the job without the day's heat or the Santee's harassment".

Fletch nodded in agreement while volunteering himself and Explorer.

It had been several hours since work had been halted for the night. The men may have quit but the current hadn't. Alanson had predicted the current would multiply the channeling effect. No white man present could have predicted the true effects. The channel already was a good five ft. deep and at least fifty ft. wide at it's narrowest. The job was completed and they were done!

To them it was a miracle but to the Indian it was simply the Missouri. They could tell stories of the channel moving a full quarter mile over night.

While returning to the Sioux the Negroes rejoiced in song. Fletch could feel the pain from where the music had originated, yet strangely it soothed. As on the banks of the Hudson Fletch couldn't help himself, the heartfelt music and honest fellowship amongst the fugitives (at least for the evening) soothed him and in the process diminished the wall separating him from mankind.

CHAPTER 16

▼

At dawn Jonas and the crew woke expecting another day of labor. Breakfast had been served and the final cup of coffee was being consumed when Fletch suggested a change in itinerary.

Cheers went up as Fletch related last night's discovery. The crew was ecstatic. These were hardened men, unaccustomed and unappreciative to waking with aching muscles.

The Santee also had noticed the channel. Inka and his two hundred some braves waited impatiently at rivers edge.

The crew was given the morning off as Jonas, Alanson, Fletch, Stroker and Rube headed toward the pilot house for discussions. Weapons would insure protection by the Santee, Fletch explained, until Inka determined they had secured sufficient means to wage war. Then the Riversioux would be their first causality.

Jonas had reluctantly guaranteed the Santee weapons in return for fuel. A bargain with the devil sometimes is unavoidable. The debate now had to do on when to cut and run. With the devil impatiently waiting several hundred yards away a decision was needed momentarily.

"We will not make Ft. Union on schedule without fuel precut and waiting on shore" Fletch directed the statement toward Alanson.

"Absolutely no way" Alanson responded as everyone expected.

"I am going to accompany the Santee. That's the way it has to be" Fletch said looking at Jonas. "I will keep you informed of the fuel pickup time and location. But most importantly I will find a way to warn when our 'friends' are no longer friendly".

"It is two days to Haddy's point" Alanson broke in "and an eight to ten day run from Haddy's Point to Ft. Tecumseh. From there it is still about two weeks to Ft. Union. This is with a dependable fuel supply. With our deadline and without fuel waiting to be brought aboard we might as well cut bait and drift back to Sioux City"!

"Stroker, please ask Jeff to join us" Jonas broke in.

Stroker soon returned with big Jeff.

"I belief I am still the one in command Fletch. You are NOT going to accompany Inkpaduta and his band by yourself" Jonas was leaving no doubt who was in control. "But if we could convince Jeff to accompany you that would be a different scenario".

Jeff was numb with anticipation. He was apprenticing under the best boiler man on the river and NOW he had an opportunity to accompany Fletch. Fletch who already was what he aspired to become.

He responded in a manner that surprised everyone. "There is almost nothing I want more then this, but Jenny and I were married in St. Joseph and we are partners. For all my life decisions affecting my life have been made by others, Jenny is NO slave. My wish is to go with her blessing and without it I can't". Jeff hesitated then asked "If you will give me a few minutes I'll be back as soon as possible with an answer".

"We'll wait" Jonas replied.

Each man was aware they were dealing with a special being. Nigger Jeff felt a need to consult his wife before making a commitment! He had certainly gained their attention, though few if any would have responded likewise. Even so most respected Jeff's decision except for one. Fletch simply shook his head knowing that where they were going a mind clouded with woman could be lethal.

Jeff returned bubbling with youthful excitement "When do we leave"?

Jenny had cried when he first brought up the proposition of accompanying Fletch. He immediately was sorry he had even considered leaving.

Jeff was learning the ways of woman. Jenny's tears were tears of love. She was being asked for the first time to make a decision in her behalf. She knew Jeff, her big lovable husband, wanted more then anything to make this trip yet he wasn't leaving without her okay!

Astounded Jeff left Jenny's embrace being showered with kisses and her blessing He didn't attempt to understand.

"Take 100 rounds for each pistol and one barrel of powder for the rifles and tell Chief Inkpaduta the two of you will be joining them" Jonas instructed. "Get your things together and be prepared to leave in the morning". Jonas was giving the newly weds a final night together.

"The skipper is alright" Jeff was thinking as headed below to 'Jenny'.

Alanson was spending the evening pampering Explorer, telling his big horse of his dreams. Tomorrow Fletch's life may depend upon his horse but tonight Explorer was Alanson's confident.

"I notice you have become friendly with the Belgian ladies big fellow". One of the mares was cycling and Alanson had made sure Explorer had access to her, hoping for an Explorer junior.

Suddenly Explorer reared up with his hooves pawing the air. "Whoa down there partner, what's the trouble"? Alanson held on for all his might but it was to no avail. Explorer would not be restrained. Explorer stared toward shore whinnying in a challenging fashion Alanson had never witnessed before.

Tying Explorer's reign to a deck tie down Alanson strained in the darkness studying the shore line. On shore a stallion leading a stable of mares was also pawing the ground, challenging Explorer for the Belgian in estrous cycle.

Explorer never retreated from a challenge but this was more then that. These horses were 'free' and that scrawny stallion was their 'leader'? New horizons were opening.

The wild stallion whinnied, pawing in contempt at the 'civilized' Explorer and then led his mares west through the tall prairie grasses.

Alanson sensing Explorers new awareness gently stroked his horses pulsating neck "You've never been a prisoner when with me my friend. You've always been my partner". Alanson spoke with a growing lump in his throat. "We have a job to do and then if conditions merit you can make your choice". Tears flowed unashamedly as Alanson curried his horse. For an instant Jeff and Jenny entered his mind.

Explorer nuzzled his master. He was comfortable and well provided for. Alanson had never abused him. Still FREEDOM once implanted within the consciousness doesn't succumb without a struggle.

THE WOOD GATHERER

RELENTLESS, OUT OF THE MIST OF ANTIQUITY,
STOOPED, STALWART, TRUDGING ONWARD, ALWAYS.
NOT BENT WITH AGE, BUT WITH BURDEN
OF THE AGES. BEARING WOOD TO THE HEARTH
FOR ALL TIME. BOWED WITH THE WEIGHT OF
THE NATIONS, SHE MARCHES FORWARD,
THE FUEL, THE POWER, SUSTAINING ALL PEOPLLES,
EVERY ERA, AGELESS.

EVERY MAN'S FREEDOM, ON HER BACK,
EVERY CHILD'S SECURITY, IN HER ARMS.
THE HEALTH OF EVERY HOME, IN HER HANDS.
AGELES, TIMELESS, MOTHER, GRANDMOTHER,
MATRON.

SPIRIT OF CIVILIZATION, HEART OF HUMANITY,
AGELESS, TIMELESS. DAUNTLESS,
FORWARD, FORWARD, FORWARD.
MOTHER, GRANDMOTHER, OF COURSE GODDESS.

—By David Alanson Bringman

CHAPTER 17

▼

Spotted Fawn, some would say now as beautiful as her mother, was married to (Oo Mato) Wounded Bear. Though it had been many seasons since being accosted on the Banks of Okoboji the haunting memory remained fresh. Fawn entered Haddy's Point, or Fort Randall as the soldiers now called it, with growing trepidation.

The Wahpekutes were obligated to trade with the white-eyes as the buffalo in their area were nearing depletion. Great herds roamed west of the river but to the east only a few small herds remained. Though the Wahpekutes were part of the Great Sioux Nation each band vigorously protected their individual hunting ground and the Wahpekutes were not yet in a position to compete with their mighty Lakota cousins.

Cloth and thread were beginning to replace scarce buffalo hide which made the trading post an uncomfortable necessity. Fawn understood she would be humiliated and most likely cheated as she entered the fort community but if she returned to camp without the needed staples she would be beaten.

Fawn struggled to keep her composure for if she smiled it was seen as an invitation and if she appeared aloof she was an uppity injun in need of education. She had already been educated for being uppity to the delight of onlookers. Fawn understood the 'game'. She was a pawn, limited to a pawn's options. What she didn't know was that this was payday.

It was Saturday, the first of the month and payday. Soldiers on the frontier have little to celebrate and in their harsh environment celebration is much in need. Alcohol removed the soldier from his circumstance and the natives provided an outlet. Celebration had started early. Spotted Fawn entered a post where restraint had exited some time ago.

Fawn carried a basket filled with berries she had picked and squash Wounded Bear had stolen from the farming Arickaras. She must return with the staples of survival. These things were on her mind as suddenly several disorderly youths in Calvary uniform grabbed the basket. What could she do? Any choice would lead to places rather not visited.

Fawn was spared the agony of choice. Not satisfied with berries the 'boys' returned for more adult entertainment. Not daring to scream, she was being dragged toward the livery stable as the 'playful' troops munched on fresh berries. Once in the past she had screamed drawing attention to her plight only to be surrounded by a crowd cheering on her antagonist. She would suffer her humiliation in silence. If she was to be violated she would provide no more then a warm corpse. For her and for her people this was now their fate. Grandfather had turned his head from the Wahpekute.

Break of daylight, the morning after the pilot house meeting, found Fletch and Jeff on their way. Though Jonas had instructed them to accompany the band of Santee, Fletch had his own idea. After having a necessary meeting with Inka, Fletch and Jeff would join the band later just above Haddy's Point. This they determined would be the first fuel stop.

If Jeff was to be his 'partner' it was imperative he teach him what he could as fast as he could.

For two days they had worked their way up the river, one teaching and the other learning. In a cram course Jeff had learned much, he was becoming less a liability and more an asset with each passing hour. It wasn't that Jeff was now a frontiersman but he was earning Fletch's trust. Two days alone in the wilderness bares many secrets which in other circumstances would remain within. The two men were bonding somewhat like the badger and fox.

The noisy din of Fort Randall warned the voyagers of civilization's proximity even before the odor. The 'outlaw' and the 'nigger' looked at each other with a shared understanding, they both longed for freedom and freedom was not here.

Outwardly Fawn made no struggle, inwardly she was in turmoil. Wounded Bear would not understand. Maybe she like her mother should fight! Would an honorable death not be preferable to this life? With these thoughts spinning in her mind once again Fawn was spared the dilemma of 'choice'.

A group of boisterous soldiers was seen dragging a young Indian Squaw into the livery barn as Fletch and Jeff dismounted. Without communication they reacted in tandem.

A huge black hand throttled one of the ringleaders as the barrel of Fletch's pistol crashed the skull of another teenage soldier who was frantically attempting to disrobe the struggling young Indain maiden.

The fort was instantly in disarray. A 'nigger' and a frontiersman were interfering with their Saturday entertainment. Most often when confronted bullies suddenly become meek boys but this was not the usual occasion. A 'nigger', probably a run-away fugitive, kindled outrage amongst a Calvary stocked with the south's best. With seething anger the camp converged upon the scene.

Their outrage was superceded by the simultaneous snap of a neck and retort of a Colt.

Fletch handed Spotted Fawn two army pistols from the downed soldiers while he pressed his Colt into the chest of the lieutenant who was apparently in command. With a learned hatred Jeff wielded two Colt pistols; his eyes expressing no niggardly characteristics.

Fletch did his best to communicate with Fawn, his hands being filled with weapons rendered sign language useless, who they were and what they intended. Fletch could communicate fairly well with the Lakota but Dakota was a somewhat different dialect, still root words were similar and present conditions didn't leave much for interpretation.

Nudging the lieutenant toward the post store he instructed Fawn to grab whatever she needed and leave what she had brought in trade. Grabbing his own sack Fletch filled it with whatever seemed useful.

"Are you ready to leave this friendly outpost" Fletch asked Jeff jamming his pistol deeper into the Lieutenant's ribs.

"We can stay while the two of you shop or we can leave, it's really your call" Jeff was cold serious.

"Soldier boy we're going to walk out that door together, we're going to take two of the best looking horses you have and hightail it. If you do as you're told in due time you will be set free, if you can't do that I might as well shoot your sorry ass right now" Fletch raised the barrel of his pistol even with the lieutenants left eye.

With unmistakable capitulation the Lieutenant vigorously nodded in agreement.

"Tell your troops to back off and stay put UNTILL you return. Do you understand"? Again a vigorous nod in the affirmative was the immediate response.

Looking at each other for affirmation, while motioning Fawn to accompany them, they headed for the door.

Fawn had no idea what to expect or what was transpiring but she did know that staying was now out of the picture. These two may not be her friends but for the present they definitely had the same enemies! Spotted Fawn fell into a tightly knit group as they exited the post store.

It was going fairly well until Fawn noticed the instigator of her attack was pointing her way with a knowing smirk and tauntingly waving a tattered piece of her garment.

Fawn carefully aimed and fired. Gut shot, the recent reveler writhed in agony as the troops stared in disbelief.

'Hold fire, Hold Fire"! The Lieutenant felt Fletch's pistol nearly impaling him.

"Jesus Christ Jeff don't cross this squaw" Fletch yelled to Jeff as much in dismay as the soldiers.

"This isn't exactly going according to plan soldier boy, we can all live or we all die. It is your move; get us out of here NOW"!

"Ten-hut! Troops stand to" looking squarely at Fletch, "a three day pass awaits any man who apprehends these criminal after my return and if I DON'T return within 24 hours there will be 7 days extra vacation for them DEAD! Until that time you are to remain at post liberty".

The troops did as good soldiers always do, obeying orders they watched as Jeff and Fletch sorted through the posts corral for the best mounts.

With Fletch leading the way mounted upon Explorer the get-away was executed. The lieutenant followed with Spotted Fawn's pistol following every bounce of his steed. Jeff brought up the rear praying the crazy squaw didn't harbor anymore pent up hostility.

Deflecting suspicion away from the Riversioux Fletch explained to the lieutenant that he and his nigger partner had been hunting for a month and had hardly seen a buffalo when they happened upon Ft. Randall. He really didn't give a damn about the army or the squaw. They needed the supplies and the squaw was a looker, after they were done with her she was possum feed.

After several hours of hard riding the lieutenant was released physically unharmed but full of verbal recriminations. He duty bound explained in detail what the army would do to the likes of them or anyone who helped them...He was still explaining when Fletch told Fawn to just shoot the S.O.B...

Jeff didn't understand what was being said but when Fawn raised her pistol he swatted her horse causing it to buck, saving the soldiers life.

Fletch laughed outrageously almost falling of his horse. To him the lieutenant was becoming obnoxious, with lots of rattle but no bite. Fawn's desire to extinguish one more soldier didn't seem unreasonable under the circumstances. The transformation from issuing edicts of death to scurrying through the under brush in an attempt to escape the squaw's fury bent Fletch over in laughter.

Jeff meanwhile had some growing doubts about his partners in this venture. Fletch seemingly valued life for what it produced while life its self was of little significance. In Fawn he sensed an all too familiar hate.

What to do with Spotted Fawn was now the question? Though physically attractive she was in no danger from these two. Neither Jeff nor Fletch, both having experienced servitude, had any ambition to exploit the situation.

Fawn was confused with the situation. She had been rescued, but for what? At Fort Randall she would have been used until they tired of the sport then she would be released to finish her trading. This was her roll in life.

The Wahpekute males were emasculated. With game scarce, depleted man power and primitive weaponry the braves weren't able to hunt successfully or wage warfare. This left the band depended upon commerce for survival. For half a century they had battled the white-eye, with memory and pride still intact the Wahpekute Brave left trading to the female.

These two would have their fun just like the soldiers and then they would release her with nothing to trade and far from the trading post. Wounded Bear would be furious. Spotted Fawn saw no good in her day.

Wounded Bear was never pleased. If Fawn succeeded in obtaining supplies his uselessness was once again on display and if she failed they hungered. She and her sisters suffered immensely at the hands of frustrated braves. Many young females had simply given up and were taking up with the white-eye. This she understood but 'she', Fawn was a Wahpekute and the sister of Chief Inkpaduta.

Inka's vision had become her vision also. One day the clear waters of Okoboji would run red with the blood of her mother's assassins...or the Wahpekute would perish. These two could use her if they managed to survive but either way judgment day was fast approaching.

Spotted Fawn aimed and fired but nothing happened.

Fletch hadn't given this wild woman an arsenal. These were single shot army issue pistols. She had used up her firepower on her uniformed antagonist, since then she had been on trial and with the click of the firing pin the verdict was in.

"Think you can secure this wildcat"? Fletch asked Jeff with a laugh.

"We risk our necks to save her and then she repays us by trying to kill us and I thought Jenny was hard to understand". Jeff didn't share Fletches humor. "What are we going to do with her"?

"You've already got one woman and I'm not wanting this one, let's give her to Chief Inka" Fletch still was enjoying the moment. "Even us up for the horse shit deal"!

The two were prepared for ridicule or even rejection but certainly not for fury from their Wahpekute allies.

Inka watched as the three entered the camp. The huge black was easily recognized and Fletch astride Explorer made his own impression. Two large sacks were strapped to the saddle horns of the first two horses and the third horse had a struggling female precariously bound to it. He didn't trust this Fletch but so far he had delivered what he had promised. Twice he could have killed him but hadn't. No he didn't trust this white-eye and he certainly didn't like him but he did grudgingly respect him. Inka understood that at present they both used the other; the secret was to be the first one to understand when the game was over.

"Greetings horse shit". Inka addressed Fletch.

Suddenly Inka was staring at the captive on the ground which Jeff had callously and unceremoniously dumped at his feet.

"GRAB THESE TWO" Inka was livid. This white-eye was loco. Yes he needed more weapons but he would not be humiliated. They had violated his sister and then publicly insulted him like this! The stakes no longer mattered and this game was over. He would personally feed their appendages slowly one by one to the camp dogs.

Spotted Fawn had always hated the white-eyes and she didn't have any affection for his buffalo headed companion either but this was wrong! Grandfather Spirit had sent them to rescue her; great catastrophe would surely be visited upon the Wahpekute if they were harmed.

"Listen my brother, white-eye and buffalo-head rescued me from the soldiers. Like you I at first misunderstood. Now I know they were sent by grandfather and they must not be harmed".

Inka had never seen Spotted Fawn more ardent. Inka loved almost no-one, Spotted Fawn his sister was the lone exception. She had nurtured Inka through terrible times therefore her wishes, although he was still confused, would be honored. Maybe Fawn was right and grandfather was returning to his people.

Jeff and Fletch had no idea that Fawn was Wahpekute and much less that she was Inka's sister. Everything about this ordeal was becoming more than a little confusing.

Jeff, with no feasible alternative, believed Jenny's faith was wrapped securely around them and had provided protection.

Fletch having once again survived savored the condiments that a life properly lived offered.

In the evening there was feasting and celebration around the camp fires. Spotted Fawn as was Sioux custom shared her enormous bounty with her village while retelling and continually embellishing the story of her capture and rescue.

As at the Riversioux picnic these adversaries by circumstance once again shared food and fun. Both understood that for now they shared a common goal but each also understood that just under the surface hate lay a smoldering. Never-the-less after sharing food and conversation Jeff and Fletch both felt a little less apprehension.

For all living things life is a journey. Though the paths are many and the means various Union Station remains the common terminal. With tickets purchased by birth most experience love, some experience freedom and a chosen few both. Some will travel the express and others the local, it is of little consequence. At destination the discussion is of experience, never the schedule. While brochures haphazardly describe scenery along the route; deportation from this life is ultimately left to the Lemming.

Jenny died relatively young but if life is measured by impact, her life left its imprint. Jenny wasn't known to complain although reasons for doing so were plentiful and neither did Jenny shirk life's duties. She willingly accepted the plantation as her vocation and she suffered unspeakable acts before taking flight. In the short time thereafter she had experienced freedom and had eagerly accepted the responsibility that accompanied it.

She had worked shoulder to shoulder with both fugitive and free-men to reroute the mighty Missouri. Her voice rang pure as she led the crew in music through the laborious work night. She had remained a woman amidst a crew of men but most importantly she and Jeff had shared love. It had been a meaningful and a fruitful life.

Jenny was feeling ill as she bid Jeff farewell. In all her days Jenny could not remember being really sick. Perhaps bidding her lover farewell made her physically sick; goodness knows it drained her soul.

Soon she was bent over with stomach cramps, and then she hung over the railing with her stomach violently wrenching as she vomited.

Finally with Jenny running a high fever the Negroes summoned Jonas. The Riversioux immediately was anchored midstream as Jonas futilely administered his limited remedies. Vomiting followed with diarrhea continued as Jenny remained doubled in agony.

Within 8 hours Jenny was bedridden and within thirty six hours from initial onslaught this vibrant display of femininity was decreed to memory.

Jonas remembered witnessing the Cholera epidemic of '49' back in St. Louis. Jenny displayed the same symptoms and succumbed to its ravages in a like manner. Jonas was fairly certain that filth and lack of sunshine were major contributors to the disease. In St. Joseph he had weighed the risk and had determined that bounty hunters were the more imminent and real threat. He would lose no sleep over his decision though he would grieve deeply over Jenny's passing. Death had made itself guest many times in Joneses journeys upon the river, life and river continued unabated.

With death growing imminent Jenny requested Jonas pen a note to Jeff. She also dictated her wishes for burial.

Jenny noticed the Sioux built resting places for their departed in high places so their journey would be shortened. She requested her remains be placed upon a small raft of sticks and then pushed into the freedom seeking waters of the Missouri, hastening her journey to eternal freedom.

Jonas read the proper passages of scripture as Jenny's remains were gently set adrift to a chorus of Gospel Blues sung by a choir of six grieving Negro men.

As Jenny was set adrift Jeff was being freed by the Wahpekutes. Though free he was beset with a sense of loss. His mind struggled for focus while his soul cried for answer. After the feast he confided his misgivings to Fletch.

Fletch also harbored an uneasy feeling, he was fairly certain it pertained to the Riversioux. Together they decided Jeff should return to the Riversioux at dawns first light.

Wounded Bear possessed the most appealing female amongst the Santee, possibly the whole Sioux nation. He also was jealous. Many times in the past he had beaten Fawn for causing other men to feast their eyes upon her. Now she had confronted her own brother in defense of the white-eye and his big buffalo head lackey. Maybe she like so many others Wahpekute squaws lusted for a white-eye, one who treated his woman in a manner unbecoming a real brave.

Jeff unable to sleep left early, well before daybreak, while Fletch snuggled next to a young Santee maiden who had graced his blanket sometime in the early morning hours. This was a custom practiced among the plains tribes, one Fletch had no problem complying with.

His relaxed morning was interrupted by the sounds of a switch and an accompanying whimper. Fletch, by nature, could not ignore the strong unleashing their shortcomings upon the weak.

As Wounded Bear brought his willow switch back for yet another strike he himself was ripped backwards. With a look of unmistakable contempt Fletch held fast to the forked ends of Bears willow branch. Dropping the branch Wounded Bear, subjugated to a cowards blighted pride, blindly charged. Fletch having no use for cowards eagerly met the challenge with intentions of pummeling Wounded Bear to death.

Like Inka, Bear was soon bloodied and like Inka he also was loaded with grit and quit was not within.

A boisterous crowd had already gathered by the time Inka arrived for this was a 'good' fight 'as nobody liked either of the combatants'. Inka along with most his band had long despised his cowardly brother-in-law and now harbored an equal dislike for Fletch. The only reason Wounded Bear had survived this long was Inka's desperate need for warriors, any warrior. Now with weapons and a promise of more warriors, Wounded Bear had become expendable.

Inka threw them both knives as he gestured with a slicing motion across his throat.

Most strangers to a situation would have waited for some instruction or a signal to commence but Fletch lived and fought on his terms.

Before Bear had a firm grasp of his knife, life's blood gurgled from his being. In one quick motion Bears head was nearly severed from his torso.

Fletch having no idea where he now stood with the Santee buried the barrel of his Colt in Inka's chest as he slowly backed away from the awed and considerably silenced crowd.

As it turned out retreat was not necessary. Inka waved off the admiring but concerned onlookers as he explained to Fletch that since he had fought an honorable fight he was free to come and go at his pleasure. "It would be better for us both if you removed your gun from my chest" was Inka's response

"Let's get wood" Fletch answered holstering his weapon.

Inka contemplating future events nodded in approval.

The Riversioux was moored between two large cottonwood trees along the west bank of the river as Jeff approached. Every door and window was open and every crew member appeared absorbed in scrubbing the 'Sioux' down.

Hobbling his horse Jeff fired in the air, gaining their attention and soon a canoe was dispatched to retrieve him. The ride over was a somber affair, with the only answer to Jeff's quarries being "better see the captain".

When Jenny didn't greet him Jeff's stomach turned cold. By the time he reached the pilot house his heart was pounding, his cloths were drenched in sweat.

Jeff didn't comprehend Jonas's words of condolence; he was adrift in a personal world of grief.

Dormant anger rose from within…an anger which cried for and then demanded anarchy within the soul. Where was this God and why hadn't Jenny been worthy of his mercy?

He had suffered indignities and inhumanity all his life but combined in their totality nothing equaled the pain he now bore. The flower of life had been tantalizingly revealed, he had breathed long and deeply of its fragrance causing hope and dreams long silenced to resurface in a beautiful and magical song. Now the flower was gone and the music silenced, nipped by an early and unjust frost. He was engrossed in these thoughts when he again became aware of the note that Jonas had placed in his hand.

Jeff felt a pressing need to be alone while on the other hand he longed for companionship.

He found himself sitting alone under one of the cottonwood trees the 'Sioux' was secured to, staring at the paper containing Jenny's final words. With fists clenched and with bursting heart he sobbed. For some time he rocked back and forth in unrestrained grief until he was startled by a comforting hand placed upon his shoulder.

Stroker had observed the big man slowly making his way to the cottonwood tree where he had slumped to the ground and then sat staring emptily at a piece of paper. Stroker assumed that Jeff being a nigger couldn't read.

Stroker not only admired the big man but he also had grown fond of him, trying to be of comfort was a normal reaction.

A mere few days earlier Jeff had been simply a 'nigger' but since being forced to work alongside the 'nigger', the 'nigger' had now become humanized.

In the work place Stroker was industrious while in life he remained common, simply reacting. He understood each wood had its own properties. Some varieties burned hot and quick while others varieties reacted oppositely yet each variety was also affected by age, dryness and the environment from where it came. He also knew there were numerous exceptions to the general rule. Some 'soft' woods would burn like a hard wood and vice-versa. For these reasons Stroker had 'learned' to size up each wood and make fuel value decisions based on individual merit as well as by sight. The Riversioux got more energy from less wood then any other paddlewheel! This ability made Stroker a valuable employee.

In life Stroker was content to remain average. A nigger was a nigger and an injun was an injun except when forced to share a common path. Being judged by results and paid accordingly in the work place Stroker adjusted his thinking as he gained experience, in personal dealings there is no such incentive. None of this interfered with Stroker's life, because he now knew Jeff he liked him and because he didn't know the others they remained niggers.

"Want me to read the note for you" Stroker quietly asked?

Jeff, though skilled in linguistics, found comfort in Stroker's offer "Yes I'd appreciate it Stroker".

Stroker spread the paper on the ground and laboriously sounded out its printed message.

My dearest Jeff:

"When abused the lord gave me refuge, with his caring hand he led me to freedom, and our days together expressed his love. Now I am called to his glory. Please do not grieve for I gladly go to a better place and a greater love, a place where sorrow is never present and peace is ever lasting. May Jesus always hold you in his hand".

Love Jenny

Jeff's face first lost coloration and then brimmed crimson as he grabbed the note from Stroker, then with neck muscles pulsating he shredded the note, compressed it into a ball and flung it into the flowing waters of the Missouri.

The white man's Jesus passively conceded the enslavement of his people and now when freedom was at hand he had removed love. He would surely Miss Jenny but the sarcastic humor of her God—never.

How could Jenny possibly believe death was enrichment?

Maybe Jenny was right. For the first time in memory HE was free!

Jeff quietly knocked and then entered the pilot house appearing as if nothing had transpired. He brought Jonas up to date on the events of Haddy's Point and their encounter with the Santee. Jeff, although he and Fletch hadn't really discussed it, assured Jonas there would also be firewood at the mouth of the Cheyenne River. He reminded Jonas rifles and ammunition would be a requirement of the Wahpekutes to assure their passage north.

Jonas thought he sensed a change in the big man when he had entered. When Jeff made no inquiry as to the well being of his fellow fugitives there was no doubt. Young and grief stricken Jeff may attempt a metamorphous but in the end

Jefferson would remain Jefferson, basically good. With a shrug Jonas returned to the business of piloting the 'Sioux'.

Upon leaving Jonas Jeff sought out Stroker. He knew Stroker would be amiss as to why he had reacted to Jenny's note in such an angry manner. Stroker in the past hadn't been a person he'd spent much time socializing with BUT he was the one who had appeared when he was adrift and it was he who had provided a crutch when one was desperately needed.

"Stroker, I owe you an explanation and an apology if you have a minute" Jeff said resting his immense hand upon Stroker's shoulder.

"You alright, if you need some time alone" Stroker didn't know what to say. He had tried to be a friend. He'd mistakenly thought that Jeff and Jenny had shared a good thing but for Christ ever lovin sake he'd never witnessed a reaction like Jeff's! Maybe niggers treated death different? In any case he wasn't about to say anything that might upset the man.

"Don't worry Stroker, things are okay now. When you came to me I was struggling under an immense burden, I was down upon my knees. When you left much of my burden went with you".

Stroker attempted to reply when Jeff gently squeezed his shoulder and continued. "Jenny was my first and my only love and I believed I was hers also. I am young lover and I am jealous. Her note was clear and unmistakable, Jenny loved the God of the plantation more then me. I willingly shared her faith but I will no longer share her ignorance; no black skin will ever darken the streets of that God's heaven. The realization of these things culminated in the fury you witnessed. I hope you can understand". Jeff removed his hand from Stoker's shoulder and gently clasped his hand in friendship.

Jeff's mastery of the English language had at first irritated Stroker and it damn sure still amazed him. Yes he did understand, though he 'liked' Jeff he didn't think Jeff or any nigger was going to heaven either.

As Jeff made his way to the canoe and a return to 'freedom' Stroker called after him "going to miss you partner".

Inka had the word spread amongst the many bands of Sioux that he, Chief Inkpaduta 'sworn enemy of the white-eye' would soon have the ability to wage a great war, a war cleansing their Dakota homeland of white-eyes for all time.

Inka was now possessed by a noble dream; a dream of leading the whole Sioux Nation in a glorious uprising.

Jeff made a wide birth around Ft. Randall in his journey up river in search of Fletch and the Santee. For most his adult life Jeff's dreams revolved around freedom. Reality and the dream often are at odds. Being constantly apprehensive of the master's daily whim and fear of the unknown are not to be compared as equals but both are wearing.

Jeff had learned much in the time he'd spent with Fletch. He had no desire to be impedance to the Indian way of life but he lacked the ability to communicate this message. Until he rejoined Fletch Jeff hoped not to come in contact with the people he so admired.

The snap of a branch as a white tail deer broke for cover brought Jeff to a reactionary defense mode. A cotton tail running thru the brush brought the same reaction and when a covey of quail broke under foot Jeff felt his heart leave his rib cage.

For three days Jeff worked himself northward. The sun was hot and the insects constantly pestered which certainly was irritating but fear of the unknown was exhausting.

Exhausted, uncomfortable and continually on edge Jeff finally gave up. He knew and understood he had become the prisoner of fear when he should be enhancing his learning process…and it was killing him.

In a willow patch on the bank of the Missouri Jeff wearily acquiesced to nature. Amazingly with his surrender the noises which had brought tension now were sounds bringing rest. With his conscious disconnected his unconscious stood watch, Jeff for the first time since leaving the Riversioux rested in peace.

It was dark when Jeff awoke. He found himself refreshed and anticipating the adventure. Inadequateness, though surely still present, now was subservient to youthful zest. he was preparing to live his dream.

New sounds became apparent while sounds from the past took on new meaning. Jeff realized that for the first time he was hearing rather then analyzing. There was a harmony which he only now was becoming aware of. Sounds of terror, predation, challenge, joy and absolute silence inundated the night air. Each species, often individually, made these sounds as the occasion arrived. Jeff couldn't identify the species but as he merged with his environment it became more and more apparent what was and was not threatening.

The feeling of freedom and 'belonging' added adrenaline to the big mans stamina. Confidence progressively replaced fear as Jeff continued his trek northward.

As the sun grew more powerful the dew weighted grasses shook of their wetness and stretched skyward to receive the suns energy. This is a peaceful time of day, with the nocturnal predators at rest the daytime birds and beast revel in a new day.

Jeff also reveled in a new day. Before being betrayed by Ebau and Nosha he had known nature and its freedom; but he had never been free of superstition and prejudice. Here in the wilderness he was what he was with no imprisonment of the past. No longer in a hurry Jeff stretched his frame in rest under the canopy of an American elm. In thoughtful daydreams of who he was and what he intended to be Jeff at last lay in peace.

A life time of solitude was not his dream; he couldn't picture himself permanently isolated from mankind but on the other hand dreams of civilization chilled his being. One dream followed another until one dream continued to dominate his thoughts.

Being Sioux was his paramount desire. If this was truly his dream, he would exert his energy toward that end.

With these thoughts intact Jeff resumed his travels upstream in search of Fletch and the Wahpekutes.

It took 2 days and a night for Jeff to be reunited with Fletch. Entering the Santee encampment Jeff not only now loomed physically superior but he also walked with that confidence.

Fletch and Inka met Jeff and began immediately explaining the past few days' events. Jeff stopped the conversation and asked it be resumed in Dakota as he preferred the Sioux way of life.

Fletch nodded in agreement as a small smile surfaced through Inka's grim mask.

For some the languages are a gift and for Jeff more then most. He found that as in nature one does not analyze language, one simply enters. Enter he did to the amazement of both Inka and Fletch.

Energy radiated from the camp as it swelled with warriors itching to acquire weapons, itching for revenge.

Jeff spent more and more time mingling with the Santee and less time with Fletch. Fletch cared little where Jeff spent his time, he preferred the Sioux way of life himself. Still if Jeff ever posed a threat to the Riversioux his frontier honeymoon would be short lived.

Spotted Fawn had never before looked upon a man with the physical attributes of Jeff. He obviously was a man of great strength and he yet was surprisingly light of foot. She noticed with pleasure how he picked up on his new environment with robust expediency.

She had made the mandatory minor attempts of self mutilation with the demise of her husband. It simply wasn't to be, if it hadn't been for the Wahpekute need of warriors she would have slit his throat years ago.

Now Fawn dreamed of the new warrior with black skin.

Spotted Fawn overheard Jeff tell Fletch he was now without a woman. He also no longer was subservient to the white-eye God hung on a cross. She was glad; here was a man with no mate, a man who was vulnerable.

For 5 days they traveled north and were now camped at the mouth of the (good river) Cheyenne. Tomorrow they would cut and stack firewood but tonight Fawn would stalk a mate.

As the fires burned low a solitary figure quietly slipped into Jeff's bedroll.

Jeff was not asleep. He had hoped for and anticipated Fawns arrival. For three days she had been flirting and this evening she had intentionally…seductively bathed within his view. Oh yes Jeff was ready.

With no words spoken Fawn encircled him. Warm and firm yet soft was her body as she gently massaged his neck. Slowly Fawn worked her fingers down Jeff's spine until she reached the small of his back. With her body wrapped tightly to his and with her wetted love nest caressing his leg Fawn slowly grasped his manhood. An involuntary shiver coursed through Fawn's body as she held his erection with both hands.

As Jeff rolled to meet Fawn she welcomed him with an encircling embrace. Though desire was great Jeff slowly and gently entered loves abode. He valiantly struggled to restrain himself but entwined in love's heat (like dry lightening upon a fall prairie) inevitably they exploded in primeval wildfire.

Later sweat soaked and spent the two contentedly drifted to where all lovers drift.

As the sun slowly climbed over the Missouri River bluffs, the camp once more burst with life. The new lovers, as is Sioux custom, met the new day with lewd razzing from the camps young adults. Jeff initially took offense but as Fawn lovingly squeezed his hand he reconsidered. If this was the Sioux way so be it; he was free and never again would he be captive to someone else's values. He and Fawn laughed good naturedly along with their tormenters.

Jeff struggled to understand the events that now entwined him. Yesterday he was content trying to make inroads as a Sioux, today he copulated with the chief's sister! Though he scarcely knew the Sioux vixen sharing his bed role he was certain she was after more then his body. She alone had engineered the chain of events which now wrestled for control of his will.

Inka also was pleased with the turn of events; good warriors were at a premium. With weapons already acquired and more promised Inka's dreams were nearing maturation. Big Jeff could be used.

Spirit Lake and retribution, always subconsciously smoldering, now openly burned in Inka's thoughts.

Fawn shared her brother's ambition for retribution. Though years had passed her mother's words, "run and don't stop" still haunted her early morning sweat wracked dreams.

But unlike Inka, Fawn now lived a life beyond hate. Fawn was in love! He was more then she had dared dream of, besides physical superiority he also 'wished' to be Sioux! In a time when capitulation was the norm, this black warrior eagerly sought her way of life.

The band of Wahpekutes was returning to health, Santee warriors were joining daily and 'her' man was destined for greatness. Fawn at long last had reason to dream.

"Momma, soon white-eye blood will become a river where your blood once trickled and the Wahpekute will run no more". These thoughts dominated as she searched for her black warrior.

"When the crew is occupied loading fuel we will attack", Inka explained to Jeff. "We may lose warriors but in return we will gain many weapons! If we succeed the reward will be great. I, Inkpaduta chief of the Wahpekute, will become war chief of the entire Sioux Nation. No white-eye will ever again be welcome in Sioux territory. If we should fail then grandfather spirit no longer walks with the Wahpekute and death will be a welcomed guest".

Jeff interrupted "Inka I agree with the goal but I can not agree with the plan. Brave men took great risk for me; repaying them this way does not seem right"!

"When one white-eye is welcomed, others come. Soon there is room only for the white-eye and those who would be his lackey; surely even a slave knows this"!

"I am slave to NO-ONE Chief". Things were getting difficult for Jeff. He had been offended and befriended by black, white and red, skin pigment it appeared meant nothing. Still Inka was right; the white man's need for control and his own fledgling notion of freedom could never co-exist.

"When still young I had a vision where the future became clear and terrible. Do you wish to know the future black warrior?

Jeff wished all things were explainable but unfortunately they just weren't. He struggled to dismiss all theology; it seemed they all ended up tools of the practitioner. But he had witnessed Jenny's miraculous flight to freedom with faith as her only means. The Sioux seemed to posses an admirable theology gleaned from the heavens though it appeared toothless. When very young he remembered his father seeking out special persons who tossed sea shells with eyes that peered into the future before making important tribal decisions.

"Tell me your vision Chief so I may determine if treachery is a proper reward for those who rescued me".

"Many moons ago I sought my vision. Not wanting to be a messenger of horror my vision hid from me but like a young lover I persisted until finally she relinquished her secrets. Now as a young lover I am slave to that knowledge. She transported me to a great height where the future was laid out beneath me. This is what I saw".

Inka's eyes filled with tears and sweat beaded. With breathing ceased and lips motionless a voice from within foretold the Wahpekute's future.

Jeff quietly listened as the Redman's story of tribulation unfolded. He had dealt with charlatans on two continents, if Inka was on stage he acted well. He also had an advantage of knowledge; he had already witnessed much of Inka's vision.

The southern streams already ran murky brown and the soil was or was becoming sterile. The white mans answer to these problems was to abandon the old earth and continually press westward in search of new earth. There was wisdom in Inka's answer and maybe the sacrifice of a few for the good of all was justified. Anyone knows that man can not impose his will upon nature…. Everyone except the imposers.

Spotted Fawn had observed their conversation and she understood Jeff's Dilemma. Her acquaintance with Jeff and Fletch was not of long standing but their experience together was telling. They had dared to rescue her from Ft. Randall through a shared sense of right.

If Jeff believed he owed the boat people, she knew it would be a major task convincing him otherwise. She loved Jeff and she loved her people's ways. Life no longer was black and white, with her new knowledge it had now become a hazy brown. If only she could reverse time, back to before she met Fletch. She now realized Fletch and Inka were quite similar only Fletch was embodied in the wrong skin. It had been simpler when she had believed all white-eyes were the same. Still the answer was clear; the white-eye must be eliminated for Wahpekute survival! Fawn didn't see the answer to this conundrum but she was determined to search until the answer was revealed.

Fletch normally could sense trouble well before trouble appeared and Jeff obviously was amidst plenty of it. His erect confident walk was disappearing and being replaced with a noticeable uncertainty. Possibly it was caused by the squaw, but it appeared to be more.

As more and more warriors joined the party instead of being pleased Jeff grew more agitated. Fletch grew uneasy knowing the welfare of the 'Riversioux' was in jeopardy if he didn't solve the puzzle soon.

"Fletch" the baritone voice of Jeff brought him back to present circumstances. "Spotted Fawn informed me there is to be a pow-wow and we are asked to attend. Now please listen well, you have taught me much and you have been a friend, for this I owe you. I understand your duty is to protect the Riversioux and you must understand my duty is to remain free. Maybe these two objectives will collide; I implore you to take this as a warning to be cautious. We must go to the pow-wow so I remind you once again, you have been a friend and hopefully this will not change but be reminded our dreams may be divergent dreams. Let's go".

The meeting commenced beneath a tall cottonwood, next to the river. Jeff and Fletch were ushered through a clearing to where Fawn and Inka were engaged in an animated and terse conversation.

Inka, never one to procrastinate, got straight to the point. "In one maybe two days the boat will be here. I have determined the original bargain insufficient, we need more in return. We need thirty rifles at minimum and three kegs of powder or my warriors will not risk passing through Arickara lands and surely not through the territory of the mighty Assiniboine"

Fletch spit, barely missing Inka's foot. "Are all Santee warriors pussies or just the Wahpekute? Possibly Spotted Fawn and some of the other squaws could lend buckets to your Crow hermaphrodite warriors to pick berries while REAL warriors procure weapons"

Fletch was merely posturing for he and all concerned knew the Santee desperately needed the weapons and they also understood attacking the Riversioux was foolhardy with the few weapons the Wahpekute now possessed.

White, red and black each looked for weakness within the other but none surfaced. With many divergent hopes resting on the outcome of this parley the atmosphere grew increasingly tense.

Fletch kept his back against the tree as the talks continued. He knew the Wahpekute needed what he had to offer, from experience he understood every dealing also veiled unforeseen possibilities. The possibility he hadn't anticipated was Spotted Fawn. While keeping the warriors in focus Fawn bashed his head with a knotted ash limb.

The 'Sioux' beached on the east side of the Missouri, across from the mouth of the Cheyenne River (Good River) as planned. Jeff and Spotted Fawn received the tie down rope from the 'Sioux' and secured her to a make shift loading dock.

"Where is Fletch"? Jonas demanded as soon as Jeff boarded.

"Boss we have some talking to do in the pilot house. Fletch couldn't be here but he asked me to deliver a message" Jeff said walking toward the pilot house.

"Sit down Jeff" Jonas said motioning toward a chair as he closed the pilot house door. Though Jeff attempted deceit, Jonas sensed trouble as he boarded.

"What has become of Fletch"? Jonas was fuming. "Straighten up young man, tell the truth and we will work it out".

Jeff had expected an uncomfortable confrontation but not this soon. The "old man" had an uncanny second sense about him. Jeff had spent his entire life in servitude, never having been involved in management decisions he was feeling less secure by the moment. He genuinely liked and respected Jonas; he owed him his freedom, but Jonas and those who would follow were death to his dream.

What had been recently clear became less so as he looked into the honest eyes now scrutinizing him. Then his thoughts turned to Spotted Fawn and doubt fled.

"Fletch is our hostage" Jeff said as he motioned toward his Santee accomplices along the river bank. "For fifty rifles and the powder required for fifty rifles he will be retuned unharmed".

Jonas was relieved. Fletch was alive and nothing had yet been done which couldn't be undone. "Leave now; we'll talk again when the fuel is on board" Jonas said escorting Jeff to the door.

The wood was being stacked aboard the Riversioux as Jeff walked down the ramp to discuss the situation with Inka.

Joshua, one of the other black fugitives, was busy stacking wood as Jeff passed. "We hear you are leaving to join up with these Indians. Jeff if you leave, we all leave". This Joshua stated as a fact.

With all that was transpiring Jeff had forgotten his fellow run-a-ways. "Joshua I'm sorry you weren't consulted but the situation is still being negotiated. What I do know is the tribe needs more warriors in their unending fight for survival. As of now this isn't your battle but if you leave this boat it will be. Talk it over with the others and remember this is about warriors not trappers. We will talk later".

With that Jeff departed.

Weight of responsibility wore on Jeff. The other fugitives looked up to him, Spotted Fawn depended on him and the Santee needed him. He owed the boat crew. To please one the other would be hurt, maybe destroyed. He knew only one person who possessed clear vision on the cloudiest of days. He would need to make another trip to the Riversioux pilot house.

Jonas graciously welcomed Jeff, he was quite certain the other fugitives would follow Jeff's lead; he also assumed no quantity of weapons would placate Inkpaduta. Likely Jeff was the pivotal player in these negotiations. He and Jeff would have to come to an arraignment where everyone felt benefited.

Offering coffee Jonas asked "Just what is it YOU want Jeff? Tell me that and we will start from that point".

Jeff was relieved, in his few discussions with the captain; Jonas had always weighed in on the side of reason. "I wish the Riversioux and her crew to be well rewarded, I wish for me and the other Negroes to become black Wahpekute, I want ample weapons for the Indian and I want to take Inkpaduta's sister as a wife. These are the things I want but how can we accomplish all this"?

"Come back in one hour. I will see what can be arraigned". Jonas opened the cabin door motioning Jeff to depart.

Fletch found himself secured to the same cottonwood that had offered shade for the pow-wow. His throbbing head was of no surprise but the young maiden swabbing his head was. Spotted Fawn sat alongside his bronzed nurse sporting a concerned look.

Though still groggy it was coming back to Fletch. Just before losing consciousness he had caught a glimpse of Fawn preparing to smash his head with a large limb.

"Who is this girl and why is she cleaning my wounds"? Jeff could see she was no more then thirteen or fourteen years of age.

"I hit you for your own good; I truly hoped I wouldn't kill you. You are being used as trade for guns. If they do trade you will be freed, if not you still will not be harmed if you do as we ask. My cousin (Mani Zintkala) Walking Pigeon knows how you rescued me at the fort. She also saw your bravery when you ridded me of Wounded Bear. She wants you for her husband".

Marriage at puberty was common for Santee females and this Walking Pigeon definitely was one good looker in a band well known for appealing young squaws.

Pigeon though blushing managed to maintain eye contact with Fletch throughout the conversation.

Love was not a thing Fletch ruminated on but being male, females were never far from mind. He felt awkward and foolish being at the mercy of two squaws, beautiful though they were. He had let his guard down, it wouldn't happen again.

"Walking Pigeon pleases me greatly and I am honored she would have me. What are the terms of this marriage?

Fawn answered as Pigeon held his hand. "Until the trade is completed you will remain bound. You will be well tended by Pigeon. If the trade is consummated you may leave and Pigeon will accompany you. It is our desire you stay with along your black friend and become a Wahpekute warrior. Although your skin is white I know your heart is red. Once adopted as Wahpekute, Inkpaduta well welcome you as a brother and I as your sister. Pigeon will make you a very good wife".

Blushing even more noticeably Pigeon placed Fletches hand upon her breast and gently squeezed as Spotted Fawn spoke.

It didn't surprise Fletch that Jeff was defecting. Hell Jeff was being offered what he had only hoped to obtain at Ft. Union. He also had the added bonus of Spotted Fawn. He was pleased things were working out for the big man. His present concern was preventing harm to the 'Sioux' and being tied to a cottonwood tree this was a major problem.

Fletch remembered a saying he had heard when first traversing Dakota Territory "The cure is in the snake what bit you". Fletch boyishly smiled at Pigeon.

Jonas poured another cup of coffee as he puzzled over Jeff's want list. He was sipping from Chauncey Maynard's cup, to Jonas a chalice of wisdom. He seemed to draw strength when drinking from his father's cup. As Jonas massaged the cup memories enveloped his mind.

Many times he had come to Chauncey with seemingly unanswerable questions and Many times Chauncey had pointed in a direction where the answer lay. Innumerable occasions since Jonas had reaped dividends from his father's wisdom, rather then rendering the answer Chauncey simply provided a map leaving the journey to Jonas.

With his mind at ease Jonas studied the 'whole' situation. He was responsible for the welfare of black fugitives who had already suffered more then anyone should. His crew who had dared much (upon his recommendation) deserved compensation. The continuation of the Underground Railroad river route depended upon the survival of the Riversioux and more importantly many lives would be impacted no matter what his decision. Chauncey had believed for every problem there was a solution if one opened his mind to all the possibilities, so did Jonas.

Jonas sipped coffee and circled the cup with his fingers while immersed in thought, within half an hour what had been a puzzle of many pieces became a clear singular portrait. Alanson was summoned with the tingling of a bell and given instructions to relay to the crew.

Jeff's knocking on the door signaled an end to Jonas's 30 minute nap. Refreshed, Jonas welcomed Jeff to his office.

Jeff was taken back by the calmness of Captain Jonas. Never had he witnessed anyone with the calm resolve of this 'good' man. He also immediately understood who was 'really' in charge.

"Jeff I doubt the free Negro trappers care where you and your partners end up as long as it is by choice. I and Edwin Denig (post bookkeeper) at Ft. Union are old friends. If I swear to your whereabouts and if each of you signs or make his mark on a document to that effect I see no problem in satisfying the free Negro trapper's demands. As to weapons I'll live up to our previous agreement, plus each fugitive who wishes to depart will also be armed. Before anything transpires Fletch must be free and upon the deck of the Riversioux! Look out the port window Jeff and you will notice there is no activity. The few Wahpekutes and all your fugitive companions aboard the 'Sioux' are in lockup below! At sundown the Riversioux heads upstream with your black companions, a few Wahpekute, a warehouse full of weapons and the end of Inkpaduta's futile dream. Take this message to your 'chief' and do what you must but BE BACK WITH FLECTH BY SUNDOWN". Jeff was escorted to the door.

In a huff of anger Jeff stalked down the gangplank toward shore. He just had been dismissed, like a child or even worse like a slave! But as he walked his anger slowly subsided and was soon replaced with an understanding. Actually nobody had been hurt and in fact everyone could still benefit. The good captain had once again come through, if Inka agreed!

Jeff was again becoming excited. He still remembered freedom across the water but he really never had been free. Superstition had imprisoned both him and his people but no more such nonsense. Here he would build a new life on his terms, free from ageless baggage. Now his dreams were only a blink away from fruition. It all depended upon Inka. Jeff approached Inka with a rekindled confidence.

Inka greeted Jeff "Black Brother you walk like one who has succeeded in his mission".

"If you red brother share my vision we have".

Inka noticed that Jeff once again spoke as his equal.

"We deal with am honorable man and a man of solid resolve. If we return Fletch he will honor our original agreement plus we may well have the addition of six more well armed black warriors. He now holds both my black and Wahpekute brothers as hostage. We could attack in an effort to free them; we would lose many warriors in a futile attempt. Inka, my wise brother, we are so near to obtaining what we covet. I agree the whites must be driven from our lands but the boat and its crew have been just in their dealings. Start your war on a weaker more deserving foe, then as we are stronger with even more warriors we can deal with the riverboats. I will do as your wish but these are my thoughts".

Inka was a man of instinct; his instincts told him Jeff was correct. The thought of six more armed warriors was a most enticing development "Get the prisoner and tell the white chief to meet us at the landing". With that Inka was off.

It was quite easy persuading Walking Pigeon to release her betrothed.

Fletch and Pigeon watched the 'Sioux' from the safety of thick marsh grass some hundred or so yards down stream. Though mostly completed the loading of firewood was halted and confusion seemed to prevail. Jonas, Alanson, the crew chief, along with Inka, Spotted Fawn and several other Santee were at the landing but Jeff conspicuously was absent.

Fletch could see the crew aboard the 'Sioux' were armed and seemingly ready for confrontation while on shore the Santee appeared just as battle ready. Though Fletch didn't know the exact situation he was positive his absence wasn't helping.

Fletch had assured Pigeon no harm would befall the Wahpekute with his release. Her supplying him with the rifle he had stored away for later use would be used for 'their' protection.

It was Fletch's duty to protect the 'Sioux' and he knew Inka was the problem as he inched ahead leveling his sight upon Inka's forehead.

Walking Pigeon saw no future for the Wahpekute, weakened by white-eye diseases their numbers continually shrunk and still they fought but they never won. Many of her Sioux sisters were marrying white-eyes to escape their dreadful and always deteriorating conditions. The more her tribe tasted defeat the worse she and her sisters were treated. Fletch had been her first and quite possibly her only avenue of escape.

She realized Fletch thought he had used her naivety to his advantage; she was ready to be used. He had promised not to use his freedom or weapons to the detriment of her people. As she had loosened the bands securing him and presented him with a rifle and powder she whispered "I am your wife to be, your wish is my wish. I will use my life to make your life easier". She sensed her words had had an impact upon Fletch; momentarily his eyes went from determined, to troubled. Then looking her in the eye (being nearly of equal height) he motioned her to follow.

She watched as her man leveled his sight upon Inka's unsuspecting frame. Pigeon held her hand over her mouth to subdue the involuntary scream about to erupt. As Fletch's rifle echoed Jeff's huge frame bowled Inka aside.

Luckily no one responded to the shot and equally luckily the Wahpekute wouldn't open fire without Inka's command. The crew was dependent upon Jonas!

Alanson placed his pistol square against Inka's temple as everyone waited for whatever came next.

Jonas broke the silence. "Jeff can you explain what has just transpired"?

Jeff still somewhat dismayed knew he must answer and answer well or all was lost. "I went to get Fletch but he had escaped. I knew his first instinct would be to protect the 'Sioux". I thought of yelling a warning but there was already so much confusion, I couldn't risk it. The only way to preserve the status-quo was to keep Inka from harm. Which I did".

Everyone looked at Jeff expecting him to continue; since he had adverted one catastrophe maybe he also would propose a strategy curtailing the catastrophe still at hand.

Again Jonas broke the silence. "Jeff I always expected you would respond well when necessity demanded nothing less, do you have any suggestions of how to break this stalemate"?

"I believe I might have Jonas, if you would ask Alanson to remove his pistol from Inka's skull, I think we are back to where we started. Inka is unharmed and Fletch is free. I see no reason we shouldn't consummate this deal as we previously planned.

Delivered from impending calamity red-man, black-man and white-man alike shrugged their shoulders in a relieved, why not?

CHAPTER 18

▼

The Montana days were becoming short and there was a definite nip in the morning air. The Riversioux having been unloaded of its cargo left the crew anxious to return south for the winter. The date was Sept. twenty eighth eighteen fifty six.

With the delivery deadline for the Riversioux fast approaching Jeff volunteered to stay aboard as a second boiler man while Flower remained with the Wahpekute. The 'riverside' standoff had drained Inka more than he dared let be known; for him all else was now superseded by an overriding desire to return to his place of birth. All his life he had waited for an opportunity to return and another month more or less waiting for Jeff was of little matter. The Wahpekute finally would winter at Spirit Lake.

At the junction of the 'good river' Flower anxiously waited for Jeff's return. Jonas had stood rigid on the negotiations and added another stipulation to the bargain while adding an extra keg of gun powder for sweetener...The final transfer of arms would take place when they returned to their rendezvous location at the Cheyenne River. Three of the black fugitives had chosen to stay with the Wahpekute while Joshua and the remaining two fugitives accompanied Jeff on the 'Sioux', preferring to pursue the dream of trapper as opposed to warrior.

Meanwhile Fletch was doing some soul searching and was perplexed with his findings. Pigeon had accompanied and served him on their trek upriver and now she required either a guardian or a mate. Fletch could not be a husband but found neither could he simply abandon her.

Unknown to anyone except Jonas Fletch had means far surpassing most anyone's expectations. True he had left half a suitcase of money with the Reverend in New York; he still was in possession of the other half.

Edwin Denig, post bookkeeper at Fort Union, had for years been friends with Jonas and with Alanson in particular as he and Alanson both were keepers of the books.

Denig was married to an Assinboine by the name of (Tahca Winyjela Conala) Deer Little Woman. He was gentle and fair in his marriage. With this knowledge in mind Fletch was determined to use Alanson's connection for the benefit of Pigeon.

Denig was a man of many talents, a long time curator for the Smithsonian Institute; he also had assisted John James Audubon in collecting bird and mammal specimens in the summer of '43'. Denig was a respected and well known author of numerous historical articles documenting Indian culture. During the long winter months he schooled local natives along with his own children. Fletch, Alanson and Pigeon had much to discus with Denig.

Alanson had wondered what would be Walking Pigeon's fate once they arrived at Ft. Union. He had never been witness to any unkindness initiated by Fletch in all his years aboard the Riversioux. He also knew it wasn't yet in Fletches character to become a domestic. It was with pleasure he now brought Denig and Fletch together.

"Where do the Wahpekute call home" Denig asked Pigeon as they sat in Denig's parlor sipping after dinner tea.

"The Wahpekute have no home; Spirit Lake was once home to our ancestors. Chief Inkpaduta still dreams of returning but I have tired of futile dreams" Pigeon answered with simple honesty.

Denig busily scribbled notes as they talked.

"What are YOUR dreams Walking Pigeon"? Denig displayed a true interest. "Would you be interested in exchanging knowledge for boarding"?

"I belong to Fletch and with this I am content".

"Pigeon you are young and you are beautiful and you please me but YOU don't belong to anyone"! The idea of indentureship hadn't entered his mind. Fletch's emotional outburst surprised everyone.

"Pigeon I simply can't take you with me and I'll be damned if I'll leave you without means. You can go back to the Wahpekute aboard the Riversioux if you want or you can stay here. I have talked with Mr. Denig and with his wife and they would be pleased if you would stay and help Mr. Denig with his research. I hope you will consider staying with the Denigs but this is for you to decide".

Fletch already had proposed a financial arrangement with Denig for Pigeons future well being.

Pigeon had always assumed that once Fletch tired of her he would leave, she had looked for a way out of a seemingly helpless position and Fletch had provided one. All Wahpekute females expected to be used and therefore young Pigeon was overwhelmed that Fletch cared.

Pigeon flew to Fletch with loving embrace, crying and…crying.

Grasped within Pigeon's embrace Fletch blushed with a growing and obvious embarrassment as she continued to cry. He had handled life threatening situations numerous times but this was beyond his experience.

Finally releasing her embrace and gently clasping Fletch's hand Pigeon spoke "I do not cry in sorrow my husband, but for my good fortune. I was asked if I had a dream, you will not understand but my dream is already answered. If it pleases you I will stray and await your return".

To 'civilized' persons Pigeons situation would seem pitiful yet Alanson and Mr. Denig understood. Walking Pigeon was one of many whose future held only heartbreak or worse. Fletch 'cared' about Pigeon and truly she was blessed.

Fletch who remained composed and keen of mind through the greatest of life's turmoil now remained without a clue. He understood responsibility and he understood debts of gratitude but he never would understand love.

Later in life as the proprietor of an 'honest' trading post in Ft. Pierre Pigeon would often reflect upon Fletch's compassion to her life's partner (also benefactor) Black Joshua.

The free black trappers had a good year, a very good year. In an ice filled cave furs and pelts lay salted waiting for shipment and now the hole of the Riversioux overflowed with bounty.

The crew was making plans for their windfall when Jonas called a meeting. "This has been an extraordinary trip. We have faced many obstacles together and together we have prevailed. The free trappers have lived up to their bargain and while they could have shipped furs without our knowledge they didn't. I propose we pay the trappers ten cents on the dollar". Jonas through rearing was inclined toward fairness and through experience had found it justified.

Alanson seconded the motion, not only was it right but it was his understanding that good deeds reaped generous reward.

With no descent from the crew the trappers were paid and the winter suddenly looked brighter for a few men of color.

On the first of Oct. the Rversioux disembarked, returning south for the season. There had been festivity and farewells which lasted throughout the night.

Denig waved the 'Sioux' and its crew farewell for a final time. Fletch, sporting his characteristic boyish grin leaned over the deck railing nursing a throbbing headache as he weakly waved Pigeon farewell. Though they never would meet again Pigeon never would want. Fletch not being capable of love; nevertheless knew he was loved. He responded as he knew how, leaving Pigeon very well provided for!

Downstream can be a swift semi-relaxing trip, easily occupied with dream. Each crew member possessed his individual and unique dream. Most dreams were of lewd women and raucous parties but a few were somewhat more complex.

Jeff was having second thoughts about the upcoming excursion to Spirit Lake. The Wahpekute may have ancestral and spiritual ties to this piece of property; even though young he already understood the inevitability of ones perceived justice versus insurmountable odds. Spotted Fawn would surely protest but they would not be crossing the Sioux River!

Fletch remained Fletch, if he did dream they were of his past however he did contemplate the future. He remembered the pitiful-ness of his mother and thought of the aged frontiersmen he knew with no means of survival; he was working on a plan to do better!

Jonas who seldom fretted now did. The river had become too hazardous. The Indian uprising was enough of a problem without the slavery issue. Militias were being formed in Missouri and Kansas and they needed supplies. The skipper of the St. Joe had relayed information that riverboats were now becoming prime targets of both the militias.

He had a moral obligation to the Underground Railroad and to the safety of his crew; perhaps another avenue of service would become available. He, after much thought, determined he would not jeopardize his crew or fugitives again. As of yet he had not shared the recent news of high jackings with his crew. Yes Jonas had much upon his mind.

Alanson was a dreamer. He dreamed when at leisure and if possible while at work as well, the present seldom offered enough to subjugate his thoughts. In his mind he had already built home and farm. The dream continually evolved as his knowledge expanded. His dreams now encompassed businesses that supplied farm needs and construction enterprises that made both possible. Most of all he dreamed of an ability to influence. America was a capitalist country with freedom of capital its foremost commitment, individual freedom was as of yet an embryonic dream awaiting blood fertilization. He understood this and he planned accordingly.

Explorer though a recipient of love and good care; daily grew more bored with the life of a 'boat' horse. His days were spent remembering a promise and dreaming of its fulfillment.

As dreams flowed so did the Missouri with the 'Sioux' riding its currents, the Cheyenne (Good River) was soon reached without incident.

Jonas suspected treachery from his Wahpekute allies. While passing the Cheyenne, with heartfelt goodbyes Jeff was set adrift in a canoe containing twenty four rifles and three kegs of gun powder. This brought the total of Wahpekute weapons to forty eight rifles and five kegs of gun powder plus twelve Colt pistols along with twelve hundred shells which fulfilled the Riversioux's commitment Not enough to wage full scale war but plenty enough to insure considerable mischief.

Jeff was free and in the heart of Dakota Territory and he knew he should be ecstatic but instead he faced a quandary as he neared shore. He knew the pilgrimage to Spirit Lake had always been Spotted Fawn's premier dream. He also dreamed of living free but he believed freedom need not be accompanied with a death wish. Crossing the Big Sioux River would with out question lead to bloodshed. He would attempt to reason with Fawn.

Looking ashore Jeff noticed only Wahpekutes remained in camp. The other bands (like him) having no wish for confrontation to procure a Wahpekute dream left upon hearing Inka's unwavering plan. This left forty seven well armed warriors and about three times that many women and children in the Wahpekute village (roughly two hundred in all).

Fawn eagerly waded out to great Jeff, showering him with embraces and kisses. "This is going to be difficult" was the thought in Jeff's mind as he passionately embraced Fawn while lifting her high above the water.

"The village is anxious to leave, we only waited for your return" Fawn was exuberant. "I never dared dream of returning to our homeland with such a warrior as you as my husband".

"I must distribute the rifles, then we will talk" Jeff handed a rifle to each of his black compatriots as he talked.

Fawn noticed hesitancy in Jeff's speech, he hadn't sounded cold but he didn't sound anxious either. "Yes, we must talk".

Jeff motioned his fellow blacks aside while whispering instructions and then motioned for Fawn to accompany him.

"Fawn please listen to what I have to say before you reply. In Ft. Union I had long conversations with the black trappers and from them I learned a great deal. The free black Sioux are becoming strong! The government supplies them with all their needs including weapons to support them in their struggle to secure a land of their own. Spirit Lake is in your past and I believe there it should remain, we would be welcomed among the Black Sioux band of warriors. There we can have a future, if we cross the Sioux River I see nothing but hardship and heartache. I know and I understand your dreams, for a time I shared this dream but if we follow Inka I fear we will not live to realize any dream".

Flower weakened and devastated remained silent for a long while, and then with a firm resolve she answered. "You are right; the Wahpekute may suffer when we return to our homeland, this time the white-eye will suffer also. Soon Inka will be exalted among chiefs, but how would you know about these things! Under his council and through his wisdom the Wahpekute will erase the sting of yesterdays defeat. Remember what could have been when you hear songs of the Wahpekute sung around your fire. Now take your slave friends and depart"!

Fawn turned and briskly walked away; her dreams once again dashed and her heart once again broken, she dared not glance back as tears welled down her cheeks.

Jeff and his partners did leave and for a time they did well. They were welcomed into the growing band of neo-Sioux. The band regularly provisioned by the government with commodities earmarked for treaty Sioux prospered. Weapons were regularly and leniently dispersed to support the band in their continued struggle for territory. This co emption continued uninterrupted until the end of the civil war, then with ample troops once again available ALL bands (red and black) became expendable.

Jeff evolved with the changing circumstances, he returned to the Mississippi delta where with his rhetoric abilities and his dominate physique he temporarily represented the State of Mississippi in the U. S. House of Representatives during reconstruction.

With his life's ambition seemingly within reach Inka and his band crossed the Big Sioux River in the fall of eighteen fifty six, well supplied and eager. It had been years since the band had camped on the banks of their ancestral lake but its spiritual significance remained intact. This was a spiritual quest and the band sought no conflict but with new their weaponry neither would they capitulate.

In a familiar willow thicket on the banks of the Rock River the band made camp. It was now cool and pleasant in contrast to the heat and humidity those many years ago.

Spotted Fawn led her brother 'Chief' Inkpaduta to a remote Okoboji beach. Since that terrible day so many years ago Inka had shed not a tear, as sand gently sifted through his fingers his tears dampened the beach. Spotted Fawn embraced her younger brother as the evening sun painted tranquil colors upon the waters.

"Enough killing, surely there is ample land for us and the white-eye. My vision obtained in youth has now dimmed and we have suffered far too long. I will go to the white-eye village in search of peace".

Inka was ageing and he was wearied from the responsibilities of a lifetime of continual warfare. Now the aging warrior was deeply moved by the placid beauty of his native lands. To his bewilderment long nurtured dreams of retribution struggled to coexist amidst such beauty.

Fawn also was moved, not by the beauty but rather by her brother's newly acquired forgiveness. "Someday we may all live in peace my brother but we now stand upon our mother's spilled blood. Her spirit will forever remain troubled unless the white-eye shows remorse for their evil deed".

"Spotted Fawn I wish you were not right, I was overcome by the beauty and temporarily blinded with false hope. Do I forget so soon Black Eagle's teaching? The white-eye has neither soul nor conscience".

With these words Inka took his sharpened blade and slit his palm coagulating with blood the white sand where his mother had been murdered.

Inka understood the paradox of white and red living in harmony; still even though his tongue spoke words of retribution the placid lakes of his native homeland moved his soul toward peace. Inca aging and weary desperately wanted to believe and therefore he lacked resistance to this new testament of peace and forgiveness.

The winter of 56\57 was abnormally cold. Winds piled snow into menacing drifts of historic proportions Buffalo, turkey, deer, elk, bear, and otter which had been plentiful disappeared. Deer didn't return with numbers for a decade, the other afore mentioned wild life never again returned through natural circumstance!!

The Wahpekute were nearing starvation and still the white-eyes sympathies were not stirred. Even so Inka steadfastly avoided conflict, since returning to his ancestral home the latent peace which had emerged from deep within simply refused to vacate.

Disillusioned with Inka's inability to respond to their growing crises Fawn and the Wahpekute band furtively searched elsewhere for leadership; Inka no longer driven with the fire of revenge also no longer reached to the Gods for wisdom.

Finally driven by starvation Inka with several other braves trekked to Ft. Dodge Iowa in a desperate attempt to trade rifles for food.

After a heroic trek through raging blizzard they reached Fort Dodge only to be greeted with ridicule and derision. The starving natives were relieved of their rifles as a safety precaution and then expelled from 'civilization' empty handed.

Hate which had lain dormant since the sandy beach of Okoboji resurfaced...multiplied 'seven times seven'. With rejection Inka's New Testament of love was discarded, replaced with the ageless covenant of retribution.

As Inka's starving and exhausted band staggered back into camp Fawn sensed her brother was once more 'the' chief.

Inka raised his hand as he addressed his desperate band "I like a mole was blind and I failed my people. Hear me Wahpekute; never again will I stray from my vision. Your chief, who departed with the vision of a mole, returns with the claws of a badger. The white-eye will understand terror and commune with fear for as long as 'chief' Inkpaduta walks upon this earth".

Rifles were loaded, paint was applied and the Wahpekute prepared for their long waited warpath of retribution!

From the winter of eighteen fifty seven until his death in eighteen eighty one Inkpaduta never again bent to the demands of 'civilization'.

Inka led his band through unparalleled blizzards of historical proportion to the town of Jackson Minnesota, slaying homesteaders, burning farmsteads and procuring provisions as they traveled...

The band made a detour to the prairie home of one settler known to the Wahpekute as broken Tongue Smith. He had always seemed to gain satisfaction from the plight of the Indain. Many times during the winter he had caused the starving Wahpekute hardship as they attempted to barter with their white neighbors for food...With speech slurred from a bent tongue he reminded the homesteaders that the Wahpekute remained heathen even as many bands were now becoming Christian. The Wahpekute despised broken tongue for his actions but truth would unleash their fury!

The story was told that as a young man Smith had fallen nearly severing his tongue while he, his brother and cousins repelled an unprovoked Indian attack near Spirit Lake. In their rush to escape reprisal the retreating cowards left a mortally wounded squaw on the Okoboji shore. The story was legend throughout northwestern Iowa but unfortunately legends have legs that will not remain hobbled. This tale of homesteader bravery and Indain cowardice was reiterated as a warning parable to Inka as he was expelled from Ft. Dodge.

Broken Tongue Smith (various body parts) was found weeks later nailed to a wooden cross on the snow blown beach of Lake Okoboji. It appeared he had been disemboweled while yet alive but really no one could say for sure. Broken Tongues demise sustained for one more season a family of disappearing Midwestern Prairie Wolves.

After routing the Village of Spirit Lake, Iowa; Jackson, Minnesota was next to be laid to siege. This time women and children were taken hostage to insure safe passage back across the Sioux River. The hostages who survived the ordeal were then sold wholesale to the always peaceful Yanctons who in-turn retailed them back to their families.

In American History the conquering hoard of invading illegals record this skirmish as the Spirit Lake Massacre. Native Americans commemorate the occasion as a heroic but futile effort to preserve an ageless sustainable culture.

For the following five years the Wahpekute savaged the tri-state area of Iowa, South Dakota and Minnesota plundering, killing and celebrating their long awaited revenge.

In eighteen sixty two Inka and his Wahpekutes spearheaded the largest slaughter of white settlers in Midwestern history.

In southwestern Minnesota Sioux once again were being forcefully removed from their treaty lands to pacify the unending white quest for 'virgin' sod…Inka, well known among Dakota Sioux as an invincible hero and amongst whites as a deviant heathen, massed the diverse bands into a cohesive unit for a 'cleansing' operation. More then five hundred whites were cleansed before the Sioux were once again forced to retreat into western Dakota.

In the badlands of North Dakota the Wahpekute and allied Dakota Sioux joined forced with their cousins the Lakota Sioux gathered by Sitting Bull and Crazy Horse! The renowned Black Elk writes "Inkpaduta was one of the 'great' men present when Custer was rubbed out". This was at the Battle of Little Big Horn in '76'.

Although strategically less brilliant then either the Spirit Lake Massacre or the Southwestern Minnesota Campaign the Battle of Little Big Horn historically dwarfs all other Indain campaigns due to the presence of one General George Armstrong Custer.

After the great victory Inka along with Sitting Bull departed for Canada but unlike Chief Sitting Bull the Wahpekutes heeded the wisdom of their Chief and remained in Manitoba.

In eighteen eighty one while dreaming great dreams of honest existence the spirit of a legendary Dakota Sioux Chief of the Santee Tribe firmly grasped brother badger's mane, ascending from the Manitoba prairie in route to eternity.

Inkpaduta had realized a rapidly disappearing dream; dieing old, proud and Wahpekute…never experiencing the humiliation of surrender!

Inkpaduta
(Artist's Rendition)

CHAPTER 19

▼

Downstream was a boring affair for Explorer. He was at liberty to roam the deck during daylight hours but since his tantrum over the ladies his nights were spent snubbed to a deck tie down.

The boredom (to the lewd enjoyment of the crew) was momentarily interrupted as Explorer 'serviced' the Belgians fillies. Three would not cycle again.

Just below Ft. Pierre the fourth filly came to heat during the most restful period of night. Passion in animals is not diminished by human association. Explorer and the Belgian filly demonstrated with fury their inability to fulfill natural instincts.

Alanson dutifully responded to the ruckus and attempted to calm the protest. "Come on big fellow, calm down 'people' are trying to sleep. Miss "B" will still be here in the morning".

Alanson reaching for Explorers reigns, stopped abruptly. Explorer was no longer focused on the deck but rather on the shore line. Realization took hold.

On shore was a familiar stallion, once again issuing a challenge to the 'domestic' Explorer. Explorer looked Alanson in the eye—pleading.

Love (absolute love) was absolutely on trial.

Alanson needed little time for decision as decision had been reached a month and a half ago. Fulfilling this commitment would take great effort and just a little more time.

Explorer's heart raced. Alanson had promised freedom and the time was now at hand. Explorer understood he had always been if not an equal at least a respected partner in Alanson's adventures but 'freedom' waited on the shore, more importantly a sorry example of stallion-hood impatiently waited an ass kicking!

Alanson slowly lowered the gangplank into the flowing waters of the Missouri river. Explorer graced Alanson with a quick parting nuzzle before splashing Hell-bent into the water, confrontation his goal.

The moon's reflection on the river momentarily rippled as Explorer thrashed his way shoreward.

With heavy heart Alanson watched as Explorer neared the bank. He and his 'friend' were now separated, both on their own. Heavy heart was replaced with heated emotion as Explorer attempted to claw his way ashore. Shouts of encouragement couldn't be restrained.

Soon Alanson was surrounded by crew mates directing their own vulgar epithets at the Appaloosa stallion on shore. Fletch, uncharacteristically, wrapped his arm around Alanson while hurling verbal abuses shoreward. Continuous vilifications and curses erupted from Fletches mouth, some phrases beyond Alanson's comprehension.

Explorer (like every crewman aboard had done at one time or another) was fighting against the odds. As Explorer endured kick after kick each man groaned in pain and responded with appropriate cursing.

It was believed but never verified even Jonas was heard issuing a swear word!

The Appaloosa alpha stallion wasn't ceded his position, he had brutally earned his monarchy and only through brutality would he relinquish his throne. Flying kicks from front and rear hoofs thwarted Explorers attempts to scale the bank. Vicious blows and snapping teethe continually blocked but did not diminish Explorers attempts to reach land.

Alanson considered 'shooting' Explorer's land advantaged opponent. His friend was being pummeled in a brutal and seemingly unfair contest. Upon raising his rifle to fire he reconsidered; life is not fair and especially life in its natural state. Explorer would overcome the disadvantage on his own or he could return. Many more challenges would lie ahead and...he would not be there.

Explorer was not being 'beaten' by this Appaloosa; he simply wasn't winning—yet! Explorer whinnied and shook his head in disdain. He'd been kicked harder than this in foreplay by 'domestic' Belgian fillies.

It was slippery on the shore line and as the Appaloosa paced back and forth it continually was getting more so, opportunity waited for the patient horse.

Appaloosa frothed and kicked and sweated as Explorer paced the river's edge feinting and then retreating. Hell the water was cool and a horse could even stop and take a sip if the notion arose.

Alanson watched beginning to comprehend where this was going. Pride slowly rose as gut wrenching apprehension subsided. Explorer was effectively executing a plan most his crew members would never fathom.

Minutes that at first had seemed hours became hours and still the battle raged. Cookie made coffee for the crew who now watched in awe. Though to the last man Explorer was 'their' combatant, a grudging respect was gradually being gained for his gritty opponent.

Finally as dawn broke an exhausted Appaloosa rose on front legs and loosed a mighty kick striking Explorer squarely with both hooves of his hind legs. Explorer who had not begun to tire met the leg volley with an unexpected charge, sending his foe sprawling in the mud.

Explorer reacted to the applause erupting from the Riversioux with a sudden rush of adrenalin. He had forgotten his audience. With an audience Explorer's performance was elevated to even greater heights. Great athletes achieve their greatest accomplishments on stage, likewise do great horses.

With teeth gnashing and hoofs flashing Explorer thrust and parried with no regard for self injury. Within minutes the reigning monarch was reassigned to serfdom.

Explorer assessed his new domain, proudly circling and getting a head-count of his newly acquired harem. He was free and he was 'the' king and he was elated. He glanced toward the Riversoux where Alanson leaned over the railing waving at him. Alanson wasn't motioning him to return but instead he had removed his hat in salute…to a friend, a worthy friend whom he already missed.

Jonas brought the crew back to the business at hand as a blowing whistle signaled the beginning of a new work day.

With conflicting emotions but definite sadness Alanson watched as Explorer led his new fiefdom into the expanse of the Dakota prairie.

For three days the river boat made its way down stream and every evening near dusk Alanson would observe Explorer and his new equine world paralleling the Riversioux in the distant prairie grasses.

Freedom is freedom or is it? What embodies freedom to one is servitude to another. Explorer could now range where and when he chose but the freedom of existence very soon becomes boring to one accustomed to human instigated drama.

Nights now were occupied with coyotes and cougars and days were occupied fending off solitary stallions with upwardly mobile ambitions. Neither was a threat but both were a nuisance.

And 'his' mares were the absolute worst! Constantly they 'pretended' leaving in search of greener pasture as he coaxed one frivolous female back another would bolt. They kept him near exhaustion and he thought he might be losing weight.

Maybe he ought to drive half of the fickle mares out! Let them try to make it on their own for a while, maybe that would teach them but No…pride excluded such rational behavior. Stallion status was maintained by numbers. You know life can be damned complicated for a 'free' stallion of merit.

On the fourth evening after the great horse battle Alanson and Fletch were leaning over the boat railing reminiscing about their experiences with the 'great' Explorer. Fletch related experiences (some true and some outlandish fiction) that he would never have dared mention had Explorer still been aboard. Alanson enjoyed hearing these exploits whether believable or not. He had never before felt this alone, reminiscing filled the emptiness. Finally both became silent, engrossed in their own individual memories, when a terrible commotion aroused them.

Explorer, as horses will do, had ruminated upon his situation. He was now free but hadn't he been free for nearly 2 months? When Alanson promised "it'll be your choice whether you stay or go" hadn't he become essentially free?

In four short days Explorer came to a realization that many men never grasp. It is basic horse sense to chose freedom with the luxury of hay and a warm stable over freedom without these luxuries but they damn sure better let down the gangplank for he was about to drown!

In exuberate panic Alanson and Fletch stumbled over each other racing to lower the ramp.

Explorer would not be 'free' tonight. Two good men fawned over the returned prodigal.

Explorer good naturedly endured the attention of his humans.

EXPLORER

CHAPTER 20

▼

'Mother' and 'father' Cheney, the preferred title of Mary's new guardians, decided upon St. Joseph as their destiny. Pastor Cheney well compensated for Mary's wagons and livestock rented a pricy but 'comfortable' home located on the bluffs over looking the Missouri River.

Mother Cheney immediately became active in St. Joseph social circles while the pastor struggled to keep the doors of his newly founded church open. Within months the 'dowry' of finery accompanying Mary was being liquidated to maintain the Cheney status.

Mary begged to keep her cross necklace from the dowry chest. Her nanny back in Virginia had given it so she could hide her secret 'stuff' while traveling to Texas. Mother Cheney believing the cross around her 'daughters' neck produced proper effects relented. Unknown to 'mother' the ends of the cross were removable where 'secret documents' could be hidden. The note from Alanson was carefully inserted.

Mary struggled to make herself an asset in the Cheney household. Finding acceptance through love unattainable she cleaned and cooked in an attempt to become a welcome member of Cheney household. Nevertheless Old Testament discipline was generously applied when Mary improperly addressed her 'parents' or ineptness in household duties was detected. For the first several months in St. Joe Mary nursed hands, swollen with welts from the pastor's rod of obedience.

Her true value became evident when the Cheneys began liquidating the George family valuables.

Mary accompanied the Cheneys on most excursions as she ran errands and totted bags filled from shopping while always remaining 'pleasant'.

Mary studied the science of barter in the many pawn shops frequented on their liquidation expeditions. In ways unnoticeable she helped procure top dollar for their wares while at the same time making certain the family always 'stumbled' unto items priced below market value.

In "53" Mary was blessed with a little sister. From the moment of birth Mary became an intolerable necessity to mother Cheney. The pastor, who was becoming aware of Mary's value, became a target of vicious verbal attack if any way Mary was favorably acknowledged.

Mary often fell asleep listening to 'mother' lamenting the pastor's ineptness. "The pittance received from Mary's stingy grandparents had become necessary for 'their' existence.

By "54" the Cheneys were nearing insolvency. With the embarrassment of a 'lesser' lifestyle being unacceptable the pastor reawakened to his calling.

Pastor Cheney exchanged correspondence with The Frontier Methodist Episcopal Diocese who once again suggested The Dakota City Nebraska mission which still was merely a dream. It would be the spring of "55" before the necessary arraignments could be completed.

Segregation was the pressing issue of the times with no clear geographic line of division. The Missouri River was presently the de-facto dividing line. On the east shore the clergy and Henry Clay revisited the words of Jesus Christ; "slaves obey your master" while on the west bank Daniel Webster quoted "all men are equal in the eyes of God" from the same gospel.

The preacher most capably articulating scripture aligning God with populist opinion prospered. Pastor Cheney grasped onto the slavery issue with intensity.

Rev. Cheney possessing intellect was woefully lacking in charisma. Throughout history spiritual orators have conned God into hewing the Devils tools. Having this knowledge but lacking the tools to implement the feat tormented the Reverend Cheney; a man already domestically sterile.

Cheney possibly lacking in originality understood the value of plagiarism. The five Brown brothers were successfully rallying jayhawkers to the abolitionist cause just across the river. Rumor was that their infamous father John would be arriving any day.

Cheney, being intelligent, educated and near bankruptcy did what many red-blooded patriots have done. The "Good Word Bible Church" became headquarters for the Missouri Freedom Militia. The church marquee was enlarged and then enlarged again as new enlistees were added to the roll. Overnight Pastor Cheney became the 'respected' Colonel Cheney.

The failing church was now a Mecca for pro-slavery zealots. With proceeds from hawking war and the status of 'Colonel' things also warmed at home.

Mary began overhearing disturbing conversations in the evening. "Colonel, my love, you at long last have awakened unto what God intended and I believe Colonel is only a beginning!" Mother Cheney suddenly was becoming a compassionate help mate to the Colonel. "Soon Mary will be back on the street where we found her". Mary listened with growing alarm amidst their reawakened wheezing sounds of 'love'.

"We're not situated just yet, my dear, but soon—very soon" pastor answered between gasping spasms of love.

Pastor Cheney fully aware he lacked leadership abilities found dismissing the possibilities of later repercussions amazingly easy; prestige is a blinding addiction.

Mary also knew her 'father' had neither the courage nor charisma to fill the shoes seemingly envisioned by Mother Cheney.

Even Mrs. Cheney long ago had abandoned any illusions of greatness for her husband but she also now nipped from the same intoxicating bottle of prestige.

All three were now secretly second guessing the wisdom of this new venture but the train was rolling and they were aboard with no one willing to apply brakes.

By early eighteen fifty five the St. Joe Freedom Militia had tired of drilling and demanded action as members began departing for 'active' units.

Colonel Cheney no longer could dodge the responsibilities of his position. Having accepted acclaim as leader he now was forced to perform. Next week they would perpetrate a daring raid on Lawrence Ks. and route out the Brown Brother's abolitionist followers, preempting their heralded father's arrival.

The church filled with parishioners waiting to hear 'The Colonels' parting sermon before leading the militia into conflict.

Mary spent the final week listening to monotonous gibberish about bravery and God's calling. She also noticed the libido of her guardians was at fever pitch.

Mary rechecked her 'cross' to see if the note was still intact as her thoughts raced…It had been so long, would the man even remember her? She was now 14 years of age, she could survive on her own. Then again being aware of what life offered girls of the street…she would stay for now.

Remembering his look of concern as she departed the Riversioux Mary read the note one more time "CONTACT A. BAKER % RIVERSIOUX AT ANY PORT ON THE MISSOURI RIVER IF YOU EVER NEED HELP". Sobbing she slipped the note back into her cross.

"The liberal left must be crushed once and for all. For too long we true Christians have stood idly by while the word of God is bastardized to fit the left's agenda. This very week as in the scriptures of old we will cross over the waters in a holy crusade. For God we will march and in God we trust". Preacher Cheney had never been so eloquent and the passion! "America's forefathers saw the wisdom of slavery. Presidents Washington and Jefferson embraced slavery and Colonel Cheney will, with God's blessings, preserve slavery. As patriotic Americans we willingly march and as believing Christians we willingly offer our earthly bodies in sacrifice to preserve our God given heritage, God Bless America, I repeat GOD BLESS AMERICA. Say it with me GOID BLESS AMERICA".

The church thundered with applause as the reverend ended his sermon. He had done it; he had given 'his' troops a message to die for. But he wasn't ready to die and this was his dilemma. "God deliver me from this pitfall" was his prayer as he walked home from church with his 'adoring' wife clinging to his arm. Mary respectfully followed at an appropriate distance dutifully carrying the baby.

"Don't you dare fail again" were the thoughts playing and replaying in Mrs. Cheney's head.

Lawrence Kansas was unprepared and unprotected as the Missouri Brigade charged. The result was mayhem and murder. The few men attempting to protect the community were easily overwhelmed. Intoxicated with victory the invaders reveled in 'unchristian' manner. Rev. Cheney attempted to minimize the rape and carnage but in doing so only succeeded in garnishing the militia's scorn.

The Freedom Brigade returned home to acclaim, Colonel Cheney returned home disgraced with his incompetence publicly exhibited and verified.

With grandeur dreams dashed, the missionaries locked the church doors and unceremoniously boarded a Paddlewheel in route to Dakota City Nebraska. The last of Mary's family trinkets financed their 'escape'.

The Cheneys embittered with circumstances each lay responsibility upon the other but vented their frustration on Mary. Stepping off the boat in Dakota City Mary was desperate; life had become a continuous cloudy day were even the chance of sunlight seemed unattainable. While mentally searching for an avenue of escape Mary unconsciously caressed her cross.

Calling Dakota City anything more than an outpost was disingenuous. The City Café, Dakota Hotel\Livery Barn and Brickhouse Mercantile constituted the entire business district which was located on the main street of 'Broadway". Broadway was a 150 feet wide rutted dirt or quite often mud trail with its eastern terminal being the Dakota City Dock and Warehouse.

Dakota City residents patiently waited hoping to become a port 'boom town' like Omaha or St. Joseph. Civilization had sprouted some rudimentary roots in Iowa but on the Nebraska side of the river which the Cheneys now called 'home' there were no gardens, neither was there a church. Things would appear bleak to a functional family, to the Cheneys words of description were nonexistent.

Driven by desperation Pastor Cheney procured a part time 'job' clerking and handling freight at the dock warehouse. Mrs. Cheney, driven by the same necessities, begrudgingly cooked and tended tables in the City Café while Mary kept house and tended her little sister.

Work hours though not pleasant were the hours Mary most looked forward to. Now fifteen years of age Mary spent the days dreaming of the prince who would come to her rescue. Would he be a handsome dashing young man as in the stories she read to baby Rachel? In her dreams he was.

Mary's grandfather George still sent regular stipends for her support. Evidently the payments were quite small for she continually was scolded for her family's selfishness. All mail always had and still did pass through Mrs. Cheney with Mary's responses being scrupulously censured. Mary despised her guardians and they reciprocated (more mother then father) but as of yet both needed the other.

Dakota City had now been 'home' for over a year and a small church was in the process of being built. The diocese as promised financed the construction of a one room auditorium structure for Sunday services. Traders, trappers, U.S. Calvary troops and river men constituted the bulk of the Dakota City Methodist Episcopal Sunday congregation.

Temporarily services were being conducted in the City Café while the church was being completed. Finances from the offering plate of the fledgling church were miniscule, which left Mary's grandparents still the major source of income for the Cheney household.

Since the birth of baby Rachel back in St. Joseph Mary had been verbally and physically abused by 'mother' Cheney. As Mrs. Cheney's dreams diminished Mary's 'faults' escalated. Week after week Pastor Cheney explained away Mary's proneness for accidents as another example of her 'awkwardness'. A month or so ago Mrs. Cheney managed her own 'unbelievable' accident, ever since Mary seemed to have overcome her teenage awkwardness but noticcably she also no longer ventured out.

Pastor Cheney never approved of his wife's treatment of Mary or little else she did but as in Lawrence Ks. though his conscience was rightly motivated his spine buckled under the weight of trial...

Ruffians were the patrons who frequented the City Café and ruffians were the souls who occupied the pews at Sunday services. Life in eighteen fifty six Dakota City offered limited opportunity for a fifteen year old girl on her own. Still Mary determinedly sustained hope through dreams.

The Riversioux docked in Sioux City with a crew anxious to celebrate. Jonas was equally anxious to see what the Frost and Todd Fur Co. was offering for hides and pelts this season. Alanson still served as clerk as well as engineer. If his manifest was correct the crew would have ample reason to celebrate.

The hole of the Riversioux held a total of 7574 buffalo robes (tanned), 740 beaver pelts, 41 elk skins, 13 bear skins, 2 moose skins and 35 misc. pelt packages. The value would be many thousands of dollars, no less then $12,000 and possibly double that amount or even more. The 'minimum' cut would be over $500 to each crew member.

Jonas had decided since he would be selling the Riversioux the crew would receive one third of the total cargo profit rather then just the free black trappers share. It would serve as a severance and help tide them over until they found other employment. He hadn't informed the crew of their impending wealth before docking; Jonas wanted sobriety when they disembarked.

While Jonas attended to the business of the Riversioux Alanson attended to personal business.

The Iowa Falls and Sioux City Railroad held the deed for most all property along the Big Sioux River from Sioux City to the future site of Hawarden, Iowa. Alanson had pending business with their land office.

As is so often the case a bureaucratic roadblock awaited. The federal government had granted huge parcels of land to the R. R. as an incentive to attract investors, enabling actual rail construction. The Iowa Falls and Sioux City cartel had already sold great chunks of its eastern property and as to date had not begun any construction. The government recently had curtailed further land sales until signs of 'actual' construction were evident.

Alanson was assured this was a temporary boondoggle which undoubtedly would be resolved by spring.

This presented a problem as Alanson had no idea where spring would find him since Jonas had confided that the Riversioux was making its final run. With so many dreams already having been invested, the deal must be consummated.

Legal papers were drawn giving the local land agent power of attorney to purchase the river property when it became available. Sufficient money was deposited in a dual account at George Weale's (Sioux City's only) Bank. The whole affair most certainly wasn't to his liking but the dice had been rolled and the game now began.

A belief in destiny played a major roll in Alanson's decision, he had much to accomplish and the river property he believed would be its Genesis.

Having completed his business Alanson sought out Jonas who was by then done tending to Riversioux business.

Sioux City was still in search of a 'main' business district. The river and river boats were the reason for her existence but 'the' business district stubbornly insisted upon its own location.

The Missouri River from Sioux City northward rambles with no permanent shore line. The river at Sioux City was little more then a flowing marshland with a usually navigable but ever-changing channel. On the-other-hand The Big Sioux River maintained a fairly constant flow through the worst of droughts with the native grasslands of its valley serving as a storage receptacle for summer rain and winter snows. Like a sponge numerous springs released waters from its immense aquifer in a steady flow year round.

The mouth of the Big Sioux therefore remained constant and navigable allowing permanent dependable dockage. This northern 'suburb' along the Big Sioux River became known as Riverside. In Riverside a wooden walkway connected the dock with Bruguier's Inn where the 'real' river men congregated.

The business establishments on the-other-hand preferred the smaller more manageable Floyd and Perry tributaries as receptacles for their waste products. Though small in population the city was spread over a five mile area between the Big Sioux and the Floyd Rivers. Tiny Perry Creek makes it's juncture with the Missouri between the Big Sioux and the Floyd rivers. Horse drawn taxies connected 'Riverside' with the 'downtown' area.

Jonas negotiated prices with F. and T. Fur Buyers situated on the banks of Perry Creek while Alanson did both his banking and real estate business in a log building at third and Pearl. The United States land Office (which brokered the railroad real estate business) occupied the street level portion of the building while George Weale operated his bank from its basement.

Finished with business Jonas and Alanson prepared to hail a taxi for Riverside. While waiting Fletch and big Rube were seen staggering toward West Seventh Street (home of Sioux City's better brothels).

"Have you broken the news to the crew yet" Alanson asked watching his fellow crew members.

"I thought it might best be approached when the full picture could be presented". Jonas replied shaking his head as the two unsteady crewman entered a "place of business".

"How did things go at Frost and Todd"? The answer impacted Alanson.

Many riverboats simply delivered their furs directly to Saint Louis; the basis for the fur market. However Jonas discovered early on he could turn considerable profit by selling at least a portion of his cargo at Frost and Todd.

Selling in Sioux City entailed more work and more headaches then a straight load to St. Louis. One must reload freight for terminals in Omaha, St. Joseph or elsewhere and then reload for St. Louis and New Orleans. Though most certainly a hassle it paid handsome dividends. Neither Jonas nor his crew shrunk from work and neither went unrewarded.

"Alanson we'll all prosper from this episode, but I'm thinking more on what's next. I have a standing offer back in Philadelphia for the Riversioux. How would you like to make a trip back east and maybe visit your former home?"

The thought of visiting 'home' hadn't crossed Alanson's mind as real possibility for years. His parents, the mere thought seemed to overload the auger of his thought process. Still excitement of the possibility couldn't be denied. At the least a trip east would get his mind off 'other' things for a while.

"Jonas you might be on to something there. I have several details to attend to while you are putting together our load. Tomorrow I'm catching the Dakota City Ferry; I'm going to attempt to look up one of your Christian compatriots. If things work out a trip east might be just alright".

A night in a bed that didn't river rock and one of Bruguier's famous 'Rivermans' breakfasts started Alanson's day properly. He'd caught a taxi to the Pierce Street Dock where a Ferry departed twice a day for Dakota City Nebraska, one ferry at approximately 10:00 am and another around 3:00 pm. Alanson looked foreword to the ride.

The Sears brothers, Walt and Dan had operated the family owned business for several years. The 'boys' came from a simple background and possessed no formal education Still Alanson considered Walt one of the more knowledgeable persons he knew. Walt, who possessed an inquisitive mind, remained humble, a rare attribute, which left him free to ask questions without embarrassment. ASK HE DID.

Walt wished to know the geography and climate of any area he hadn't visited, which was almost everywhere. He talked local politics and inquired about politics beyond. Most of all he was a judge of character which left him under-impressed with social status. Walt understood who he was and was comfortable with his findings.

Dan on the other hand was less philosophical and more social. Dan worked hard, was honest to a fault and once a friend he remained loyal. A good day for Dan would be spent in congenial conversation while toiling at work.

The 'boys' as they were called actually were in their early forties. Walt had noticed a business opportunity and a public service need as the cities of Dakota City and Sioux City expanded. In the cold of winter, travel between the cities was quite easy as the Missouri usually froze by Dec. 1 and stayed that way until March 15th but nature is not predictable. When someone made the journey across the river without incident the winter season officially opened and when teams or lives were lost come spring thaw the winter travel season officially ended. In the warmer months travel was left to the individual which greatly reduced interchange between Nebraska and Iowa.

Walt created a methodology which could safely determine when and where crossing the iced over river was safe. The city businessmen when approached eagerly salaried the Sears boys during the winter for 'flagging' a safe route each morning or closing the river to travel if deemed necessary. This left the boys with dependable winter employment; their summers were occupied with numerous odd jobs.

Dan, never afraid of work, came up with the scheme of operating a summer ferry. At first he was never short of passengers but rowing upstream from Dakota City to Sioux City was taxing and unpredictable. Passengers were left waiting (sometimes for hours) at the Pierce Street dock while Dan battled winds and loads. A passenger with weighted luggage made the trip upstream nearly impossible and yet Dan could not find it in himself to turn a passenger or his luggage away. Soon the business dwindled to the point where it no longer was feasible.

Walt as he was known to do came to the rescue. "Dan why don't you make both trips down stream"?

"Why don't I grow fins and just carry them on my back" was Dan's incredulous reply.

Walt wasn't one to poke fun at another's situation without also having a solution. "Let's customize our wagon so your boat can be winched onto it. We can back the wagon into the river, and then pull it ashore enabling passengers to disembark on a permanent dock high and dry".

"Great idea but how do I move Sioux City upstream and downstream according to my whim"? Dan was getting a little exasperated.

"Since the boat is already on the wagon and we do have horses why not head on up the road and disembark at Harney City just above Sioux City".

The Missouri River from St. Louis to Kansas City flows generally westward. At Kansas City the river makes an adjustment and flows northerly to Sioux City where once again a westward direction is maintained until near Ft Randall South Dakota. At Ft. Randall a northern route is procured to the Montana line where the river again flows westerly until it finally disappears into a maze of springs and creeks.

Dakota City is slightly down stream from the river bend and Harney City is just above the bend, both on the Nebraska side. Sioux City lies at the apex of the bend on the Iowa (north) side of the river. The landscape is gentle and the distance short between Dakota City and Harney City, an easy half hour trip.

Harney City was added as a terminal and Sears Brothers maintained a regular schedule thereafter.

Sears Brothers Ferry arrived at 9:30 am with six passengers aboard.

The ferry was larger then Alanson remembered, now with a capacity for twelve passengers plus the Sears boys on the oars. There were also oar locks for two more row men if conditions warranted.

Alanson paid his nickel (the trip was a nickel, you could return within 24 hours for the same nickel) round trip fare while shaking hands with the brothers.

"Looks like you boys are going into competition with the Riversioux". Alanson was pleased to see things going well for his friends.

"Thought we might add Ft Randall as a terminal next week but first we need a relief oarsman. We had you in mind". Dan always had a ready reply.

"Well I may soon be in need of employment so I'll consider your offer but right now I'm in need of a lift to Dakota City. I hear you Nebraskans have a resident preacher and presently I'm in need of one".

"Yep, we have something like that but I doubt he's what you're after" Dan answered with a peculiar grimace.

"What do you mean; doubt he's what I'm after"? Alanson was uneasy.

"First off he and his Mrs. landed here mad at the world and secondly something is strange about their oldest daughter. The girl never leaves the house except for church and I have never seen anyone so unsure of her self as that one, she acts like she's a prisoner or something".

Alanson was no longer uneasy he suddenly felt weak. "What's the preachers name Dan"?

"I've never darkened the church door but the marquee says Rev. Cheney".

"How old is the girl and is she alright"? Alanson's heart raced as sweat beaded on his forehead.

Walt, after securing the boat and having taken several reservations for a return trip the next day, now joined the conversation.

"Why the excitement Alanson"?

"I think I'm acquainted with your Reverend Cheney and if so the excitement may have only begun"! Alanson related his experiences with a Rev. Cheney and a little girl named Mary back in '49'.

The Sears Brothers exchanged troubled glances and Alanson knew his hunch was right.

Alanson turned cold as he demanded "Walt is her name Mary"!

"Yes, but we've got to keep our emotions in check and think this problem through. If you are right the girl deserves better then some emotional half baked kidnapping".

Alanson shook his head in agreement while pondering the situation. If he remembered right she should be in her teens by now. Maybe the boys were wrong, hadn't he given her a note? He'd plan for the worst while praying he was wrong.

"Is there any form of law around the Dakota City area"?

Both shook their heads no.

"That's not all bad; the law often is a hindrance to justice in affairs such as this. How much would it take to have you boys make an extra trip if needed"?

Walt ran his hands through his hair looking pained "money isn't really the issue Alanson, the girl is. No-one can just snatch someone's child without some substantial evidence or something".

Alanson understood what Walt was getting at, Mary could end up worse off if things weren't handled properly. Still he KNEW that S. O. B. Cheney and he had just figured where she would be welcomed! There was a good Quaker home in Kansas that he knew positively for sure would be happy to be of assistance. Yes that would work but Mary would have to want his help and he would have to be able to provide immediate transportation. She wouldn't spend another day under that preacher's roof if things actually were as he feared.

Alanson ran these things through his mind with his feelings and desires continually in flux. Little Mary had been a ray of sunshine on an otherwise trying first trip aboard the Riversioux. It would be great to have someone who depended upon and looked up to him; especially since he had no family he called his own. On the other hand what if she wasn't the same sweet child? Living that long without love could leave scars, he knew this all to well.

If she was being mistreated and she wanted help she would get it! His life experiences left him no options; if later problems arose well that's when they would be handled.

The three talked the situation over, with Alanson doing most of the talking until several other passengers boarded.

Dan and Walt conversed with their regular passengers while Alanson contemplated what he was getting into.

The Sears Ferry would be available for a special run if needed, the decision rested upon him. With transportation and destination determined Alanson pondered upon his possible life altering decision.

Many folks would pray in such a situation which Alanson in his own way now did. Simply and quietly, with eyes closed and mind open he let the situation sink into his consciousness. For the forty five minute trip to Nebraska Alanson remained motionless drawing slow deep breaths as if day dreaming on a warm summer's afternoon. As the ferry was being winched unto the wagon the problem which had been submerged reappeared with resolution. As surly as destiny waits destiny also now is, 'he would simply react'.

The nearly completed church was in sight as Alanson stepped down from the ferry. He was not angry nor was he calm, he was resolute.

Since her altercation with mother Cheney, Mary was forbidden to leave the house for any reason. Pastor Cheney offered no safe harbor; long ago he had abandoned any semblance of self determination and now simply did as bade. Mary understood she would unquestionably suffer as never before if she was not completely submissive in every detail.

For two grueling weeks she had suffered. When sleep would temporarily relieve her drudgery she experienced fitful dreams of guilt. Nightmares of slaves writhing in pain while being 'disciplined' on her grandfather's plantation haunted her sleep. Mary woke exhausted, soaked in sweat and having to face another day without hope. A cross still hung around her neck but 'he' was from a time long ago. Life had abandoned Mary and Mary had abandoned hope.

Alanson recognized the reverend as he passed him in the warehouse. For a man of God he appeared in need of intervention. His eyes were sunken and dark. No emotion seemed plausible from such a limped vassal and none was forth coming as Alanson passed within arm's reach.

Alanson had prepared himself for human brutality but not for ghouls. Walking close to the man sent shivers through him; he unconsciously picked up his pace. He tried not to imagine what lay ahead but reality is hard to submerge. If Mary appeared anything like the reverend could he honestly offer haven?

The City Café was directly across the street from the church. The parsonage was next to the church which enabled Mrs. Cheney to keep a motherly eye upon her home while she worked. While Mary and the pastor withered from their environment 'mother' now thrived.

The Dirksons, proprietors of the City Café, had considered letting Mrs. Cheney go even if she was the wife of the new preacher but in the past couple of weeks Mrs. Cheney had become 'less' unpleasant.

Mrs. Cheney saw Alanson approaching on Broadway; something seemed familiar about the man. He would soon be entering the café as there was no other business beyond, then she would get a better look at him.

Walt had given Alanson (you can't miss) directions to the parsonage; in Dakota City directions aren't overly detailed.

Since he was here…there was no use standing around contemplating, he'd already done more then enough of that.

Mary also saw the stranger approaching, it couldn't be. She hadn't sent for him, it probably was another lost soul in search of the minister but he looked awfully familiar…She opened the door with one hand while grasping the cross with the other.

"My name is Alanson".

Mary threw her arms around a stunned Alanson.

He didn't recognize Mary. This girl was now considerably taller than him and certainly no longer a little girl! She looked so worn and tired. He had observed abused wives and children in the past with this 'beaten' look. His blood ran ice cold.

"Are you Mary, my little friend from the river boat"? Alanson couldn't believe the robust fiery Mary was now so…'plain' looking. She was certainly big enough for her age and apparently from her hug which she still hadn't relinquished was also plenty strong.

The dark circles around her eyes and slumped shoulders of defeat were betrayed when he finally looked into eyes.

Her 'prince' was here, just like in the fairy tales she read to Rachael. Mary crying and now holding on with desperation looked down into Alanson's eyes. She who had given up somehow had been found.

Mary, 15 years of age believed Alanson understood her situation and was here for that purpose. Feeling no need to explain Mary continued clinging to Alanson while also continuing to cry.

From across the street Mrs. Cheney had been watching the episode and this had gone far enough! "Take your hands off my daughter you-you beast".

Alanson was desperately trying to decipher exactly what was going on while Mary was just as desperately clinging to salvation.

Neither saw Mrs. Cheney approach.

Mother Cheney was screaming as she attempted to separate Mary from the intruder.

From an early age Alanson had always been a 'proper' gentleman. Females usually enjoyed wide latitude in their dealings with Alanson BUT his own mother had been less then a model parent and he also had been abused by a man hiding behind the auspices of God.

"Remove your hands from my daughter NOW"!

Alanson like many individual's possessed several ignition points; unfortunately Mrs. Cheney ignited them all…

Mrs. Cheney who had never been challenged within 'her' own boundaries badly misjudged the situation. Screaming she lashed out at Mary.

Alanson no longer deciphering, now reacted. Even so Alanson could not bring himself to strike a lady; he grabbed the hand pulling Mary's hair and twisted 'hard'. Bones snapped and an arm dangled from the elbow.

Mrs. Cheney formerly wailing in anger now screamed in terror…and ran.

Mary young and confused looked to Alanson for direction while encircling him ever more tightly with her arms and began crying in earnest.

The chaos woke Sister Rachael from her afternoon's nap, who also started crying.

Alanson was amiss and faced with a continually escalating situation. Mrs. Cheney was across the street screaming and pointing his direction, Rachel stood in the door crying and Mary draped herself around his neck with no indication she intended to relinquish her hold.

"Mary come inside and tell me what is taking place here". Alanson grabbed Rachael's hand while whisking Mary inside.

Mary pulled the end off her cross and thrust the note into Alanson's hand. She knew she had to leave this place and leave it now but she couldn't explain in a 'few' words why!

Alanson looked at Mary and then glanced at the infuriated banshee across the street. He recalled the sweet little Mary aboard the Riversioux's maiden voyage as he read the note.

CONTACT A. BAKER % THE RIVERSIOUX AT ANY PORT ON THE MISSOURI RIVER IF EVER YOU NEED HELP.

Tears formed as Alanson's once more looked into the eyes of the broken child desperately clinging to 'him'. He suddenly realized that for years this simple note may have sustained Mary through, Lord he didn't want to imagine.

"Mary, you're coming with me! Pack whatever clothes you need".

Mary had known she was going with Alanson as soon as he had first introduced himself. She was throwing her few clothes in a sack as Alanson picked up Rachael and headed for the door.

"Get your things together and wait here until I get back and Mary please stop crying, I meant and still mean every word written in the note. 'We're' going south on the Riversioux"; with these parting words Alanson strode resolutely toward the City Cafe.

A small crowd had gathered around the café by the time Alanson arrived. Pastor Cheney, the Dirksons and several others now surrounded him in a threatening manner as he reached for the café door.

Alanson thrust the squalling Rachael into Mrs. Cheney's remaining good arm and held his hand up for silence.

Mrs. Cheney started to speak until Alanson glared her direction with unmistakable intentions; she then grabbed her dangling arm and retreated behind the haven offered by the pastor.

"I first met Mary approximately nine years ago. She was the sweetest child anyone ever met". Alanson was struggling to restrain himself. "She has been imprisoned, enslaved and abused by the Cheney's for all these years. This past year right here in Dakota City while you-all stood by and watched! I should have come for her years ago". Alanson struggled to continue, "I am ashamed and if anyone doubts what I say look for yourselves"!

Mary still sobbing was standing in the parsonage door way with her cloths packed in a pillow case.

The Dirksons had held suspicions about the Cheney family for some time but hadn't wanted to get involved and from the looks of the others they weren't necessarily innocent either.

"Since nobody troubled themselves to help Mary in the past I assume nobody wants the trouble of standing in our way as we exit this pigsty of Christendom".

It was clear Alanson yearned for atonement through aggression.

Shamed and sensing the stranger's resolution no resistance was forthcoming.

The crowd now stepped away from the Cheneys who immediately were shunned by the gathering as newly discovered pariahs.

Alanson shaking his head in disgust spit through the café door and then did a military about face before re-crossing the street.

Alanson offered Mary his arm, who was no longer crying. Mary hugged Alanson in a noticeably more adult manner and then with an unmistakable look of "dare you to say something now" Mary grasped Alanson's arm as the two walked through the stunned crowd toward the pier.

Mary, as young girls may do, once more was dreaming, this time grown up dreams!

Alanson was feeling a little uneasy with this sudden turn of events. To him Mary was still the little sister he never had. She would probably get over this infatuation, after all she was a good 15 years his junior.

It was 1:30 pm when they reached the dock. The Sears ferry wagon which departed at 1:45 for Harney City already had three passengers when they arrived.

"Who is the lovely lady with you Baker"? Walt knew but he had never laid eyes upon Mary in the year she had lived Dakota City.

"My long lost sister Mary and you ruffians better treat her accordingly".

"Mary, meet Walt and Dan Sears, old friends of mine".

Mary smiled and shook their hands while squeezing Alanson's arm "I'm not 'really' his sister".

While Mary boarded Walt caught Alanson's eye for a moment and smiled a knowing smile.

Alanson shook his head in defiant denial.

The wagon trip to Harney City and then the ferry ride to Sioux City for Alanson seemed like eternity. 'Little' Mary couldn't sit close enough to her hero. Every now and then Alanson sheepishly would glance at Dan or Walt who seemed to thoroughly enjoy his discomfort.

Mary meanwhile experienced a completely different concept. For the first time since childhood she was without fear—anticipating the future! She had rubbed her cross and like a genie Alanson had appeared. Happiness and dreams filled Mary's journey as the trip ended much too soon. In these few short hours Mary already was beginning to exude rays of sunshine which had lain dormant for nearly a decade.

Alanson couldn't deny he enjoyed the attention of his young companion but at the same time he couldn't help but wonder what he was getting into.

The Sears brothers wished him well as they parted at the Pierce Street Dock. No longer was Alanson the object of humor, he was in a position that would surely test him. The boys understood the gravity of the situation as Alanson grasped hands in parting handshakes…seemingly unwilling to relinquish his grip.

The two hailed a taxi for Riverside, Alanson waving to the Searses as Mary snuggled close.

Damn Walt and Dan were giving him that silly look again as they pulled away.

It was nearing supper time when the taxi reached the Bruguier Inn.

"Mary grab us a spot at the table and I'll see about rooms" Alanson said already hurrying toward the desk.

After having asked a patron if he minded moving over one spot Mary procured a couple of adjacent chairs near the end of the large communal dining table.

"Only one room was left, it well have to suffice for tonight" Alanson shook his head apologetically.

Momentarily Mary's heart raced until Alanson continued. "This definitely is no place for a young lady to be left un-chaperoned so I asked Mr. Bruguier to set up a cot in the hall just outside your door for me".

"What ever you say big 'brother'" Mary teased.

Alanson recognized 'little' Mary's humor had returned but damn it all she wasn't so little anymore!

Mary enjoyed the evening more than any she remembered. Some day she would be the wife of Alanson. Until that day she would make certain he would never again be content. Stubborn determined Mary had reawakened.

Alanson, always a disciple of destiny was now destinies object.

Alanson walked Mary to her room. "Why don't you change clothes and freshen up and then we'll walk over to the Riversioux and claim you a room". Alanson reached for her cloths sack to help her unpack. Mary shyly resisted saying she could do it herself. "It's alright Mary I only wanted to help".

Mary covered her face with her hands and began sobbing.

Alanson was in unfamiliar territory with no apparent avenue of retreat. "Don't cry Mary I'll just step outside a minute so you can change".

Embarrassed Mary dumped her bag on the bed; it contained one severely worn dress and a few equally worn under things!

"Is that ALL you have"?

Mary nodded yes, still sobbing.

Alanson never swore in the presence of 'ladies'. "Damn it, I should of wrung her scrawny neck instead of simply breaking her arm and for good measure slapped that man of God around for awhile"!

"I'm sorry I'm such a burden" Mary still cried.

"Listen Mary there are two merchandise stores in Sioux City, well one operates from a tent but nevertheless tomorrow you and I are going shopping. It would sure be a pleasure dressing you up properly. When we reach St. Joseph we'll do it up even better. Please don't cry".

Mary must cheer up as he had no idea what else to do.

The sobbing slowly ceased. Mary was also in new territory, no-one had ever considered her wishes before. She didn't have any idea on Alanson's financial status. All she had heard since '49' was how expensive she was to provide for.

"Do you 'really' want to go shopping"?

"Truthfully I would rather split elm wood then go shopping but this also is the truth. Nothing would please me more then spending a day watching you buy pretty clothes. So do we have a deal?"

Once more Alanson was assaulted with hugs from an adoring young admirer.

"You know what? You're already the prettiest girl in Riverside. With a new dress every mate in Bruguiers will be at your bidding and we will never make it to the Riversioux. If you are feeling ready let's go and check in with Captain Jonas Maynard".

"Alanson you know you're not my brother". Mary was practicing her wiles.

Jonas was at the captain's desk comparing figures when the two arrived. "Come on in and who is this young lady Alanson"? Jonas stood up and offered his hand.

"Remember my friend little Mary who boarded with the pastor Cheney and his wife on our maiden journey, well this is Mary and she intends on going to St. Joseph with us".

"It surely is going to make our final trip more enjoyable with you aboard Mary. It seems fitting since you were on our maiden voyage that you would accompany us on our final voyage; and how are the Pastor and his wife"? Jonas directed the question to Mary.

Alanson gently squeezed Mary's hand. "We'll discus the Cheneys later but right now Mary needs a room fitting a young girl, Jonas do you think we could take care of that"?

While Mary was engrossed studying a long list of figures on Jonas's desk Alanson grimaced indicating all was not well. Jonas didn't need any more hints; he remembered the pious Cheney pair.

He also noticed Mary's intrigue with his shipping rates and costs analysis sheets. "Do you have an understanding of the shipping business Mary"?

"I have always enjoyed figures and comparisons, even father Cheney used to say I was gifted". Mary was looking at the tabulations on Jonas's desk. "I believe you would receive more compensation from proposal 'A' than from 'B' Captain Maynard".

"And why would that be young lady"? Jonas knew why but didn't believe Mary could grasp the concept that quickly.

"Proposal 'A' doesn't pay quite as much per hundred weight as proposal 'B' but more than half of the load is destined for Omaha where I see you can take on merchandise going to St. Joseph which will more then makes up the difference. Am I right"?

Alanson, a skilled clerk himself was amazed while Jonas, less skilled in finances, rubbed his head in disbelief.

"Alanson your job would be in jeopardy if this wasn't our final voyage; this young lady is destined for the business world."

"Let's find a room for Mary before she decides to look for work elsewhere". Alanson no longer saw Mary as simply a little girl, she may be young but she definitely wasn't a child.

Mary could see that Alanson was surprised and also obviously pleased with her business astuteness. "I am no longer your 'little' sister Alanson; you'll see I've grown in many ways".

Mary snuggled up closer as Alanson retreated.

Alanson glanced at Jonas with a 'help me look'.

Jonas simply grinned.

Alanson was beginning to believe he had chosen his friends unwisely!

The room that Jenny and Jeff had shared seemed the most fitting for Mary to Alanson and Jonas.

Mary really wasn't that interested in the accommodations, she was reveling in freedom and attention!

With the room agreed upon the party walked back toward Bruguiers.

Jonas excused himself and returned to his figures while Alanson and Mary walked back to Bruguiers. It was a crisp fall evening with new fallen leaves crunching under foot. An orange moonlight shimmered upon the Big Sioux River.

"Mary would you like to take a walk along the river before calling it a day"?

"It is such a gorgeous night it would seem terribly wrong not to partake".

As they walked Alanson told of his dream estate some twenty five miles northwest on the banks of the Sioux River. Mary was a willing listener so he continued to talk, telling stories of the river, about renegade Indians and fugitive slaves but mostly about his dreams.

Mary could not restrain her heart's racing pulse.

Why wouldn't she be enthralled? Never had anyone confided in her nor could she remember having a conversation simply for conversation sake. Only this morning (hours ago) she had lived without purpose.

Since six years of age she had lived in servitude, somehow managing to survive on a dream until finally even the dream died. Miraculously in her darkest hour Alanson had appeared!

Mary was a fifteen years old young lady, impressionable and star struck! She hung on every spoken word as if gospel.

Alanson's care for Mary deepened as the night wore on. She was intelligent and bubbly and she worshipped him. It became abundantly apparent he alone was responsible for Mary's well being. A wrenching responsibility for an idol!

Being a man, as Mary flirted, thoughts unwillingly crossed his mind. He shuddered at his base subconscious instincts. Mary was vulnerable, no not vulnerable but even worse as she now had replaced her will with his. He and he alone toed the line between honor and barbarism.

"Mary this is a night that shouldn't end but you and I have some shopping to do tomorrow. Truthfully shopping wears me out worse then an honest day's labor. How would you like a night cap of coffee and Bruguier's berry pie before we tuck in for the evening"?

"I don't think I can sleep but it probably is time. I haven't been out after dark since well I can't remember when. Alanson I'll never be able to repay you…really" and Mary again began to cry.

Alanson understood that Mary's crying was not in sadness but it still was unsettling.

"What are we going to do Mary? It hurts to see you cry when you are sad and it doesn't feel a whole bunch better when you aren't sad. Either you are going to have to stop crying or I am going to have to go deaf and blind"!

Mary stopped crying and laughed. "Let's get that pie and some sleep and prepare for tomorrow".

It had been years since Mary looked forward to tomorrow!

Mary again made what seemed a mandatory attempt to entice Alanson into her boudoir with the same results. Alanson unable to hide his uncomfortable-ness, remaining very much a gentleman excused himself…. Which oddly seemed to please Mary?

After considerable time Mary Finally fell to sleep, she dreamed of the plantation and slaves once more. Mary unconsciously gripped her pillow anticipating a rerun of horror. As always before a slave was being lashed to a post in preparation for a whipping with the entire slave population compelled to witness the consequences of 'running'. Mary once again a little girl peeked out the window crying "Don't grandpa, please don't" but as always in the past it was to no avail. The whip rippled backward with a lashing sound until it's reached its apex where it cracked in readiness.

A muscular arm grabbed the whips tongs, ripping the whip from the hand of the whip master. Alanson strode foreword now with the whip in his hand lashing out at any who stood in his way. "You can stay in this place or you may leave, in any case there will be no more whippings" Alanson addressed the gathered slaves as he tossed the whip into the smoldering forge pit.

Alanson made an about face and then walked over to the window that Mary peeked out of, he motioned her to back up as he kicked it out. "It is time for us to leave Mary" was all he said as he gently lifted her out the window into his arms. "I will take care of you from now on. Be assured there will be no more whippings"! Mary woke gently caressing her pillow, her nightmare conquered.

Mary opened the door just a crack to reassure herself, Alanson lay sound asleep on the cot. Softly squeezing through the door she tiptoed over and gently kissed his cheek, then retreated in great haste. She had never kissed a man before!

Mary did not sleep again that evening; she was much too busy with 'girl' day-dreams to sleep.

The Riversioux slipped passed Dakota City on its final journey down the Missouri river. Mary and Alanson stood leaning over the railing watching the Nebraska port city fade away thinking entangled but necessarily different thoughts.

Mary wore a freshly purchased colorful flower print dress with a matching bonnet. She had purchased 'many' other dresses but Alanson seemed to favor this one. She wore it to please him, it certainly wasn't her favorite!

Alanson had broached the idea of her staying with some of his Quaker friends in Kansas while she finished her schooling. Of-course she had agreed, now she hoped they would like her.

Everything was so new and exciting; it was difficult not to shout in exubera-tion. She now understood that she wouldn't be marrying Alanson right away. She loved him all the more, he wanted her to have choices and experience some FUN. Alanson truly cared about 'her'. She had loved him when he first came to get her but now she also respected him If Alanson thought it was in her best interest to pursue more education and experience some life without the burden of responsi-bility, well she trusted him. When the time was right she would have him; there was no way he'd ever escape!

Lord she looks beautiful in that dress, it's good I insisted she purchase it. Neither she nor the clerk seemed to really favor it but once again I was right. Just look at her! I'm even more thankful we're only days from St. Joseph, in fact tomorrow wouldn't be too soon. She enjoys teasing me and damn I'm only human! She absolutely the most intelligent person I've ever run across. She's beautiful and witty and God knows what else. I usually don't pray but please Lord deliver us to St. Joseph soon.

"Face it you old reprobate she's reeling you in and your resistance is absolutely pitiful".

The Samuel and Jane Clemons family now had two additions, James six years of age and Ruth two years of age. The Clemons through hard labor and a tight budgetary policy now operated a dairy business employing several blacks, blacks that routinely were being replaced by other blacks.

Mary had been welcomed beyond her wildest expectations. Mary loved children and the children reciprocated. She was 'family'.

Finding schooling for girls was difficult but understanding the dividends Quakers usually found a method. A school master who excelled in math was employed to tutor Mary in the Clemons home. Immediately new texts were ordered, Mary was a prodigy extraordinaire.

Alanson and Jane spent late night hours discussing Mary's special circumstances and her unconcealed 'love' for Alanson. To his surprise Jane didn't downplay Mary's girlish feelings.

"What do you expect "lover boy" have you forgotten I found you quite attractive also and by the way I still do" Jane added laughing.

Alanson had forgotten how much he enjoyed Jane's simple unassuming humor. It struck him, Mary entertained the same qualities. "You know that she is out to lasso me, and maybe that's alright I really don't know. She is only half my age and maybe I'm being selfish but I don't want to take advantage of circumstances only to see either of us hurt later on".

"You worry too much and you always have. Listen Alanson Mary and I will have many heart to heart conversations before your return next year. If something comes up that could sway Mary in another direction and it if seems for the best I'll certainly not council against her best interest".

Jane smiled "I don't think you better count on it, you undervalue your self Alanson, maybe that is why we girls find you so attractive'?

Jane was no more helpful then the Sears's boys or Jonas had been. In most any other situation they all would have been helpful but with Mary they simply set him adrift and damned if they didn't all seem to enjoy his dilemma.

"Are you really going back to Pennsylvania"? Jane had been anxious but hesitant to ask. "Are you going to visit your parents"?

Yes I've decided I'm going to at least go past the homestead, I don't know if I can bring myself to actually enter the Baker house. I suppose I won't know until the time comes. I know you must be wondering whether I'll be visiting Rev. Satterday, the answer is the same. I hope I have matured since then but truthfully I just don't know".

"If you do please tell him I feel no animosity toward him. He lived with a terrible secret in a most unforgiving society. Tell him I and Samuel pray he finds comfort in our loving father. The scriptures are filled with love and forgiveness if one is inclined to search".

"If he finds any of that in 'his' Bible I'll bake you a Dutch Apple pie upon my return".

The time to part had arrived all too soon. As much as Alanson anguished over Mary and her constant teasing he was torn as to whether he should really leave. Yes he wanted Mary to have the childhood that had been denied them both and sure he wanted her to become strong and independent but now he doubted his wisdom. Mary was precious, why had life suddenly becoming so difficult?

Mary cried as Alanson boarded the Riversioux on its swan song voyage. She had planned on teasing Alanson with a story about her 'handsome' tutor. She so wanted him to be jealous all the while he was away. The look of total devastation on her 'fiancées' face thwarted such treachery. She would be anxiously waiting when he returned, by then an educated 'woman'.

CHAPTER 21

▼

Stiff, sore and suffering from sea legs Explorer 'finally' was ashore. Alanson initially had entrusted him to Mary's care but at the last minute discovered he simply couldn't bear leaving both Mary and Explorer.

A light snow was drifting across the trail that ran westward from Philadelphia towards Cambria County Pennsylvania. They were returning to the land of Alanson's childhood and still home to his parents. Two hundred and fifty miles this trip and Alanson seemed to be in no hurry. They had stopped at Valley Forge, barely out side Philly, where Alanson studied manuals as he walked the area. For two days Alanson strolled the site, Explorer sensed he was procrastinating more then anything else.

"I'm beginning to understand what General George and the troops went through here" Alanson said to Explorer as he pulled his collar up around his neck. "At least they froze anticipating action; I'm freezing trying to postpone it. Remember back in the Big Sioux Valley when I asked you to make the trip to Sioux City in one day. Don't you even think of duplicating that feat! I suppose we're going to have to do this thing but I sure am not in any hurry".

In St. Louis most of the crew had departed from the Riversioux with hefty severance pay. Fletch, Stroker, Rube and Alanson comprised the 'coastal' crew accompanying Jonas on to Philadelphia.

Other then the upper Missouri five or six men could suffice as a river boat crew, the upper Missouri required extra man power to wench through sandbars and there always the matter of hostile Sioux.

Goodbyes were heartfelt, after six or seven years together the crew had become family. Jonas was presented a gold watch with skipper of the Riversioux 'from the crew' engraved into its face. Placid faced Jonas broke down unable to complete his parting speech. For the crew Jonas's final speech would remain his most memorable; Jonas once again had performed well!

Jonas and his friends were welcomed to Philadelphia in a manner similar to the returning of the prodigal's son. Old business associates and members of the Philadelphia Society of Friends couldn't seem to toast their old friend too often or too graciously.

Jonas as had been promised sold the Riversioux for near new price (around the seven thousand dollar figure). This along with proceeds saved from years on the river rendered Jonas a moderately wealthy man. Wealth, although not unwelcome, had never been Jonas's life ambition.

The Underground Railroad desperately needed funding but even more needed was meaningful employment for its ever burgeoning cliental.

Through the 'Friends' Jonas became acquainted with a group of sympathizers from Canada who had proposed a most interesting proposition, he was presently on his way north to investigate the opportunity.

Hamilton, Ontario which lay on the western shore of Lake Ontario was becoming a major port. It was brought to Jonas's attention that a ship refurbishing business not only would be profitable but was also badly needed in the area. With Jonas's previous experience in ship refurbishing (and after examining the rebuilt Riversioux) the group was anxious to help finance a ship repair business using Negro fugitives as employees.

Alanson harbored little doubt the venture would mature and prosper.

Meanwhile Fletch had 'hatched' a brainstorm of his own which Alanson would have gladly invested in if he already hadn't made commitments.

Fletch, (still possessing a goodly share of his New Jersey gambling proceeds) Stroker and Rube (who had their severance pay) were going to Hartford, Connecticut with the intention of purchasing stock in the reopened Colt Revolver factory. (The idea had come to Fletch after observing the Santee actually willing to 'work' for a multi-shot colt)

It was a pristine idea if the boys carried through but when last seen the three hadn't been sober for days. Alanson doubted little if any money would actually reach Connecticut. It remained a puzzle to Alanson how these three who were rock solid employees became adolescents when unencumbered with responsibility. He hoped fate would intervene in their behalf.

It was late December when Alanson rode into Altoona, Pa. upon Explorer. Altoona lay barely east of Amsbry, Alanson's place of birth.

Altoona was a bustling community with canals and the railroad intersecting at the heart of the city. The Logan House, the cities finest hotel, occupied the square where these means of transportation interlocked. Alanson intended to spend the evening in the luxury of The Logan House.

Explorer was entrusted to the Logan Livery while Alanson explored the city on foot. The entire city was new. The emergence of the railroad in '49' had changed a country livery stable into a city almost overnight. The convergence of rail and canal were of special interest to Alanson. The Big Sioux was possibly navigable and the railroad certainly was coming to northwest Iowa. His property bordered on both!

Still he understood his immediate interest was to a great extent motivated by his uneasiness of going 'home'. Could he even make the final ten mile journey?

Remembrances of his childhood flooded his head. His father, I wonder if he still sits in a pious manner with nothing to say and had his mother ever evolved beyond appearance. Frankly he seriously doubted it but still…. How could one be sure?

Alanson walked back to the stable seeking the reassuring presence of Explorer. "Are you ready to meet my parents big fellow? Tomorrow we either do it or we turn back and hopefully leave Pa. and its memories behind us once and for all".

Explorer nudged him forward as if to say you can't turn back. Explorer already knew what Alanson still searched for. "I misunderstood freedom until you let me experience it and you will remain in doubt if you let fear end your search". Explorer lovingly nuzzled Alanson. "Fletch had certainly been a trip and Lord didn't he still miss the excitement, but Alanson had loved him enough to set him free". Explorer would sacrifice life for his human.

"You are right big fellow. If you stick with me I believe I can do this". They hadn't spoken words but had communicated. This is not an experience exclusive to this man and this horse; many have the opportunity but most through 'education' refuse to partake.

It was late in the morning the 24th of December when the travelers reached the Baker homestead. A cold bitter wind swept the Pa. countryside as a troubled middle aged man stood watching smoke curl from a farmhouse chimney.

"It was the Christmas season some fifteen years ago when I left here. I was young with no intention of ever returning and you know I still can't force myself down that driveway, anyway not right now. Let's go".

Alanson nudged Explorer westward toward town. "We might have made a long trip for nothing big fellow; I still don't want to confront the memories. I don't remember Christmas as a pleasant time in the Baker house, of-course no other time was either".

Alanson wasn't bitter, maybe a little disappointed but he'd come prepared to feel his way through this homecoming. Right now he didn't like the feeling.

"Whoa up big fellow". They were in front of his old church building but something, no everything was wrong! The marquee read 1rst Universalist Church of Cambria County \ Rev. David Satterday minister. "Come help us celebrate the joys of Christmas"

Alanson could see reminisce of a garden plot. From the residue it appeared as if it had been a dandy. Dormant rose bushes grew along a neatly swept pathway and behind the church was a small milking parlor with several Jersey cows contentedly chewing their cud in the barnyard. Everything appeared gentle and welcoming.

Alanson actually never harbored any intention of stopping but seeing this how could he pass? He dismounted and stood reading the marquee over and over. The preacher's name was right but nothing else was. Flowers, contented cows and a sign which shared the words Rev Satterday and joy!

"Can I help you" brought Alanson back to reality. A gentle, friendly voice and a smiling face greeted him.

No, he recognized the face but it couldn't be. A weathered compassionate appearing vicar possessed old Satterday's body.

"Do you know me"? Alanson asked the question searching for something to bring the visual present into focus with the known past.

"This is truly Christmas if you are who I think you are" the reverend answered offering his hand.

Alanson didn't respond. Maybe he looked pleasant but the lowly S.O.B. was still Satterday!

"What is your game you phony—God Damn you. What is a Universalist Church, what's happened to everything and why would you be HAPPY to see me"?

Long submerged rage rushed to surface. This asshole who nearly had destroyed both his and Jane's lives was glad to see him! "Don't touch me again preacher"!

Rev. David Satterday stepped backward slowly shaking his head 'no'. "I understand your resentment Alanson but things aren't now what they were and YOU are the reason. I know I don't have the right to ask anything of you but please give me the opportunity to explain".

The man looked sincere; he sure didn't look or act like the old Satterday.

"I've got to get my horse out of this wind and then you've got a minute".

"He is a beautiful horse Alanson. Let me open up the milk parlor where it will be warmer for him".

Alanson was confused. He despised Rev. Satterday but seemingly this wasn't the same person.

For sanity sake he had to listen to the man's story.

After leading Explorer into a warm dry stall Rev Satterday invited Alanson into the parsonage.

"Please sit down. Jason would you bring Alanson a cup of Christmas eggnog please"?

So the story was told.

That Christmas 15 years ago when Alanson and Jane had fled, oh the congregation was furious. Alanson's little ditty left on the easel board certainly hadn't helped!

Their preacher was a homosexual! This abomination of human kind had defiled the church pulpit rendering it forever tainted with blasphemy.

The congregation hastily departed leaving him with a church but with no congregation. It seemed as if his world had ended, shunned and with no friends he took a sabbatical to Meadville, Pa. where he understood a Universalist Church thrived.

He had preached sermons condemning this blasphemous cult on several occasions. They taught that infants were born in innocence and worthy of heaven by birth. Their doctrine was of a loving God who through his sacrifice on the cross offered universal salvation for all mankind rather then Calvin's exclusionist doctrine of born into sin and in need of atonement.

Now 'he' sought forgiveness and needed inclusion.

The meaty gossip of a fallen homosexual fundamentalist preacher travels rapidly. Confrontation waited the reverend upon his arrival in Meadville (a full one hundred and fifty miles northwest). His presence on the streets of Meadville at first perpetuated virulent demonstrations but to David's dismay, even knowing his past, the Universalist congregation extended a 'cordial' welcome...

Of all the revelations garnished from divinity school or through life experiences for David this was the greatest, freed from pretense and guilt he no longer was servant to anger!

In time David sympathized for those who taunted him. It appeared they suffered from a sickness similar to the one he was in the process of being healed.

Possibly man 'was' sinful by nature and maybe a homosexual was an abomination, this he didn't know. He did know he hadn't chosen this lifestyle! For a Christian man of faith the Universalist seemed his only haven.

Approximately one year and six months later he returned to Amsbry and 'his' deserted church with his new life partner Jason and a divinity degree from Meadville Theological Seminary.

Several weeks were spent cleaning and refurbishing the building. Flowers and a garden patch were planted and the yard was re-sown. A few dairy cows were purchased and the 'couple' reopened the church for services…with little expectation.

The church marquee proclaimed. "Where love frequents God abides. Where God abides most certainly all are welcomed".

For weeks nobody entered. Then one Sunday evening a battered mother and her children entered seeking asylum which readily was granted. Several persons who lived similar lives (although not openly) to David and Jason began attending. Then a few alcoholics searching for 'real' acceptance started attending and later a few brave souls who truly believed love and forgiveness 'was' God's doctrine actually became members. The congregation was slowly becoming a theological 'underground railroad' for Amsbry's social outcast and its free thinking theist.

"Alanson if you hadn't penned that awful note I'd still be submerged in a life of misery. God works in ways that only a chosen few will ever understand, most certainly I don't understand. For me you were his messenger. Although my behavior was reprehensible and I will understand if you can not bring yourself to forgive me, I have fervently prayed you will".

Alanson had seldom dealt with a moral dilemma of equal depth and never in such circumstances. Usually he instinctively knew what was right from what was wrong, even-so at times the cost of doing right was simply too demanding.

He closed his eyes and sat quietly pondering the situation for some time. He wasn't by nature a bigot; on the other hand he didn't understand how anyone could forgive such an abuse of positional power—with a child! The reverend truly seemed a changed man, possibly even a good man but his life had been forever tainted by his uninvited intrusion.

He himself couldn't make moral decisions based on a rigid two thousand year old doctrine, these teachings undoubtedly influenced his notion of right and wrong but experience led him down another path. People harvested right here upon this earth what they sowed right here on earth, his interpretation of this knowledge still left moral dilemmas. On one hand it could warrant his damnation of the preacher or on the other hand it might mean if he himself expected forgiveness and understanding he must first plant its seed.

"You know Pastor I never expected to see you again and I certainly didn't expect to be sipping eggnog in your parlor. Truthfully I do understand a person trapped by circumstance, I suppose to a degree we all are. What you are and what you have done aren't agreeable to me, seeing the two of you I wish this wasn't so. Still I don't give a Damn what you two do with each other as long as you understand what you did to me was an abomination! I don't know if that is forgiveness but it works for me. Since I have no intention of ever returning to this place it might eases your mind knowing I have gained a little understanding which I didn't come with. If your conscious can live with that, possibly we both will have gained from this Christmas Eve homecoming".

"That works for me Alanson". Reverend David Satterday offered Alanson Baker his hand which this time Alanson firmly clasped in hand shake.

"Christmas Eve services will be commencing soon, we would like you to attend Alanson". Jason asked and Alanson having nothing better accepted.

As they did chores David asked if Alanson knew how 'poor' Jane had fared.

Alanson explained that she had married a man of Quaker faith, which probably wasn't legally binding but definitely was morally sanctioned. It didn't seem to be an issue to either of them. They now had two children and they interestingly also operated a dairy farm. He then remembered the message he was asked to relay. "Jane and her husband said they wished you well and prayed for your well being and peace of mind".

"You mean Jane harbors no anger? Surely God has bathed her in the healing waters of his mercy, there can be no other explanation".

Alanson shook his head in disgust.

"You do agree Alanson"?

"Preacher I know Jane is one of the most loving forgiving persons I've ever met and you know what else, she can also be a lot of fun. Jane most assuredly would agree with you that God is responsible for the pleasing aspects of nature and the laudable achievements of mankind but I believe you asked for my opinion.

If God is so perfect and all powerful his creation should at minimum be relatively glitch free which we both through mutual experience know is heifer dung; anyway didn't he drown the inhabitants of his first creation attempt? I have no quarrel with your spectator God; he never has been a factor.

My problem is with you preachers who interpret for this mute deity espousing conflicting and self serving messages, the only commonality being a self possessed knowledge of the truth".

"I understand your skepticism much better then you probably think Alanson, experience and education has a tendency to widen oncs vision but at the same time it can dim ones 'in' sight. Still many of us (even experienced men of education) feel we need more then what we are physically endowed with to meaningfully survive in this inexplicable world. I now understand truth is not within mans grasp, still the search for meaning does not subside. I yearn for meaning and understand this need in others.

Between the two of us, I have no special insights into spirituality nor do I think special insight is of great significance. My calling is to offer comfort to those in need of comfort. This simply takes compassion. Having suffered greatly I have much to give, I pray daily that I may have the strength to emulate the example of Jesus Christ our Lord".

The Christmas Eve program was 'meaningful'. People, in good cheer, brought gifts of food and clothing for the less fortunate in the community (viewing some of the congregants Alanson thought less fortunate must be hard to come by).

Hot cider and sweets of many types filled a table in the basement R.E. room.

The revelers placed their gifts on the floor and in return received refreshments from Rev. David and Brother Jason.

Alanson couldn't help but reflect on the significance of gifts being placed on the R. E. floor. Years earlier he had been gifted on the very same floor; inwardly smiling (while shaking his head and looking at Reverend Satterday) he conjectured his life truly had been altered for the better.

The evening ended with the singing of carols, followed by prayers for peace and understanding.

The only scar upon the occasion was Alanson's inability to erase the memory of 'old' Satterday from his mind.

Alanson saddled Explorer, headed for town and a night's sleep at the inn. Tomorrow (Christmas Day) he would visit his Mother and father.

It wasn't Bruguiers breakfast extravaganza but the inn did provide an appealing Christmas morning buffet. Alanson dawdled the morning away until he suspected the inn keeper might perceive him as a thug a-waiting opportunity. Finally noticing some left over pastry, he purchased the sweet rolls and departed.

Thankfully Explorer had spent the night in the livery barn as a full fledged blizzard ravaged the western Pennsylvania countryside. Slowly and methodically Alanson saddled and blanketed his big horse in preparation for the couple mile jaunt to his parent's house. He was glad they didn't know he was coming; he still wasn't secure in his resolve.

"Let's get this over Alanson, fool around much longer and I'll be too arthritic to bend my legs". Explorer whinnied in disapproval of Alanson's procrastination. "Sometimes you're plain pathetic, Fletch would have had this thing skinned and on the stretching board by now".

"Okay know it all, we'll see how anxious 'you' are when I open the barn door"!

He threw the door open, Explorer disgustedly snorted clouds of steam, stamped the stiffness from his legs and the two bull headed mammals were off.

"Do I have to?" Alanson asked of God and Explorer as he momentarily sat shielding his face from the sting of the north wind while staring down the Baker farm lane.

He knocked on the door lightly, kind-of hoping no-one would hear.

"Merry Christmas mother" Alanson said offering her the sweat rolls he'd purchased from the inn.

"Alanson, fifteen years and now you've come home". Elizabeth Baker noticeably was experiencing breathing difficulties.

"Why didn't you write"?

Alanson was opening his arms to his mother as his father entered the room.

"Come home finally, huh son"? John offered a stiff hand.

It had appeared as if mother was about to reciprocate but she had drawn back when John entered the room.

John instinctively wanted to grab and hug his son but Elizabeth might see it as lack of resolve or even craven capitulation so he resumed his pose of piety.

Meanwhile Elizabeth cried out for Alanson but her words never left her heart, therefore unheard by the one who desperately needed to hear them.

"Remember those Dutch apple pies you used to make for church bazaars mother, they were unquestionably the worlds best. Do you suppose you could show me how to bake one up"?

Alanson assailed himself with most bitter recriminations for ever having stopped. If possible things were worse now then back then! Still he'd have to spend some time before just LEAVING.

His mother had never baked anything for home consumption 'but' for church affairs she was known as one of the better cooks in a Pennsylvania Dutch congregation. He was going to have to bake Jane a pie upon his return to Kansas so why not spend the day doing something that wasn't too painful for either of them.

"John, would you get some cobs for the kitchen stove please?

I didn't think you would still remember Alanson. Did I bake for you very often? It was so long ago I seem to have forgotten".

Elizabeth absolutely remembered but hoped Alanson wouldn't.

"I do remember how great they were mother".

"What is taking your father so long"?

Elizabeth hoped he would experience difficulties as she wanted to 'be' with Alanson but it wasn't to be as John was already back.

"Where did you spend Christmas Eve Alanson"? John asked as he set the cob bucket down.

"Actually I was at 'our' old church last night for evening services and I couldn't believe the difference in the church or in Pastor Satterday".

They might as well know the truth and get the "what-ever" out of their systems.

John and Elizabeth exchanged uncertain glances and then Elizabeth spoke.

"After all the grief that man has caused US and still you saw fit to step foot in that church"!

"Mother I don't recall either of you thought so lightly of the man back then".

This is not going in a good direction were Alanson's thoughts but he no longer was a child and he wasn't about to back down.

"He was immoral, both a Letcher and a blasphemer. How could you ever visit 'him' before visiting your own parents"?

Elizabeth wanted to say 'I don't care I'm happy you are home'—but didn't.

"Mother I really wasn't sure how well I would be received after being gone all these years, but most of my doubts have vanished". Alanson was no longer an immature willow that bent with the wind; he also had become mature Baker hardwood.

John and Elizabeth once again looked to each other searching for some indication of which way to take this situation, both unsure of the other returned to the norm,

"Here is the recipe you wanted so badly son" Elizabeth thrust it into Alanson's hand.

John broke in "It is shameful you haven't matured some in all these years Alanson. Since you bring nothing but heartache to your mother and I it's probably best you leave".

John appeared more pained then angry to Elizabeth, in fact she had never seen John look so distraught.

Alanson, heart broken saw nothing but rejection.

"Merry Christmas to you mother and to you also father and a jolly GOOD BYE". Alanson grabbed his coat, jerked open the door and slammed it shut as he departed.

Alanson jumped astride Explorer and viciously kneed him into a gallop. "Well I came, I saw and I'm Damned glad to be leaving"

"At least the visit rekindled some emotion and the trip wasn't a complete failure" were Explorer's thoughts as he showed Alanson speed, Fletch type speed.

Alanson let Explorer have his way for quite a good spell. "Whoa up there big guy, I'm not really out to commit suicide and I see no need for you to either".

"I guess it's kind of getting out of my system big fellow, my parents no longer exist. From now on it is you and me and with the gentle kiss of luck a young lady back in Kansas".

With the slamming of the front door Elizabeth immediately ran to the bedroom while John just as rapidly retreated to the barn where he began smashing everything upon the workbench.

Why didn't she just for once forget about appearance and simply be human? John cried for the first time in his adult memory. To hell with it, I am finally going to confront that lizard hearted woman, John stormed towards the house.

Elizabeth lie on the bed crying, if only she could have been strong and told John her real feelings. It was too late now, Alanson would never be back! So she continued to cry.

"ELIZABETH we need to get a few things straight right now! Where are you"?

He heard crying from the bedroom, with a renewed hope he ran into the bedroom.

"Why are you crying Elizabeth, don't you think it is time we stop pretending"? He desperately hoped she cried for the same reasons as he.

"John he's gone, I let our son leave with out him ever knowing I loved him"! Elizabeth burst uncontrollably into tears again.

"Good God woman that is my precise feeling also. The only person we ever truly cared about has gone. Get your coat on while I hitch up the buggy. By-God we're going to catch our son and MAKE him come back home! Elizabeth at this moment I remember why I first loved you".

He had never said he loved her since, well she didn't remember when. Why should he, neither had given the other cause!

"John, no matter the outcome of this Alanson has given us a Christmas gift beyond compare; I have waited so long to say, I love you too".

"We have a life time with which we can catch up but I have a feeling Alanson needs us right now. Let's be off", John flung Elizabeth into the buggy.

They flew down the snow drifted road with absolute abandon but of-course they never had a chance of catching Alanson.

Explorer had let it all hang out at the most inopportune moment!

After many miles of pursuit John and Elizabeth finally abandoned the futile chase and returned home heartbroken but not defeated. Their son's homecoming would not be without meaning.

"It is still Christmas John, NOW is the time for US to start anew". Elizabeth was determined to resurrect something from her son's return.

"John would you please start the fire in the cook stove, I'm baking Dutch apple pies, maybe Alanson won't be here to enjoy them but I know who will."

Sad, broken hearted but Baker gritty they determined life henceforth was to be lived in full.

David and Jason received the most surprising of Christmas Guests bearing pans of Dutch Apple pie along with an appeal for forgiveness.

The 1rst Universalist Church of Cambria County became the church home of John and Elizabeth Baker for their remaining years. Their belated enlightenment couldn't bring Alanson back home but it did plant a seed that for years produced with abundance.

The Bakers financed and personally did most the work remodeling the church R. E. room which was aptly renamed the A. Baker R.E. room!

The one time austere and judgmental Bakers were remembered by their many friends as caring 'fun loving' individuals long after their passing.

The unusual inscription upon their grave stone reads "eternally indebted to our beloved son".

Alanson remained in Philadelphia throughout the winter working for several of Jonas's former associates in various accounting and procuring positions.

There were reasons for his staying in Pennsylvania other then shedding his lingering hostility towards his parents before retuning west. The slave issue was bubbling over and conditions along the Kansas\ Missouri border were deteriorating rapidly. Mary needed a safe haven until things settled down.

Jonas had introduced him to reputable persons who would gladly be host to a young lady such as Mary, even-more-so when informed of her remarkable business abilities.

Alanson made arrangements for Mary to work as purchaser for the same syndicate of Quaker ship repairers he now worked for. He also procured boarding for her with a family Jonas had recommended, her stay would terminate only when hostilities subsided.

Alanson bid his friend, the skipper of the Yellowstone, farewell as he walked down the gang plank at the Port of St. Joseph Missouri in May of '57'. He immediately caught the cross-river ferry to Ellwood, Kansas.

As he walked up the farmstead lane Mary spotted him.

Alanson was greeted by a vibrant enthusiastic beautiful (in his eyes) young lady in the fullness of life. Gone were her sunken eyes and stooped shoulders, now replaced with sparkle and a marked posture of confidence. (In truth Mary was a young lady of radiant personality, 'pleasant' appearing and endowed with sparkling intelligence).

Hugs and kisses and embraces, Alanson was once again embarrassed by all the affection. Jane stood watching the event from the front porch obviously delighted!

Jane and Mary had spent many evenings in girl talk. Jane at first was hesitant to rush the affair believing Mary was simply blinded by first love.

Mary told and retold of her dramatic rescue and fearless rescuer, then later how he had protected her. How she had tried to repay her hero the only way a girl with nothing to offer could but instead Alanson had placed her on a pedestal, like a fairytale princes. He wanted her to have some childhood 'fun' and get education and meet interesting people. He thought about 'her' welfare and her life, nobody before had even ever considered what she needed. She could spend her entire lifetime looking for the right man when she 'knew' she'd never find one who'd measure up to the one who'd found her. Yes he was twice her age, they had better not waste any more time. She was going to marry Alanson, both he and Jane had better get used to it!

Jane didn't need much convincing since she thought Alanson, though obviously awkward with the opposite sex, was a great catch. Jane explained Alanson's childhood to Mary as best she could. The scars inflicted by parents and parson would most likely remain throughout his life.

Nevertheless Jane soon was not only thick in the plot to hog tie Alanson but busily co-planning the assault. Instinctively as a woman she understood what was in Alanson's best interest.

If not for the unset of calamity the plot no-doubt would have come to fruition on schedule but calamities seldom proceed on man's schedule.

Scrimmages between pro-slave and freedom forces escalated daily. John Brown was now in Kansas Hell bent for blood retribution while the Missouri Militia was equally intent on extraditing the Yankee interloper and his entire ilk…Being on the border Ellwood Kansas was becoming a tinder box. With Samuel deeply involved in the Underground Railroad Alanson couldn't rest until Mary was removed from 'harms way'.

Amidst determined but futile argument Mary was 'sent' east for the duration of conflict. Devastated by turn of events Mary was not in the least disappointed in Alanson (in fact she openly adored him); once again her welfare was his priority. Even-so Mary 'wouldn't' leave until securing a solemn oath from Jane that Alanson would be constantly inundated with subtle reminders of her.

When boarding the paddle wheel for St. Louis, where various other modes of transportation would then take her east, Mary 'left' Alanson with a remembrance. Standing on the loading platform Alanson was reciprocate of a passionate farewell kiss, not an embarrassed peck of a girl but an unmistakable kiss of mature commitment.

Jane's subtle reminders were instantly and forever rendered no more than inadequate redundancy!

Alanson baked Jane the promised Dutch Apple pie, telling her all about the Rev. Satterday and his new partner as they sat and enjoyed his mother's family recipe.

Jane was ecstatic about, although hardly able to imagine, David's involvement in Universalism! She and Samuel had agreed that if they were ever where a Quaker community didn't exist Universalism certainly would suffice quite well since both seemed solidly based upon their understanding of 'Christian' principles.

Unable to alleviate empty nest syndrome in the same house that Mary had just vacated Alanson soon embarked on a north bound river boat with Sioux City his destination.

Soon after entering the land office Alanson learned he had on the first of May 1857 become a property owner in Plymouth county Iowa!

With new title in hand he and Explorer made an inspection of their new premises. It was an excursion of pleasure with of no financial reward on the foreseeable horizon. With no railroad or settlements, opportunity for development still was a thing of the future.

While riding along the most western bend of the river (an area later called Riversioux Park) Alanson noticed a familiar band of Indians camped on the Dakota side of the river. They seemed to be making sport of a white woman who apparently was being held prisoner until they saw Explorer, whom they immediately recognized. Luckily once again the Big Sioux was running high from spring rains! Inkpaduta raised his fist in defiant gesture appearing (if possible) more hostile then ever. With the river high and Explorer underneath Alanson knew Inka held no chance of overtaking him so smiling he returned a middle finger salute. He was confident remembering his Christmas ride through western Pennsylvania…It wasn't until returning to Bruguiers that he became aware of the recent Spirit Lake Massacre. He shivered remembering his childish display of ignorance

Dakota City dock and warehouse was in need of a clerk as their former employee (an ephemeral minister) had recently fled in disgrace.

Alanson, in need of employment, engaged himself in the warehouse business waiting for the inevitable. The war had been raging on the western front for some time but it would never be settled until it engulfed the entire nation. He must keep busy while he pined for the end of what still hadn't officially begun; he desperately hoped Mary would be still be waiting 'after' the CIVIL WAR!

THE BUNDLE

On the snow swept short grass prairie
Of the Dakota's last resort
In a cold tarpaper cabin
For Mrs.' Elk Head, time grew short.
Her lips were dry and matted
She could neither eat nor speak,
Couldn't rise to stoke the fire
Her legs were now so weak.

How many years had passed
(Could it be so long)
Since the drummers and the dancers
had produced a joyous song.
The shaman are all dead now
Their knowledge lost, their culture shattered.
The sacred objects mostly stolen
What remained ignored and scattered.

In a corner of the cabin,
Leather wrapped and neatly tied,
Lay the most precious of the sacred
Of what had now been cast aside.
The last request of her dear brother
Was to protect this as her life
That no-one cared or noticed
Cut more deep then any knife.

On a blanket on the floor
In the center of the gloom
She was praying in the old way,
"guide a seeker to this room".
Though her voice had long been silent
As though her mouth was gagged and bound

Lamedeer heard her urgent message
As clear as any sound.

A hundred miles he came walking
For two long days and a weary night.
Guided through the blinding snow storm
By her prayers now flickering light.

Came directly to that room,
Through the door without a pause,
Wet her lips and built a fire
had no need to state the cause.

The next day when he returned
His eyes beheld a wondrous sight.
The old woman who had been dieing
Was now vibrant, poised and bright.

Took him to the precious bundle
Sat him down upon the floor
Showed him how it should be opened,
Explained all the pertinent lore.

Patiently she showed him
What to do, which way to face
The atmosphere of the cabin
Was infused with awe and grace.

The young and vital Lamedeer
rapt in reverence of the hour
Held the baby buffalo bone pipe
said the prayers and felt the power.

That spring and many after
midst the poverty and blight

The old woman was seen walking
her back erect, head held upright.

For of-course she was the keeper
(one of the last of that rare type)
for of-course she was the keeper
keeper of the pipe.

—By David Alanson Bringman

CHAPTER 22

▼

Like a young boy anticipating but dreading a new school year Alanson waited. In the halls of congress enraged congressmen grew tired of debate and caned each other into submission. The western Border States practiced democracy off destruction, both tallied votes with spilt blood.

The 'war' simply wouldn't start.

Mary sent a letter once a week, each night an entry was made until the document became a lengthy epistle at which time it would be posted. She was physically and monetarily doing 'quite' well but she longed to be with Alanson.

After work Mary was being tutored in the arts and in return she tutored math.

School for girls was difficult to obtain and advanced schooling was as of yet a dream. Elite educators in the Philly area held school three nights a week for 'special' students of notable talent. Being female and a business\mathematical genius Mary qualified for the evening classes.

Within months new text in calculus, physics and advanced mathematics were ordered for the new prodigal mathematician. When her questions surpassed her tutor's understanding Mary became instructor through default.

On the school off nights Mary attended forums discussing the issues of the times. Dorthea Dix lectured on mental health reform one week while the next week Ralph Waldo Emerson would take the audience on a transcendental journey. James Russell Lowell, William Lloyd Garrison and Frederick Douglas passionately cried for abolition. Horace Greeley espoused the values of labor unions and co-ops while Adam Bailou condemned the entire capitalist enterprise!

Dearest Alanson:

"I am blessed to be living in a time when many persons of liberal thought are conjoined in honest debate. Every day my mind is challenged with new thoughts from great persons! Today Clara Barton asked 'me' to assist in procuring funding and administering financial arrangements for her 'Red Cross". My bosom literally burst with self admiration, then think I of my indebtedness to your gracious care and I am humbled. Nothing can be 'right' until once again I hold you. I 'pray' constantly for this war's end and your continued safety. Every night while drifting into sleep I clasp the cross containing your life sustaining note firmly to my bosom.

With fondest memories and undying love

Always yours Mary   Oct. 4, 1862

This along with 6 conveyances of similar content arrived in a single envelope at Dakota City on the 18th of October.

Alanson left the following day for Omaha. Finally he was going to war! He and the several other local Nebraska male residents had waited and waited for a 'Nebraska' unit to be formed in their area. Their wait now ended.

Alanson and the Sears boys signed papers of enlistment on October, 23, 1862 in Omaha Nebraska—well almost anyway. Walt was rejected for reasons of commerce; the fathers of Sioux City had signed and delivered a petition stating the ferry must be operated!

After a short period of basic training Private 1rst class Alanson Baker 2cnd regiment, 1rst Nebraska Calvary of the Union Army reported to Fort Kearney, Neb. for service to his country astride his great horse Explorer.

The posts mission was to protect emigrants along with stage and telegraph lines from insurgent Indians. The west no longer was afforded protection by the scarce frontier federal army. Volunteer units were being pressed to protect the settlements yet alone scattered homesteaders.

Northern Nebraska and the entire northwestern Iowa area was slowly but grudgingly being seeded by default back to Indain control.

Alanson was pained with his assignment. He had no quarrel with the Indain inhabiting what little he still possessed, his passion targeted the Confederacy. Still the detail was certainly hazardous and he supposed it did free others to do something 'worthwhile'.

Until June the 23rd action had been limited to routine placement of troops for the sake of visibility. Hopefully the mere presence of Calvary would detour hostile aggression.

The Pawnee band lived a subdued life of capitulation on the Pawnee agency. Their price for commodities was mandatory service to the military when called upon. Since the outbreak of The Civil War the Pawnee had become surrogate militia through out the upper plains.

This practice caused derision around the 'still' hostile Sioux camp fires.

Captain Henry L. Edwards was commandant of the agency on June, 23rd when approximately fifty Brule 'Sioux' attacked at dawn wounding Captain Edwards and killing several Pawnee.

1rst Lieutenant Henry Gray led thirty five Calvary (Alanson made thirty six) and three hundred fifty Pawnee in pursuit. For fifteen miles the Brule warriors remained just out of harms way as they led the pursuing troops farther into rough and forbidding terrain.

While crossing a small gorge Lieutenant Gray suddenly found himself staring up into the fearsome eyes of four hundred and fifty battle ready Sioux warriors. Immediately Sgt Joseph Dyson became a war statistic with Pvt. George Osborn receiving a mortal wound soon after. When several Calvary horses were destroyed the Pawnee fled which left Lieutenant Gray and the remaining thirty four volunteers battling for survival.

For over an hour the regiment stubbornly maintained their ground until Capt. Edwards, though wounded, came to their aid with twenty more troops and a howitzer. The howitzer sadly soon had to be abandoned due to the terrain. Hostilities seized when darkness offered cover for the hapless troops to 'sneak' back to the safety of their encampment.

Alanson was frustrated and growing concerned; experienced capable officers were engaged fighting the 'real' war while the western volunteers were left with young inexperienced officers looking to make a name. This time their outfit had been relatively lucky, he knew the Sioux from past experience. Worse could be on tomorrows horizon.

Explorer didn't relish life in the Calvary either. His abilities which had been so valuable to Fletch were of little consequence in this man's army. Drill and formation may appear fine to an onlooker but he envied the Sioux ponies where individual skills remained a factor. Alanson needed him or he would've split after the first day of mundane drills in Omaha. It seemed Alanson became more and more distraught each passing day. These were serious times and Alanson was obviously loosing his edge. Explorer fretted while Alanson deteriorated.

Explorer was not doing well either; Alanson watched helplessly as his big horse withered. Alanson, having lost all faith in his superior officers constantly worried whether Explorer might become a fatality to some career driven battlefield judgment.

As each insisted on carrying the others load, they both soon suffered from battle fatigue. Dan Sears tried in vain to bring some cheer into Alanson's life but alas Alanson continued to spiral downward.

He knew the war was not going well in the east and he spent his days chasing Indians through the western plains! Someone in high places was completely insane. Left alone the red man had never been a threat but Robert E. Lee and the Confederate Army certainly were and they didn't seem ready to roll over as many had predicted. Men, good men were fighting to end the black mans slavery while he fought to impose it upon the red man.

Sleep never came easily anymore, what had seemed unquestionably the right thing to do was now clouded with doubt. Still Dan probably was right, do what your country asks of you and that is all anyone can do.

Try as he might Alanson couldn't make it feel right; he was on a foolish mission under God-awful leadership; he fretted night and day.

Finally a reprieve came in the form of orders to relocate. The second regiment was ordered to Sioux City where General Alfred Sulley was amassing a massive army of volunteers from Iowa, Nebraska and Minnesota to 'punish' Inkpaduta and his Dakota for their recent slaughter of homesteaders in west central Minnesota.

Inka's Santee Sioux having retreated to The Dakota Territory were regrouping and were rightly perceived as an imminent threat to the whole northern plains.

From the staging area in Sioux City General Sulley led his army northwesterly in search of hostile Indians. Immediately Alanson along with most the volunteers perceived Sulley as a pompous individual at best and an arrogant asshole at worst. Almost no man among the ranks retained high hopes for their upcoming mission.

Dearest Mary:

The 'war' if that is what it is to be called drags on. We now head west under the command of a General Sulley, a man of questionable character. We finally do have an objective I feel less contemptible then any other we have so far 'failed' to carry out. Dan Sears (remember the ferry) accompanies me on this venture. Somehow he manages a better humor then I.

I entered this conflict believing it a war of moral values; I now question that earlier judgment. The lowly Negro is not even warranted worthy of fighting for his own independence. Though not actually involved I understand thousands of men have died for what? The war seems to be a contest between rival moneyed interests with slavery being its moral cover, the sugar that draws us flies into their conflict. I see very little sympathy for the black man among the troops I serve with. In fact I don't believe a democratic vote would sustain the conflict 'IF' that were the issue. Mary I am so confused and TIRED. And Explorer, I shouldn't have brought him into this conflict as he looses weight every day. It saddens me to look upon my once magnificent friend...I am truly worried about the big fellow.

Many things I was sure of, I now doubt. The only thing that remains constant is my continued love for you.

I am sorry for seeming so negative when I know you are engaged in so many worthy endeavors. Please believe that this knowledge and your letters keep me sane, I read them to Explorer. He 'acts' as if he knows who sent them!

Must close for now.

Always keeping you in my thoughts

Alanson   August 20th, 1863 Sioux City Iowa

Fat Snake (Wasing Zuzeca) lay sprawled in the afternoon sun day-dreaming. He was old and his life had been mostly pleasant. Many years ago Chief Ioway had sought peace with the white-eyes and this had been good. Many of his cousins in the Sioux nations still fought the insurgency of the homesteaders in an attempt to live as in the past but instead of living a free life they had become a people engulfed in perpetual warfare. He had never known war nor great hunger, the white-eyes although not without prodding, furnished commodities in the lean years as had been agreed to so many moons ago.

There would be no need of commodities this year as the fall hunt had been very successful and the coming winter would bring no starvation to his people, the Yancton Sioux. For as long as memory the Hankpatina (also treaty Indians) and the Yancton had rendezvoused on the Dakota prairie in preparation for winter. Tomorrow would be a celebration to commemorate an extraordinary successful fall hunt. This year the celebration would be even greater than in past years as a huge army of white-eyes had been spotted making their way toward their camp at Whitestone Hill. This harbored grave consequences for his wayward cousins but for the Yancton and Hankpatina it would mean even greater celebration as undoubtedly the soldiers would join in the feast and games. Tomorrow would be a great day.

Fat Snake beckoned his granddaughter Little Rascal to his side. He loved Little Rascal more than he had known possible and so on this warm fall day with a winters supply laid in they played as grandpas and granddaughters have played for millenniums.

Little Rascal full of youthful joy frolicked with Fat Snake until she finally collapsed, instantly asleep cradled in Fat Snakes arms. Her little body twitched as she dreamed excitedly of tomorrow's festivities.

Officers competed for influence with 'the' man as a great victory with national acclaim was near at hand. The chain of command changed from day to day according to the 'Generals' daily whim. Discipline 'begrudgingly' remained intact among the Calvary Troops while the upper chain of command was becoming frayed.

On Sept. 3, 1863 near a spot called Whitestone Hill in south central North Dakota the combined volunteer forces happened upon a gathering of 4000 Indians.

The Yancton and Hankpatina bands were in their yearly fall jamboree making final preparation for winter. Both tribes had for decades been 'treaty' Indians living in peace with the whites. Neither had participated in the Minnesota rampages.

'General' Sully didn't care; his mission was to eliminate the Indian. "If they were peaceful it only made the job easier"!

There was (intentional) confusion among the officers as to a battle plan; meanwhile the tribes remained unarmed expecting a friendly visit from their longtime white comrades.

Sully dispatched The Iowa 6th Calvary to the far side of the encampment to engage in the festivities which would culminate in games of marksmanship and races with the young Indian males.

On one side of the encampment the Iowa 6th Calvary shook hands and shared buffalo meat with the young Indian braves of the tribe who anxiously anticipating the games that would surely follow…

Not so for the Nebraska 2cnd Regiment on the opposite side of the camp. With the sound of the trumpet the regiment charged into the encampment of women and children (the men of fighting age were on the other side sharing buffalo meat with the Iowa Calvary).

Fat Snake watched in horror as the Nebraska Calvary charged. He had never been a warrior but he was no coward and his people were being slaughtered. Quickly he retrieved his hunting bow and yelled for the other elderly males to do likewise.

In the middle of the Yancton encampment several dozen determined elderly braves prepared to make a stand. A line was hastily formed as mothers and children were instructed to squat behind the line of 'warriors' until the soldiers arrived, then make a desperate break for the tall grasses during the confusion of conflict.

Alanson had no intention of inflicting injury, in fact he was irate BUT he was a soldier and he would 'act' as one.

Alanson and Dan hurriedly pushed through the village yelling and waving bayonets in a ferocious display of aggressiveness while never firing a shot or lowering their sabers. Not slowing to participate in the slaughter they were the first of the Calvary to approach Fat Snakes line of defenders. Already sickened by the ensuing action he soon would become horrified.

After a final glance back at their grandchildren the old men made a death charge directly at Dan and Alanson. Alanson could see terror and determination in the old man's eyes as he determinedly pulled the bowstring taught.

Suddenly time lost dimension and the ongoing din was stilled as if God had clamped his hands snuggly around his ears. In a detached semi-frozen or under-water state Alanson watched as Little Rascal cried and frantically struggled to join her grandfather in battle.

Alanson's mind was not present nor could it be. Sane people do not kill old men and children. He 'was' aware that these were 'people' and that the little girl loved her grandfather and now her grandfather was preparing to die so she might live.

Thoughts of past and future flew through his mind in micro seconds. For Alanson this instant rearranged his life's ambitions. He never again would trust his voice to the arena of public discourse. 'He' was party to something he could never pretend justifiable! He entered this war believing he was part of a noble cause, he had been so wrong. If only he would have emulated Jonas Maynard, he WAS doing something noble. He had been harboring growing doubts but realization now broke his will! These and many other thoughts raced ran through his mind in those micro seconds.

He watched as the little girl freed herself from her mothers grasp and ran toward her grandfather. In the confusion he momentarily forgot the immanent threat at hand but Explorer ever watchful for his partner rose on hind legs to receive Fat Snakes arrow full in his chest. Alanson by instinct fired point blank at the old warrior, instantly exploding his skull. He heard the shriek of a little girl and watched in shock as the terrified child splattered with her grandfathers blood dashed toward the tall grasses.

Never, even in the blackest days in Pennsylvania had he felt so low. He was going to have to put his friend Explorer down! His great horse lay mortally wounded and now suffered in atrocious agony.

Explorer though struggling to remain conscious was cogent of the situation. He hopelessly strained to raise his neck as he looked to Alanson for forgiveness, his brown eyes pleading. He knew his life was spent and he had let his human down…Alanson had lost his edge and he would not be there to watch over him.

You have been what I strive to be big fellow, always a worthy friend. Nearly blinded with tears Alanson placed the 'Colt' next to Explorer's temple, closed his eyes and squeezed the trigger. The sound deafened him and for a second he was numb, when realization finally emerged all semblance of sanity vacated. Alanson cursed his God, his country and then himself before emptying his revolver in a blind frenzy, with the revolver empty he fell upon Explorer weeping uncontrollably.

Fortunately 'big' Dan Sears was there to restrain the distraught Cavalryman. Alanson could not block out the images of dead and dieing women and children, the old mans terrified yet resolute eyes, the little girl screaming in a horror beyond imagination and…. Explorer. He was overwhelmed with a primeval hate that demanded release.

The company medic placed a frantic Alanson on a medication commonly used to calm soldiers suffering battle fatigue.

Alanson being confined to sick bay was spared the final episode of atrocity. For 2 days the 2cnd regiment was detailed to gather the Indian belongings including five hundred thousand pounds of buffalo meat (the entire winter supply) along with all teepees, buffalo skins, utensils hatchets and every belonging available for a great victory bomb fire.

More then three hundred unarmed Indians were slaughtered before the execution was brought to a halt by gunfire from the disbelieving Iowa Calvary. In the process several Nebraska Volunteers were wounded by 'friendly' fire from their neighboring state to the north. Some historians claim the Whitestone Hill Massacre to be the largest mass execution in United States History.

The 2cnd Regiment of the Nebraska 1rst Calvary was mustered out December 23rd 1863 in Omaha Nebraska, a disillusioned and broken brotherhood.

Neither Yancton nor Hunkpatina Sioux would ever again inhabit the Dakota plains as free peoples. Many long time allies died of starvation and exposure the following winter. The surviving tribal members would for generations live in despair—perpetually imprisoned by mistrust.

General Sulley proudly and justifiably proclaimed these tribes never again would be perceived as a threat to the white settler. Neither the elite general nor the elite bounty hunter gains renown through a sense of fair play. Honor and the killing profession are not now nor never have been kin.

The dichotomy remains; General Sully as a military tactician remains a genius while in the eyes of a humanitarian a reprobate. To the blind eye of history he appears as both!

CHAPTER 23

▼

April 9, 1865—the war was finally over! Lee's surrender at Appomattox for practical purposes ended hostilities and reconstruction began. Alanson and the nation desperately needed healing and fortunately he and his fellow Nebraska volunteers had been afforded an eighteen month head start.

After receiving Alanson's depressing letters Mary pleaded to come 'home'. Obviously suffering from battle fatigue he needed her care but Alanson steadfastly refused her request insisting time and 'occupation' would suffice.

When mustered out Alanson and Dan Sears returned to Dakota City. Dan rejoined Walt in the ferry business while Alanson was welcomed back to The Dakota City Dock and Warehouse.

Dan smoothly rejoined society while on the-other-hand Alanson struggled. Disillusionment weighed heavily upon a man who for forty years had believed destiny illuminated his pathway. The war had forever erased this illusion.

Tallying expenses and receipts soon grew into an insurmountable task. Figures no longer could compete with the images of terrified squaws clutching their babies while squatting behind a determined line of primitively armed old men. When the rest of the Nebraska regiment arrived upon the battle scene nearly every Indain present instantly died in a deadly hail of rifle fire! He wasn't sure whether the little girl had escaped or not. Sleep when it rarely came offered no rest.

With the continued torture of unending migraines Alanson reluctantly resigned from his clerking duties at The Dakota City Dock and Warehouse.

He needed rest. The farm home of Samuel and Jane had always offered respite in the past. In desperation Alanson booked passage on a riverboat bound for St. Joseph, by-now a very sick man.

Alanson noticed recent war devastation on both sides of the river but more so in Kansas as the riverboat neared St. Joseph.

Smoke arose from, it appeared, the Ellwood area as the cross river ferry slowly chugged towards the Kansas shoreline.

He hadn't believed emotion still resided within but as thoughts of Jane and her two children resurfaced his heart pounded and his migraine imploded, nearly rendering him blind.

He had to get off the boat and he had to get off now, vomiting as he ran Alanson raced down the ramp even before it bumped the dock. Jumping from ramp to dock Alanson hurried toward the farmstead, only pausing momentarily as he continued to vomit.

The house was destroyed but still smoldering. He searched through the rubble, though he wasn't sure for what. The barn!

His head was exploding and the dry heaves wouldn't subside but he had to find Jane!

He ran to the barn where the door hung open, freely swinging in the Kansas breeze.

Horror! Samuel lay face down in a coagulating pool of blood—Alanson rushed to him but when rolled over it was obvious he was dead.

Unconsciously Alanson wiped the thickening glue like blood on his trouser legs, already soaked with regurgitations.

Where were the children and where was Jane?

He heard a faint whimper coming from the loft, a child's whimper.

Alanson assisted by adrenaline scurried up the loft ladder and peered over the ledge. The sight bludgeoned him backwards off the ladder, consciousness vacated upon impact.

He awoke crying uncontrollably God NO NO; please God no no no 'in descending and weakening decibels'.

He attempted to rise but found his strength insufficient for the task. For some time he sat sobbing while holding his head in his hands until once again the realization of 'what' had transpired again became cogent.

Sobbing Alanson struggled up the ladder into the loft once more; the child's whimpering had by now subsided.

Both children were now dead, frenzied terror etched into their still cooling corpses. Jane, poor wonderful, fun-loving, forgiving Jane had suffered the worst,

Oh-God, it appeared she had been brutally raped in the presence of her children and then all three had been savagely hacked to death.

Overwhelmed by nausea and weakened by continued vomiting Alanson again lost consciousness. It was dark when he finally re-awoke.

He struggled through the remaining darkness and into daylight preparing a common grave in which to bury the family.

These loving people who from violence had abstained, how and why?

When finished with the task Alanson dropped his spade and ran (his senses had already fled, his physical body now simply followed).

Several days later hungry and tattered Alanson found himself sitting on the St. Joseph dock as the Yellowstone (captained by his old friend) tied to.

Whip thin with drawn taught skin and facial lines accurately portraying a man emptied of purpose Alanson enlisted his services on the Riverboat Yellowstone. He searched for purpose while inviting death.

Dearest Mary:

There is no way I can easily explain what I now feel compelled to do. For your welfare I must insist you pursue a life apart from my own. You have been and will remain my only 'true' family. I once thought me too old for you to consider as matrimonial material, recent experience renders age irrelevant. People live life with no guarantees, leaving one obligated to partake of life in abundance. I now have nothing positive but many negatives to offer you. Though it pains me dearly I must inform you no more correspondence will be forthcoming.

Continue expanding the life you now posses; meet it with your usual gusto. I beg of you do not feel I have abandoned you for this I could never willingly do. Abandonment is no option for one who life has already abandoned. It is with the deepest of concern that I refuse to pull you into this downward spiral which now possess me.

My will along with a few other documents are in safe keeping at George Weale's Bank in Sioux City. After 10 years any existing assets revert to you, you are also listed as my beneficiary.

Eternally grateful

Alanson   May 29th, 1866

For several years Alanson worked the river trade, steadily amassing wealth while immersing himself in the physical aspects of boat life. The physical body quickly responded to his 'therapy', muscles once again rippled and labor derived fatigue induced sleep.

Meanwhile the mind searched for reason but its where about remained illusive.

Books rescued Alanson! Initially hours were spent reading the Bible which seemingly always was available. Though the reasoning eluded him, tales of lost souls searching for 'something' while wandering through a wasteland initiated the healing process.

Gradually he amassed a small library containing contemporary and classical writings. It was the Greek philosophers who finally grasped the weighted sponge of his consciousness, squeezing self into acquiescence. With the concept of 'all' replacing the self indulging concept of singular his heinous war involvement eventually lost its intensity.

Man reacts to circumstances as best man can, as do societies and nations. Both terrible events and wonderful achievements occur from these reactions with only God and History being enabled to differentiate between the two.

Theology initially offered comfort, while reason eventually restored sanity, combined the processes required seven years of the veteran's life.

With sanity returning Alanson longed for Mary's company but he dared not initiate correspondence. Mary by now would most certainly have reestablished a life of her own; he cared too deeply to intervene.

Mary was frantic when she received Alanson's letter. Life without Alanson seemed unthinkable!

She read and reread the letter and then read again his previous letters. Without variance her interest constantly remained Alanson's primary concern, better she should die in waiting then abandon unquestionable love. No matter the time required she would wait!

Neither did she take lightly his advice; Mary renewed her commitment to academia and vocation. She determined to live an even more frugal life; scrupulously saving and investing for the future she still fervently believed would be theirs.

Mary continued to sleep with her cross pressed tightly to her bosom.

May of "76" an unexpected but welcome visitor knocked on the door at Mary's place of business.

"Mary, I expected you and Alanson would be in Iowa with a small family" then Jonas paused believing possibly Alanson a war casualty.

"The war left Alanson with life but without soul Jonas, he is I pray at this moment somewhere searching to reclaim meaning. I know I belong at his side if only I knew where". Mary broke into tears.

Jonas embraced his old friend's true love and then noticing the cross hanging from her neck asked. "Mary, do you still carry Alanson's note in your cross"?

Mary reached for the cross and carefully opened the 'secret' container. "I am embarrassed by my foolishness Jonas, all this time the answer hung around my neck"!

CONTACT A. BAKER % THE RIVERSIOUX AT ANY PORT ON THE MISSOURI IF EVER YOU NEED HELP

"I will be on my way to Sioux City myself as soon as I wrap up a few details here. I certainly would welcome you as another female companion".

Mary hugged Jonas as if he were Alanson; until Jonas gently reminded her he wasn't Alanson.

Jonas had recently been appointed Federal Judge of Iowa's western judicial district. He would be accompanied west by his new bride Barbara, who had patiently waited these many years.

U.S. Grant was nearing the end of his second term as president. His administration rocked with scandal left Grant desperately searching for some means to resurrect his place in history. "I am not plagued by lack of ethics but rather I am plagued by lack of judgment in appointments" U.S. GRANT

Jonas having amassed an impeccable resume also possessed NO previous ties to the president. Having appointed old friends and army subordinates to high positions now Grant suffered from the predictable consequences, Jonas as judge would offer positive testimony to an otherwise inauspicious administration.

The Bruguier Inn brought back fond memories, and great news! Alanson was presently aboard the Yellowstone and if operating on schedule should be returning most any day.

Mary secured a room for an indefinite stay while Jonas and Barbara departed for Ft. Dodge, site of the federal district courthouse.

Mr. Bruguier clearly remembered Alanson sleeping in the hall 'fatherly' protecting young Mary. It was an occasion worth notice since Alanson was not a 'lady's' man, in fact with matters concerning the opposite sex he was quite restrained. The event still often came up in their conversations. Mr. Bruguier and Alanson by-now had a long established relationship which now benefited Mary. Mary was treated with unusual dignity.

June 10th, 1876 Alanson walked down the Yellowstone gangplank into the waiting arms of Mary George. Pretense was not present; their love which had endured war and matured through grievous circumstance was beyond childhood pettiness.

June 15th the two exchanged wedding vows in the newly rebuilt (the former building having burned) Dakota City Methodist Episcopal Church. Only the Maynards, who made the one hundred and twenty mile trip and a few friends (including the Sears boys), were in attendance.

The couple spent their honeymoon night at Bruguiers Inn sharing their joy with his best man Jonas and Mary's attendant Barbara Maynard.

Jonas once again managed to beat Alanson in a very close, hotly contested game of horse shoe. Alanson had pitched his best game in front of his new bride but 'luck' still favored Jonas!

The Maynards returned to Ft. Dodge while the newly weds returned to Dakota City where they were guests in the Sears home as together they drew up blue prints for their home on the 'Big Sioux'. Money was no issue; both eagerly brought many years accumulated wealth into the 'partnership'.

The railroad had finally become reality. The Chicago\Milwaukee and St. Paul purchased the defunct Iowa Falls\ Sioux City property and 'built' a railroad. The village of Portlandville was now adjacent to the Baker property on the northeast. The railroad bordered the entire eastern extremity while a sparkling creek ran from east to west serving as a northern border. The Big Sioux River served as the western property line.

The Bakers built their home in the northeastern corner of their property approximately a quarter mile west of the R.R. tracks and opened for business in the fall of '76'.

Alanson received a quarter section of adjoining property as a veteran's bonus for Civil War service. The original property was located in Westfield Township while the recent addition lay just within Portland Township. The couple began operations with three hundred and twenty acres free and clear.

With resources saved from past enterprises men were hired and machinery was purchased. Alanson was in a hurry, he was no longer a young man and much remained to be accomplished. The first few years were spent in the back breaking proposition of turning sod of ancient origin; as soon as the soil was properly mellowed crops were planted.

As had been expected the virgin bottom land produced prodigiously. More land was rented and more men were hired. With the crop land in full production livestock became of interest, if one grew crops for livestock feed shouldn't one also raise and feed his own livestock? Alanson thought yes and soon hog pens and cattle yards became prodigious testaments to the fledgling enterprise.

Soon eggs from laying hens and milk from dairy cows guaranteed a regular and reliable source of revenue. These enterprises also kept men employed year round, a unique fringe-benefit for the times. With year round employment Alanson attracted and maintained the cream of the local labor pool. MANY OF THESE INOVATIONS WERE PRODUCT OF MARY'S VOLITION.

The area was growing and the need for sand, rock, and gravel grew in equal proportion. The Baker property laying adjacent to the river had vast reserves of sand, rock, and gravel; a railroad siding was laid and soon The Baker Pit shipped gravel for roads and sand for concrete to Akron, Sioux City and the entire 'Siouxland' area.

Mary and Alanson still harboring memories of trying times reveled as their dream evolved into reality. They naturally prospered, Mary (Alanson to a somewhat lesser degree) was born with natural business instincts and though business was a shared endeavor it certainly was not their life's purpose.

The Bakers were an educated people with a vastness of experience between them. While gossip and talk of mundane life experiences may be the norm, around the Baker dinner table conversation was an experience in enlightenment.

Discussions erupted spontaneously and at times evolved into episodes continuing for days. Any and every subject at one time graced 'dinner' conversation. Two stubborn individuals, with considerable experience and learning, regularly engaged in monumental verbal jousting matches. Unless the discussion pertained to the families well being it usually ended with "Alanson most likely you are correct", Mary's respect for 'her' Alanson never waned. Alanson understanding this inherent advantage struggled mightily not to abuse his privileged position. Mary, Alanson and later on the children always looked forward to times around the 'table'.

Meanwhile Alanson still struggled to overcome the lifelong affliction suppressing his ability to be 'naturally' outgoing. He read profusely on the subject but the answers were not stamped in concrete, instead it seemed everyone had an opinion and many opinions were in contradiction.

Mary believed the root of this phobia was buried along with his childhood memories; together they dug deep into his past where roots long buried and forgotten were once again exposed. Several unsavory suspects were apprehended and thoroughly grilled but alas the 'main' culprit remained at large.

It seemed strange that Mary, with all she had endured, suffered no similar emotional effects. Heredity, gender, or factors yet unknown may have been the reason who knows; in any-case theirs was a love that transcended wrinkles. Alanson's affliction was Mary's affliction and visa-versa. If one was weakened the other simply pulled harder, together as partners they lived, dreamed, and matured.

Hardship, happiness, babies, business triumphs and down turns all visited the Baker household. Some issues were dealt with in a unique and admiral fashion while others presented real log jams, little different than average 'except' blame was never an issue. When life itself has been the opponent and the opponent has thrown its best punch and fought its greatest round the survivor reveling in mere existence offers no excuses and appoints no blame. Mary and Alanson both survivors understood winning or loosing for the most part is merely an apparition of the mind.

Life finds its own path regardless of plan or individual, leaving participants no option but to adjust. Mary regularly entertained (never having lost her southern graciousness) and attended civic and social functions while Alanson remained content dealing with business associates. Still at times loneliness (present whether invited or not) forced him to town for coffee with the locals, it seemed no matter how divergent his and his peers goals and desires were he 'needed' their company. Alanson loved his fellow man but the message could not be communicated, over time a toll is extracted.

They worked it out as best they could; social events came under Mary's auspices. With Mary as a buffer Alanson attended the necessary events and as for Mary a time never existed when she wasn't proud of Alanson.

Coffee in town and the few shared community functions sated Alanson's appetite for social interaction between their visits to and from the Maynards. At least twice a year, once in Akron and once in Fort Dodge, the old friends got together and at least twice a year Alanson got thumped in a game of horseshoe. Damn that Maynard remained lucky!

As the farm business prospered Alanson found pastimes. FISHING, the sand pit was stocked with trout and bass and blue gills and fishing as many have found out (good fishing) can become a passion. Corn, wheat, oats, and soot from the fire place…you name it Alanson fed it to the 'pit' fish. At first new fangled spin reels were purchased and then after a successful cast of spindly line on a flimsy pole FLY FISHING ruled! Catching a single Carp in the Sioux River on a fly rod could make a week of rainy weather suddenly seem insignificant.

Work of-course was still attended to BUT fishing was always on the mind. Hurry to feed the fish, take a mental count of species and numbers in the feeding frenzy, then get the pole and attempt to reduce the count number.

Alanson was content, with a loving…even doting wife. Socially things— were—what—they—were. The business enterprises had prospered beyond either of their expectations, and they made their home near the river. Water, running water, was a common life sustaining thread for Alanson. It seemed all his life the river had inexplicably helped fill a void. For Alanson the river provided the only evidence of life's continuity, the river remained real and constant where family had been shallow and illusive. For Alanson Mother\father River was more than a cliché of ancient origin.

Baker House
1900

In the fall of "81" Alanson attended an auction in Elk Point, South Dakota supposedly with intentions of seeking 'quality' milk cows but actually it was a nostalgic repast more than a business event; it was an opportunity to sit upon the banks of the 'Mighty' Missouri where occasionally a riverboat would be seen.

Animals of every stripe were herded into the ring where soon they soon left with new owners. Alanson had arrived late and sheep, cattle, hogs and mules already filled the auction barn's adjacent roads where they were in the process of being driven to their new premises. As he entered the auction barn the horses already sorted according to use (work or saddle back) were now entering the ring.

Midway through the procedure a lone horse that had no clear category was being prodded into the arena, being large and strong enough for the plow but also possessing the physical attributes of a saddle horse.

Alanson's heart raced as "Explorer" defiantly stood in center ring blowing strings of mucus while challenging man or beast to close within striking distance.

While moored at Bruguiers on the Riversioux's final journey one of Joneses parting chores was to unload livestock no longer needed. Jonas not being or wishing to be a livestock trader sold the Belgian mares to a Mr. Callander who was.

As Callander had expected each mare later birthed a colt. Mr. Callander resold the mares and their colts except for one which he kept for stud purposes. For several years colts of good pedigree resulted from this decision.

In the spring of '79' the final foal from the Callander\Explorer line was born. Try as he may he could not break this outlaw colt. Local cowboys were approached to ply their trade and each had their go at young Explorer but he simply wasn't intended to be a domestic.

Callander, now willing to bite the bullet, brought the animal to the Elk Point auction hoping for a gullible bidder who would rid him of a problem. The Explorer transaction in totality had already been quite profitable.

"Fifty dollars who will give me a fifty dollar bill for this magnificent animal" was the auctioneers call.

Alanson's hand went up involuntarily, not having even heard the opening bid figure. Most auctioneers start the bidding on the high side hoping for a novice bidder, usually when no bid is forthcoming the bid is dropped to a continually lower figure until bidding resumes.

Alanson owned the beast for the outlandish high price of fifty dollars.

With the help of several auction ring 'would be' cowboys the brute was subdued and tethered to the rear of Alanson's buggy.

The trip back was memorable. Young Explorer, though hobbled, managed to nearly rip the carriage from its frame. While the physical strain on the buggy's team was telling the emotional strain upon Alanson was brutal. He felt compelled to communicate with Explorer's offspring but as he looked to the horse with love hate was its reflection.

Mary was in town with the babies when at last he arrived home. Alanson, always a man of reasoned caution, now responded to a remembered love. 'Explorer' bled profusely from the hobbles restraining his desire for freedom. Alanson remembering Explorer's desire for freedom and the resulting bond forged when freedom was granted temporarily was rendered insane.

Any man can look back at certain past actions with puzzled amazement, as later Alanson surely would. Driven by a past love Alanson loosened the hobbles of a horse presently inflamed with rage.

Mary returned amidst mayhem. Alanson's carriage was literally pulled apart with the rear portion of the frame being flung around the corral by a crazed 'familiar' horse of large proportion. The buggy team, still hitched to the front axel was frantically trying to elude the rear axel attached to young Explorer; meanwhile Alanson laid unconscious half way under the corral fence in peril of being trampled by horses or bludgeoned by buggy parts.

Mary frantically ran for the house, cradling her babies in her arms, and returned with Alanson's Colt Revolver. She fired at the crazed horse as he raced past and then fired and fired again. Young Explorer lacking his sire's temperament did possess his will, refused defeat. The crazed animal now snorting misty clouds of blood from his nostrils raced toward Alanson determined to extract retribution.

Mary, who Alanson had schooled in firearms, knew she had but one shot remaining as she placed herself between the charging animal and her husband. Leveling Mary squeezed off the final round from the pistol sending a spiraling projectile into the frontal lobe of the charging horse. Young Explorer caved, rolling uncontrollably toward Mary and of-course Alanson.

A neighbor lady making her daily visit to purchase eggs and milk found a frenzied Mary lying on top of Alanson under a huge dead horse. Neighbors were summoned and in short time Alanson (still unconscious) was carefully laid upon the parlor couch.

Mary escaped with bruises and some painful scrapes but luckily suffered no serious complications. No doctor was summoned for at the time; once again no doctor was practicing in the villages of Akron or Westfield.

Alanson apparently suffered a minor comma for he lay unconscious the next twenty six hours. Pain, physical stabbing pain awakened Alanson from his rest. He recalled reaching to cut young Explorer loose from his hobbles but from that moment on it went blank. Oh God his back ached and white hot piercing darts shot through his skull as he struggled to open his eyes. Finally after several futile attempts he forced his eyes open. "Mary, what happened to you"?

Mary and the children had been sitting or lying beside Alanson for the full twenty six hours, leaving only for food, drink or bathroom. With blackened, puffy eyes and large swollen lips Mary was not a comforting sight. "Never mind Alanson I am completely healthy and with you once more conscious my mind is at ease.

Alanson listen closely I want you to slowly lift each foot, one at a time and then slowly attempt to move your toes back and forth and then I want you to wiggle your fingers on each hand".

Mary always well read and now a wife and mother on the frontier attempted to keep abreast of medical developments. In Philadelphia she had attended many lectures, some by Americas most gifted learners and some of these lectures pertained to the medical practice. Books, newspapers and magazines of every description frequented the Baker post office cubby hole. She now drew upon her vast knowledge.

Damn it hurt and yet at the same time Alanson felt relief as he slowly lifted his right leg. Gently he let his leg fall back to the couch.

He smiled at Mary and she repaid his efforts with a gentle kiss upon his forehead. It was so comforting to have Mary at his side, he was strong and usually equal to most any tasks but with a wife like Mary who wouldn't be?

Okay, with regained confidence it was time for the left leg. He slowly lifted and then all the sudden LORD JESUS, the pain was unbearable. Spasms in his lower back cramped and then twisted into a knot that seemed on the brink of exploding! Sweat beaded, then poured from his entire body as the spasm some how continued to intensify.

Then suddenly just like that the spasm was gone. Thank God it was gone; he couldn't stand anymore pain like this…. Embarrassed at not being able to mask the pain he attempted to raise him self and assure Mary things were alright.

Mary had read about the unpredictable and possibly crippling effects of back injury. "God please don't let this happen to my Alanson"!

A cry of excruciating pain escaped from Alanson's mouth before he was aware of its presence. His whole back writhed in ever tightening knots of bolting pain. Afraid to breathe, for even breathing escalated the now unbearable pain, he lay rigid consciously struggling not to make even the slightest of moves.

Then for no apparent reason the pain once more subsided but now fear had a grip; was he being teased or was the ordeal over. He lay desperately trying not to move while at the same time wanting to reassure Mary things were alright, nevertheless movement could not be thwarted nor the excruciating pain accompanying it.

Sweating, oh Jesus was he sweating! His cloths were soaked and now dampness was beginning to saturate the bedding.

Mary, even though the neighbors had suggested otherwise, insisted Alanson not be moved anymore than absolutely necessary. His cloths had not been removed. Now a couple of days later the manure stained garments were stiff with dried sweat and blood, becoming obnoxiously odorous.

A decision had to be made. Lying in filth is not a prerequisite for healing but on the other hand movement seemed to completely paralyze Alanson.

Several hours elapsed with Mary continually massaging Alanson's pulsating back muscles but apparently to no avail as Alanson continued to experience spasms of here before unimaginable magnitude.

Mary would watch no more suffering." Alanson, do you hear me"? Mary had come to a decision. Massage was not the answer, she must get him up!

Never had Alanson experienced such physical pain and it simply would not subside, Oh momentarily it would ease off, only to resurface once again with gathered intensity. He remembered Mary giving birth to Sarah and 'little' Alanson, her arcing back and pained blood-shot eyes. Her pain did not subside until birth was accomplished, he also had come to a decision but he needed Mary's help to implement it.

"Mary I don't know what will be the result but you must get me on my feet, no matter how loud I protest you must try to get me upright".

Mary had reached the same conclusion. This was not an unusual happening for the couple, many times under trying conditions the same answer simultaneously had come to both.

Paralyzing pain shot through the small of his back and raced down through the back of his right leg in throbbing—crippling shock waves. Of its own volition a scream erupted (which had lain evolutionary dormant since primeval times) from deep within Alanson's soul.

Though determined and well known for his grit, Alanson's legs folded uselessly as pain triumphed over will. Mary, who should have succumbed to circumstances many times in her youth didn't because she was a willful woman. With every available resource Mary 'willed' Alanson to his feet.

Now with weight being transferred to his feet the spasms slowly resided, replaced with a severe but more bearable pain.

The relief from spasm to mere pain is unexplainable but damn sure real. Alanson, leaning on Mary shuffled across the room regaining confidence with each step. The lessoned pain was wonderful, still when he reached the parlor doorway he had had enough.

Exhausted he asked for a chair. Slowly he lowered himself into a sitting position, experiencing crippling spasms as he willed himself into a sitting position.

For weeks the healing process continued with the spasms becoming continually less frequent and less severe. Still every time Alanson attempted to return to work he would without fail make a wrong twist; his back immediately would protest with acts of terrorism. Still he remained encouraged realizing every time the relapses seemed less severe.

After 'many' attempts to work and the subsequent relapses Mary finally had had enough!

"Alanson I know you always do what you think is right BUT sometimes Baker stubbornness replaces common sense and I refuse to sit and watch while you seem intent on becoming an invalid"!

Alanson was placed on a regulated schedule of walking and stretching intermingled with ample periods of rest. He outwardly pouted but inwardly was grateful for intervention; he knew his routine wasn't working. A mans pride can be lethal.

Mary 'truly' loved Alanson. By nature a female is maternal and by nature her love is possessive, though this time she saw through his pretended objections she would have had her way in any case!

Books, Mary's immense library, filled Alanson's idle time until he began to realize idle time actually was the time spent away from the library. When regaining his sanity after the war books had been instrumental, once again knowledge gleaned from the ages was to have an impact.

With his mind temporarily off business matters many lingering thoughts from the past resurfaced; the same thoughts and questions he had pondered in younger days but NOW he had access to answers and time for research. History and politics and religion, things a business man has little time for now occupied his mind.

Though not formally educated Alanson always was inquisitive and in a 'learned' world this is not always welcomed.

History and tales of the Revolution always had been troublesome, though the reasons were not clear. The ability to read and then consciously struggle to reach a reasoned comprehension of the content leaves one at odds with the commoner. The attractive seclusion of Walden Pond for Emerson and Thoreau would soon became abundantly clear.

American History texts proclaimed the revolution a war for liberty and freedom but didn't the father of this revolution own slaves…many slaves! What kind of libertarian keeps his fellow man in bondage?

The American Indain was saved from perdition and graciously civilized to European culture but nine out of ten of these joyful reciprocates were sacrificed for this enlightenment.

Carefully hidden between the lines, history mentions mistreatment of the Native American BUT the Spanish conquistador and 'the church' is castigated with special vilification; then why only in Catholic Canada and the Catholic Southwestern Areas did the native survive in any substantial numbers?

At first it seemed only America flavored its history to accommodate its pallet and then Alanson delved into world history. It soon became apparent all history is tainted by the teller.

Realization that truth does not subtract from ones heritage and then garnering the courage to accept this fact separates one from general society. Average preachers and common politicians rapidly build their platforms upon a foundation of sand, concrete takes time to cure and the public is restless. The world is saturated with common persons and woefully short of Walden ponds. Knowledge and its acceptance can leave solitude a congenial partner.

Alanson regained his health although he continued to hike with a walking stick throughout his remaining years; rough farm terrain remained an obstacle better tackled with a 'third' leg.

Mary, already possessing much of Alanson's new knowledge welcomed this new and exciting chapter in their life. Alanson had always been of liberal mind and he now possessed a reasoned basis for his idealism.

With a shared knowledge of the past they enthusiastically discussed current affairs; generally concluding with a shared opinion…still Alanson refused to enter public dialogue.

Any politic was singularly Mary's affair. Measure twice and cut once goes the adage. In the (60's) he had cut without proper measurement, he and the nation still suffered. Now he did measure and he found him self lacking. As Jonas had stated many years ago, if you make the judgment you must also do the tallying.

Jonas, Fletch, Stroker, Big Jeff…. He missed the men and honesty of the times but he knew that even nostalgia couldn't miscue the obvious "no dream of the past equaled the reality of the woman he was now married to"!

Mary was returning from shopping as these thoughts were evolving.

"Mary, let me help with the groceries" Alanson, simply a man, had ideas.

Together they packed a lunch, grabbed a blanket and each carried a baby as they trekked westward toward the Big Sioux River.

Sarah and Alanson both possibly had been conceived on the banks of the Big Sioux and Avis was presently becoming a twinkle in Mary's husband's eye.

Mary gently kissed Alanson's cheek while spreading the blanket on the ground. Even though her man was far from debonair he overflowed with substance and she loved her prince with all her heart.

As babies frolicked amongst the scent of green river grasses their aging father once again lay entranced in the arms of his only love. The valley held its breath in reverent silence as ageless notes of love echoed from her bosom.

For the following quarter century wealth accumulated. Two blocks of property in the village of Portlandville (renamed Akron) joined the tax rolls, plus the 'prominent' Baker Building on Reed (main business street) street, five hundred and twenty acres three miles south of the original homestead and the largest sand\rock and gravel pit in the area boasting its own rail road siding were also on the rolls. The family operated a well drilling business, a threshing business and leased an additional five hundred acres adjoining their southern (Westfield) holdings.

Eventually three more 'prominent' houses were added to the Akron farm estate and a large 'principle' house to the Westfield estate. (A solid half dozen smaller shacks were interspersed for hire hands) The Bakers never once accumulated debt.

Still business never 'consumed' the Baker household as their family materialized. Sarah in August of '77, Alanson Jr. in July of '80' and then Avis in '1882 became Alanson's 'grandchildren' children (Alanson was 49 at the birth of his first child).

The partnership (based upon mutual respect and 'adoration') flourished. Alanson, though he no longer relied upon destiny, regained his zest for life. Alanson remained a man of vision while Mary had no peers in the business world. Love (genuine love) overcame socially engrained gender bias and Mary became CEO; evolving a century before their contemporaries the Bakers harvested the fruits of their enlightenment. Accumulating wealth under these circumstances was no encumbrance, leaving abundant energy for social endeavors. Mary (unquestionably a genius) had married Alanson, a man secure enough for both to reap the benefits.

Alanson suffered with two social handicaps. He who had dreamed of political influence now fervently avoided involvement in politics of any social magnitude. The war had settled nothing; the Negro was still a subservient existing in a country still divided. The 'war hero' General and later President Grant sat placidly as the victorious northern financiers plundered the southland with ruthless abandon. Alanson had once argued and later killed for this unconscionable outcome.

The other handicap was a self imposed wall around his inner self that after these many years refused to crumble.

The Bakers compensated in numerous 'un-noticed' areas. A church was mandatory for community legitimacy and Akron was no exception. The significance of denomination isn't to be underestimated. The Bakers understanding more then most this significance determined the 'first' church in town would be of liberal persuasion. The northern (American) Baptist Church under the guidance of Roger Williams (founder of Rhode Island) had fervently supported separation of church and state. American Baptist had supported abolition early on and the Negro was determined to 'posses' a soul (many denominations debated this theological conundrum). The Baptist had no 'established' doctrine of equity between the sexes but neither was there a doctrine emphasizing inequity. It remained troublesome that females couldn't 'officially' occupy positions of leadership; no major denomination had yet made that leap, sanctioned or not there was never any doubt who ran the church.

Mary and Alanson were MAJOR donors to the building fund and of-course became charter members of The First Baptist Church of Akron Iowa. (They rarely attended but regularly and generously tithed)

A full city block was maintained as a public park providing picnic tables for summer festivities which was certainly enjoyed BUT winter was a time of exceptional pleasure. An ice skating rink was maintained for the city youths. Hockey teams proliferated and just 'plain' skating became an Akron municipal past time. (Upon their death the block was donated to the city for public use) On the banks of the Sioux, a river park with trees, picnic tables and benches was maintained for public use. Few locals realized these 'niceties' were privately owned and maintained.

These were a few of the things Alanson felt 'comfortable' doing. He and Mary felt a connection to 'their' community and both believed they owed their fellow man.

CHAPTER 24

▼

JUDGE MAYNARD VISITS AKRON (Akron Tribune)

In June of 1904 the Milwaukee R.R. offered means of transportation for a passenger of note to the village of Akron. The Honorable Judge Jonas Maynard (retired) would spend the night at his old friend Alanson Baker's Estate.

Mary who very seldom exhibited signs of inadequateness now did as Alanson's only remaining friend from his river days would be spending the night. The Judge must surely be nearing 90 years of age.

"It's simply Jonas Mary; don't embarrass the old man with preposterous preparations". Alanson continued pitching horse shoes hoping to finally beat old Maynard! Maybe at long last Jonas really 'was' getting old, Alanson smiled. The old codger always managed in the end to somehow just 'barely' win.

To Alanson Maynard would always remain captain, Judge sounding a little too socially restrained but to Mary Jonas was 'Judge'.

"Alanson you look better then when you stepped off the Yellowstone" Jonas said extending his hand to Alanson.

"I'm grieved you lost Barbara Jonas, I can't imagine life without my Mary" Alanson shook Jonas's hand while at the same time squeezing Mary's hand for reassurance.

"We get old Alanson; Barbara hadn't been able to really enjoy life for quite some time. For 'her' sake I suppose it was for the best".

"Mary, do Alanson and I have time to settle a pressing issue before dinner"?

"To think I actually worried about your visit judge. Yes go ahead and play your silly game of horse shoe". Mary was pleased to see Alanson actually enjoying company.

Though Alanson seemed to tolerate whatever came his way he no longer sought companionship other then family. The world had changed as he had aged.

Both contestants suffering from exertion and more then a little pain competed as if life itself hinged on the outcome. Either would have proclaimed the stakes were rather higher.

The judge insisted the farmer demonstrated Neanderthal era ethics and the farmer proclaimed the judge was corrupted with both thoroughly enjoying the contest. The game deteriorated even further as neither could remember the score from one set to the next!

"Supper" Mary yelled to the squabbling boys.

"Showed you this time huh, Maynard" Alanson snorted while entering the house.

"How do you put up with this childish old man Mary? Not only is he a totally incompetent horse shoe pitcher, the truth remains foreign to his continence".

Mary so enjoyed the judges presence, his visit temporarily restored youth to Alanson (and seemingly to Jonas). Age no longer could be denied.

After dinner Mary served the 'men' coffee in the parlor, before she made her daily jaunt into town to visit Sarah and their new granddaughter Ruth.

"Alanson we're getting old and each visit certainly could be our last. With Barbara gone little seems to peak my interest anymore. Can you imagine being alone 'all alone' in this new world"?

"I live in your world Jonas and with out Mary, well no I simply can't imagine. Since you're actually being reasonable for a change there is something I need to confess.

Remember in the cabin house of the Riversioux, seems so long ago, when you and I discussed war and the necessities of armed conflict. If only I had listened, for once YOU were right"!

"What do you mean right? If you boys hadn't forced the issue, slavery would still be a fact of life. Haven't you noticed I am now a Methodist"?

"You mean to tell me that 'now' you believe in the necessity of war? Of-course you weren't apart to innocents being slaughtered at the alter of justice"!

"No of-course I wasn't but then you didn't see hundreds of slaves scarred both physically and mentally and many thousands more risking everything for just a chance at freedom. I left the 'friends' not because I differed with their commitment to right—Good God man they willingly died for their beliefs. As you once said Alanson sometimes you must spill the other man's blood to get his attention".

"I suppose no man can rationalize another's experiences still I have concluded no man can truly understand the terror of war without personally experiencing its horror; another man's blood is just not an appropriate resume".

"And just what do you mean by that"?

"Jonas have you ever hit your thumb while driving a nail, where the thumb nail breaks loose from the entwining skin and blood oozes out the side and with every throb of your heart your thumb expands and then retreats in excruciating pain?

If you haven't stick your thumb out and let me whack it real good with a blacksmith's hammer, then tell me which leaves the more lasting impression.... Experience or hearsay?

On-the-other-hand I suppose it is just as ludicrous for me to draw conclusions without having had your experiences, what ever the Hell they might be".

Alanson was smiling but no more so then his old friend.

It was late and old men get tired.

"Jonas I shipped a load of hogs to Sioux City this morning and tomorrow I am taking the early south bound passenger train to observe the stock yards in action and of-course pickup the proceeds from my Livestock Commission Man. I've been led to believe an old timer like me will be completely overwhelmed. I might need the old skipper to lean upon; I wonder if maybe you would make the trip with me"?

Regretfully Jonas was already committed as guest speaker for a Republican fund raiser in Sioux Falls the following evening.

In the morning the two old friends shook hands for a final time, without Barbara's companionship Jonas simply slipped away.

The 'boys' parted happy, Jonas believing he had won at horse shoe once again while Alanson waved good bye believing he had finally showed the old coot a thing or two!

Jonas departed for Sioux Falls on the 6:16 am express while Alanson was scheduled for the 8:29 am Sioux City local (picked up and dropped the U.S. mail). It had rained all night canceling field work for the day so Sarah had insisted her husband Merrill accompany her aging father to Sioux City.

Alanson just didn't 'like' his new son-in-law, oh he was friendly enough and everyone else seemed to think him debonair. He came from a ne'er-do-well family and he had lived that life style quite well until he'd married Sarah! Now he always picked up the meal ticket when with his old friends, Merrill simply liked playing the big shot. Possibly he was being overly critical of the man who had married his eldest daughter but he 'doubted' it.

They boarded right on schedule. Alanson picked a west window to sit by. He wanted to observe the scenery while Merrill preferred to impress his fellow travelers with 'impressive' talk from an isle seat.

Alanson watched the farm at first slowly and then more rapidly slip by as the train accelerated. He remembered the tall wetland grass nurtured by springs that never ceased flowing. Now everything was crop, of-course today everything was mud because of the overnight rains. His head drooped; he knew he had helped perpetuate this change.

They whizzed passed the southern farm four miles south of Akron or perhaps a mile and a half north of Westfield according to whether a Westfield or an Akron resident was giving directions.

Alanson remembered stumbling across the plotted R.R. Village of Westfield nearly a half century ago. He now owned the property where the village had first been plotted; the plot had been moved (when plans for an adjoining R.R. line directly west to Vermillion fell though) to higher ground a mile and a half west.

Now Akron boasted nearly a thousand residents with Westfield claiming half that many. Farmers with 'large' families dreamed the American dream, each reaching for their rightful share of prosperity on quarter section plots. It was a population boom and small communities thrived.

As Riversioux Park came into sight tears rolled down the old man's cheeks.

Passengers looked at Alanson and then hurriedly readjusted their sight elsewhere as Alanson glanced their way. Merrill slyly shook his head and winked at fellow passengers as the old man wept.

Alanson knew he was considered an old fool by this sophisticated group of travelers, it hardly mattered as Alanson watched Riversioux Park fade away.

The mighty Dakota Chief Inkpaduta had raised his fist in defiance just across the river; Alanson smiled remembering returning middle finger salutes while firmly grasping Explorers reigns. Inka had made his mark, from Spirit Lake, to Minnesota and right on to Little Big Horn. He had certainly garnered his revenge; he hoped the old chief had come to a decent ending being so few of his contemporaries had.

Then as he thought of Explorer, tears once again replaced the smile.

Explorer had sacrificed his own life so he might live. Even mortally wounded Explorer had managed to fall gently to the ground assuring no injury to Alanson. Alanson's chest ached and a growing lump in his throat nearly strangled him as he relived the memories of relieving his greatest friend from excruciating pain.

The old Indian at Whitestone once again looked him in the eye, facing sure death in an attempt to save his granddaughter. The blood splattered little girl running in terror—she must have been about the same age as his little cricket 'Ora'. Once again the past was becoming too much he simply had to let it go.

Those days were gone forever; the horse was being replaced by the train (Merrill even had an 'automobile') and the high cost of freedom was being replaced with the comforts of 'civilization'.

The train made a short stop in Westfield where several passengers boarded; Alanson could see a couple of old Westfielders, he thought he recognized local businessmen J.B. Pope, and Harry Feltis conversing in front of Burnight's Grain Elevator which sat just west of the tracks. It certainly looked like old Pope with that bent cigarette barely hanging from his continually flapping mouth but he hadn't been to Westfield for quite some time and he just wasn't sure anymore. Since both depended upon the horse for business survival they had much to discuss. Mail was transferred and the trip was resumed.

The natural beauty of the valley which had enchanted him and Mary was now reformed in mathematical precision. Fields were mostly perpendicular, mostly squared, mostly in rows methodically spaced and always impeccably straight.

Man had coerced nature to comply with his wishes without first consulting God. Alanson looked down into the murky Sioux River as the train continued its frantic pace, crossing over the bridge connecting Iowa with South Dakota on its way to Elk Point.

He and Explorer had 'drunk' sweet water from this river of sludge not that long ago. What had happened? He had barely even noticed these monumental changes until today.

'Get hold of your self old man' Alanson castigated himself for once again believing HE alone occupied the throne of responsibility.

A short stop at Elk Point for mail exchange and a few more passengers, then off again. 'Elk Point' where Jeff and fellow fugitives first made their appearance on the Riversioux was now a village of nearly one thousand persons, unbelievable!

Alanson sat back in his seat wondering what had ever become of big Jeff or that rascal Fletch.

The train made a short mail stop in the French Catholic community of Jefferson and then re-crossed the river back into Iowa. They rolled into Riverside, past the former Bruguier Inn where the tracks made an abrupt left and then pressed tight against the Missouri River bluffs. They now passed through shadows below War Eagles Grave.

The river still ran wild and free, three quarters of a mile wide in places and still without a discernable stable channel. The juncture of the Big Sioux and Missouri had changed little, except the Sioux which had seemed a river of murky filth a few miles upstream actually now appeared clear as its 'pure' waters resisted but eventually disappeared into the muddy 'Mo'.

No it couldn't be, Alanson was suddenly aware of a horrible stench. Surely Sioux Indians weren't still rotting on the bluffs above. He hated to ask his SON-IN LAW what the stench was but he needed to know.

"It's the smell of prosperity gramps" Merrill was pleased to inform his father-in-law.

"I have never smelled prosperity before Merrill but after this morning's train trip I won't quibble with your answer".

Alanson's answer made no sense to Merrill who thought the old man was well past his useful years. "You're smelling the stock yards and the packing plants Alanson, which are about to make Sioux City into the Chicago of the West".

Alanson wasn't sure that was necessarily a good thing either.

The Milwaukee train depot was on Pearce Street just south of George Weale's Bank.

George was no longer on Pearce Street nor was the Sears ferry doing business at the Pearce Street dock as a new 'combination' bridge (the center section pivoted enabling river traffic to pass through) now connected Sioux City with South Sioux City Nebraska. Merrill and Alanson waited for and then caught the appropriate trolley running past the depot which terminated at the yards.

The stock yards were not overrated! The Sioux City Stock Yards Company occupied a full 80 acres. The packing giants Armour and Cudahy along with their subsidiaries who were mostly situated on the eastern extremity of the Stock Yards property employed 'thousands' of Siouxlanders and it was rumored Swift would soon be joining the Sioux City boom!

Many of these new Siouxlanders were papist who spoke with unfamiliar dialects. It seemed each new wave of employees searched for and found an area to claim as their own. Sioux City like Chicago had become a city of contrasting neighborhoods.

Riding in the trolley Alanson enjoyed the contrast while Merrill flamboyantly verbalized his disgust. Both embarrassed the other and both were relieved to arrive at the yards. Railroad cars were backed up for blocks waiting to be unloaded. Men swore and whips cracked while hogs squealed and cows bellowed, though not humane it was undeniably efficient. Alanson had never before witnessed anything like it.

The noise and the odors combined with all the human energy overwhelmed Alanson.

"Merrill, do you suppose we could find a place to sit a spell"? Alanson was exhausted and they had only just arrived.

"Pretty impressive isn't it Alanson, you probably do need a respite with all the commotion". Merrill seemed pleased with the old man's inability to handle 'modern' commerce.

"We'll go over to the Live Stock Exchange Building, that's where The Steele Commission office is anyway. You'll really be impressed when you get inside that building".

Alanson was impressed, ornate stone floors laden with manure was beyond his comprehension! Hurry, everyone was in hurry and everyone talked at once. Seemingly everyone had something so important to say that no-one had time to listen. He understood why Merrill enjoyed the place.

"Let's try to get our business settled and then sit down to eat if there is such an establishment anywhere nearby"? Alanson now wished he hadn't come but had to admit as much as he disliked being with Merrill, he was glad he wasn't alone.

Merrill laughed "You know what, just down the hall from the commission office are the best steaks in the whole of Sioux City".

They received payment for the hogs and were assured their business was greatly appreciated. Alanson conjectured the man in the suit definitely did appreciate the stockman's business judging from his expensive cigar, polished cowboy boots and rotund figure.

"Can we find a place to sit a while Merrill, I really am becoming tired"?

Merrill (whose character was grievously flawed, nevertheless possessed an uncommonly soft heart for persons of like ethnicity) felt sorry for the old man. "If we can elbow our way through all the commission men and if the Café isn't already filled we've almost got it made".

But it was noon and it was busy, leaving standing room only.

"Let's go down stairs, I need a haircut and there are always chairs in front of the cigar stand" Merrill suggested.

They walked down an elaborate, very wide handsomely divided stair case which also was ornately inlaid with colorful stone. The farmers found the steps handy to rub off their manure and mud laden boots. The whole concept reminded Alanson of an Old Testament story where a lowly herdsman sacrificed his only remaining goat in jewel embedded surroundings to support the lifestyle of obese priests. He knew under what conditions many of these farmers lived, once he had killed Indians for another man's profit and now he just wanted to go home!

Merrill poked him in the side and pointed. "Did you ever see such a big nigger pops"? Near the end of the hall a black shoeshine man was bent over polishing a broker's shoes, even bent over the silver haired man appeared enormous.

"I think I'll have that 'boy' shine my shoes if he can bend over far enough" Merrill snickered as he walked toward the shoeshine stand.

Merrill noticed Alanson all the sudden no longer appeared exhausted, instead he now walked with an energetic pace!

"Got time to shine my shoes boy" Merrill asked?

"You alls wants jus a polish or the whole business mistah" Jeff asked?

'The whole business and don't dilly dally around, my father-in-law seems to be getting weary from all this big city life" Merrill demanded.

"It's been quite awhile since you and I rechanneled the Missouri Jeff. I'm confused as to what's transpiring here? I can't understand why you are shining shoes and what's with this language, if I remember properly you might have given William Shakespeare honest competition in proper English usage"?

Merrill thought the old man had finally crossed over into insanity. "Alanson do you want to grab a seat over next to the wall while this boy finishes his shining job" again Merrill slyly shook his head signifying to those around the old man had lost it.

Alanson reached into his pocket for some change and paid Jeff for the shine while motioning for Merrill to dismount from the shoeshine chair.

Merrill started to speak when Alanson reiterated his request only this time with unmistakable authority "I said get your ass off that chair"!

Merrill was struck dumb. Never had he seen the old man react in such an aggressive manner.

In his mind Alanson had returned to different times. He no longer was an old man but instead he was Alanson Baker and this was Jeff Davis, both better men then Merrill could aspire to. "Merrill go do something worth while until the 5:00 pm train leaves for Akron, I'll meet you at the Pierce Street depot".

Merrill left in disbelief, wait until he told Sarah!

"I'm nearly starved Jeff, can you leave the stand long enough to get something to eat" Alanson really needed to eat.

"Well Mistah Alanson where does you spose we gonna eat" Jeff asked only this time he was the one in disbelief?

"I don't understand Jeff, you never called me Mr. on the Riversioux so please don't start now. Let's go upstairs, my son-in-law says they have good steaks and that he 'would' know".

"Where you been Mistah Alanson on some bean farm? The last negraw walked in der ain't nevah been seen gain. There's no place in dis town gonna fed the likes of me. Tells you what, my woman is commin wid some vittles and we can share space and grub behind this heah buildings if you's want. Few white mens goes back der".

"Have it your way Jeff, I'll order some take-out food from upstairs and we can share it out behind if you wish, but you must stop this gibberish".

Jeff smiled while nodding in the affirmative, "I always was pretty adept with the languages; right now I find gibberish serves me quite well".

Alanson went upstairs and ordered while Jeff went out back to wait.

Remembering Jeff's appetite and figuring his children's needs Alanson soon appeared around the corner of the exchange building carrying enough food for six good men.

Jeff and a much 'younger' lady of mixed parentage waited with several children and plenty of their own food.

"Alanson this is Marguerite and these are our young ones" Jeff motioned toward the several children playing along the railroad track.

They all sat down with their backs next to the Exchange building wall soaking up the sun as they shared their food.

"Would you explain to me what I just witnessed inside" Alanson asked while washing down the last of his food with a cup of Marguerites bitter but satisfying Creole coffee. He was still obviously puzzled.

"How would you rate your son-in-laws social intelligence" Jeff asked and then answered his own question without giving Alanson time to respond…"Well I'll tell you what, he is an average American. There aren't many Captain Joneses or Alanson's in this world or even Strokers for that matter. I must confess I've been guilty of some of the same oversights as them; it seems we at times get caught in the immediate and overlook the whole. People are simply people Alanson and pigment is simply color but unfortunately color is 'very' important. I'm wrapped in black and you in white, it gets very tiring pretending differently. White talk from black wrapping isn't popular at present. If you haven't noticed I've gotten some older and I guess I'm just becoming too tired to continue pretending".

"I understand perfectly well, I'm more tired today then even yesterday. It 'IS' good for me and for my daughter's sake to be reassured you believe my son-in-law is average".

"Alanson have you seen Captain Jonas? You know at the time I was so young, I so wish I could redo those days, I didn't appreciate it but looking back he very well could be the only truly 'honest' man I've ever known".

Strange you mentioned Captain Jonas since I had a visit from him just yesterday and would you believe I finally whipped him in a game of horse shoes" Alanson sported a wide pleasurable grin.

"I would have to hear that from Jonas himself Alanson, in competition you've always lived in a world of your own" Jeff laughed remembering Alanson valiantly trying to place logs in the Missouri channel so many years ago.

They both laughed but Alanson still knew he had won!

As the day passed the two exchanged their life stories, filled with many highs and an equal amount of lows.

Jeff's believed his greatest regret was not sticking with Inkpaduta. He had wanted to be Sioux but when given the chance he'd settled for being half Sioux, opting for the comforts of 'race' instead of accompanying the Wahpekute and Chief Inkpaduta!. This also had also been his greatest learning experience; through his own ignorance he now understood that ignorance was not synonymous to hate.

When asked his greatest regret Alanson wavered. He should of written Mary and he should have just hugged his mother.

"So what are you going to do now Jeff" Alanson seemed to suggest since he and Jeff were having 'this' conversation the world had also changed. Alanson was getting old and he was very tired, brain waves of low wattage were beginning to take short cuts instead of making the full journey.

"Well mistah Alanson ah's goin back inside and shine me a few mor white boy's shoes. Be pleased to shine yours foe old times sake if you'd like".

Alanson shook his head no and then offered his hand in a parting handshake, which Jeff of-course heartily shook. With this the two old acquaintances returned to their adjacent but separate worlds.

The train ride back to Akron was a quiet affair as Merrill wasn't quite sure his father-in-law had regrouped all his marbles and Alanson wasn't motivated to demonstrate otherwise.

Mary was concerned for her Alanson when he returned. Never had she seen him so thoroughly worn out.

Alanson really was tired upon his return from the stockyards; he had lived seventy six hard years and each year now showed. Between Jonas, Jeff and of-course Merrill the past two days had been epic and had taken a toll.

Alanson showed change in the days following his return from Sioux City. It wasn't a change that caused Mary great concern for if anything Alanson now enjoyed life more then ever.

He at times appeared to act silly but if pressed could be as lucid as he 'wanted'. He now enjoyed playing with Ruth and Ora (the tom boy) more than ever. Baby Muriel was a contented baby and he found great solace in simply holding her, the two could spend long moments just smiling at each other. She was the happiest child he had ever seen, took after her grandmother Mary! Alanson always played at his granddaughter's level and they each looked forward to the others visits.

Business was by now completely in Mary's hands. Alanson seemed disinterested in business but for the first time in their marriage he took interest in people. He talked to people; anyone he met was 'interesting'.

Like most elderly persons Alanson cared little about pretense and he could be so embarrassing to those around him. When meeting an imposter he seemed obligated to expose it.

Of-course Merrill now avoided the old man like disease; unfortunately Merrill depended upon the old man for life substance.

Mary, though at times she surely must have been tried by his shenanigans, never criticized Alanson and Sarah's pleas for intervention on poor Merrill's behalf went unheeded.

A few 'gifted' individuals understand love and what it entails but to the many others it seemed a pity that a woman of Mary's remarkable ability was anchored to a man who spent his days playing as a child with children except of-course when sitting on the banks of his beloved Sioux River.

If any were foolish enough to verbalize their thoughts to Mary, well it was a poorly thought out proposition.

Mary 'decreed' Alanson had become a 'transcendentalist". If this didn't end criticism of her Alanson they were courtly sent on their way, their sympathies now lying with Alanson.

Alanson certainly understood what people thought but he no longer cared. Mary handled things quite well and if she wasn't pleased he would of-course do whatever it took to resurrect the situation. Mary enjoyed the business world and lord she had a head for it, he no longer enjoyed the competitiveness and truthfully he seemed to get confused so easily anymore. They were there for each other, of this neither doubted and they had grown old together which had always been their wish.

Alanson lived 'elsewhere' more then in reality by the spring of ought eleven, not that he couldn't live in either but elsewhere sufficed for a man of eighty three—except with Mary. Their love was a constant where nothing less then reality would ever suffice.

By fall he was rapidly slipping away, Mary knew and understood and dreaded the thought. She was filled with energy while Alanson now struggled with simple personal hygiene. It no longer was a matter of if...but when.

On good days Alanson would be able to walk the farm and check on the 'pit' and at times even fish but mostly if he did anything he simply sat on the river bank.

October the 30th 1911 was a typical sunny cool Iowa autumn day; Alanson spent the morning enjoying the river when an unusual weakness suddenly came upon him. He struggled to get home, shaking and soaked in a feverish sweat he managed to crawl through screen door onto the front porch.

Mary immediately sent Alanson Jr. to Westfield for Dr. Merenes the family doctor.

"Mary he simply is worn out, I'm sorry but really there is nothing I can do. My advice is that you send for your minister and gather your family".

Dr. Merenes departed, with many more house calls ahead, hoping for patients he could be of assistance to.

Alanson smiled peacefully as he dreamed of his three loves Explorer, Mary and Jane...all were aboard the riverboat Riversioux.

The room which had been cold and even combative now warmed and was peacefully inclusive.

EYE OF THE NEEDLE

Life whisked by instantaneously, yet easily manageable! He stopped to view and then sped on; he knew what he looked for but not what it was. The Riversioux lay in harbor surrounded by Wahpekute but 'no' that wasn't it.

There was Fletch, maybe that was it?

For a 'mille-moment' he hesitated to observe…

Fletch was old and wracked with disease yet steel still flashed from his blue eyes.

It was August of '76' and Fletch had won another hand. Deadwood South Dakota was wild, lawless and ripe for picking…Fletches kind of town.

Hickcock lived off reputation; Fletch was the one who merited attention. They had played since late morning and now it was evening—near dusk, Fletch held most everyone's money as he prepared to call it a day.

"You leaving so early old timer" Hickcock asked attempting to once again use his reputation in bluff.

"Yep, I'm old and it seems even you ought to be old enough to understand when your hands already been dealt Hickcock". There was no misunderstanding the message.

"Have it your way little man. We adults stay up past dark". Hickcock knew he pushed a little beyond his want but without reputation he was nothing.

While keeping a wary eye on Hickcock's whore Jane, Fletch softly spoke "It's your call Wild"…. The sentence remained incomplete.

Three youthful prospectors burst through the front door dragging an elderly Indian. The Indian struggled to stay erect as the 'gent' dragging him continually jerked the rope looped around his neck.

"You gentleman ever see a drunken injun piss up a rope"? The man with the rope also was the spokesman for this trio of 'bad' hombres. "We're going to entertain you gentleman tonight. Bar keep set this injun up with all the liquor he can drink in say the next couple hours". A gold piece was tossed to the bar keep. "Then he is going to get the chance of his life time right here in Deadwood South Dakota the spiritual home of the Sioux". He gave the rope a quick jerk as an exclamation point causing the old man to stumble while gasping for air.

'Most' everyone within the saloon roared with laughter.

"See the knots on this rope". One of the trio had tied the rope snuggly to a fix-ture above the bar while leaving the other end looped around the Indians neck. The rope was knotted every few inches. "After two hours of free drink he is going to get a chance to piss up this rope every fifteen minutes, every time he pisses higher he gets another drink, when he doesn't we use his cock for target practice".

Fletch had been suffering for months, his bowel movements were becoming blackened putty and lately with the distinct odor of decay. He had seen others die from this rot. This seemed as good a time as any.

Fletch drew 2 'Colts' which he leveled at the ringleader "Big man there with the rope, drop your drawers…. All the way now I want to see asshole—asshole".

A vacuum suddenly sucked all sound from the room.

This was Deadwood in "76" and someone was drawing final breath!

Fletch was once again the badger, simply attending to business. People had tread where no-one should but now it was too late, the curtain had already drawn closed.

Fletch threw the old Indain a knife "cut your self loose there old timer" which he quickly did, "now slip the gun out of big mouths holster and lay it on the bar…. Yea just out of his reach".

The other two hombres eyed Fletch, who seemed completely at ease with the situation. "Keep your guns handy boys, but don't attempt anything foolish"!

Fletch kept a gun on each of them, he no longer worried about their loud mouthed leader since the elderly Indain now impatiently fidgeted while holding the knife to his throat.

Fletch casually pointed one Colt at the Indain "Injun whack his pecker off"! He motioned toward the ringleaders genitals with his pistol.

Then without warning Fletch fired both Colts effectively pureeing the scrotums of the two lesser hombres.

Throughout the bar room hardened men grimaced as they stared in disbelief.

The Indian (fresh from little Big Horn) dropped the knife and fled. Later he would ponder on what would be the outcome if the great Chief Inkpaduta and this crazy white-eye were ever to meet!

The 'bad hombre' still butt naked dove for his revolver…too late.

Fletch simultaneously fired both 'Colts', first into "butt naked" and then continued firing until empty at the remaining two. Innards and appendages commingled with blood across the bar room floor.

Their deaths would be slow, painful and certain.

The three hombres fired back determined to empty their pistols before succumbing to a life draining pain.

Bystanders at the "Deadwood Cockfight" would forever remain puzzled by the climatic ending. The three 'bad' hombres seemed to die content watching Fletches demise while Fletch appeared content with the entire proceeding.

Mary felt Alanson gasp for breath then clinch his fist as the trio emptied their weapons into Fletch.

Alanson swore, as Mary wiped his forehead which now was weeping sweat. "Fletch" and a few more inaudible swear words and Alanson was off again.

Time no longer was restricted; time was now flat. On the 'planet' time had been circular, beginning with birth and eventually reconnecting with death. There were big circles and small circles, with none being a greater circle. Now from the in-between world Alanson observed time on a flat plane with a panoramic overhead vision of time eternal. He sped forward and backward, still not knowing what he looked for but knowing Mary depended upon him finding it!

Jeff appeared in the hole of a slaving vessel gasping for breath but that wasn't it, then Jonas appeared instructing fugitive slaves in ship refurbishing but that wasn't it either.

He was pitching horse shoe with Jonas for the final time; now maybe he could see who actually had won but Mary was his mission and he found 'really' he didn't need to know.

Time was running out. Alanson could see the in-between worlds' road rapidly coming to finality.

He had to find it NOW!

It was a Pennsylvania blizzard and he was back in his childhood home. Earlier he had left in a huff but after reconsidering he had returned and now stood shaking off snow while rubbing his aching hands together in an attempt to regain blood flow.

No, though he begged to rewrite life's script from the celestial vantage point he presently occupied he found the pen was now removed from his hand and he no longer was the playwright…If only he would have returned…but he hadn't and now he watched as his mother cried. She was in his her bedroom with his father standing over her.

"John he's gone, I let our son leave without him knowing I loved him" Elizabeth burst into tears.

"Good God woman that is my precise feeling also. The only person we ever cared about has gone. Get your coat while I hitch up the buggy. By-god we're going to catch our son and MAKE him come back home! Elizabeth at this moment I remember why I first loved you".

"Mother, mother—slow down Explorer God-Dammitt Explorer please slow down. They loved me, they LOVED me" but now Alanson was himself a spectator.

Alanson slowly opened his eyes and motioned for Mary to lean closer to his mouth. Barely audible he whispered "Mary they loved me".

Alanson held Mary close as he wiped her tear stained face. Weakly he gestured toward her cross and whispered "with all my heart I am yours". He finally could complete the rescue…without reservation.

Mary, it seemed, had waited all her life for this moment. Though now she was losing him, she also now had found him. She clasped the cross close to her bosom as she unashamedly wept tears, tears originating from her soul.

Love, contented yet vibrant love exuberated from the old man as he caressed his wife, at long last with unencumbered affection.

Mary lived another fifteen years; remaining astute and alert. If temporal desire becomes eternal design in August of '26' Mary packed one final picnic lunch that she and Alanson forever share upon the banks of the Big Sioux River.

From Akron if one takes Iowa highway 12 north (towards Hawarden) past Dunham Prairie Reserve, up the hill almost to the curve in the highway and then turns left into the community cemetery, in the first row (next to the fence) immediately to your right after entering the premises sets an aging but prominent grayish white stone (about in the center of the first row).

> "Pioneers of note lay at rest in this hallowed spot
> Forever looking down upon the Big Sioux River"
> A. Baker born sept. 26 1828—Mary E Baker born Dec. 25 1846
> Died Oct. 31 1911   died Aug. 21 1926

> ***They loved—they prospered—they shared***

> They and their kind are greatly missed

"Granddaughters after the funeral, Nov. 1911"

ADDENDUM

Truth sears the soul, in the process pain is more then a byproduct. In writing and researching this "story" truth remained the object. Jesus states in the scriptures "slaves obey your masters" was he referring to 'niggers' in the cotton fields of Mississippi or possibly using a metaphor beyond mortal understanding? Truth is illusive and momentary and often bastardized.

In this story many will infer references to crisis of 'our' times; more well read folk will realize no crisis today is 'of today'. History and theology are built upon the past, denying fact leaves truth unaltered.

In this tale some hard decisions were made (for me), Is a graphic description of sex necessary? Of-course not but on-the-other-hand neither is a detailed description of a river or a tree. This is a tale of young men on the frontier, leaving either out would be insincere and adolescent. Both are of nature and both are nature.

I confess on another issue I reluctantly acquiesced to accepted norms (and pressure from people I care about) as the offending episode was of minimal consequence in this 'story', still if one runs from truth for convenience sake when does one stop running?

Grandfather Alanson and his legacy has always been a puzzle to the Peccary. Few persons have done more for a community with less recognition. Did he really covet no recognition or financial rewards? The question defies a logical reasoned answer which leaves one fumbling through the misty realm of theology\psychology...

Clarifications:

Walking Pigeon—"Mani Zintkala" actually translates as walking bird in the Lakota Dictionary. The proper word for pigeon is difficult to translate in Sioux dialect.

Spotted Fawn—Glega Hehaka actually translates as spotted female deer for the same reasons as stated above.

In Sioux dialect adjectives as a rule follow the noun but for ease of reading in this tale words of description precede the noun. (Example: pretty flower vs. flower pretty)

Following are historical facts of this tale:

Alanson worked the river boats of the Missouri River for many years.

The 'Riversioux' though a fictional name is of the exact dimensions of 'one' of the paddlewheels Alanson actually served on.

Alanson knew Mr. Denig well and had numerous business dealings with Edwin Thompson Denig although 'NOT' in 1856 as portrayed in this story. Mr.

Denig and family left Ft. Union in search of better educational opportunities for his children in late summer of 1855...

The fur and hide tally listed for the Riversioux is 'almost' identical to one of Alanson's many tallies. (Documented and taken from the Sioux City archives)

He purchased the original 1\4 section in 1857 and received an additional 1\4 section for Civil War duty.

Alanson's enlistment, discharge and duty assignments are factual.

The Civil War battles described are as accurate as possible.

The listing of assets is correct but incomplete.

References to Chief Inkpaduta's conflicts and place of birth and death are from historical documents.

The where about of the different tribes mentioned (including black Sioux) are factual (although debatable, as differing memoirs exist) and documented.

The slave stories are researched and historically feasible while the individual stories are fiction.

Grandmother Mary 'lost' her family in the St. Louis Typhoid Epidemic of 1849 while crossing the Mississippi. The family was on the way to East Texas with plans for a new expanded plantation. (My own personal take on a family history contrived from various and divergent recollections)

She was raised by a 'mercenary preacher' in Dakota City Nebraska.

The 'preacher' was subsidized on a regular basis by Mary's grandparents.

****If one notices Mary's age in this saga does not coincide with her grave stone birth date. The dates she lived in Dakota City purposely 'may or may not' be accurate. The fact remains she was treated unconscionably. I have no desire at this date to reveal names.

The church mentioned in this story for afore mentioned reasons 'may or may not' be the actual church. (Did the missionaries go directly to Dakota City from St. Louis or make a detour as in the 'story'?)

Mary was a genius, nearly unparalleled in business. During her time she was referred to by locals as an astute business lady!

Merrill, although locally very popular, was a character with glaring deficiencies. In the 20's he and many other 'notable' local businessmen formed a local chapter of the K.K.K.. The Negro, although not appreciated was not of great local concern. The Jewish "money conspiracy" and the growing fear of Papist political influence in American politic had become a phobia.

Riverboats actually traversed the Big Sioux to the village of Sioux Falls South Dakota for a number of years during the spring raise. The practice was halted in the late 80's when flow due to farming practices became unpredictable AND trees of girth began growing along the river. Fallen trees in a small channel are not conducive to riverboat travel but most significantly THE RAILROAD finally extended to Sioux Falls.

In research I visited several river boats of that era for documentation and for 'feel'.

Leonard Bruguier (head of American Indian studies at the University Of South Dakota) was kind enough to be interviewed twice in 1998 by this author.

Note: Leonard is a grandson (many greats) of the great Chief War Eagle and also of Mr. Bruguier (first white settler of Sioux City). The original Mr. Bruguier married War Eagles daughter.

I entered the University of South Dakota building of Indian affairs (the entrance was tucked away behind and down a flight of stairs in the basement, fitting for this story!) with puffed chest and unjustified pride, announcing that my great grandfather had purchased land along the Big Sioux River in 1857 and worked the river boats long before and after that date. I wanted to 'write' a story of the times and wondered if he would be of help.

Leonard appeared genuinely interested as he patiently listened to my story and then asked if I wished to hear his family story. Thanks for being a 'kind' person Leonard! He was very helpful, not only with the interviews but also for giving me access to The Library of Indain Studies (containing invaluable documents).

I attempted to contact Leonard again in Dec. of 2004 but unfortunately (for me) he had retired and his where about was unknown,

The Bruguier Inn of Riversioux is fictional!

I owe much to the historical writings of Alexander Culbertson and also to Mr. Edwin T. Denig.

These are some of the people and places I am indebted to:

> The Sioux City Public Library and staff
> The Branigan Memorial Library of Las Cruces, New Mexico
> The 'fabulous' "Coas My bookstore" in the downtown Las Cruces Mall
> The Sioux City Public Museum.

God Bless the internet!

Mostly I owe my family for memories and recollections.

I can not adequately express my gratitude for the illustration genius of "ART AND GRAPHICS BY ALMA HATFIELD"

Thanks to David Bringman for bringing "soul" and adding dignity to an otherwise earthy epistle and also a 'reluctant' thanks for abrasive but effective criticisms.

I took the liberty of using several familiar 'area' names in the story; the names were used as a tribute to century families in the Westfield\Akron area and NO factual accounts of these families is intended. (If by coincidence they are factual GOD BLESS YOU)

My intent was to honor these pioneers in story.

Now the difficult task, why did Alanson who gave so much ask for so little?

Just as with "slaves obey your master' no one can say with authority. After much study and agonizing several theories developed.

As the story evolved so did 'my' theory. He obviously was a 'good' man and also obviously was socially a quite man.

I attempted to place myself in Alanson's mindset and then simply react accordingly. Hopefully the Baker blood is not too diluted.

He (I) volunteered my services to advance a noble cause in a vicious life and death struggle between good and evil; instead of advancing justice I was used to advance the illegal interest of eastern expansionist. I slaughtered the helpless and innocent on their own 'deeded' lands. After the war even the façade of a 'noble' cause was bastardized.

I am left with little faith in my government's morality and have no faith in my own ability to judge morality or governments.

Still…. I am doing well under this system and I understand no man is 'truly' self made.

Adding to the enjoyment of my community not only satisfies a natural and laudable desire to give something back BUT it also helps clear my conscious. "Giving without receiving 'recognition' is difficult and for me nearly impossible; therefore it also is soul cleansing". I, who have participated in possibly the most hideous massacre in the annals of U.S. Calvary History, can never forget!

I wish to thank my friends Blaine Parker and Harry Brink for keeping my nose to the grind stone. It took much research (more then I ever imagined) and several extended "recesses".

This 'tale' is dedicated to my friend David whose family farmed and lived in peace "just cross" the river from the Baker Westfield farm for more then a century. These were and still are remembered as good times.

In the end this work possibly harbors much fiction and little truth; nevertheless it is from the heart which renders it honest!

TRIBULATION

As we pass through this forest of magnificent lie
Decaying yet grasping for what has long passed us by.
Educated to comfort but shackled by greed
We pillar this earth with accelerating speed.

We the icons of freedom in a land blessed more than most
Raising glasses to mirror, we offer a toast.
Honoring our greatness, the red, white and blue
Providence our destiny, divine is our hue.

If it was in the past, then so shall it be
They who now serve must dream to be free.
Nations and citizens of privilege by birth
Are necessarily harangued as a test of their worth.

Can an obese nation no longer obliged to produce
Maintain in old age from earnings of youth.
Or will environment and its dwellers, long plundered and used
Join in the savagery of those we've abused.

The answer to these questions and so many more
Are being put to the test but "who's" keeping score.
"The meek shall inherit the earth" if the gospel holds true
Leaves one grasping for time with much to undo.

—By—the peccary

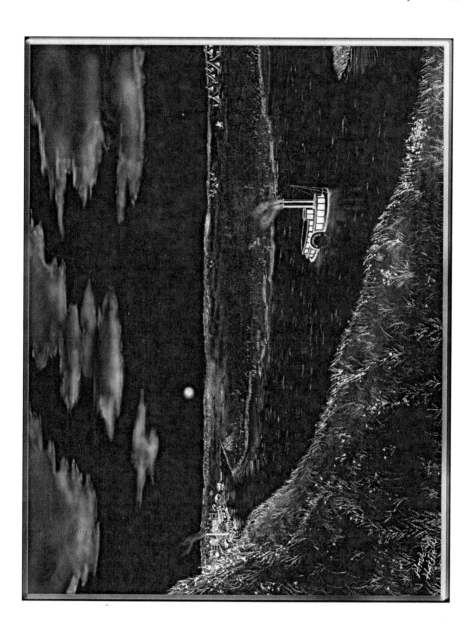

978-0-595-36885-3
0-595-36885-9